Praise for
ON THE ROAD WITH D͟   ͟UISE

"A would-be Bonnie and Clyde v   keyring dan-
gling from the rearview mirr͟   ͟hy not? These
linked short stories are by t͟   ͟ɹ, at times, touch-
ingly poignant as Del an͟ᵈ   ͟om a life of crime to
one of solid respectabil͟   ͟ they succeed, the other
half is ready for another ͟ᵢ   recommended."

— Margaret Maron,
Edgar Award-Winning Autʜ͟ ͟ of the Deborah Knott Mysteries

"Warm yet unsentimental, down-to-earth and pragmatic without
being cynical—Art Taylor's characters, like his voice, are a breath of
fresh air. Don't miss the chance to go on the road with Del and
Louise."

— Donna Andrews,
Agatha Award-Winning Author of the Meg Langslow Mysteries

"Taylor is expert at capturing small details that bring to life settings
and scenes. He has a natural talent for storytelling, hooking readers
from page one with his characters' potential to do the unexpected.
The compelling voice in which his stories about Del and Louise are
told artfully creates reader sympathy for a couple who recurrently
flirt with crime; it's a voice that will remain in readers' minds long
after the book is closed."

— Janet Hutchings,
Editor, *Ellery Queen's Mystery Magazine*

"If there's a Raymond Carver of short crime fiction, Art Taylor
would be him—but, you know, without the chain smoking and
boozing."

— Keith Rawson,
LitReactor

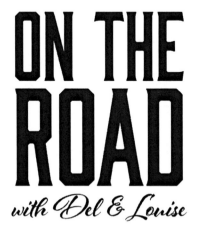

ON THE ROAD

with Del & Louise

Books by Art Taylor

ON THE ROAD WITH DEL & LOUISE
A Novel in Stories

ON THE ROAD

with Del & Louise

ART TAYLOR

HENERY PRESS

ON THE ROAD WITH DEL & LOUISE
A Novel in Stories
Part of the Henery Press Mystery Collection

First Edition
Trade paperback edition | September 2015

Henery Press, LLC
www.henerypress.com

Copyright © 2015 by Art Taylor
Author photograph by Evan Michio

ISBN-13: 978-1-941962-89-3

Printed in the United States of America

For Tara Laskowski,
with memories of the road trip
and the writing challenge
that sparked this book's journey

And for Dash at three,
already teaching me that
every day can be an adventure
—as long as it includes cars

ACKNOWLEDGMENTS

I once believed that writing was a solitary art. I no longer believe this.

Thank you most immediately to the people who read and reread these stories in various drafts and helped to give them both better shape and more substance, especially Tara Laskowski, Kyle Semmel and Brandon Wicks—a loose but long-standing writers group and my dearest friends—and also my now-once-a-month writers group: Donna Andrews, Ellen Crosby, John Gilstrap, and Alan Orloff—particularly Alan for reading and commenting on the entire manuscript in record time.

Thank you to *Ellery Queen's Mystery Magazine* for having published two of the stories in this book in an earlier form: "Rearview Mirror" in the March/April 2010 issue and "Commission" in May 2014. And even greater appreciation to Janet Hutchings, my editor at EQMM, for having given me a home in the mystery community and for all her unsurpassed support and encouragement over the years.

Thank you to everyone at Henery Press, particularly Kendel Lynn and Rachel Jackson for their fine editorial guidance and patience each step of the way—and to Kendel as well for that spur-of-the-banquet-table friendship at Malice and where it's led. Thanks too to Art Molinares for his exquisite attention to detail.

Thank you to Bill Miller, Laura Scott, Susan Richards Shreve, and Debra Lattanzi Shutika at George Mason University and to Angela

Davis Gardner and John Kessel at North Carolina State University—mentors, cheerleaders, and friends all; to Rob Drummond and Ryan Effgen, fellow MFA peers at Mason who set high standards for all of us, and to David Feiner, one of my roommates at Yale, whose own commitment to creative excellence continues to inspire; and way back to Grant Kornberg at Episcopal High School in Alexandria, VA, who gave me that first burst of confidence that my writing might amount to something.

There are many, many people in the mystery community whose names should appear in these acknowledgements—too many for me to include them all, and I'm so certain I'll forget someone important and dear to me that I'm hesitant to even venture a short list of people who've encouraged and inspired me. However, some of them demand personal mention here—most emphatically Margaret Maron, my first friend in the mystery world and still one of my biggest supporters, but also many others including Ed Aymar, Louis Bayard, Paula Gail Benson, Dana Cameron, Carla Coupe, David Dean, Barb Goffman, Douglas Greene, Toni L.P. Kelner, Nik Korpon, Linda Landrigan, Con Lehane, Terrie Farley Moran, Keith Rawson, Daniel Stashower, Steven Steinbock, B.K. Stevens, Marcia Talley, and Steve Weddle. I also want to thank everyone in the Mid-Atlantic Chapter of Mystery Writers of America and in the Chesapeake Chapter of Sisters in Crime for their friendship, support, and enthusiasm. All of us who are members surely count ourselves lucky.

Finally, the most important thank-you to my parents Gene and Jenny Taylor, to my brother Jason Taylor, to my wife Tara Laskowski, and to our son Dashiell. I would not be who I am—as a writer or as a person—without my family. All my love to you.

REARVIEW MIRROR

I hadn't been thinking about killing Delwood. Not really. But you know how people sometimes have just had enough. That's what I'd meant when I said it to him, "I could just kill you," the two of us sitting in his old Nova in front of a cheap motel on Route 66— meaning it figurative, even if that might seem at odds with me sliding his pistol into my purse right after I said it.

And even though I was indeed thinking hard about taking my half of the money and maybe a little more—literal now, literally taking it—I would not call it a double-cross. Just kind of a divorce and a divorce settlement. Even though we weren't married. But that's not the point.

Sometimes people are too far apart in their wants—that's what Mama told me. Sometimes things don't work out.

That was the point.

"Why don't we take the day off?" I'd asked Del earlier that morning up in Taos, a Saturday, the sun creeping up, the boil not yet on the day, and everything still mostly quiet in the mobile home park where we'd been renting on the bi-weekly. "We could go buy you a suit, and I could get a new dress. Maybe we'd go out to dinner. To Joseph's Table maybe. Celebrate a little."

He snorted. "Louise," he said, the way he does. "What's it gonna look like, the two of us, staying out here, paycheck to paycheck, economical to say the least"—he put emphasis on *economical*, always liking the sound of anything above three syllables—"and suddenly going out all spiffed up to the nicest restaurant in town?" He looked at me for a while, then shook his head.

"We don't have to go to the nicest restaurant," I said, trying to compromise, which is the mark of a good relationship. "We could just go down to the bar at the Taos Inn and splurge on some high-dollar bourbon and nice steaks." I knew he liked steaks, and I could picture him smiling over it, chewing, both of us fat and happy. So to speak, I mean, the fat part being figurative again, of course.

"We told Hal we'd vacate the premises by this morning. We agreed."

Hal was the man who ran the mobile home park. A week before, Del had told him he'd finally gotten his degree and then this whole other story about how we'd be moving out to California, where Del's sister lived, and how we were gonna buy a house over there.

"Sister?" I had wanted to say when I overheard it. "House?" But then I realized he was just laying the groundwork, planning ahead so our leaving wouldn't look sudden or suspicious. Concocting a story—I imagine that's the way he would have explained it, except he didn't explain it to me but just did it.

That's the way he was sometimes: a planner, not a communicator. *Taciturn*, he called it. Somewhere in there, in his not explaining and my not asking, he had us agreeing. And now he had us leaving.

"Okay," I told Del. "We'll just go then. But how 'bout we rent a fancy car? A convertible maybe. A nice blue one." And I could see it—us cruising through the Sangre de Christos on a sunny afternoon, the top tipped back and me sliding across the seat, leaning over toward him, maybe kicking my heels up and out the window. My head would be laid on his shoulder and the wind would slip through my toes and the air conditioner would be blowing full-blast since June in the Southwest is already hot as blazes.

Now *that* would be nice.

"No need to waste this windfall on some extravagance," he said. "No need to call attention to ourselves unnecessarily. Our car works fine."

He headed for it then—that old Nova. Flecks of rust ran underneath the doors and up inside the wheel well. A bad spring in the seat always bit into my behind. Lately, the rearview mirror had started to hang a little loose—not so that Delwood couldn't see in it, but enough that it rattled against the windshield whenever the road got rough.

He'd jury-rigged a hitch under the bumper and hooked up a flat-as-a-pancake trailer he'd rented to carry some of the stuff that wouldn't fit in the trunk. A tarp covered it now.

I stood on the steps with my hip cocked and my arms crossed, so that when he turned and looked at me in that rearview mirror, he'd know I was serious. But he just climbed in the car, then sat there staring ahead. Nothing to look back at, I guess. He'd already packed the trunk and the trailer both while I slept. The mobile home behind us was empty of the few things we owned.

"A new day for us," he'd whispered an hour before when he woke me up, but already it seemed like same old, same old to me. When I climbed in beside him, I slammed the passenger-side door extra hard and heard a bolt come loose somewhere inside it.

"It figures," I said, listening to it rattle down. The spring had immediately dug into my left rump.

Del didn't answer. Just put the car in gear and drove ahead.

When I first met Del, he was robbing the 7-Eleven over in Eagle Nest, where I worked at that time. This was about a year ago. I'd been sitting behind the counter, reading one of the *Cosmo*s off the shelf, when in comes this fellow in jeans and a white t-shirt and a ski mask, pointing a pistol.

"I'm not gonna hurt you," he said. "I'm not a bad man. I just need an occasional boost in my income."

I laid the *Cosmo* face down on the counter. I didn't want to lose my place. "You're robbing me?" I said.

"Yes, ma'am."

I bit my lip and shook my head—no no no—just slightly.

"I'm only twenty-eight," I said.

He looked over toward the Doritos display—not looking at it, but pointing his head in that direction the way some people stare into space whenever they're thinking. He had a mustache and a beard. I could see the stray hairs poking out around the bottom of the ski mask and near the hole where his mouth was.

"Excuse me?" he said finally, turning back to face me. His eyes were this piney green.

"I'm not a ma'am."

He held up his free hand, the one without the pistol, and made to run it through his hair—another sign of thinking—but with the ski mask, it just slid across the wool. "Either way, could you hurry it up? I'm on a schedule."

Many reasons for him to be frustrated, I knew. Not the least of which was having to wear wool in New Mexico in the summer.

He glanced outside. The gas pumps were empty. Nothing but darkness on the other side of the road. This time of night, we didn't get much traffic. I shrugged, opened the cash register.

"You know," I said, as I bent down for a bag to put his money in. "You have picked the one solitary hour that I'm alone in the store, between the time that Pete has to head home for his mom's curfew and the time that our night manager strolls in for his midnight to six."

"I know. I've been watching you." Then there was a nervous catch in his voice. "Not in a bad way, I mean. Not voyeuristically." He enunciated both that word and the next. "Surveillance, you know. I'm not a pervert."

I kept loading the register into the bag. "You don't think I'm worth watching?"

Again, with the ski mask, I couldn't be sure, but he seemed to blush.

"No. I mean, yes," he said. "You're very pretty."

I nodded. "There's not much money here we have access to, you know? A lot of it goes straight to the safe. That's procedure."

"I'm a fairly frugal man," he said. "Sometimes I need extra for...tuition."

"Tuition?"

"And other academic expenses."

"Academic expenses," I repeated, not a question this time. I thought that he had a nice voice, and then I told him so. "You have a nice voice," I said. "And pretty eyes." I gave him my phone number, not writing it down because the security camera would have picked that up, but just told him to call, repeating the number twice so he would remember it. "And my name is Louise."

"Thanks," he said, "Louise."

"Good luck with your education," I called after him, but the door had already swung closed. I watched him run out toward the pumps and beyond, admired the way his body moved, the curve of his jeans, for as long as I could make him out against the darkness. I gave him a head start before I dialed 911.

I know what you're thinking. You're thinking I was some bored, bubblegum-popping, *Cosmo*-reading girl, disillusioned with the real world and tired already of being a grown-up and along comes this bad boy and, more than that, literally a criminal and...Sure, there's some truth there. But here again, you'd be missing the point.

It wasn't exciting that he robbed convenience stores.

It was exciting that he was brave enough to call me afterwards, especially in this age of Caller ID when I had his phone number and name immediately—Grayson, Delwood—and could have sent the police after him in a minute.

That *Cosmo* article? The one I was reading when he showed up in the ski mask? "Romantic Gestures Gone Good: Strange but True Stories of How He Wooed and Won Me."

Not a one of those stories held a candle to hearing Del's voice on the other end of the phone: "Hello, Louise? I, um...robbed your 7-Eleven the other night, and I've been percolating on our conversation ever since. Are you free to talk?"

That takes a real man, I thought. And—don't forget those academic expenses—a man who might be going somewhere.

But it had been a long time since I believed we were going anywhere fast. Or anywhere at all.

We took the High Road down from Taos. That figured: two lanes, forty-five miles per hour.

"Afraid they'll get you for speeding?" I asked.

"One thing might lead to another," he said. "And anyway, the rental place stressed that it was dangerous to exceed the speed limit while pulling the trailer here."

As we drove, he kept looking up into the rearview mirror, nervously, staring back across the sweep of that trailer, as if any second a patrol car really was gonna come tearing around the bend, sirens wailing, guns blasting. He had put his own pistol in the glove compartment. I saw it when I went for a Kleenex.

"If we get pulled, are you gonna use it?"

He didn't answer, but just glanced up again at the mirror, which rattled against the windshield with every bump and curve.

I was doing a little rearview looking myself.

Here's the thing. Even if I had become disillusioned with Del, I don't believe I had become disappointed in him—not yet.

I mean, like I said, he was a planner. I'd seen my mama date men who couldn't think beyond which channel they were gonna turn to next, unless there was a big game coming up, and then their idea of planning was to ask her to pick up an extra bag of chips and dip for their friends. I myself had dated men who would pick me up and give me a kiss and ask, "So, what do you want to do tonight?"—

none of them having thought about it themselves except to hope that we might end up in the backseat or even back at their apartment. I'm sorry to admit it with some of those men, but most times we did.

On the other hand, take Del. When he picked me up for our first date, I asked him straight out, "Where's the desperate criminal planning to take the sole witness to his crime on their first date?" I was admiring how he looked out from under that ski mask—his beard not straggly like I'd been afraid, but groomed nice and tight, and chiseled features, you'd call them, underneath that. Those green eyes looked even better set in such a handsome face. He'd dressed up: a button-down shirt, a nice pair of khakis. He was older than I'd expected, older than me. Thirties maybe. Maybe even late thirties. A touch of gray in his beard. But I kind of liked all that.

"A surprise," said Del, and didn't elaborate, but just drove out of Eagle Nest and out along 64, and all of a sudden I thought, *Oh, wait, desperate criminal, sole witness.* My heart started racing and not in a good way. But then he pulled into Angel Fire and we went to Our Place for dinner. (Our Place! That's really the name.) My heart started racing in a better way after that.

Then there's the fact that he did indeed finish his degree at the community college, which shows discipline and dedication. And coming up with that story about his sister and why we were moving, laying out a cover story in advance, always thinking ahead. And planning for the heist itself—the "big one," he said, "the last one," though I knew better. Over the last year, whenever tuition came due, he'd hit another 7-Eleven or a gas station or a DVD store— "shaking up the modus operandi," he said, which seemed smart to me, but maybe he just got that from the movies he watched on our DVD player. He'd stolen that too.

That was how we spent most of our nights together, watching movies. I'd quit the 7-Eleven job at that point. It was dangerous, Del said—*ironically*, he said—and I'd got a job at one of the gift stores in town, keeping me home nights. Home meaning Del's mobile home, because it wasn't long before I'd moved in with him.

We'd make dinner—something out of a box because I'm not much of a cook, I'll admit—and I'd watch Court TV, which I love, while he did some of his homework for the business classes he was taking over at the college or read through the day's newspaper, scouring the world for opportunities, he said, balancing work and school and me. Later we'd watch a movie, usually something with a crime element like *Bank Job* or *Mission: Impossible* or some old movie like *The Sting* or *Butch Cassidy and the Sundance Kid* or all those *Godfather* movies like every man I've ever been with. I suggested *Bonnie & Clyde*, for obvious reasons, but he said it would be disadvantageous for us to see it and so we never did.

"Is that all you do, sit around and watch movies?" Mama asked on the phone, more than once.

"We go out some," I told her.

"*Out* out?" she asked, and I didn't know quite what she meant and I told her that.

"He surprises me sometimes," I said. "Taking me out for dinner."

(Which was true. "Let's go out for a surprise dinner," he'd say sometimes, even though the surprise was always the same, that we were just going to Our Place. But that was still good because it really was our place—both literally *and* figuratively—and there's romance in that.)

"He loves me," I'd tell Mama. "He holds me close at night and tells me how much he loves me, how much he can't live without me."

Mama grunted. She was in North Carolina. Two hours' time difference and almost a full country away, but still you could feel her disappointment like she was standing right there in the same room.

"That's how it starts," Mama would tell me, "'I can't live without you,'" mimicking the voice. "Then pretty soon 'I can't live without you' starts to turn stifling and sour and..."

Her voice trailed off. *And violent,* I knew she'd wanted to say.

And I knew where she was coming from, knew how her last boyfriend had treated her. I'd seen it myself, one of the reasons I finally just moved away, anywhere but there.

"I thought you were going to start a *new* life," she said, a different kind of disappointment in her voice then. "You could watch the tube and drink beer anywhere. You could date a loser here if that's all you're doing."

I twirled the phone cord in my hand, wanting just to be done with the conversation, but not daring to hang up. Not yet.

"Frugal," Mama said, making me regret again some of the things I'd told her about him. "Frugal's just a big word for cheap."

"Are things gonna be different someday?" I'd asked Del one night, the two of us lying in bed, him with his back to me. I ran my fingers across his shoulder when I asked it.

"Different?" he asked.

"Different from this."

He didn't answer at first. I kept rubbing his shoulder and let my hand sneak over and rub the top of his chest, caressing it real light, because I knew he liked that. The window was slid open and a breeze rustled the edge of those thin curtains. Just outside stood a short streetlight, one that the mobile home park had put up, and sometimes it kept me awake, shining all night, like it was aiming right for my face, leaving me sleepless.

After a while, I realized Del wasn't gonna answer at all, and I stopped rubbing his chest and turned over.

That night when I couldn't sleep, I knew it wasn't the streetlight at all.

For that big one, that *last* last one, Del had roamed those art galleries in downtown Taos after work at the garage. He watched the ads for gallery openings, finding a place that stressed *cash only,* real snooty because you know a lot of people would have to buy that artwork on time and not pay straight out for it all at once, but those weren't the type of people they were after. He'd looked up the address of the gallery owner, the home address, and we'd driven past that too.

I liked watching his mind work: the way he'd suddenly nod just slightly when we were walking across the Plaza or down the walkway between the John Dunn Shops, like he'd seen something important. Or the way his eyes narrowed and darted as we rode through the neighborhood where the gallery owner lived, keeping a steady speed, not turning his head, not looking as if he was looking.

We had a nice time at the gallery opening itself. At least at the beginning. Delwood looked smart in his blue blazer, even though it was old enough that it had gotten some shine at the elbows. And you could see how happy he was each time he saw a red dot on one of the labels—just more money added to the take—even if he first had to ask what each of those red dots meant.

I hated the gallery owner's tone when he answered that one, as if he didn't want Del or me there drinking from those plastic cups of wine or eating the cheese. He had a sleek suit, and his thin hair was gelled back dramatically, and he wore these square purple spectacles that he looked over when he was answering Del. I couldn't help but feel a little resentful toward him. But then I thought, *Square Specs will get his*, if you know what I mean. And, of course, he did.

"I like this one," I said in front of one of the pictures. It was a simple picture—this painting stuck in the back corner. A big stretch of blue sky and beneath it the different-colored blue of the ocean, and a mistiness to it, like the waves were kicking up spray. Two people sat on the beach, a man and a woman. They sort of leaned into one another, watching the water, and I thought about Del and me and began to feel nostalgic for something that we'd never had. The painting didn't have a red dot on it, but it did have a price: $3000. "With the money," I whispered to Delwood, "we could come back here and buy one of them, huh? Wouldn't that be ballsy? Wouldn't that be ironic?"

"Louise," he said, that tone again, telling me everything.

"I'm just saying," I said. "Can't you picture the two of us at the ocean like that? Maybe with the money, we could take a big trip, huh?"

"Can't you just enjoy your wine?" he whispered, and moved on to the next picture, not looking at it really, just at the label.

"Fine," I said after him, deciding I'd just stay there and let him finish casing out the joint, but then a couple came up behind me.

"Let's try s on this one," the woman whispered.

"S," said the man. "Okay. S." They looked at the picture of the beach, and I looked with them, wondering what they meant by "trying s." The man wrinkled his brow, squinted his eye, scratched his chin—like Del when's he's thinking, but this man seemed to be only playing at thinking. "Sappy," he said finally.

"Sentimental," said the woman, quick as she could.

"Um...Sugary."

"Saccharine."

"No fair," said the man. "You're just playing off my words."

The woman smirked at him. She had a pretty face, I thought. Bright, blue eyes and high cheekbones with freckles across them. She had on a gauzy top, some sort of linen, and even though it was just a thin swath of fabric, you could tell from the texture of it and the way she wore it that it was something fine. I knew, just knew suddenly, that it had probably cost more than the money Del had stolen from the 7-Eleven the night I first met him. And I knew too that I wanted a top just like it.

"Fine," she said, pretending to pout. "Here's another one. Schmaltzy."

"Better! Um...sad."

"No, *this* is sad," she said, holding up her own plastic wine glass.

"Agreed," he laughed.

"Swill," she whispered, dragging out the s sound, just touching his hand with her fingers, and they both giggled as they moved on to the next picture. And the next letter, it turned out.

T was for *tarnished*, for *trashy*, for *tragic*.

Del had made the full circuit. Even from across the room, I could see the elbows shining on his blazer. Then he turned and saw me and made a short side-nod with his head, motioning toward the door. Time to head back home.

I looked once more at the painting of the couple on the beach. I'd thought it was pretty. Still did.

I'd thought the wine had tasted pretty good too.

But suddenly it all left a bad taste in my mouth.

A bad taste still as we continued south now.

The steep turns and drop-offs that had taken us out of Taos had given way to villages, small homes on shaded roads, people up and about, going about their lives. I saw the signs for the Santuario de Chimayó, which I'd visited when I first moved out this way, picking Northern New Mexico just because it seemed different, in every way, from where I'd grown up. I'd found out about the church in Chimayo from a guidebook I'd ordered off the internet, learned about the holy earth there and how it healed the sick. When I'd visited it myself, I gathered up some of the earth and mailed it off to Mama—not that she was sick, but just unhappy. I don't know what I'd imagined she'd do with it, rub it on her heart or something. "Thanks for the dirt," she told me when she got it.

"Do you think they've found Square Specs yet?" I asked Del.

"Square Specs?"

"The gallery owner," I said. "Do you think the cleaning lady found him, or a customer?"

We were nearing another curve and Del eased the Nova around it slowly, carefully.

"Probably somebody will have found him by now. Like I told you last night, I tied him up pretty good. I don't think he'd have gotten loose on his own. But by now..."

He sped up a little bit. I don't think he did it consciously, but I noticed.

A while later, I asked "Are we gonna do anything fun with the money?"

"What kind of fun?"

"I don't know. Clothes, jewelry...a big-screen TV, a vacation. Something fun."

He scratched his beard.

"That's just extravagance."

"Are you gonna make *all* the decisions?"

"All the good ones," he said. He gave a tense chuckle. "Don't you ever consider the future?"

But again, he missed what I was saying. The future is exactly what I was thinking about.

After we bypassed Santa Fe proper, Del had us two-laning it again on a long road toward Albuquerque: miles and miles of dirt hills and scrubby little bushes, some homes that looked like people still lived there and others that were just crumbling down to nothing. The Ortiz Mountains stood way out in the distance. We got stuck for a while behind a dusty old pickup going even slower than we were, but Del was still afraid to pass, especially with that trailer stretched out behind us. We just poked along behind the truck until it decided to turn down some even dustier old road, and every mile we spent behind it, my blood began to boil up more.

I know Del was picturing roadblocks out on the interstate, and helicopters swooping low, waiting for some rattling old Nova like ours to do something out of the ordinary, tip our hand—picturing it even more after I asked about that gallery owner getting loose. But after a while, I just wanted to scream, "Go! Go! Go!" or else reach over and grab the wheel myself, stretch my leg over and press down on the gas, hurl us ahead somehow and out of all this. And then there was all the money in the trunk and all the things I thought we could have done with it but clearly weren't going to do.

Once or twice, I even thought about pulling out that pistol my-self and pointing it at him. "I don't want anybody to get hurt," I might say, just like he would. "Just do like I ask, okay?" That was the first time I thought about it—not even serious about it then.

Still, it was all I could to hide all that impatience, all that restlessness and nervous energy. None of it helped by that tap tap tap tap tap of the mirror against the windshield. I felt like my skin was turning inside out.

"I need to pee," I said finally.

"Next place I see," said Del, a glance at me, one more glance in the rearview. I looked in the side mirror. Nothing behind us but road. I looked ahead of us. Nothing but road. I looked around the car. Just me and him and that damn mirror tapping seconds into minutes and hours and more.

We stopped in Madrid, which isn't pronounced like the city in Spain but with the emphasis on the first syllable: MAD-rid. It used to be a mining town back in the Gold Rush days, but then dried up and became a ghost town. Now it's a big artists' community. I didn't know all that when we pulled in, but there was a brochure.

We parked lengthwise along the road by one of the rest stops at one end of the town—outhouse, more like it. Del waited in the car, but after I was done, I tapped on his window. "I'm gonna stretch my legs," I said, and strolled off down the street before he could answer. I didn't care whether he followed, but pretty soon I heard the scuff scuff of his feet on the gravel behind me. I really did need a break, just a minute or two out of the car, and it did help some, even with him following. We walked on like that, him silent behind me except for his footsteps as I picked up that brochure and looked in the store windows at antiques and pottery and vintage cowboy boots. Fine arts in the mix as well. "Wanna make one *last* last job?" I wanted to joke. Half-joke. "Get something for *me* this time?"

I walked in one store. Del followed. I just browsed the shelves. The sign outside had advertised "Local artisans and craftspeople," and the store had quirky stuff the way those kinds of places do: big sculptures of comical looking cowboys made out of recycled bike parts, close-up photographs of rusted gas pumps and bramblebush, hand-dipped soy candles, gauzy-looking scarves that reminded me of the woman at the gallery the night before. I browsed through it all, taking my time, knowing that Del was right up on me, almost feeling his breath on my back.

One shelf had a bowl full of sock monkey keychains. A cardboard sign in front of the bowl said, "Handcrafted. $30."

"Excuse me," I called over to the man behind the counter. He'd been polishing something and held a red rag in his hand. "Is this the price of the bowl or of the monkeys?"

"Oh," he said, surprised, as if he'd never imagined someone might misunderstand that. "The monkeys," he said, then corrected himself: "Each monkey," he said. "The bowl's not for sale at all."

I turned to Del.

"Why don't you get me one of these?" I asked him, holding up a little monkey.

I tried to say it casual-like, but it was a challenge. I felt like both of us could hear it in my voice. Even the man behind the register heard it, I imagine, even though he'd made a show of going back to his polishing.

"What would you want with a thing like that?" Del said.

"Sometimes a girl likes a present. It makes her feel special." I dangled the sock monkey on my finger in front of him, and Del watched it sway, like he was mesmerized or suspicious. "Or is the romance gone here?"

"It's kind of pricey for a keychain."

I leaned in close for just a second, whispered, "Why don't you just slip it in your pocket then?"

Del cut his eyes toward the man behind the counter, then turned back to me. His look said *hush.* "I told you last night was the last time," he said, a low growl.

I just swayed that monkey back and forth.

A woman in a green dress jingled through the door then and went up to the counter. "You were holding something for me," she said, and the man put down his polish rag, and they started talking.

You could tell that Del was relieved not to have a witness anymore. "C'mon, Louise," he said. "Be serious."

But me? For better or worse, I just upped the ante.

"Suppose I said to you that this monkey"—I jerked my finger to make his little monkey body bounce—"this monkey represents love to me."

"Love?" he said.

"The potential for love," I clarified. "The possibility of it."

"How's that?"

"Suppose I told you that my daddy, the last time I saw him, me only six years old, he comes into my bedroom to tuck me in and he gives me a sock-puppet monkey, bigger than this one, but looking pretty much the same," (because the truth is they all do, handcrafted or not), "and he says to me, 'Hon, Daddy's going away for a while, but while I'm gone, this little monkey is gonna take care of you, and any time you find yourself thinking of me or wondering about me, I want you to hug this monkey close to you, and I'll be there with you. Wherever I am, I'll be here with you.' And he touched his heart."

I wasn't talking loud, but the man behind the counter and the customer had grown quiet, listening to me now even as they pretended not to. It was a small store, they couldn't help it. Del wasn't sweating, not really, but with all the attention—two witnesses to our argument now—he looked like might break out in one any second.

"And Mama was behind him, leaned against the door watching us," I went on. "Anyone probably could have seen from her face that he wasn't coming back and that it was her fault and she felt guilty, but I was too young to know that then. And I dragged that monkey around with me every day and slept with it every night and hugged it close. And finally Mama threw it away, which told me the truth. 'Men let you down,' she told me when I cried about it, because she'd just broken up with her latest boyfriend and had her own heart broken. 'Men always let you down,' she told me. 'Don't you ever fool yourself into forgetting that.' And I stopped crying.

But still, whatever Mama told me and whether my daddy came back or not, I believed—I *knew*—that there had been love there, there in that moment, in that memory, you know?"

Del looked over at the wall, away from the shopkeeper and his customer, and stared at this sculpture of a cowboy on a bucking bronco—an iron silhouette. The tilt of his head and the nervous look in his eyes reminded me of the first night we'd met, at the 7-Eleven, when he'd called me "Ma'am" and I'd told him my age. Seemed like here was another conversation where he was playing catch up, but this time he seemed fearful for different reasons.

"And maybe," I said, helping him along, "just maybe if you bought this for me, I'd know you really loved me, for always and truly. Now," I said, "would *that* get it through your thick skull?"

Out of the corner of my eye, I saw an embarrassed look on the storekeeper's face—embarrassed for Del and maybe embarrassed for me too. His customer, the woman in green, cleared her throat, and the shopkeeper said to her, "Yes, just let me find that for you."

Del shifted his lower jaw to the side—another indication, I'd learned, that his mind was working on something, weighing things. He really was sweating now, and still staring at that bucking bronco sculpture like he felt some kinship with the cowboy on top, like staring at it might give him an answer somehow.

"What was your monkey's name?" he asked me.

I gave out a long sigh, with an extra dose of irritation in it. He was missing the whole point, just like always. "I don't know," I told him. I sighed again. "Murphy," I said.

His look changed then, just a thin crease of the forehead, a tiny raise of the eyebrow. "Murphy the monkey?" he said. He wasn't looking at the sculpture now, wasn't looking afraid anymore. "Louise," he began. "I don't really think that this monkey represents the love we share, and the truth is that thirty dollars seems like quite a bit for—"

But I didn't hear the rest of it. I just put that monkey down, then turned and walked out the door, slamming it behind me the way I'd slammed the Nova's door that morning.

I can't say whether I wanted him to call for me to come back or rush out after me, something dramatic like that, but if I did, I was indeed fooling myself, just like Mama had warned. That wasn't Delwood. When I got in the car, I saw him through the window, slowly coming back—those sad footsteps, scuff scuff scuff. No hurry at all, like he knew I'd be waiting.

We rode on in silence after that—a heavy silence, you know what I mean. More ghost towns where people used to have hopes and dreams and now there was nothing but rubble and a long stretch of empty land. I wasn't even angry now, but just deflated, disappointed.

"Men will do that to you," my mama told me another time. "After a while you feel like it's not even worth trying." I'd known what she meant, theoretically. Now I knew in a different way.

Soon the two-lane widened, and the strip malls started up and fast food restaurants—civilization. I saw a Wendy's, and asked if it was okay to stop.

"I'll pick from the dollar menu," I said, sarcastic-like.

Del didn't say anything, just pulled through the drive-thru and ordered what I wanted. He didn't get anything for himself. I think it was just out of spite.

Late afternoon, we cruised through Winslow, Arizona, which I guess would get most people in the mind of that Eagles song. Standing on a corner and all that. But it had me thinking of the past and my old high school flame. Winslow was his name, Win, everybody called him, and I couldn't help but start indulging those what-ifs about everything I'd left behind. It was a fleeting moment; Win and I had had our own troubles, of course, but it struck me hard, discontented as I was with things and people—thinking myself about running down the road and trying to loosen my own load.

Then toward evening, we stopped at a motel in Kingman, one

of those cheap ones that have been there since Route 66 was an interesting road and not just a tourist novelty—the ones that now looked like they'd be rented for the hour by people who didn't much care what the accommodations were like.

Del checked us in, pulled the Nova around to the stairwell closest our room, and parked sideways across several spaces since that was the only way we'd fit.

"Get your kicks," I said.

"Kicks?" he said, baffled.

"Route 66," I said, pointing to a sign. "Guess we couldn't afford the Holiday Inn either, huh?"

He stared straight ahead, drummed his fingers light against the steering wheel. He curled up his bottom lip a little and chewed on his beard.

"You know those court shows you watch on TV?" Del said finally. "And how you tell me some of those people are so stupid? You listen to their stories and you laugh and you tell me, 'That's where they went wrong' or 'They should've known better than that.'"

"Do you mean," I said, "something like a man who robs a convenience store, then calls up the clerk he's held at gunpoint and asks her out for a date?" I felt bad about it as soon as I said it. Part of why I fell in love with him and now I was complaining about it.

"There were extenuating circumstances in that instance," he said, and this warning sound had crept into his tone, one that I hadn't heard before. "I'm just saying that we need to be fairly circumspect now about whatever we do. Any misstep might put us in front of a real judge, and it won't be a laughing matter, I can guarantee you that." He turned to face me. "Louise," he said, again that way he does. "I love you, Louise, but sometimes...well, little girl, sometimes you just don't seem to be thinking ahead."

It was the *little girl* that got me, or maybe the *extenuating* or the *circumspect*, or maybe just him implying that I was being stupid, or maybe all of it, the whole day.

"Del," I said through clenched teeth, putting some bite into his

name, same as he always did me. "I love you, and when I say that, I
mean it. But sometimes, Del, sometimes, I could just kill you."

He nodded. "You'd go to jail for that too," he said, slow and
even as always, but still with that edge of warning to it. He handed
the room key across to me. "You go on in. I want to check that
things haven't shifted back in the trailer."

"Fine," I said, toughening the word up to let him hear how I
felt. He stared at me for a second, then went back to get our bags.
In the rearview, I watched him bending open the tarp covering the
trailer, but still I just sat there.

I don't know how to describe what I was feeling. Anger? Sadness? I don't know what was running through my head, either.
What to do next, maybe. Whether to go up to the room and carry on
like we'd planned, like he seemed to expect I'd do, or to step out of
all this, literally just step out of the car and start walking in another
direction.

But then I knew if I really did leave, he'd come after me. Not
dramatic, not begging, but I knew he wouldn't let me go. Can't live
without you, that's what he'd said, and like Mama said, sometimes
that kind of love could turn ugly fast. I'd seen it before.

"You just gonna sit there?" Del called out.

He'd opened the trunk now, blocking my view, just a voice behind me. More rearranging.

"No. I'm going up," I called back. Then just before I stepped
out of the car, I opened up the glove compartment and slipped the
gun into my purse.

In the motel room, I locked the door to the bathroom, set down my
purse, and turned the water on real hot before climbing in. I stood
there in the steam and rubbed that little bitty bar of soap over me,
washing like I had layers of dust from those two-lane roads and
that truck we'd followed for so long.

I thought about what would happen after I got out. "Sometimes people are too far apart in their wants," I could say. "I do love

you, Del, but sometimes a person needs to move on." It was just a matter of saying it. It would be easy to do, I knew. I'd done it before back with Win all those years ago, and I hadn't needed a gun then. But the gun showed I was serious in a different way. More than that, it was protection. "I'm not taking all the money, Del," I might say. "That's not what's going on here. That's not the point." As if he had ever got the point.

I took both towels when I got out of the shower. The steam swirled around me while I stood there drying myself off—one towel wrapped around me and one towel for my hair, leaving him none.

Would he try to talk me out of it? Would he try to take the gun away? Would I have to tie him up the way he'd left that gallery owner back in Taos? Even thinking about it made me sad.

He was sitting there when I came out of the bathroom, sitting on the one chair in the room, staring at the blank television, the screen of it covered in a light layer of dust. I hadn't taken the gun out, but just held my purse in my hand, feeling the weight of it. Thinking that I might have to use it. I suddenly wished I'd gotten dressed first. I mean, picture it: Me wrapped in two towels and holding a gun? Hardly a smooth getaway.

Del's face was...well, *pensive* was the word that came to mind. He taught me that word, I thought. I wouldn't have known it without him. And that kept me from saying immediately what I needed to say. I just stood there, feeling a single drip of water sneak past the towel around my head, race down my back.

"You never talked much about your daddy," he said, breaking the silence. "He really leave you when you were six?"

"Yes," I said, and I realized then that I felt like I was owed something for that.

Del stared at the blank television. I turned my own head that way, toward the gray curve of the screen. I could see his face there, reflected toward me, kind of distorted, distant.

"He really give you a sock monkey when he left?"

I thought about that, but I was thinking now about what I owed Del.

"No," I told him, and I could hear the steel in my own voice. "But what Mama said, she did say that."

I stared hard at the dusty TV screen, at his reflection there. I saw then that his fists were clenched, and that he clenched them even tighter at my answer. I could feel myself tighten. I knew then that he knew the pistol was gone. I didn't take my eyes off that reflection as I pulled up the strap of my pocketbook, just in case he stood up quick and rushed me. But he dropped his head down a little, and I saw his profile in the reflection, which meant he'd turned to see me straight on.

"You lied to me, then?" He was clenching his hand hard, so much that if I'd been closer, I might have backed away. But there was a bed between us. And the pocketbook was open now.

"If that's what you want to take from it."

His eyes watched me hard. Those green eyes. First thing I'd really noticed about him up close.

"Do you believe Cora was right?"—meaning Mama. That's her name.

"I don't know. Do you?"

Those eyes narrowed. Thinking again. And it struck me that I could just about list every little thing he did when he was pondering over something: how he sometimes stared hard at the wall or other times stared off into space with this faraway gaze, running his fingers through his hair or through the tip of his beard, biting at his bottom lip or chewing on that beard or just shifting his jaw one way or the other. Usually left, I corrected myself. Always to the left. And sure enough, just as I thought it, he shifted his jaw just that way, setting it in place.

I almost laughed despite myself. *Men always let you down,* Mama had said, but Del had come through with his jaw jut exactly like expected. At least you could count on him for that. And all of a sudden, I felt embarrassed for having taken that gun from the glove compartment, just wanted to run out in my towel and put it back.

"Do you want a surprise?" he asked, and I almost laughed again.

"It's a long drive back to Our Place."

"A new surprise."

"Sure," I said.

"The story we told back at the mobile home park, about me having a sister out in Victorville," he said then. "I really do. Haven't talked to her in a while. We were estranged." He stretched out the word. "She's in real estate. Got us a deal she worked out on a foreclosure. A house. Said she'd let me do some work for her, at her company, now that I have a degree. It's all worked out. I needed to get the down payment on it, so I figured, one more job. One big one and that'd be it." He tapped his hand on the side of the chair, like you would tap your fingers, but his whole hand because it was still clenched. I think it was the most words he'd ever said in one breath. "That's my surprise."

Part of me wanted to go over to him, but I didn't. *Don't you ever fool yourself into forgetting*, I heard Mama saying. I stood right in the doorway, still dripping all over the floor, all over myself.

"I stole that painting you wanted too," he said, as if he was embarrassed to admit it. "We can't hang it in the house, at least not the living room, not yet, not where anyone might see, but you can take it out and look at it sometimes, maybe, if you want. It's out in the trunk now if you want me to get it." He gave a big sigh, the kind he might give late at night when he was done with talking to me, done with the day. But something else in his face this time, some kind of struggle, like he wanted to go quiet, but still had more to tell. "But I was serious about that being the last one," he said finally. "This is a fresh start and I want to do it right. That's why I paid for this."

He opened his fist then. The sock monkey keychain was in it. Crushed a little in his grip, but there it was.

"I knew that story wasn't true, about your daddy," he said. "I knew it while you were telling it. But it being true or not, that wasn't the point, was it?"

I smiled and shook my head. No no no, that wasn't the point. And yes yes yes too, of course.

*   *   *

Needless to say, I didn't kill him. And I didn't take my half and hit the highway.

When we got in the car the next day, I almost didn't see the rust along the wheel well, and I closed the door so soft that I almost didn't hear that loose metal rolling around inside. While Delwood packed the trunk and rearranged stuff one more time under that tarp, I slipped that pistol into the glove compartment, just like it had been in the first place. I didn't touch it again.

As Delwood drove us along 66 and out of town, I rolled down the window and kicked up my heels, leaned over against him.

You might imagine that I was stuck on that $3000 painting in the trunk and that house ahead, and partly I was, but again you'd be missing the point. It was the sock monkey that meant the most to me. Light as a trinket but with a different kind of weight to it. When I hung it from the rearview mirror, the rattle there died down almost to a whisper, and it all seemed like a smoother ride ahead for a while.

COMMISSION

Find yourself a solid man—that's what Mama always said. A simple man too, the simpler the better. "Hitch yourself to a dreamer," she warned me more than once, wagging that finger of hers, "and *his* dreams are gonna become *your* nightmares, Louise. You mark my words."

I don't know that I'd call Del a dreamer. A planner, yes, and a doer. He's the kind of man who follows through, not just the kind who sits there thinking about it, a beer in one hand, the remote in the other, top button unhitched on his jeans.

And I'd never call him simple. Not me.

But sometimes dreams aren't where you expect them—by which I mean to say, sometimes what looks like a plan turns out to be a dream. Other times, someone else's plans and dreams get all caught up with your own so you can't tell which is whose and whose is which. And then other times it's not somebody else's dream that knocks you with a firm wallop but your own, sneaking up on you when you least expect it.

By the time the police showed up at Brenda's office, I'd lost track of it all, who wanted what, who was responsible, and why. But what I'm saying now is this: Sometimes, you've got no one to blame but yourself.

*   *   *

The afternoon the police showed up was nearly two months after we'd moved to Victorville, California, on Del's idea of a fresh start—nearly two months of working for nothing at his sister Brenda's real estate firm, of Del desperate to drum up even one listing or make even one sale, of us stuck in separate bedrooms at Brenda's house. Nearly two months of both of us making a lot of sacrifices trying to put Del's life of crime far behind him.

Or so I thought.

That was about the third thing that crossed my mind after the two detectives walked in the front door of Brenda's office—plainclothes, but just screaming cop, you know—and Del stiffened up all of a sudden, straightened his tie, brushed the bottom of his beard, glanced toward the back exit.

Old reflexes. That was my first thought. *Habit.*

"We're looking for Ms. Grayson," one of the cops said. "Is she in?" The two of them looked almost exactly alike: same height, same firm jaw and no-nonsense haircut, same swagger. But the one that spoke first seemed lumpier in the face than the other one—his left cheekbone just a bit higher than his right. *Jekyll and Hyde*, that was my *second* thought, and it struck me kind of funny, but only until I saw how pukey green Del's face had turned.

Before either of us could answer, Brenda poked her head out of the back office, that beak nose of hers and another of these floral print dresses she'd apparently bought in bulk. "I'm Brenda Grayson. Can I help you?"

"Just a few minutes of your time, ma'am," said lumpy Mr. Hyde. "If we may."

"Of course." Brenda turned on that fake smile of hers—everyone a potential customer, just the way she'd been lecturing Del for weeks. "Come right in."

Jekyll swung a hard look back at Del as they went into Brenda's office. The door swung shut hard behind them.

Del hadn't been speaking to me for about a week—that's how

bad things had gotten—and I hadn't been much better, meeting silence with silence. But this seemed the time to break it.

"What was that about?" I asked.

Del shrugged, but he was biting that bottom lip, chewing on his beard.

"Del," I said. "They wouldn't have tracked you from New Mexico all the way up here. And even if they did, wouldn't they have just asked for you?"

"This wouldn't pertain to New Mexico. This is about something here."

I didn't want to bring up the next thing, the very thing we'd specifically *not* been talking about, but I did. "Are you worried about that night in the foreclosed house?"

Del stiffened up again.

"Can't we just forget that happened?"

"I'm just trying to figure out why you think any of *that*"—I pointed at Brenda's office—"would have something to do with you."

"Louise," he said, and gave me his "Louise Look" too—double-barreled, so to speak. Then he shook his head, which, given that green tint, was probably not a good idea.

About the same moment that Brenda's door opened again, Del gave me a quick shush, and Jekyll and Hyde came out with their eyes trained directly on him. That was when the third thought hit me about whether Del hadn't entirely embraced a life of *not* crime like he'd planned—and a whole lot of questions followed that one: Had I been the one who'd set him back into his old ways? Was it those dreams I'd been talking about? And the big one: Why hadn't he just told me?

Looking back over our trip from that mobile home park in Taos, New Mexico, to Del's sister's house in Victorville, I see now how I'd indulged in some pretty hefty daydreaming about the life ahead of us, even if I didn't think of it as such at the time.

"If you could meet any movie star in Los Angeles, any one,

which one would you want to meet?" I asked Del, somewhere just past Needles. "You can pick a pretty girl. I won't be jealous."

That had been our second day on the road, Del at the wheel of that creaky old Nova, those big meaty hands of his precisely at ten and two, and me in the passenger seat watching mile after mile of the Mojave Desert blurring past as we finally began to pick up speed again.

Don't get me started on what it was like watching Del white-knuckle that trailer through all those sharp turns in the Black Mountain Range back in Arizona. A couple of times, I took down the sock monkey keychain hanging from the rearview mirror, the one he'd given me the night before, and squeezed it tight—my talisman, Del had already started to call it.

"We're not going as far as LA," Del said, his eyes not leaving the road.

"I know that." I mean, I did have a map in my lap, didn't I? And I was perfectly capable of reading it. "But it's not that much further, is it? No one would be looking for us in LA any more than Victorville." By which I meant the police, of course. "We could have a getaway, just the two of us."

"Brenda is expecting us tonight. Sunday dinner, and work first thing tomorrow."

"A fresh start," I said, echoing the way he'd been talking about it. "A fresh start which could also wait until Tuesday, couldn't it?"

He dwelled on that, chewing his beard then too.

"Things haven't always been easy with me and Brenda," he said, then took a deep breath. "She had to take care of me a lot when we were younger, and I...I was never the most responsible about returning the favor. I told her that we'd be there for Sunday dinner, and I want to adhere to the schedule as planned. I need to prove that I can do right by her, that family can do right by family."

That conversation did two things: 1) surprised me, because Del really is the most conscientious person I've ever met, and 2) left me a tad apprehensive myself about that sister of his, hinting already at something I maybe didn't want to know.

But fine, if Del felt strongly about it...no pressure. I didn't even ask him again about his movie star.

In case you're interested, however, my own answer is Joaquin Phoenix.

Instead of thinking about a night on the town, I started picturing instead the big welcome that Del's sister was probably gonna be giving us, her little brother and his new...well, I'm not sure how he would've described me to her. Girlfriend? Partner? For all the words Del was master of, it seemed like *fiancée* hadn't yet made it into his vocabulary. I'm not the type to push in that direction either, but still, wouldn't it be nice to be on the *family* end of the spectrum instead of the *floozy* one?

"This house she's got us set up with," I said. "Is there gonna be room for a swing on the porch?"

Del shrugged. "Brenda wasn't entirely communicative on those particulars."

Taciturn. That's what Del had called himself, always liking the high-dollar words. I called it *terse.*

"I hope that the kitchen has some of those tall cabinets, with the glass on front, and granite countertops. And room in the—what do they call it? The master suite, for a king-sized bed."

Dreams, like I said. Just setting myself up to get knocked on my butt.

Whatever Del might've thought later, I never blamed him for the fact that there was no house. That was all Brenda, and when I finally met her, all that apprehensiveness just got deeper and uglier.

"Oh, Delwood, I couldn't help but move that listing when I had the chance," Brenda told us that first night with a lot of sighing and head-shaking and all this heartache about the bubble bursting, foreclosures and short sales everywhere, people scrambling to make payments, selling at a loss. "These people are losing their homes, they're desperate, they're angry. Some of them, after the evictions are served, do you know they break back into those very same houses and vandalize them? Just to punish...I don't know who. The banks? Us? Because we can't sell that." Then again with the head shaking. "When an opportunity presents itself...you do what you have to in this market, Delwood, and do some things that, I'll admit, you might have some conflicting ideas about."

That was Brenda pure and simple—right down to the way she kept up that smile even through all the head shaking and everything. *Emotional contagion*, she'd explain later. *Affective communication*. Some book she'd read, but apparently not close enough to pick up on my own very real emotions while she was laying the bad news on us.

I didn't blame Del either for being all starry-eyed himself about the life that Brenda was leading and what it seemed to promise for us. She looked the picture of success, her hair in this suave 'do and rings on almost every finger and a blue silk dress that was more a going-out dress than a staying-in one. Her house had a Lexus in the front and a view of Spring Valley Lake in the back, all this blue water and fancy yachts, and the inside looked like it came out of one of those magazines that I used to read on the late shift at the 7-Eleven. The art on the walls had gold frames, like real gold flecks it looked like, and the carpet was vacuumed in two directions, and she'd turned all the couch pillows up on their corners like a row of diamonds. (*Divan*, she called it—like brother, like sister.) She'd decorated the place with all these porcelain cows and deer and monkeys and whatnot, like a ceramic zoo had exploded and took the farm with it.

I had been starry-eyed in my own way, like I said, but with the doubts creeping in, I was beginning to feel more than a little uncomfortable. Some of it seemed personal: how Brenda gave me the once-over before I sat down on that *divan*, like I might've had something on my backside, and how she kept darting glances my way when I picked up a blue and white pig—afraid I'd drop it or pocket it or I don't know what. And the big welcome? Nothing but cheese and crackers and some veggies and dip—on a silver platter (no lie), but tasting like it had all been in the fridge a day too long.

When Del finally got down to business that first night, threading his fingers almost like in prayer, he looked across Brenda's mahogany coffee table and asked, "What's our overall strategy for trying to make the best of the bubble burst here?" and she met his gaze just as squarely.

"Delwood," she told him. "You *make* your business, that's all I have to say. Confidence is the key. You do what it takes. *We're* going to do what it takes."

To be honest, maybe I do blame Del for that, because who couldn't see that it wasn't a real answer?

"Well," I said finally, "should Del and I just get a hotel for now?"

"I wouldn't even consider it!" Brenda said. "You'll just stay here."

"Oh, I wouldn't want to be indebted," I told her, hoping that Del might pick up on it.

"Not at all." Brenda turned a big smile Del's way. "Delwood's family, after all."

The way she emphasized Del's name only confirmed, of course, which "F" I probably was, just like I'd expected.

I shrugged. I sighed.

"Which bedroom is ours?"

Which then led to Brenda's big surprised "Oh!" and "*Ours?*" and "I hadn't even *considered* that..."

Del looked like a teenager caught with a *Playboy*. I had to hold myself back from shouting *Man up, buddy!*

It wouldn't have mattered anyway. All Brenda had was her kids' old rooms, a twin bed in each of them. Superman sheets on one, Star Wars on the other—the kinds of things they'd probably outgrown long before they'd moved out themselves.

"Your sister doesn't like me," I told Del the next evening, after our first day in the office. We were unloading our stuff into a storage warehouse that he'd rented—the very place Brenda had recommended, of course, like she'd laid out yet another plan that Del was gonna follow to a T.

"She likes you fine, Louise."

"Then how come you can't look at me when you say that?"

"I'm looking at where to put things."

"Where to put things!" I said. "Take your pick!" I swept my arm around. The place was big enough that we could've backed the whole trailer into it and shut the door—maybe the car itself. I wasn't helping him unload: spiteful, I guess. "Why'd you have to rent such a big one anyway?"

"It was the only unit they had available," he mumbled. He lifted up another box from the trailer and carried it over to the corner, plopped it down. "Louise, what difference does it make if Brenda doesn't like you?"

"Aha!" I said. "You admit it!"

"It was just a theoretical question." I wasn't sure whether that was upping the ante on *hypothetical* or not.

"My *theory* is that your sister doesn't think I'm good enough for you." Sisters and moms. That's how it's always been. Nitpicking this, clucking their tongues over that. As if those men—their brothers, their sons—were doing me a favor by dating me.

"She's giving me a good job," he said. "And look how she offered you some work."

At breakfast that morning, Brenda had asked if I had any receptionist skills, and before I knew it, I'd been shuttled along to the office with them.

"Delwood," I said, and hated myself for using his full first name, just like his sister had been doing. "That's not work, that's the terms of the rent—*indentured servitude*, if you ask me."

I enunciated the term, throwing it in just for him. He wasn't swayed.

"And that wasn't any spur-of-the-moment generosity," I went on. "Seemed like she had it planned from the start, with that little script ready and all." She'd already written out instructions on a pink index card—"RECEPTIONIST" in black Sharpie at the top and beneath it a quick scrawl of how I was supposed to answer the phone. "Good [morning, afternoon]. It's a beautiful day at Grayson Realty. How may I direct your call?" And beneath that, she'd written: "If someone is coming in the door, instead say: 'How may I help you?'"

"What if it's raining?" I'd asked her, and Brenda had shook her head like she felt sorry for me.

"Attitude is everything, Louise."

And here was Del now, probably thinking *bad attitude* himself.

As I watched, he unloaded the gun from the glove compartment and was tucking it behind our old TV—a symbol of putting that old life behind him. *Let's go back*, I started to say, even then, even if it meant a life of crime sometimes.

"Did you hear what your sister said last night when you told her we had a lot of stuff to put into storage?"

"She said she could recommend a storage facility that she uses herself."

"She said, and I quote, 'What woman doesn't travel heavy?' And she was glancing at my hips as she said it."

"You're reading too much into this, Louise."

"And why does she need a storage unit anyway, with everything she's got crammed in that house? Does she rotate out those porcelain cows or what?"

"Louise," he said, and gave me the "Louise Look"—the start of that trend.

"And it's not just me, Del. Look at how she's treating you. The way she walked you through using the Multiple Listings Service like you'd never seen a computer before. How she made it seem like a real favor that she was giving us those fancy cell phones to use, stressing that they'd stay in *her* name. It was like she was talking to a third-grader how she introduced you to that lockbox key and all, told you where to keep it, not to lose it."

When Brenda left the office, I'd mimicked her about it. *This may look like a walkie-talkie, but it's actually solid gold and it*

does magic tricks! Not only will it open any door, but if used cor-
rectly, it will let you walk through walls! Remember, though: With
great power comes great responsibility...

Del hadn't been amused at the time. He wasn't any more
pleased now.

"She was just setting me up," he said.

"You got that right," I said. "Both of us, best I can tell."

All Del's talk about "fresh starts" and "better lives" might've
been more convincing if he hadn't ended up unloading the painting
he stole for me: a couple sitting together on the beach, leaning into
one another and looking out at the big water and the big sky like it
was all there just for them.

Nostalgia is funny. You can even get it for something you never
really had.

When we got back to Brenda's, I yanked that sock monkey off
the rearview mirror. Something was going to stay mine, no matter
what.

To hear Brenda and Del talk over the next few weeks, good times
were just around the bend. You'd have thought they were gearing
up for some Glamour Shots portrait to get posted on signs and
shopping center benches and billboards, all smiles and some fancy
tagline like "The Siblings That Sell!" She kept him pumped up on
positive thinking and kept him on a strict work schedule: familiarizing himself with the properties during such-and-such hours,
searching the listings during this very specific time, covering an
open house for one of her listings on a Sunday afternoon, recording
almost every move he made in a slick journal she'd given him—and
then checking through it herself about twice a week, tsk-tsking like
a schoolteacher.

"Here's a schedule for cold calls," she said one day. "Two hours
on Tuesday afternoon, two on Thursday morning, these exact
times."

Del pulled at an earlobe.

"But Brenda, is anyone home then? Housewives?"

"Housewives are a target audience." She gave him a firm nod.

But no matter how many times Brenda reminded us that Victorville had once been the second fastest-growing city in the nation, and no matter how many tasks and tactics she recommended for Del, the truth kept slapping us in the face. Brenda's office was swanky ("I added the chair rail to dress it up," she said), but the storefronts on either side were hung with faded "For Lease" signs, and the whole city looked dry and dusty and sometimes a little done for. She kept talking about "redevelopment" plans in Old Town, but I didn't see much action in that direction, and the only places doing any real business were the thrift stores and the food pantry. The real estate listings all advertised "drastically reduced" prices and "extremely motivated" sellers, and that phrase "MAKE ANY OFFER!" seemed less enthusiastic than just flat-out desperate. Del finally gave up counting the houses moving into foreclosure. All those cold calls ended in a lot of hang-ups or else with someone bending his ear with hard-luck stories about how much they owed and how little their house was worth or how it was already on the market and how long it had been there and how they'd lost their jobs and when was it all gonna change?

That last one was a question I'd already been asking myself.

My job was relatively easy. Mostly I just transferred calls to Brenda, or else jotted down the names and times of other realtors calling in to schedule appointments to show some of Brenda's listings—courtesy kind of stuff, but it helped me get to know, at least by name, a lot of the folks in that community: Stanley Weissbratten, Margo Johnson, Kevin Middleton, Della Busch—a bunch of names, that was all, and those hints of desperation in their own voices.

The smartphone Brenda had given me was registered in her name, so I didn't want any charges on it for downloading a game, but I'd found a free version of hangman on there, and that kept me busy. Meanwhile, Brenda spent a lot of time on her own phone, holed up in her office, and sometimes I could hear her almost shouting behind the closed door: "We've got to be on top of the foreclosure market" and "Vandals beat us to it? How could that happen?" and "No, no, the window has to be clear." She seemed awfully upset about that one. "Windex," I wanted to tell her when she came out, but I held my tongue.

I didn't have much luck trying to steer folks Del's way, either the call-ins or the walk-ins—and one guy was downright rude about working *only* with Brenda. He sauntered through the office like he owned the place, with this greasy comb-over and this smarmy attitude, and he called me "sweetheart" once when Del wasn't around. Marvin was his name, and Brenda turned on that same fake smile whenever he came around, but I had the feeling that whatever he was looking at, he wasn't ever going to buy.

As much as Brenda shut Del out sometimes, she'd also suddenly drag him out the door other days, real urgent-like: a sudden walk-through, prepping a comp, taking some measurements, hardly any of it going anywhere.

"I'm learning things, I am," Del said. "But it does seem an...uneven apprenticeship."

"Don't most apprentices get *paid*?"

"Commission only," he said. "That's what realtors work on, you know that. And Brenda's resolute on that point."

Ruthless was the word I'd use.

Every time I talked to Mama, she asked how "Mr. Real Estate Tycoon" was doing. The one time I mentioned it to Del, he said, "Tell Cora how much I appreciate her support," snarky-like himself.

It takes time to be a success, he told me. Patience. And meanwhile, the days ticked off one after another, and the nights too. We found out pretty quickly about those stale crackers and cheese and that veggie plate Brenda had given us for dinner that first night— leftover from the "soirees" she hosted several times a week for potential clients. "A key part of the business, dears," she told us. For special clients, she even broke out some pickled asparagus.

What she wanted us to see was a professional woman wooing and wowing potential clients—setting us an example. But what I heard was the same story about a zillion times: Brenda's whitewater rafting adventure and her "new perspectives on risk and reward," how her divorce made her a stronger woman, and the biggest deal she ever closed ("the Sotheby's listing," she said in a hushed voice) and how she did it. Maybe some of those folks had heard them before themselves—lots of sideways glances and glossed-over eyes—but at least they seemed grateful for a meal, even if just a light one. My own attention kept turning out the window, watching the boats on the lake, their lights drifting by, so close but so far away. Even Brenda seemed a touch disinterested sometimes. More than once, I caught her checking her watch, like she was counting down the minutes herself.

"It's an investment," she'd tell us later, wrapping up the cheese and bagging the crackers for the next group. "You'll learn quickly enough how to strategize small talk to your benefits."

A lot of our conversation was like that, advice and pronouncements and goading. She tried to urge Del to join the rotary club and tried to get me to consider a bridge league, though I'd never played bridge my whole life. Time and again, she asked Del about selling the Nova and getting a new car. "Delwood, to be a success, you have to look a success."

"Anything I could improve?" I asked with a smirk, but Brenda wasn't much for picking up sarcasm.

"The fashion is for longer skirts in the business world," she said. "And sometimes you slouch in your chair."

After six weeks of that, nothing had changed, not at work, not at home, at least not in a good way. Even without having to pay rent, the "nest egg" from that last robbery was dwindling pretty quickly, cutting into a possible down payment on a house if a good one became available—or into the next round of moving expenses, if Del ever realized this was going nowhere.

Staying long term in someone else's house is never easy. Del liked some time each day to read the paper, but Brenda never gave him a minute's peace from all that scheduling and strategizing. Whenever I tried to turn on the TV for one of my court shows, she rolled her eyes and remarked that surely there must be something better on. Most of the time, I felt like it would be best for me to just sit very still and not touch anything.

Through it all, Del and I seemed to be growing further apart— and not just because of the sleeping in two different rooms, but that was a big part of it. Any red-blooded American male might tell you that women can go without sex, but any red-blooded American female will let you know that it can be just as hard on us. And a quick roll in the hay on those Star Wars sheets when Brenda was out didn't feel giggly illicit but just rushed and distracted and lonely.

I'd say that it's funny how quickly something temporary can become something permanent, but really, it's not funny at all. It's one of the saddest things I know.

Even when Del finally tried to give us a break from the routine...well, that was when all this really started, that late afternoon he came back to the office and announced, "Louise, I've made some plans," the way he used to back in New Mexico when he wanted to go out for dinner. (Our Place it had always been, over in Angel Fire, and I missed it now.)

This was a Friday, when Brenda kept the office open later, and it was already beginning to get dark outside. Del had supposedly been out "familiarizing himself with the product," but since he smelled like cologne, I knew he'd been by the house.

"Do I need to dress up?" I asked.

"Don't you worry," he said. "I've got everything you need"— which clearly didn't answer the question.

"Dinner plans?" Brenda asked, stepping out from her office.

"It's a date night," Del said, terser than he'd been with her since we'd been there. "A surprise." He didn't look at her as he said it, and I tried not to look myself when she started nosing around about it all—some restaurants that were her own favorite and how she could get us a reservation maybe and then "You kids don't be out late," wagging her finger all joking-like, but all along like maybe she was hoping to be invited herself.

"No need to wait up," Del said, and it felt good to see him standing up to her for a change. "You ready, Louise?"

Even before we were out the door, my own curiosity had got the better of me. Were we going to dinner? Sort of. Was it far? No. Would we be gone long? Overnight. Overnight! Shouldn't I have packed something? He had it handled: a toothbrush, some toiletries, a nightgown. (Now that *was* romantic.)

"A bed and breakfast?"

"Nope."

"A country inn?"

"Closer."

"A cottage?"

"What part of *surprise* don't you understand?"

When we drove under that Old Town Route 66 sign that stretches across 7th, I felt for the first time in a while that sense of adventure and opportunity like I'd felt along parts of that same Route 66 coming from Taos—at least the second half of that drive. *Another* fresh start maybe, at least for the night.

I don't want to tell you exactly where we went, not given everything that happened afterwards, but it was a neighborhood in one of those newer subdivisions that had gone up right before the real estate bubble burst—slick looking houses, some of them never even lived in, some of them already turned back to the bank. It was past twilight by the time we got there. Those vacant houses were dark as the tomb, but lights shone out of the ones that had been sold, the TVs on I could tell from the way some of the colors played through the window.

Suddenly, Del just pulled over and stopped at the curb.

"Ready?" he said.

"Here?" I asked.

"Trust me." He smiled that boyish smile of his, then pulled a flashlight from the glovebox and opened the door.

I did trust him. Still, I couldn't help but notice how he kept looking side to side and over his shoulder as we walked up the street. Just as quick, he seemed totally focused, turning us toward a house on the left with big "For Sale" and "Bank Owned" signs out front. He touched my arm just lightly as we stepped up on the big front porch—affection or just hustling me along, I wasn't sure. There was one of those lockboxes on the front door, and Del used that walkie-talkie electronic gadget to open it.

The inside of the house was empty—big rooms, blank walls, and that echoey feeling. The moonlight and streetlights through the windows gave it all a spooky glow. When I flicked the light switch, nothing happened.

"A foreclosure," Del said. "Most times, they cut the power." He turned on the flashlight and led me into the kitchen, holding it up just enough to reflect off those stainless steel appliances and those shiny granite countertops and those tall cabinets with glass fronts. It was beautiful—and, I realized pretty quickly, just like the house I'd described to him. I could picture a pair of rockers on that porch we swept past. I knew there would be a big master suite. Even in the dark, the whole place felt like potential, like it was just waiting for someone to move in and give it some life.

Suddenly, I knew what the surprise was.

"Like Brenda was telling us," Del was saying, "a lot of the fore-closed houses, the owners get mad and trash things before they leave, but this one wasn't the case. Looks like they kept it all nice and neat and orderly. And in here..." His hand rested on my arm again, and I could feel a tingle there now. "Watch your step."

Just off the kitchen was a sunken living room bathed in moon-light, and in the middle of it were two sleeping bags, some tall can-dles, and a picnic basket. Off to the side, just at the far edge of the light, stood my suitcase, the one he'd packed.

As Del leaned down to light the candles, I felt the first flush of real happiness that I'd felt since we'd gotten to California. I know, I know: Del hadn't sold anything, Brenda was a bitch, and I'd pretty much decided against staying in Victorville, so a new house? But the important point was that Del had been listening.

"The candles are romantic," I said.

"Practical."

"Since you haven't got the power turned on yet, you mean."

"Yet?" he said, and he laughed. "That would've taken some magic, but even if the power was on, we probably shouldn't turn on the light. The neighbors and all."

"*Our* neighbors, right, Del?"

His head popped up.

"I don't know what you mean."

"Del," I said. "You're planning on buying this place, that's the surprise, isn't it?"

"Oh," he said, and even in that dim light, his expression told me everything. "I don't think we could afford this *particular* place at the moment, especially not with the business like it is right now...but I thought, like you've said, what does it hurt to dream some?"

I nodded like I understood, like I agreed. But really that was the first I saw clearly how dreams like that really can hurt. The whole thing just smacked me upside the head. And I didn't want to tell him what else was running through my mind, the sudden memories of Win, that old high school boyfriend. How I'd thought that ours was the truest kind of love, that we'd get married and start having babies, the way you think when you're a teenager. And now here was Del kneeling on the floor, the way guys are supposed to do when they're getting ready to ask you to—

"All this," I said. "It's like a promise ring, that's what you were thinking, right?"

"That's not precisely how I'd articulate it. But yes, maybe a trial run, a sample of how life *might* be someday. A getaway, just like you'd talked about on the way up here."

I looked around, trying to catch a glimpse at what he was seeing. But those big empty rooms just seemed less like potential than just empty promises now, all of it echoing hollow a long, long way into the future.

"C'mon down here," he said, picking up the champagne and twisting off the seal. "We've got the night to ourselves, a big time ahead of us."

With the moonlight and the candles and him popping the champagne, I know he was expecting me to run over to him and put my arms around him, giggling like a schoolgirl. But I didn't move. I couldn't. Finally, Del just stood up himself.

"Here," he said. He tilted his own glass toward mine. "To us."

I didn't feel like it but I took a sip anyway.

"It's best at room temperature," I said, and even I could hear the bitchiness in my voice. "Hot and fresh, like champagne oughta be, right?"

Del looked at me like I'd slapped him. Maybe I had.

"Louise, this is supposed to be fun." That pleading sound in his voice broke my heart a little.

"Del," I started, not sure what I was going to say. "Del, I—"

But before I could answer, blue lights cut through the moon-light, a police light flashing and circling just outside the front windows.

Del fell to the floor and blew so hard at the candles that he was almost spitting. "Get down," he said, half-shout, half-whisper, and when I didn't move, he reached up and pulled my arm, tipping my glass and spilling all that warm champagne into the carpet. I landed in the puddle, of course, and felt my side go all bubbly as the champagne spread across my pants.

And all he packed me was a nightgown?

That's not all I was thinking, of course. A lot of things were running through my mind, and those blue lights just reminded me even more of Win back in high school—Sheriff Earl or one of his deputies tapping on the driver's window of Win's Camaro when we were parked by the lake or down some dusty road, searching for privacy wherever we could find it. We weren't the "it" couple, but we had been steady and solid, made it through two years of proms without any meltdowns. Everyone believed, the way you do then, that we'd always be together.

But the day after he'd given me that promise ring, I gave it back to him. "We're not in junior high," I said and walked away.

I looked at Del, crouched beside me.

The moonlight and that pulsing blue strobe glinted against the silver that was already beginning to appear in Del's beard. I thought: We get older but we really don't.

Del crawled commando style over to the window and peeked out. Then he turned and leaned back against the wall. He pulled the back of his hand across his brow—maybe wiping real sweat away but probably just signaling that everything was okay. It was still several minutes before he dared to crawl back.

"He pulled a car over across the street, that's all"—still a whisper.

"Aren't we lucky?" I said, sitting up.

"I'll say." Del laughed. "For a minute there I thought this evening was going to be a bust." He took my hand. "I'll wait to light the candles until he's gone. After all, we've got the full night ahead of us. So where were we?"

"Del," I began again, and this time I did know what to say. "The truth is I don't know where we are, or where we're going. I would tell you I want to go home, but we're living in a house that's not ours, sleeping in separate bedrooms with teenagers' sheets, and now we're ducked down in another house that's also not ours and won't ever be. We're in the dark, the police are outside, and the only thing good about that warm champagne is the fact that my backside at least isn't cold, and—"

"Louise, I love you," Del said—and it brought me up short for a second. He never said it much, that taciturn nature of his. "And I'm sorry. I know that things..."

I'm not sure what all Del said after that, what else he was going to say, but I can imagine it. He was working on all this. He meant well. Give him time.

I never let him finish.

"All I hear from you these days, Del, is a lot of empty words. And when I look at you, all I see is an empty place where the fella I loved used to be."

When Del grew even more distant after that, I just gave him his space.

When he started taking his few calls at the office all hunkered down with his hand over the receiver like I was a nosy officemate instead of the love of his life, I didn't let it bother me. When he took to staying out of the office more regular—busying himself somehow, despite no buyers in sight—I tried not to take it personally.

Even when he began excusing himself from Brenda's soirees, I let her be the one to ask where he was going and why—confronting and questioning and pulling out all the stops while I just said, "Have a nice night, Del," and resigned myself to yet another tray of stale cheese.

"That boy needs to listen to me," Brenda would complain after he left. "A lot depends on it." When I didn't answer, she'd just dump a bag of crackers onto a platter, spread out another array of browning vegetables. "None of this is helping."

Maybe I should've been more worked up about Del myself. I'd seen this kind of thing happen to Mama, of course—seen it happen to me. Men who began wandering away, preferring a bottle of Bud at the bar to the nagging woman back home. One day, those men just didn't come back.

But it never crossed my mind what he'd really gotten himself into—both of us.

Never crossed my mind until the police showed up, that is—then the bigger picture started to come into focus: me wanting something more and him not being able to provide it, our falling out that night in the foreclosed house, Del's being away so much since.

"We can resolve this fairly quickly," Brenda said as Jekyll and

Hyde followed her out of the office. "Delwood, do you have your lockbox keycard?"

"Is there some trouble, officers?" Del asked, the way you do when you've been pulled over and pretend you don't know how fast you were going.

"Burglaries," Brenda said before either of the detectives could speak. "Someone is breaking into vacant houses and stealing...microwaves, you said?"

"Various small appliances," said Jekyll. "Fixtures too: faucets, doorknobs, cabinet knobs. Some of it high end."

"Even granite countertops, just ripped off," said Hyde, and his expression made his face look even lumpier. "We've seen a lot of this with all the foreclosures and evictions. The owners come back to break a window, jimmy a lock, take back what's theirs."

"But these haven't been break-ins," said Jekyll. "This guy—"

"Or woman," said Hyde.

"Agreed," said Jekyll. "Whoever it is just seems to open the doors and walk right in. Several houses, same M.O."

Brenda crossed her arms.

"They even brought up the possibility that a realtor might be involved, can you imagine that?"

Jekyll was staring pretty hard at Del again. His green had paled, but his expression still looked unhealthy.

"We're just dropping by to confirm no one is missing a keycard," said Hyde with a smile. "Because that would help explain things here."

No smile from Jekyll. "We've got a subpoena out for the usage records."

Listening to them, I wondered for a moment about the idea of overcompensation: good-looking Jekyll didn't have to be nice. Hyde meanwhile had to find other ways to charm. Or maybe it was just good cop, bad cop, like they do on TV.

Then there was Brenda, overcompensating in her own way—boisterous and bossy. A big sister complex, even at her age.

"Delwood," she said with a flourish of her hand like she was finishing up a magic trick, "please show the man your lockbox card."

Del reached into his desk and held it up. "Right here," he said, but I had a sinking feeling that he wished he'd lost it.

"Our rule is to keep the keys in our respective desks when we're not using them," Brenda said.

"And do you keep your desk locked, sir?" asked Jekyll.

Del shrugged. "I wouldn't know how."

"The building itself is locked," Brenda cut in, "unless someone is actually here in the office. And when Delwood and I are both out, Louise is here, isn't that right, Louise?"

I didn't want to, but I said yes—feeling like Brenda and I were setting Del up, her unwittingly, me unwillingly. "Sometimes I step back to pee without locking the door," I said, trying to give Del some breathing room. "But since hardly anybody ever comes—"

Brenda had started shaking her head at the word *pee*. "Attitude," she said. "That attitude and that level of carelessness are simply unacceptable. This is *exactly* the reason I had to let that last girl go. And if it turns out that—"

"Brenda," Del said. "You're jumping on Louise like she's to blame somehow. The key's here."

"But has it been here *the whole time*? How can we be sure, what with—" Brenda was already cutting her eyes my way.

That's when Jekyll stepped in. He was finally smiling now—an ugly thing to see.

"If I understand correctly," he said, "then it's possible that your brother's key may have been misplaced."

Brenda nodded, Del shook his head, I didn't know what to do. Either way was bad news.

"I should tell you, officers," said Del, "that I've been, um, spending a fair amount of time looking at properties. Most afternoons I'm out looking at houses, and—"

Seemed like Brenda couldn't let anyone finish a sentence. "Oh, even on the *very* off-chance that Delwood's key has been associated with these...burglaries, I can assure you that it's not *him* committing these crimes. He has kept a detailed record of everything he does during the day. You'll find all of his time accounted for."

Another dark smile from Jekyll. "Would you mind sharing that with us?" he asked.

"Actually," said Del, giving a quick look my way, "I haven't been writing everything down. Some nights I've stopped by a house, just an empty one and—"

That was the last straw, of course—Del about to admit to what had happened in the foreclosed house, it seemed like.

Brenda interrupted first, starting up again with all this talk about procedure and protocol. Jekyll and Hyde cut in asking more pointed questions about where Del had been and what he'd seen, clearly wondering if he was the man they were looking for, even if nobody said it straight out. A lot of talk, a lot of suspicion in the air, but I'd moved past it myself. I *knew*.

Del had always had a rationale for the crimes he pulled back in New Mexico: only when he needed a little extra and only if no one got hurt. And wasn't that the case here? Working on commission hadn't earned him pea turkey from his sister. Heck, he'd probably made more holding up that 7-Eleven I was working at than he'd made the whole time in Victorville. Really, no wonder all this was happening, right?

Recidivism. Now that was a Del word if ever there was one.

Even after the police left, Del and I didn't immediately get the chance to talk. Brenda just kept yelling about everything we should've thought about, should've done differently, should've done for her (and clearly hadn't). She stomped and shook her finger and slammed her door. I could hear her on the phone making calls to some of those other realtor friends, comparing notes, all of them in an uproar it seemed like. "As if this business isn't hard *enough*," I heard Brenda shout through the walls.

"When were you planning to tell me?" I asked Del.

"Tell you what?" he said.

"You know."

"I *don't* know." But his look told me he did.

"Listen to me, Del," I said, whispering to make sure Brenda couldn't hear. "I don't care if you're a criminal, not in the least. If that was a deal-breaker for me, would I have gotten involved with you in the first place?" I leaned forward across my desk. "But when was I supposed to find out about all *this*? When they came to arrest you for real?"

Del listened, he gritted his teeth.

"For God's sake, Louise. I'm not stealing toasters."

"Neither of them said anything about *toasters*," I said. "Something else we need to talk about?"

Del sighed. "Could you have a little faith?"

I pointed my finger at him. "Del, you just keep missing the point."

But it was clear he'd tuned me out by then.

And what was that point?

The way I see it, if a man can't fess up to his woman that he's been out stealing small appliances...well, that relationship is just not working.

And if we weren't working, then what was I gonna do to fix us?

I don't need to go into all the technical aspects, but suffice it to say, the CIA may have nothing on RadioShack when it comes to surveillance technologies.

A few days later, I swapped the phone that Brenda had given Del with the one she'd given me (they looked the same, after all), said I needed some time off for some quick shopping, and headed to The Shack over at the Mall of Victorville. Fifteen minutes and one tracking device later, I was out the door again. Swapped it back with Del's at lunch, and he never knew the difference.

While I was out "shopping," I swung by the storage unit Del

had rented. The size had always struck me as fishy, and now I wondered how early Del had been considering these heists. Had it only just come to him that night with the champagne and the candles? Or was it back when Brenda was talking about homeowners vandalizing their property after getting evicted? Or even back during our drive from New Mexico? Del always surprised me with how far ahead he planned. He might indeed have worked out this whole scheme from the start.

But I didn't find any microwaves or plumbing fixtures. Just our stuff and a lot of empty space. And the gun was still there, wedged behind the TV. No chance he was using that.

Still, even if his plans were unclear, my own was slowly coming more fully into focus.

Now Del needed to make the next move.

For the next couple of days, Del mostly just laid low, making cold calls on the phone (on his own initiative this time), hunkering down at his desk, everything back to normal, or at least to the point that anybody passing by on the street outside might've thought so. For me, it was just more words unsaid, distrust in the air, and a lot of watching and waiting.

Hyde stopped by the office alone one afternoon, showed Del some pictures of houses, asked if he'd been to such and such address and if he'd seen anything suspicious—pretending Del was potentially an eyewitness and not suspect number one. Other times—I can't be sure—I thought I caught sight of him or Jekyll through the plate glass window, standing down on the corner or sitting in a car on the curb. Each time Del went out to look at more property or follow up with a potential customer, I got the feeling they were hot on his tail.

They weren't the only ones following him, of course. Day after day, I was getting practice on the tracker I'd picked up.

The RadioShack clerk hadn't been wrong. It was easy to follow Del's route on my own phone—a tiny blip on the map. All I needed

to do was cross-check his moves later with whatever name and address he'd written in his journal, which he was suddenly keeping up
with again. Brenda's orders, of course. The final destinations always
matched, but a lot of times he seemed to follow a pretty wild route.
Was he just trying to shake Jekyll and Hyde off his track? Or was
there some extra stop on the way? Either way, it was suspicious,
even if not enough yet to act on.

That weekend, Del tried to skip out on Brenda's evening soiree, but she put her foot down, ranting and raving. "You *need* to be
here," she said. "Several of our fellow realtors are joining us tonight
to discuss this situation." And sure enough, all those names and
voices I knew only from the phone started showing up: Stanley
Weissbratten and Della Busch sauntering in together (a couple, I
saw now, and a good match for one another, both of them as big as
prize pigs and with these hefty jowls on them), and Margo Johnson
whose red hair was clearly straight out of a bottle (and whose gaudy
rings rivaled Brenda's) and Kevin Middleton who was short and
blinky-eyed behind thick glasses.

Piggies One and Two zeroed in on the cheese and munched
down while the other three compared notes on what Jekyll and
Hyde had told each of them. The same explanation in each case,
same request for records and promise of a subpoena, same suspicions. Everyone seemed addled by it all.

"I'm thinking of getting out," said Blinky, his eyes going into
overdrive. "Getting out of the business completely. I haven't had a
sale in weeks, and now to have the police coming to the front door."

"I knew it was going to happen," said Red, nervously twisting
about four carats on her middle finger. "As soon as I saw the way
the newspaper was covering some of the break-ins, I knew the direction it was gonna go. Once the reporters start following a story
like that—"

"But why come to us?" said Mama Piggy. "When the boom
came, suddenly everyone was signing up for real estate classes, taking the exams, getting their licenses. Money grabbers, get-rich-
quick greedy." She reached for another thick bit of cheese. "Those

new agents, they would be the ones *I'd* suspect of being unscrupulous."

"Della's right," said Red. "Were they in for the hard work like we'd put in? The work we'd done to build this place? We have *reputations* in this town."

"They have to interview everyone, I'm sure," said Brenda coldly. "And Del's a new agent, don't forget."

I don't think anyone had forgotten. All through the talk, several of them had cut their glances Del's way, and I wondered if Brenda had told them everything about our police visit: the questions about the keys, about the office being open, all of it. Here in front of them, Brenda didn't say a word about it, and she didn't whoop or holler like she had at us back in the office. She was all about reputation herself, about being in control.

For his part, Del didn't speak. He just nodded here and there—even at that "new agents" comment—and shifted now and again in his seat, his eyes darting around at everyone. Everyone but me, that is.

He could probably feel me watching him. Wondering what he was thinking, and where he'd planned to be instead of here.

Clearly an opportunity missed—for both of us.

"I blame the vandals *first*," said Red. "The homeowners. They're the ones who started all this, and now it's coming around to us."

"It's this subpoena threat that's bothering me," said Blinky, his eyes all atwitter again. "And it is a threat, no other way around it. It's a violation of our rights. Suspicion of guilt before being proven innocent. I have half a mind to get my attorney involved."

"You have half a mind period," Mama Piggy said, with a laugh. "And anyway, what do you have to worry about?"

"I couldn't tell you now whether I've been to any of those houses or not. I haven't even kept track of which ones were hit or on what days, except for seeing it in the newspaper sometimes, but I'm sure going to pay attention now."

"Vigilance is key," said Brenda. "Confidence. You do what it takes. All of us need to remember that." This time, she was the one cutting her eyes Del's way. He just nodded again.

"Do you have any more of that cheese?" Papa Pig asked. As he readjusted his bulk, he squashed one of the pillows on the divan. Brenda winced, but didn't say anything.

Finally, late one afternoon, dusk coming on, Del got a call—not the office phone, but that cell phone Brenda had given him. A lot of whispering, his hand cupped over his mouth, and I knew the time had come.

"Tell Brenda I'm stepping out for a minute," he said, when the call was done. "And don't wait up on dinner." He paused near my desk like he expected me to say something, but he was looking the other way.

"I'll call if anything comes up," I said. "Be sure to take your phone."

Part One of the plan was in action.

I waited ten minutes, called for a cab to meet me a block over, then knocked on Brenda's office door.

"Del had to step out, and I just remembered a hair appointment."

Brenda rolled her eyes. "Are you telling me I'm on my own here?" There was a tut-tut in her tone.

"Almost closing time anyway," I said, and left quick with her still calling after me about *responsibilities* and *dependability* and *didn't I know that she had plans herself?*

Out on the street, I activated the GPS tracker, and there was Del, still not too far away. The cab pulled up three minutes later.

Follow that car has taken on a whole new meaning these days, I imagine. I had to redirect the cab driver to keep up with Del's moves: under that Old Town Route 66 sign and a ways down 7th, a quick dog-leg past some tennis courts, then more turns until a big intersection with a McDonald's and a CVS before more scrubland, nothing but those big power lines soaring overhead. At every intersection, I checked behind us for Jekyll or Hyde but saw no one.

"Lady, are you even sure where you're going?"

"Not yet," I said, flashing him the phone. "But we'll get there." Like I said, I can indeed read a map.

"Poor guy," I thought I heard him say, and I could imagine what he thought: cheating husband, vengeful wife, that old story.

"Pull over," I said finally, when I saw that the blip had stopped out by one of those big struggling developments—a couple of houses sold, others empty, and construction at a standstill on the rest. We were around the corner from Del's signal. I paid the cab driver and sent him on his way.

When I turned the corner myself, what I didn't expect was to see Del's car parked on the curb by a house with a "For Sale" sign out front. He was still in the driver's seat. I ducked into the garage of one of the half-built houses and hid behind a flap of construction paper. The place smelled awful, like wet sawdust and a box of those Sharpie pens Brenda liked, but at least I could keep an eye on Del, who was sitting there in the almost-dark like he was waiting for someone.

Waiting for who, though? A client maybe? It could've been that simple, and for a second, I chalked up the evening as a waste and started to call another cab.

But then why all the whispering and secrecy?

It came to me what he'd told me time and again: *Boldness is key.*

Hiding in plain sight. Waltzing in the front door, and walking out with a microwave. After all, what was suspicious about a real estate agent sitting outside a house for sale?

But then I realized something else: the someone he was waiting for, the reason there was nothing in the storage room. If he was just letting another person in, then he hadn't stolen anything himself—just allowed someone else to do it. Jekyll and Hyde wouldn't see much of a distinction, but wasn't that Del's way around the truth? How he could tell me he wasn't stealing anything himself?

I looked around again to see if Jekyll or Hyde had shown up

yet, but there was no sign of them. Then a minute later, a car pulled into the driveway of the house where Del was parked—even bolder than he was—and I was surprised to see a woman get out and wave to him. A tall blonde, leggy even, in this sleek green dress. Del climbed out of his car and headed toward her. He carried a flashlight—the same one he'd carried the night he'd taken me to that foreclosed house—and something about it gave me a shiver of sadness, thinking about how badly that night had gone. He and the woman talked briefly, I thought I heard a laugh of some kind, then he touched her arm just lightly as they stepped up on the porch.

It was just the way he'd touched my arm. Then that shiver of sadness turned into something else. After all, Del had told me not to wait on dinner—same as he'd told Brenda not to wait up the night he and I went out on our surprise date night.

The two of them went up on the porch and into the house, and I could see that flashlight playing around behind the windows. I walked up to the house, brazenly myself, and looked in a window, catching them just as they disappeared into what must have been the master suite. I tried to run around to the back of the house and look in there, but the slope out back left the window too high to peek through. I couldn't see anything but the faint glow of the flashlight, darting here and there, then going still.

Maybe she *is* just a client—that's what I kept trying to tell myself. That's all. Or maybe she really was the thief I'd imagined. Why couldn't she be? Women could do it, couldn't they? Even young, pretty blondes, right?

But that was the thing—how pretty she was, and how skinny, and how young. And how charming Del had been to me way back when—charmed the pants right off me, like they say.

Here I'd been wondering how stupid Del could be. What I should've been thinking was how stupid I was being myself.

Part Two of my plan? I'll admit it now, it had been fuzzy at best. Something about catching him on one of these break-ins and calling the police and giving them the house number just next door or right across the street, and then Del getting all panicky like that night with the champagne and the sleeping bags. And who knew, but maybe he'd just come home and confide in me like he had that night, tell me he loved me, and this time I'd be more supportive—handling my own self different than I had the first time.

We'd be together again.

But when he and the pretty blonde stayed in that bedroom for so long, what I did instead was to call the police and give them the *right* house number, then hung up and called another cab to take me home.

All of it would get back to Jekyll and Hyde soon enough. And served Del right, didn't it?

"Your hair doesn't look any different," Brenda said when I walked into the house. She was sitting in the center of the divan, with the pillows propped up like diamonds on each side of her and the phone in her hand. The latest round of cheese and crackers had already been laid out on the coffee table.

I'd been doing a lot of thinking on the ride back—about Del and me, about where we'd been going, about what this new turn meant—and it took me a moment to remember my own cover story.

"I was wrong," I said. "About the appointment." Wrong about a lot, it seemed.

Brenda gave a humph. "And do you have any inkling when Delwood plans to return?"

I shook my head. Had the police caught Del and the woman in the act? (Which act, I didn't want to imagine.) Would the police have taken them in, or just run them off?

And the most important questions: What would Del do afterwards? And what was I going to do?

"Can't keep track of anyone," Brenda said, "and all this a waste," looking at the spread of food. There was even asparagus.

"Somebody will eat it," I said. Like on cue, the doorbell rang.

"Can you answer that, dear?" Brenda asked, punching the keys of her phone.

"Off the clock," I called over my shoulder, and I could feel that ugly glare of hers following me down the hallway to my room. But no time to spare. Her comment about keeping track of people had reminded me that I still had Del right there in my pocket.

I kept the door cracked and listened to Brenda start up the old dog and pony while I fumbled to pull up the map. Del was already on the move, and the guilt hit me hard when he stopped and the map symbol showed it was a police station. For the next hour or more, the signal stayed there.

Wasn't that what I wanted? Wasn't that why I'd called the police? In the heat of the moment, sure, but suddenly it was like the worst I'd imagined back in New Mexico each time Del had headed out on a job, except now it was my fault. My mind kept careening back and forth between that guilt and fear about the trouble he was in and anger about whatever he was doing with that blonde and justification about my reaction and back around again to the guilt. And through it all, despite myself, this sense of loss about how far Del and I had come and how far we'd gone wrong. Those plans of his, those dreams of ours—those dreams of mine, at least, and whatever was going on with him that I wasn't a part of anymore.

Trying to keep from staring at the map, I looked out my window, searching in vain for those same boats that had once seemed like a dream out on the horizon. Nothing but darkness tonight. I pulled out that sock monkey and rubbed it near bout to pieces, praying for luck. A talisman. Del's gift. Del's word. Now I just needed Del himself.

About the time Brenda's soiree was dying down, the blip finally started moving again. Soon it was headed our way, but I still didn't know what to feel.

When I heard the Nova pulling into the driveway, I came out. Whatever guests there'd been were gone. Brenda was in the kitchen, washing up. Del's shadow loomed through the glass panes on the front door. The key turned.

What would he say to me when he came in? What would I say to him? Would the truth finally come out? Or more lies? And which ones?

Turned out Del and I didn't get much of a chance to talk to one another. He looked at me with a blank expression, announced "I've been at the police station" in a flat tone, and quick as a blink, his big sister stepped into the room and took charge.

"This is *exactly* what I've been afraid of," said Brenda, and the way her face twisted up, it wasn't just fear or even disappointment but anger behind what she was saying. I thought back to what she said once about emotional contagion, and I didn't want any part of it. "Ever since those policemen came to the office, and I learned that you'd been going into houses without keeping track of it and at night of all things, I've just been waiting for this. Honestly, Delwood, I thought that the two of you were going to be an *asset* to my work. I don't know why you couldn't just listen to me, just do what I said. If you had, then none of this would've happened, none of it."

Brenda had been cleaning a spoon, and she started waving it at us, emphasizing key words in her tirade. That expression on her face, I felt glad it wasn't a knife.

"This won't ruin me," she said. "No, sir, and no, ma'am. This is exactly what we were talking about the other night. I've worked too hard, and whatever mess you've made of all this, I'm going to fix it. And I'm not letting you go down either, Delwood. I won't let that happen, would never have let it happen. That's not who I am."

She stepped back into the kitchen, dropped the spoon in the sink, and started scrubbing at the cheese tray—her elbows flying.

"I've already arranged for legal representation," she said through the doorway, her back to us. "As soon as the police came by that very first day, I called up my attorney and explained to him how Delwood was new to the business and uncertain about proper protocol and about Louise and all her carelessness. 'Some keys have most likely been misplaced,' I told him, and 'That girl hasn't been keeping an eye on things. If there's any trouble, *she's* the one to blame.'"

"Me?" I said, stepping into the kitchen.

Brenda whirled around and shook a soapy finger at me. "Of course *you*, Louise." She spat the word *you*—spat my name. "Wouldn't that make the most sense? And oh, wasn't my lawyer interested indeed to know about your history in this department. The way you just let that convenience store in New Mexico be robbed. That was the first thing I saw when I looked you up online, that newspaper article—"

"You looked me up?" I said. "You're blaming *me* for that? And now for this?" I stopped short of pointing out that it was Del himself who'd robbed that convenience store, but I felt like I was sputtering on about almost everything else.

"Oh, don't be surprised, dear. Would I possibly have someone like you in my home without vetting her thoroughly? And what an unexpected bonus I got for *that* work, I'll tell you."

"Do you hear this, Del?" I asked. He'd stepped into the kitchen, but he just stood there nodding—same as he had with everything Brenda and her realtor friends were saying the other night, same as always these days. "Del!" I said again and glared at him—the way he'd give me that *Louise* sometimes—but he stayed quiet, like I was hardly even there. I turned back to Brenda. "If you think Del's gonna let you throw me under the bus—"

"I don't hear him speaking up for you, Louise." A smile played around the corner of her lips. "The two of you can hardly stand one another. Or haven't you noticed? All these silences, all this fuming, and Delwood going out all the time. I thought he might even have a woman on the side, which would at least have been another alibi."

Which made me think, of course, of that tall leggy blonde, and what Del was doing with her, and what I'd done. Maybe Del being quiet and him not looking at me...maybe that was because he already knew. Or because he simply didn't want me anymore.

"Don't worry," Brenda went on. "I don't think they could hold you as an accomplice, since you were simply negligent, not an actual accessory to all this—to whatever has happened with those keys. And Del, whatever they might charge you with, I'm sure that the evidence will exonerate, and you'll be mighty glad that I had you keep that journal. But we'll need to fill in the other times that you didn't keep track of." She clucked her tongue, thinking. "We'll get all the dates and the times. We'll get witnesses. Even if there are some lapses…"

Brenda just kept talking, and Del just kept standing and listening, nodding every once in a while, not saying a thing. *Taciturn* again—that word I'd grown to hate. And between the two of them, I'd finally gone quiet myself, stunned into silence, not sure what else to say.

Then a funny thing happened. As I started listening instead of reacting, I began to hear something else in all those plans that were rolling out of Brenda, and Del's taciturn nature suddenly seemed like it might have an upside.

Ever since the beginning, Brenda had been trying to take charge of me and Del, and I thought it was just bossiness: what Del should wear and what he should drive and when he should make cold calls and jerking him in and out of the office at a moment's notice and don't forget tonight's soiree, of course, and the same with me. But now, a lot of that bossiness from the past took on a different look: her being so particular about Del and that notebook, all those wine and cheese parties and her looking at her watch mid-conversation like she was bored with it all, the phone conversation I overheard about the window needing to be clear, that shady character who came by the office with his greasy comb-over and smarmy attitude, the fact that she'd already called a lawyer and laid out a big story for him, and how happy she was about what happened at the 7-Eleven.

Really, all of it sounded different this time around.

Finally, Del spoke. "Misplaced keys," he said. "I have indeed stepped out of the office and left it in the desk. Oftentimes, it does seem to be sitting differently in the drawer when I come back."

"That's exactly the kind of detail they'll need," Brenda said, smiling wide like she'd just closed a big sale. "Oh, Delwood. Confidence. Confidence! *We're* going to do what it takes, for both our sakes!"

"Family looking out for family," he said. "It all comes together nicely, doesn't it?"

When he finally met my eyes, his expression looked like about a hundred miles of bad road and about eighteen layers of unhappiness. But this time none of it was directed at me.

After Del excused himself and headed back to the bedroom, I stayed out for a couple of minutes. Brenda moved on to the living room, walking past me like I wasn't there. She swiped a cloth across a coffee table that already looked spotless, straightened those pillows again. Part of me just couldn't take my eyes off her, the obsessiveness, the unreality of her. Part of me couldn't let go of wanting to smack her for what she'd done.

But the bigger part just didn't want to go face Del.

I needed a minute for myself, like Mama used to say—but the truth was, even if you could get a minute for yourself, you couldn't get one *from* yourself. Not hardly.

When I finally headed back, Del was just sitting on those Superman sheets like he'd been waiting for me. He patted the bed, and when I sat down, he leaned into me. It was the closest he'd been to me in a while, and I couldn't decide if this was reconciliation or if he was just easing me into a breakup. All night the picture of that pretty young woman had been running through my brain, images of whatever was happening between them, and now Brenda's words were echoing right alongside.

"My sister was right about one thing," he said finally. "You do what you need to do." There was just the slightest sting to his words, and it didn't go away with the next ones. "Louise, there's something I need to tell you." He took a deep breath, and I felt myself tremble, bracing for the truth. "Since I haven't been making any money, I reached out to some banks about those foreclosed houses—the ones that the owners had really messed up somehow. Odd jobs most of it. Handyman work. That's where I've been all those afternoons away from the office, some evenings. A lot of those bankers didn't see it was worth the investment, but I offered to work cheap. Some money's better than none."

I didn't realize how hard I'd been gripping the edge of the bed until I let go of it. It was a relief, sure, sudden and real, to have been wrong—twice wrong, really—but just as quick I was mad at myself again because of what being wrong had led to. And mad at him as well, because wasn't the same issue at the heart of it? A lack of communication, no two ways about it.

"Del, why on earth wouldn't you have just told me that?" I asked, trying not to make it sound accusatory.

"And admit to being a failure? After everything we'd invested in that fresh start?" He'd folded his hands together and started rubbing at a finger, distracted-like. "Maybe I should be glad someone called the police. I was meeting with one of the bankers, a hole someone had kicked in a bedroom wall. Those same two detectives came out, thinking this was one of those burglaries, and if it hadn't been for that..."

"Then the truth wouldn't have come out," I said—though part of that truth still gnawed at me, the part I was hiding. I couldn't go there yet. "When did you begin to suspect what was going on with Brenda?"

"With Brenda?" he said. "Since the first time the police visited the office—since even before then. But I wasn't sure about the rest of them then."

"The rest of who?"

"Her realtor friends. That old guard. Stanley and Della. Kevin. Margo."

"They're in on it?" I pictured them: The Piggies and Blinky and Red. A ring of criminals? They didn't look smart enough for it.

"Probably," Del said. "I didn't realize how widespread it might be until the night she got us all together. And I wasn't certain about any of it until tonight. The police got their subpoena back."

"And every one of those places that had been hit was on your key, right?"

He snorted. "They wouldn't have let me walk out of there if that had been the case. Brenda's not the only one who can swap keys. I had hers, which were clean. But I didn't want to let her know that, not until I'd heard her out." He ran his fingers up through his hair. "They'll be coming by tomorrow to check the other one."

"I hope they throw her *under* the jail. Trying to set up her careless little brother who didn't know what he was doing. And how about that bimbo with him, right? The one with a history of letting someone rob her blind?" My turn to snort. "A person like that deserves whatever she gets."

Del stiffened beside me, and I could tell that something was up.

"There's more to Brenda than that," he said. "Or there used to be. You don't know it but...she was there for me when I was younger. When I needed it. That's what's disappointing here. All her talk about family and taking care of family. All that may be hollow for her now, but those words still mean something to me, and for her to use that to set me up for this—set us *both* up like this? You're *my* family, Louise, more than she is these days, and—"

I couldn't stand it anymore. "Del," I said. "I have something I need to tell you." And then I did: me following him, me not trusting him, me calling the police—all my own wrong steps and unfairness.

Del just listened. I couldn't tell from his expression if he was angry or disappointed or what. I wouldn't have blamed him if he'd cut me loose himself, said enough is enough and moved on. But even though I knew the risk, I had to fess up, because you just can't live a lie. Brenda was proof of that.

"Oh, Louise," Del said, and for the first time in a while, he made my name sound all sweet and beautiful. "I know you may sometimes want something else, maybe someone else, dreaming of Hollywood Stars and Rodeo Drive"—he pronounced it Rode-e-o, bless him—"and it's okay to dream. But I'm not much of a dreamer myself, not like that. I don't need a Lexus or a big home either, because it's not the size of the car or the home that matters. It's..." He turned those green eyes my way, the ones I'd first seen between the wool of a ski mask—clear and beautiful and wide open now in a way he'd hardly looked at me the whole time we'd been in California. "You're my home, Louise, that's what I'm trying to say. You're where I want to be, who I want to be with. No Hollywood actress, no done-up housewife, none of that."

Maybe Mama was right. I'd never call Del simple, but he was solid, he was real. A real man, I was reminded again. Sometimes, I realized, it's best if you keep your dreams to yourself and your focus on the person in front of you.

"I've been thinking about it a lot, what to do with Brenda," he said. "Even though I don't think you'll like it, I plan to take the high road. But I also mean to take the road out of here. Are you with me?"

As if that question needed an answer, right?

Since most of our stuff was still in storage, Del and I didn't take long packing. Brenda had regained her composure by the time we went back into the living room, and she kept refixing her smile again and again as she tried to explain to Del why he couldn't leave. But this was a sale she just wasn't going to close—which finally hit her when Del handed the keycard back.

"The police checked through this one tonight," he said. "But it's not mine, it's yours. I swapped them yesterday."

She held it in her hands and turned it over, like she was inspecting it for something. Finally that smile fell apart.

"It's going to look like *my* key was...It's going to look like I've...They'll never believe that...Oh, Delwood, what have you...?"

There was a lot of ways I could've helped her finish most any of those sentences, but I held my tongue.

"*You* did this to you, Brenda," Del said, and it was like the anger he'd been holding in burst out suddenly. "You did this to *us*, putting your friends ahead of your family, your flesh and blood.

And for what? With five of you splitting whatever you got from—"

"But Delwood, you were never going to get into trouble," Brenda said, as if she really believed it. "Not if you'd just done as I'd asked, if we'd followed the plan."

"Your plan had too many coincidences," he went on. "It was far-fetched to have a key go in and out like that without someone inside knowing. It was stupid, start to finish. You're just not cut out to be a criminal."

I think that word *criminal* hurt Brenda worse than *pee* had. Her face contorted for a second and you could see her trying to get it back together. When she did, she sat down and started rearranging a group of porcelain elephants, fingering at them like they might just get up and run away if she didn't herd them tight.

"Criminal," she said. "I never thought I'd be called that." She looked around the room, like she was looking at it for the last time. "But even *before* the bubble burst, the business was going downhill. Ever since my husband...He was a good real estate agent, had a way with the clients, a way with words. He was the one who built this, and when he left me and I got the business...What am I supposed to do now, Del?"

He rolled his shoulders, adjusting them, trying to get his anger under control, but now that he'd let his feelings out, he couldn't really put them back away.

"All that talk about family may not mean anything to you, but it does to me," he said, same as he'd explained it in the bedroom. "Tomorrow, when the police come by, you can tell them I swapped my card for yours—and you'd be telling the honest truth." *For the first time,* I could've added, but I was so stunned by what Del was saying that I couldn't speak at all. "And with us leaving, they'll think we're guilty. You and your friends are off the hook."

"I couldn't do that to you, Delwood," Brenda said. "To family. I can't let you—"

"You're not letting anything," Del said. He was breathing heavier again, big heaves of air. "But we're even now, do you understand me? It's done. *We're* done."

*   *   *

Brenda watched from a distance while Del and I packed our bags in the Nova, her on the steps and the two of us standing out in the dark driveway, the moon overhead lighting up the street. The night air, the distance, the silence, Del still simmering with some kind of heat—all of it felt thick, tense. After a while, I couldn't take it anymore and darted back in the house.

"One more pee before the road," I called to Del as I passed Brenda—and one last nudge at her, I guess, with that word.

It was the last thing I said in her presence. None of us said goodbye.

"What did you mean by 'we're even'?" I asked, as Del pulled off.

"Another story," he said. "Another time. Not now."

His tone told me to let it go. I did.

There was only one rental place open that late, and they had only one trailer to rent, even larger than the one we'd gotten before. Del fretted about it, but I told him to go ahead and splurge.

"And let our stuff careen around back there?" he said.

"Del, will you ever just do what I ask?"

For once, he did, but again, everything else was closed.

"Last time I'll be using this ID," he said as he was hooking it up, giving me my first glimpse at the life ahead for us. But there was no one else I'd rather be on the lam with.

We drove to the storage warehouse then and loaded up our stuff. It felt good to see it again, especially that picture he'd stolen for me. Nostalgia felt a lot better when you were reconnecting with the past instead of walking away from it.

On the flipside, of course, was the gun he shoved back in the glove compartment—maybe another glimpse of the near future.

Once everything was packed, Del started to climb behind the wheel, but I stopped him.

"We're not quite done yet," I said, and I headed over to another storage unit, a half-dozen doors down.

"What's that?" he asked.

"Not what," I said, holding up a key. "Whose."

I popped the lock and lifted the door. Inside stood stacks of microwaves, boxes full of brass faucets and knobs, porcelain sinks, even a full granite countertop just like the one I'd pictured for our own house. Except ours would have actually been connected to the house, of course.

"This is Brenda's unit?" Del asked.

"She kept the key on a hook in the kitchen. I grabbed it when I went back in. I figured if you're going to take the blame, you might as well keep the goods, right?"

Del looked at it, percolated on it, then said, "We'll take half. Call it a final settling of the ways."

It was a compromise I could live with.

Del backed the trailer in and we loaded it up quickly, both of us together, as much as we could, before we got back in the front seat.

"Know where we could get rid of this stuff?" I asked, pointing toward the back.

"Not a clue," he said, but that didn't stop him from putting the car in gear and pulling us out onto the road, those big hands once more on the ten and two. "Where do *you* want to go?"

The map was there in the glovebox, but I didn't even pull it out. "Isn't that the beauty of a fresh start?" I said. "You never really know where you might end up." I reached up to the steering wheel and pulled his right hand down, clasped it in my own. "Let's just enjoy the ride for a while, okay?"

PROVENANCE

My home state of North Carolina was once the biggest producer of wine in the entire United States—sometime back in the plantation days. Then the Civil War happened and it all went south for a while. Or, well, north. And then there was Prohibition, and after that a lot of NC counties still chose to stay dry, which kept a plug on the whole business even longer.

When I was in college, the wine industry seemed to be on the rise again. I remember a bunch of us girls heading out for a tasting one summer afternoon. Several of us had just hit twenty-one, and going to a wine tasting had seemed like something different— something different being the one thing we all wanted back then. A winery had opened up two towns over, out on the new bypass—this barn-like house in the front and all those trellises in a field out back, vines twisted all around them. The day we went, you could see the grapes out there, plumping themselves up—at least that's what I remember, though I've been told since then I probably couldn't, that all I could've seen were the leaves.

The tasting was two dollars a person, refundable if we bought a full bottle, and most of the wine was real sweet—which was fine by us, having come up on wine coolers in our teens, all that sticky sugariness that seemed like a good way to ease into the brand new world of drinking. (The Southern Comfort would come later.) Scuppernong was one of the grapes, I remember, since my girlfriends and I made a joke out of it. Scoping out boys all the rest of that summer, we kept whispering to each other, "I'd sure scupper his nong," which always got us to giggling like...well, like the kids we still were.

We'd giggled too at the old man who ran the winery—talking to us about the health benefits of wine with each thimbleful that he poured. He reminded me of some huckster selling snake oil out of the back of a wagon: Good for what ails you! Cures headaches, backaches, joint ache, poor circulation in the feet, indigestion, menstrual cramps! Actually, he just said cramps, but we knew what he meant, and my friend Charlene swore he was leering at us as he said it.

At the end of the tasting, we bought a couple of bottles of white, which earned us our two bucks back, then had a fine time with them on the porch back home, sitting on these fold-out chairs with our feet in a plastic kiddie pool.

The next time, we went back to wine coolers, which might explain why the business was still trying to find its groove back then, at least in our neck of the woods.

That was my one and only experience with wine tasting.

None of it prepared me for Napa Valley—and Del certainly had no idea what he was getting into either.

We'd been in the area less than half a day when we visited our first winery in Napa. A six-hour-plus drive from Victorville, check-in at one of those extended-stay hotels, then a quick nap for Del, who deserved it. Not only had he been driving all night after an already-long day, but his Nova was straining to pull this big trailer filled with microwaves, granite countertops, copper pipes, and a lot more. Del himself seemed to be straining with the steering wheel, and to top it off, he was edgy and nervous the whole time—waiting for the authorities to catch up with us, since all that loot in the trailer was hot.

You might think from those words *loot* and *hot* that I was already getting into the spirit of our life on the lam—and add *on the lam* to that same list. But I'll admit it, I was watchful myself. Even after Del's nap, when we left the trailer at the hotel and went out for some vacationing—him rallying for me—I couldn't shake the idea there was trouble ahead.

"This one look good, hon?" Del asked, slowing past a flat-roofed building behind a gravel lot.

"Any one would be fine, I'm sure."

Given what happened later, I'm not going to tell you the name of the winery, but in case you want to track it down, the sign out front was purple and had grapevines running up each pole. I couldn't tell at a glance if those vines were real or what, but the whole thing looked a lot like that place back in NC.

"We should've brought some ones for the tasting," I said.

"I've got cash," Del said—which I knew. Everything cash now. No paper trail.

Del pulled the Nova between the only two other cars in the lot—a silver Mercedes convertible and this sleek red Acura. I was careful getting out not to bump the Acura on my side. It was shiny and squeaky clean, and I could already imagine the driver checking his door when he came back out.

We followed the "Tasting Room" sign to a side entrance (what was wrong with the front door, I never found out—just decorative maybe), and if the outside of the building was bland, the inside made up for it. A long mahogany bar stretched in an L shape, and a brass footrail ran the length of it. They'd arranged these plush leather chairs and sofas into several semi-circles, one group set in front of a fireplace that seemed to have been swept spotless. Over-sized artwork on the walls, just swirls and colors, and these tall candleholders in the corners.

Two men in dark suits stood behind the bar, one of them serving two couples who already had wine glasses in front of them. Mercedes and Acura, I imagined.

The other bartender smiled and held up a hand, a quick welcome. He was a good-looking guy and seemed to know it, all big shoulders and dark tan, with his blonde hair swept back and moussed up.

Del sidled up to the counter in front of him. "We'd like to take you up on a tasting, my good man."

"Certainly," he said. (I couldn't quite tell how he took it, being called "my good man" like that.) "Would you prefer the bar or the salon?" He gestured to those leather chairs.

Del looked at me. I shrugged. Why not?

"The salon it is," Del said, and I could tell from the way he said *salon* that he was warming to the place.

The barman introduced himself as Trevor as he led us to our seats—two big chairs facing out a back window and across a small porch to those trellises.

After we'd sat down, he handed Del a leather-bound folder. "On the menu here, you'll find two flights to choose from, and the premium tasting does include two vintages that took gold at the Concours Mondial—highly recommended. I'll be back in a moment once you've had time to consider."

I was still admiring the view—leaves thick on the vine, hills rising real steep just beyond—while Del opened up the folder.

"Good lord, Louise," he whispered. "It costs twenty-five dollars for three wines—and that's for each of us. For fifty, we could get nearly a whole case at the grocery store."

I reached over to take it from him. "We don't have to do the premium, Del, just the regular is fine."

"That is the regular tasting," he said. "The premium is forty dollars a person."

The regular tasting was actually labeled "Cruising Altitude," and the other was "Higher Elevation." Even the three wines at the, um, lower elevation had won a bunch of awards: gold at the San Francisco International Wine Competition, silver at the International Wine Challenge, a score of ninety-two from Robert Parker. (Before we left, I pulled the slip of paper from inside the menu and tucked it into my purse as a souvenir—figured we'd paid enough for it by the time we were done.)

"This must be a mistake of some kind," I told Del. "This is probably for three full glasses of wine, not for those quick sips like you get."

Del just snorted at that. I knew he was right. When I glanced over at Mercedes and Acura, I saw these thin swallows in each of their glasses—and they seemed pretty delighted with that much, the way they seemed to be chewing at each sip, all these facial contortions and crazy expressions.

"Should've just kept on sleeping this morning," Del said.

"You would've regretted it," I said. "It's like they always say with jet lag—better just to push through, get back on a regular schedule."

Del shook his head.

"First, Louise, we are still in the same time zone that we left last night. Second, we didn't actually take a jet anywhere."

Like it is with many relationships, what we were talking about wasn't what we were talking about.

"Twenty-five bucks a person." He laughed, no pleasure in it, then stared out that back window across the fields.

"Should we go somewhere else?" I asked, but Del had clearly gone somewhere else already. A little pensive, that was the way he would've explained it. *Contemplative* if he was thinking something really deep. And I could imagine what he was thinking now, what these last months had been like. Scrimping and saving, expenses going out, no income coming in, and now all we had to show for it was a lot of stolen merchandise that we still needed to find a way to unload somewhere.

"Maybe Trevor could take a microwave in trade, you think?" I whispered, trying to be funny, but Del acted like he hadn't heard me.

He was still staring out that back window when Trevor returned, a wineglass in each hand.

"Have you made a decision?"

"Listen," I started to say, still working on how to back out of this without embarrassing anybody, but Del roused himself up first.

"Just two at the Cruising Altitude, please." He said it with such a straight expression that even I would've had trouble seeing what it cost him to save face.

Once Trevor was out of earshot, I leaned Del's way. "I'll pay you back."

"Our money is our money," he said. "There's no yours and mine." Which made me regret sometimes looking at it that other way myself.

The wines, I should explain, seemed really good—at least to me. As I said, I'm hardly a wine connoisseur, and I still remember the sting I felt back in New Mexico at that exhibition opening the night Del robbed the art gallery—me sipping the free wine and feeling all sophisticated before I overheard that fancy couple calling it swill.

Sitting there in Napa that first day, I felt that way all over again. Mercedes and Acura looked like they'd gussied up for some fancy dinner on the town, the women in these silk dresses, the guys in sports coats. Del and I were just in our jeans.

But as Mama says, "The only way to get an education is to ask the dumb questions," so I dove right in—especially after Mercedes and Acura left, and I didn't feel like I had to whisper.

"What exactly do you mean by minerality?" I asked Trevor. "I mean, should I actually be tasting the rocks or the ground or what?"

And: "Is that a hint of black cherry in there? Like with Cheerwine?"—which isn't wine, I know, but still.

And: "Is there really that much of a difference between these wines and the ones you get for seven bucks at the grocery store?"

Trevor was patient with all of it—even that last question, but maybe it was the way I smiled when I asked it.

"The more experienced your palate becomes, the more you're able to taste the small nuances of quality," he said. When he smiled back, these dimples showed up in each of his cheeks. "And I can tell you'll be a very quick learner."

It seemed just a mite flirty to me, especially with Del sitting there and all. But Del just sipped and sat, didn't say hardly anything. Maybe his attention was focused elsewhere, since I caught him mouthing some of the words Trevor was using—*sommelier, appellation, provenance*—collecting vocabulary the way he does.

Poor Del, though. For all the words he was learning, he didn't seem to have much in the way of tastebuds to go along with it.

"It's got a real minty taste to it, spearmint or peppermint maybe?" he said about this Chenin Blanc we tasted, but really I think it was psychosomatic, as Del might say, since he'd been swishing it in his mouth like a swig of Listerine.

Trevor nodded, but it was in that tight-lipped way that English teachers do when you interpret a poem wrong but they don't want to stifle you.

"I don't know, hon," I said. "It's got a sweetness to me, almost like—" I looked at Trevor. "It may be silly to say, but it's almost like a Krispy Kreme doughnut, the way that glaze is sweet and crisp at the same time."

"That's very astute," he said, surprising me. "The sweetness comes from the extra sugar here, because of how we stop the fermentation process early."

Del dutifully jotted something down on the "tasting notes" sheet that Trevor had given us.

"What do you think about this one?" Trevor asked, pouring us the next glass. Looked like he'd tipped some extra in this one.

Del swigged again. I sipped and just let it sit there in my mouth, like I'd seen Mercedes and Acura doing but without the histrionics. Really, I just wanted to enjoy the flavor, that's all.

Del spoke before I could: "It seems to be very fruit forward," he said. I wasn't sure where he got that phrase from since I hadn't heard Trevor use it. "A bouquet of watermelon and something more citrusy."

Because I could tell Del was just feeling some pressure here, I didn't point out that you actually wouldn't put watermelon into a bouquet.

"It makes me think of mowing the grass on one of those first spring days back in North Carolina," I said. "You always had to wait to mow until the dew was gone, but you didn't want to wait too long in case it got hot. And something about that smell of cut grass when it's moist...it's nostalgia, I know, but somehow that's what pops to mind. It's a good memory."

Trevor nodded again, but this time it was with real enthusiasm. "Exactly, exactly," he told me. "That grassy quality is just what we strive for in a Sauvignon like this."

"Highway robbery," Del said after he'd paid the bill and headed for the car. "At least I got this." He tossed a bottle on the seat beside me.

"When did you get that?" I picked it up. A Cabernet Sauvignon.

"Swiped it while you were flirting with your new boyfriend," he said, shifting the Nova into gear. "Figured you might want to try something from that Higher Elevation."

The extended-stay hotel we picked wasn't *too* too far from Route 29—that main drag of Napa Valley, stretching from St. Helena through Yountville and down to the city of Napa itself—and it suited all our needs at that moment. It was cheaper than a regular hotel but not as semi-permanent as a lease someplace, and Del was able to negotiate a cash deposit in lieu of a credit card. "No paper trail" seemed like it was going to determine almost everything about our lives those days: not just where we slept but where we ate—so it helped that the room had a kitchen and a dining table.

I won't say it felt like home, but it felt homey in its own way, especially when Del took down the picture over the bed—grapes, of course—stashed it in the closet, and hung up the beach picture he'd stolen for me back in New Mexico, those two people looking out to the horizon, the waves and the sea oats and all. It made the place feel like ours, and no one from the hotel seemed to mind—at least not that we heard.

There was a continental breakfast, just doughnuts and coffee, and about four evenings a week, the hotel hosted a happy hour and light dinner for folks who got there early enough for the first-come, first-served limited supply. Nothing fancy—meatball sliders, chicken wings, mini tacos, stuff like that depending on the night—but it was good for our limited income (at first, no income at all). To make sure we got our fill, the two of us started showing up at five on the dot, like senior citizens catching the early bird special—though Del's already further along in years than I am, so maybe he truly appreciated this new schedule.

"A smidge of raspberry in this one, I think," I said one of those first nights, tasting some of the white zinfandel the hotel had put out for the happy hour. "Or maybe it's strawberry, but with some tart behind it. What do you think, Del?"

Del smacked his lips. "I don't know, hon. I'm getting a bleachy taste here."

"It's from the kitchen," I said, pointing to the door behind Del's seat. "I can see how it would mess up the bouquet. Next time, we'll get a table on the other side of the room."

"At least we know the place is clean," he said—though when we got a lemony fresh undertone to the pigs in a blanket, I began to wonder how close they kept the cleaning supplies to the cooking itself.

To get the taste out of our mouths, we went back to the room and popped open that bottle of wine Del had stolen.

"To our future," Del said.

"Whatever it brings," I added, and we clinked.

It tasted like liquid velvet—and I mean that in a good way. And I have to admit, Del having swiped it like that somehow made it extra sumptuous.

Maybe life on the lam was going to be fun.

We celebrated in other ways too, I'm happy to say. Now that Del and I had a place of our own again and not the two separate rooms we'd had at his sister's, we started reacquainting ourselves with one another, so to speak. In fact, we were making a pretty regular acquaintance in that way, and it felt good to move past that rough patch of suspicion and miscommunication that had caused such trouble back in Victorville—felt like a vacation from the people we'd become during that bad spell.

But as much as this was a vacation, there was also business to attend to—both what to do next and then business of a more existential sort, as Del put it.

"Robbing those convenience stores was supposed to be a means to an end," he told me after our first reacquaintance sessions, the two of us lying in that hotel bed, staring at the ceiling. "It was a way to get the tuition to earn the degree to get the better job and the better life. It wasn't supposed to orbit back on itself like this." He meant the trailer out back, the bottle of wine we'd just drunk—easy to slip back into old ways.

"You're a good man, Del," I said. "An honest one. And I understand that you want to live a good and honest life, but..."

"But?" he asked, when I didn't go on.

"But whatever fresh start we're aiming for, sometimes the path ahead gets determined by a lot of other things."

A moment passed, then the pillow jostled from where he was shaking his head.

"No," he said. "It's still a choice. And I know I made my choice when it came to my sister. That path you're talking about, that's only the consequences of the choice."

Sometimes after a conversation like that, it took both of us a long time to nod off to sleep. But that first night, Del fell right off to bed, the long days still taking their toll or maybe all the existentialing he was doing.

I couldn't sleep, and after a while, I got up and headed down to the hotel's small business center—a single computer and printer in a room you needed your key to get into. I searched stuff about Victorville and real estate crimes and both Brenda's name and Del's. I expected to see the story pop up somewhere. Victorville Vandalism Solved. Local Realtor Arrested. Burglar Brother Missing. Statewide Manhunt for Criminal Couple.

Nothing yet, and nothing later on other nights that I checked in. And truth to tell, maybe that bothered me more. I'm always better at dealing with what I know rather than the things I don't see coming.

As for that immediate path ahead, whether it was choice or consequence or us being thrown down it, Del made a checklist of what was next.

Eliminating our paper trail wasn't difficult, since Del had always traded mostly in cash. We'd already ditched the smartphones that Brenda had given us—too easy for someone to track us down, as I'd proved myself. Even though the Nova was pretty conspicuous (not many like it on the road), Del was hesitant to give it up, so he just swapped license plates with another car—"camouflage," he called it. We'd need to get new identities for ourselves, he said, fake licenses and social security cards. Then there was the trailer.

We visited a few pawnshops, percolating over options there to pass off some of the goods, but really, how would that work, taking in those microwaves one at a time? Cops trolled those places. One had a big sign "Discount for Law Enforcement." Guns and ammo were the biggest inventory.

All of which took us to this dive bar down in Napa that Del had learned about—"Someplace the locals would go for cheap beer and whiskey?" he'd asked the front desk. "Nothing fancy. In fact, maybe just the opposite."

We got what he asked for.

If that first winery we went to was upper crust, the bar in Napa was sure the bottom of the pie. The inside was dark enough that it took a second for our eyes to adjust. Neon signs hummed along the back wall—that off-kilter Budweiser bowtie and "Jack Lives Here" with "Old No. 7" just beneath it. Dim fluorescent tubes hung low over a pair of pool tables in the back. A couple of guys were playing, the first one bent over the table in mid-stroke, his beard grazing the green felt. A second man—with long stringy hair and a mechanic's shirt on, a name patch on the chest—stood to the side. Two more guys stood nearby, just watching, and several others leaned against the bar or sat on one of these tattered stools, wobbling back on their seats.

Del got us Budweisers, and we grabbed a booth not far from the door, benches with no cushion and a heavy wood table. I ran my fingers along some of the letters carved into the top, wondering if CV still loved DG these days.

"Del, do you really think this is going to work?"

"Worth a try," he said, tipping back his beer. Some foam clung to the center of his mustache. "Crime is a business, and we've got to think smart, like businesspeople."

"And we're networking here, right? What was it you said? Integrating yourself into the criminal community? Diving down into Napa's underbelly?"

"That metaphor is pretty mixed, hon," Del said. "And I think I said *insinuate* not *integrate*."

The jukebox had been playing that old Billy Squier song—stroke me, stroke me—and I looked over when I heard the pool players laugh. They were holding their cue sticks up and rubbing them like a bunch of adolescent boys. Like I've said, most people don't change, even as they get older.

"I don't know, Del. These fellas don't really look like part of some criminal network. And aren't all the real criminals wearing suits and ties these days and sitting behind a computer somewhere in their big swanky offices? This strikes me as stereotypical, don't you think?"

About then, the stringy-haired pool player in the mechanic's shirt turned my way. I smiled—don't back down in a staring contest, that's what Mama always said—but I'll admit it, I shivered when I saw his eyes, which had this cold, snake-like look to them. Despite what I was saying, I wondered if maybe there was indeed some criminal element lurking here.

The song shifted on the jukebox then, a ballad. Stringy Hair headed toward us, still hefting his stick.

I saw Del tighten the grip on his beer bottle. I felt my own body steeling up for whatever was going to happen next.

Then Stringy Hair pulled up his pool cue like a microphone.

"La-dy," sang the voice on the jukebox, and stringy hair mouthed the word extravagantly, looking at me like he was serenading me and singing along silently about being my knight in shining armor and loving me and all that. He added a curtsy here and there and swung his head in this exaggerated way, all earnest-like. It was clear again how much he'd been drinking, the goofy expression, that glossy look to his eyes less scary than just silly.

Stringy Hair had come closer now, and I could see that the patch on his shirt said "Carl." Behind him, some of the other guys seemed to be laughing, and I thought, it's a dare, that's all it is. When an instrumental section kicked in, Carl leaned forward and reached out for my hand.

"May I have this dance?" he asked.

His breath had that hoppy smell to it. There was a whistle over at the bar, this smatter of applause. I looked at Del and could tell he was getting steamed. He's not a violent man, not really, but he's hefty and could surely do some damage if he put his mind to it.

"Thank you," I said. "But my boyfriend and I here were just enjoying our beers—"

But Carl was singing again, out loud now and with some real feeling about being lost and brokenhearted. He moved around in circles as he sang, dancing with that cue stick, coming back to gesture my way at choice lines.

I turned to Del, raised my eyebrows. What now?

Del nodded, like he was agreeing with something I didn't know I'd suggested. When he stood up, I thought things were gearing toward a fight.

Then Del just started to clap.

The song went on, but Carl had stopped singing. His glassy expression didn't look goofy anymore.

"I don't think I was singing to you, was I?" Carl said, his voice calm—too calm, I thought. Before Del could answer, Carl shook his head just lightly. "No, I'm pretty sure I was singing for that little lady you brought with you."

"Either way, this has certainly proved the highlight of our visit," Del said. "But we were just stopping in for a quick drink." He held up the bottle, almost empty now. "And it's probably time for us to head on."

"I think she oughta give me at least one dance before you go, at least to reward me for giving her the highlight of your visit." He put a twist on the phrase—and a tighter grip on his cue stick, the move almost like a tremor or a spasm. "Don't you think that's only proper?"

"I don't want trouble," Del said. His own hand was tightening around the Budweiser in his hand.

"Then don't go looking for it," said Carl.

I know how easily a bottle would break when you slammed it against a bar—and not just from the movies. I'd seen it firsthand, bar fights like this one, and usually over some woman. Once, it was over me, and at the time, even in the middle of all the craziness and chaos, it had made me feel special. But I didn't think I'd feel that way these days. Maybe people did change, at least some.

The song finished up then and another one started, a quick riff of the guitar, bouncy and easygoing.

"Boys, boys," I said. I stood up and stepped between them. "I sure appreciate your offer to dance," I told Carl, "and the song. It was all very nice. You really shouldn't have gone to any trouble just for me."

"Honey," Del said behind me.

"Now that I'm done with my own beer," I told Carl, "I'm sure my boyfriend won't mind if we have a quick dance, as long as I let him know I'm okay with it." I turned toward Del. This time it was me nodding and Del clearly not sure what my plan was. "Just one dance and we can go?"

Del hesitated, then shrugged.

The guys in the bar applauded as I took Carl's hand and he led me in a short dance there between the booths and the pool table.

That hoppy smell was stronger up close, but those are the kinds of sacrifices you make. When he spun me around, stumbling just slightly, and pulled me closer to him, I took it as my signal to open up the conversation.

"Tell me," I whispered into his ear. "You wouldn't happen to know where someone might get rid of a truckload of microwaves, would you?"

There's this saying: Love isn't two people gazing into one another's eyes, it's two people looking together in the same direction.

I'm not sure who said it originally, maybe a philosopher or maybe an advice columnist or maybe it was just somebody at the greeting card factory, trying to come up with something new for Valentine's Day. The truth can come from any number of places.

"That's a lot faster than I would've risked it," Del said later, after we'd left the bar, "but good work." Because it turned out that Carl might indeed be able to help.

Back in New Mexico, Del had always operated on his own, so having me as an accomplice was a new step for both of us. And it wasn't just me here, but others. It was risky, Del admitted that, especially given how little we knew about Carl. He'd lived in Napa for four years, he worked in the storage warehouse for one of the big wineries, he admitted to having been arrested a couple of times on drunk and disorderly, and he told us about some burglaries that he hadn't been caught for.

Actually, listing it all out like that, I guess that's knowing a lot. Not only did the beer give Carl a boost toward homemade karaoke, but it also made him chatty, and he'd told us all that and more when he'd joined us in the booth after our dance. Still knowing *about* someone and *knowing* them are two different things in the end. We all felt cautious moving ahead—all but Carl.

"Wow," said Carl when Del opened up the back of the trailer

and showed him everything inside. It was still propped up at the back of the hotel, and we had the parking lot to ourselves for the moment. It was mid-morning, the sun already beginning to heat up the day. "Big haul. How'd you manage it?"

Del hesitated. Who would want to admit all the backstory here: his sister's bungled attempts at a life of crime and her attempt to pass off the blame on us; how Del and I had tangled at cross-purposes over it all; that late-night escape from his sister's house.

"I'm not sure the provenance is important," Del said.

Carl pointed to the inside of the trailer. "You're a real pro. And ballsy, keeping it parked here like this." He gestured around him. I looked at the windows to see if anyone was watching us, kept an eye on the corners of the building for cars circling around.

"Um, yeah, about that. Do you mind if we pull down the door?"

"Not at all, man. Not at all."

As Del closed the trailer, Carl gave me this big grin and did a quick sway like he was dancing.

"You know someone who might like to take this off our hands?" Del asked.

"Oh, yes, I think we can manage that," Carl said, but he was cagey about the who and the how and the when. Del said he'd prefer to meet directly, Carl insisted he'd just take it over from here.

"Collaboration," he said. "You be the mastermind, let me handle the middleman stuff. But here's the real question, big man. Do you know anything about the wine business?"

Carl proved to be a good resource. We got a fair windfall from the fence he was using—not as much as we'd hoped from the Victorville stash (microwaves aren't high-dollar items anyway), but Del had also let him pass along some of our own stuff. "Necessary streamlining," he'd said. Carl had also used his own truck to deliver the trailer back to Victorville, covering our tracks and keeping Del from showing his face, in case the police had found out about the rental.

"Everything okay in Victorville?" Del asked.

"Shouldn't it have been?" Carl asked.

"I'm just saying no trouble returning the trailer, getting the deposit back and all."

"You mean my service fee?" He gave this sly smile, like he'd pulled one over on us. A small price to pay, Del said.

Carl also arranged our new licenses and social security cards, though maybe Del regretted letting me work that part of the deal myself.

We were at the hotel's evening happy hour when I showed the new IDs to Del. Chicken wings that night, and his mustache and beard had bits of hot sauce clinging to it. I held up the licenses, not wanting him to get them smeared.

Del peered at them, then cut his eyes at me. "Don't you think these names are a tad conspicuous?"

"Clyde is a good name, Del. It's strong and solid and distinguished."

"But yours is Bonnie."

I smiled. "You've always said it's best to hide right there in plain sight, haven't you? And if anyone asks, we'll just tell them we get that all the time. Truth is stranger than fiction, we'll say. We can tell them that maybe it was fate that brought us together."

Del shook his head, picked up another wing.

What bothered me was that he hadn't mentioned the other part. Bonnie and Clyde there on those IDs—us, I mean—we had the same last name: Graysmith now, not far from his own.

He hadn't even commented on the fact that I'd married us.

Once Del had come to terms with his new identity, Carl also helped to get him a job in one of the warehouses, basically just helping to move cases around, prep them for delivery. He knew how to run a forklift, and it wasn't like they needed someone with a resume. He was learning the basics of the operation, seeing how it worked, setting the stage for whatever plan Carl was hoping Del would "mastermind."

Mornings, I dropped Del off at the wine warehouse. Some evenings, I picked him up, and other times Carl drove him back and joined us for the hotel happy hour, which gave him no end of pleasure. ("The goods without being a paid guest," he boasted, savoring a hot dog. "Tastes even better that way.") Those nights, he and Del would gather around the kitchenette table in our room and make notes and maps and charts about the warehouse—the plan evolving.

"I've scrutinized it from a variety of angles, and we could strategize getting a case of wine or two out of the warehouse," Del said. "It's all a matter of timing—and luck. We'd have to dodge around the inventory schedule and one particular manager's shift."

"I know who you mean," Carl said. "Jackass."

"We also need to hope that the spot checks by ATF officials don't introduce any complications."

"Hard to predict those visits," Carl said. "The surprise is part of their whole plan."

"Which messes up any of *our* plans." Del sighed. "In any case, I'm struggling with the idea of a bigger haul all at once. Unless we intercepted a shipment as it was being transported somewhere, it might be a real challenge."

"But wouldn't several bottles at a time be tougher to catch than if a whole truckload went missing?" I asked.

"Maybe," said Del. "But the way I see it, we're exposing ourselves to risks each time—cumulatively, in fact—and it would ultimately take us too long to accumulate enough critical mass for any real windfall."

"So it's a question of enough quantity on the one hand," Carl said, talking to me.

"And a dose of risk calculation on the other," Del finished.

Carl promised he had a connection to handle the next stage of it all—a wine brokerage with some "questionable scruples," as Del put it, ready to "relocate" well out of the area whatever they could smuggle out. But smuggling it out seemed to be the issue.

I tried to play accomplice, but there wasn't much I could contribute, not having been inside myself. Sometimes I stepped down to that business center for another search on Victorville (still no news) and other times just settled down on the sofa to watch my court shows or some movie. I was working my way through a bunch of heist films: *The Thomas Crown Affair*, *The Italian Job*, *Inside Man*, and *Ocean's Eleven*—the original, the remake, and all those awful sequels—keeping myself in the spirit of things.

"You've heard the story about the man stealing from the construction site where he works and taking it right past the security guards every day?" Del asked Carl one night, and I tuned in myself.

"Can't say it rings a bell," he said.

"I forget where I read it, but this man, he works at this big construction site, and security's pretty tight. Every day the workers have to check in and out. And about once a week as he's clocking out, the man walks up to the security checkpoint with a wheelbarrow full of dirt. After awhile, one of the guards gets a funny feeling about it and starts checking the dirt, sifting through it to make sure nothing's hidden there."

"And what was hidden in the dirt?" Carl asked.

"That's just it. Nothing. Ever. The guard just waves the guy past each time. And that's how the guy got away with it."

"With what?" Carl said.

"Stealing all those wheelbarrows."

Carl just about jumped out of his chair. "I can see it!"

I couldn't.

I paused the movie I was watching. "That can't be a true story," I said.

Del shrugged. "Maybe not, but it's something to think about for what we're planning."

"It shouldn't be," I said. "You can't bring out a case of wine without someone noticing it, can you? I mean, it's not like the wine would be carrying something else."

"She's got something there," Carl said.

"And wouldn't someone notice a bunch of missing wheelbarrows after a while? Wouldn't they keep inventory on that sort of thing?"

"I'm still thinking about it all, Louise," Del said, all huffy. "I wasn't saying this was the answer. It's just something to consider."

Del's smart, I know that, but I was beginning to think that the mastermind thing might be going to his head.

After I dropped Del off at work each morning, I took the Nova and went exploring, furthering my education sip by sip at some wine tastings and seeing more of Napa in the process.

Parts of the area were just beautiful—about what you'd expect. You'd get these pretty-as-a-postcard views of acres of vineyards, the gentle roll of the hills, sometimes this golden sunset turning it all amber and magical. The wineries themselves were a mix. A lot of it was in what they call Mission style, looking like a cross between the adobes we'd left back in New Mexico and these big churches, but you could see a little of everything, even some places that looked like just a house there off the side of the road. Parts of Route 29 seemed like travelling down the midway at the State Fair—winery after winery, sign after sign hawking a tasting, open now, groups welcome.

I couldn't afford a regular diet of those twenty-five dollar a pop winery visits like we'd done the first day, of course, but there were other opportunities. The hotel sometimes passed along some fliers and coupons to wine tasting bars or to wineries themselves. A couple of times, I splurged and signed up for a half-day tour on a small coach bus, with stops at about four wineries—but only after we'd gotten rid of all the merchandise and pocketed some extra money. Del did indeed join in sometimes, which was the best—nice breaks from those nights when Carl stopped over for a planning session.

"Have y'all been stomping around in a grape barrel yet?" Mama asked one morning on the phone. With the time difference between California and North Carolina, it was one of the best times to catch her anyway.

"That may just be in the movies," I told her.

"Looks messy anyway," she said. "But I was thinking about it when I was in the grocery store the other day and looking at the wine section. Lots of California on the shelves. I bought a bottle of red, actually."

"Did you like it?"

"Tasted like sock. Maybe that company still does the foot stomping, yeah?"

"I like some of it, mostly the whites. I'm learning a lot, and Del's picking up some good wine terms."

"Him and his words." Mama snorted. "What kind of terms?"

"Oh, I don't know," I said, sorry I'd mentioned it. "Wine words."

Oenophile, I could've said. Or any of those tasting terms he just ate up: *aggressive* and *astringent*, *buttery* and *peppery*. *Herbaceous* had been a real favorite. *Minerality* and *transparency*. He really perked up when he heard a champagne called *biscuity*, and bless his heart for sidling up to that phrase *boutique vineyard*, even if it was slightly feminine for his taste.

I didn't tell Mama about any of that. You have to be selective with her.

"He's been practicing them on me," I told her instead. "He said I'm voluptuous. And complex."

"Always the smooth talker," Mama said—double-edged, of course. Smooth talkers made her suspicious. "He found a job yet, now that the real estate market has proved not quite his thing?"

She was throwing my own words back at me. I'd tried to be vague about Del leaving his sister behind. And had to be vague again now, but in a different way.

"He picked up a job in the storeroom for one of the big wineries here." Working on another job in the process, I could've said, but I didn't. "But really this is like a vacation for us, and Mama, it's really beautiful here. Almost like a honeymoon."

From the deep breath on the other end of the phone, I already knew what was coming.

"Last I heard about honeymoons," Mama said, "you need to get married first."

Which would be the way she'd look at it, literal-minded like that.

"Does Cora ever have anything nice to say?" Del asked me whenever I relayed any part of a conversation.

"Mama means well," I said. "It just sometimes comes out rougher than she means."

"Abrasive as sandpaper," Del said. "Do you ever wonder if you'd be better off not telling her everything?"

I didn't stop calling her. Just cut back on telling Del about it.

Back when I was a teenager, even before that, I remember that it meant everything to be the first to know something or to be the closest to whatever was new and fresh and fun. "Girl, You Know It's True" on the radio, and all my friends talking about it and memorizing it and arguing about which one was Milli and which one was Vanilli. Or me memorizing all the names of Bryan Adams' back-up musicians because I thought *he* would appreciate it, then searching the mall for a jean jacket just. like. his. When Mama got me a subscription to *Tiger Beat*, I felt like I was the coolest kid on the block, but later, when my friend Amanda got a subscription to *Rolling Stone* before anybody else, I felt like I'd been left behind, and those *Tiger Beats* seemed suddenly embarrassing.

Maybe that's why it had bothered me back in Taos, feeling like a fool drinking that bad wine and not knowing it. And maybe that other feeling I was feeling now, learning everything, realizing even from that first day that I might be good at this, was the flipside: knowing, belonging.

All of which was how I got the offer to stand on the other side of the tasting table for a change.

Here's how it happened.

One afternoon, I splurged on one of those coach trips—didn't even know where we were going, just signed up for the half-day, climbed onboard, and figured on an adventure. The group with me came from a lot of different backgrounds. One couple on the bus carried this big black binder, looked like a lot of maps of the area and brochures for wineries stuffed in it, along with pages for tasting notes and I don't know what all else. Mr. and Mrs. Binder were very studious and serious—connoisseurs clearly, or at least trying to be. Right across the aisle were some younger couples, fraternity and sorority-looking types, about the age I was with that first winery visit back in North Carolina. Everything about them said that they were gonna get their drink on. And sure enough, between the first two wineries we'd visited that day, one guy chugged almost a full bottle of pinot.

In the middle of all those shenanigans, I didn't even notice the third winery until we'd pulled into the parking lot: the same purple sign with the grapevines twirling around it, the same gravel lot just without Mercedes and Acura parked out front today.

As soon as I walked through the door, I spotted Trevor and his moussed-up hair. A quick smile curled up at the corners of his lips when he, in turn, spotted me.

You can't say I went looking for trouble, but I will admit to being flattered that he remembered me.

"Welcome back," he said, singling me out as the whole crowd of us gathered at the bar. "Alone today?"

I laughed. "Not hardly."

Down the line, one of the frat boy types called out, "This round's on *me!*"

With all of us gathered together, Trevor and his coworker Cindy, bleached blonde and very buxom, tag-teamed a short presentation about the winery: the history, the wines they specialized in, the selection prepared for the day. Cindy enunciated and projected her part of the pitch like she was part of a beauty contest and hellbound to win, but I mostly tuned her out until she mentioned that we had the chance to upgrade to the more expensive flight.

Trevor caught my eye and cocked his head at me. Yes?

And again, why not?

When I ended up being the only one who took up the offer, Trevor eased me down to the far end of the counter, then shuttled back and forth between helping out Cindy and chatting more one-on-one with me.

I told him about visiting some other wineries, getting tons more information about wine, developing my tastebuds. I dropped some wine terms I'd learned, some of the ones that Del had liked the best—hoping I was using all of them right.

"And coming back now to let me take you to the Higher Elevation?" he asked.

"I think my palate is up to it," I said.

I didn't realize how that might've sounded until Mrs. Binder just down the counter stole a glance my way, raising an eyebrow. She raised that eyebrow again when Trevor lined up three clean glasses in front of me while everyone else down the line got just a single glass for their whole tasting. If he was trying to impress me, he wasn't endearing either of us to the rest of the group.

Instead of explaining each of the wines—the varietal and all of the awards and what I ought to be tasting—he just asked questions about each one, my impressions, my perspectives. It got to where the tasting seemed like a test in some ways.

"How would you describe the color of this first one?" he asked.

"It's a white wine," I said, and laughed.

"Seriously," he said, and he did look serious. Earnest even.

I picked up the glass by the stem and looked at it, then held it up to the light.

"Whites are really kind of yellow," I said. "And this one...I'd call it golden, but a paler gold, like a ten carat ring instead of a fourteen maybe."

Trevor laughed. "It's a good thing that the wine doesn't rank the same way. This one is a pretty high quality."

"Eighteen carat?"

"At least," he said. "Now give it a taste."

I closed my eyes and took a small sip.

"Back in North Carolina," I said, after a minute, "one of our neighbors had what looked like a wall of vines along the back edge of her yard. During the winter it was just these twiggy shrubs, but in the spring and summer, it was all green leaves and covered in flowers." I tasted it again. "Honeysuckle, definitely. Just a hint of it, but that's the first thing I thought about, that wall of honeysuckle vines and that summer afternoon. There was a boy I liked then, and I remember the two of us pulling the backs off of the flowers and sipping out the nectar." It gave me a shiver to remember it. So many years trying to get away from the state, and here I was being nostalgic about it again from a whole country away from home.

"Anything else?" Trevor asked. He was pushing me, wanting more.

"Something citrus maybe? Orange?"

"Orange blossom," he said. "You really are a natural."

I did okay with the next two wines. The second one had a bit of a ruby color to it, like a ring that Mama used to wear when I was a kid—evidence of a slightly younger wine, Trevor told me, and he beamed at me when I said I could taste the plums in it. "Some other berries, I'm sure, and a bit of sweetness—more brown sugary than regular sugar—but it's the plums I taste most."

By the time I'd picked up the tobacco in the last one, it was pretty clear I'd passed—not that I really liked that one, even though Trevor said it was the star of their line-up. I'd only worked tobacco one summer back when Mama was dating a guy who oversaw some fields, but that was enough to turn me off of it for good.

The rest of my group was still finishing up their tastings (I heard a "Chug, chug" further down the line) while Trevor started tucking away my wine glasses.

"Listen," he said. "I don't know what your plans are for next Saturday, but the winery is taking part in this street festival, and..."

I was already gearing up to tell him that as much as I appreciated him asking me out, I couldn't make it, I was obviously seeing someone else, etc. and all that. But that wasn't where he was going.

"...and I was wondering if you might like to help us with the tasting." He motioned toward Ms. Buxom. "Cindy is away for the weekend, and those events need all the back-up help we can get."

I laughed. "I don't think being able to pick out the tobacco taste in a wine is enough to help sell it."

"Really this is less about wine expertise than about good PR," he said. "Most people just taste it and move on, and if the questions get tough, you can just ask someone else."

"Like you."

He smiled. "Like me."

"Meanwhile, I just look pretty and keep the glasses full?"

"Not full," he said. "But the pretty part..."

This time it was him that blushed—a light salmon color, I'd say, if it was a wine I was trying to describe.

"Look," he told me. "The, um, owners are gonna be out of town, and we've got to keep the winery here open that day in addition to staffing the festival. We're really needing some extra help. They put me in charge of staffing the festival—told me to get some friends to help."

"And I'm your only friend?"

"The only person lately who can pick honeysuckle out of a wine." He was running his hands along the stem of a wine glass. "It would be fun to have you along. No great pay, I should mention, but you could probably make a good deal if there's anything you're interested in taking home with you."

I know there are different ways to read what he said right then. I'm not oblivious. And if I had been, the way one of those sorority girls was staring at me and nodding with this fool grin on her face— *say yes!*—would've clued me in.

"The price may still be bit steep for that," I said, "but..."

But what? I wasn't being seductive on purpose. And honestly, if I'd known where it would all go, I think I would've just said no.

As it was, with Del working, getting his plan together...

"Okay," I said finally. "If you're able to clear it with the owners, I mean."

This sly look crept up on his face. "Since those owners are really my parents, I think it'll all be fine. But just let me get your number, and I'll give you a call when it's squared away." Then that sly-ness deepened a little. "And you know, you'll need to give me your name."

I held out my hand, dainty-like. "Bonnie," I said.

His handshake was gentle, warm.

"It makes me happy to think we'll be working together, Bon-nie," he said. "And I gotta say you look really happy yourself these days. You're just radiating it."

My turn to blush? I was probably garnet.

I was picking up Del that night. All the way to the warehouse, I felt my insides beginning to twist and turn at the thought of telling him about it—the guilt working at me about how it might look.

But by the time I got there, I had something more to worry about. Just outside the entrance to the warehouse sat a pair of black and whites, their blue lights slowly turning.

Nothing to do with Del, I told myself. They weren't planning anything today. Were they?

Other people left, walking right past the police cars. Other people went in—the usual change of shift. But each minute that passed without Del appearing left my insides queasier. No Del, no Carl either.

I didn't dare go in. Del had always said to take off at any sign of trouble. *Vamoose*, that was the word he used.

After a while, I couldn't look at those twirling lights anymore.

I backed up, headed to the hotel.

By the time Del got back to the room, my stomach was truly in knots. What was I supposed to do? Start packing? Wait there for him? Head somewhere else for him to call or to find me? I'd just sat on the bed, letting those questions churn.

"Carl got caught," he said, as soon as he came through the door.

"Caught?" I said. "How? Doing what?"

"The plan. Or part of it." Del had been carrying a paper sack, the bottom greasy. He pulled out two cheeseburgers, tried to hand one my way, but I waved it off. "He made a trial run—unbeknownst to *me* at the time, I should add, but the timing was everything we'd talked about. Inventory had just been finished, and ATF had done a spot check yesterday. The floor manager was suddenly out sick, the one who was circumspect about everything." He shook his head. "Then one of the forklifts got stuck, the lift way up midair with a crate of wine at a precarious angle, and when several workers went over to try to look at it, Carl made his move. Boldness is key, that's what we'd been discussing, but..."

"What happened?"

He held up his finger as he took a big bite of his burger. Stress always gave him an appetite, while it made me want to *not* eat—and all this new stress was on top of what I was already feeling about Trevor.

"Carl's lazy," he said. "It's no secret. He's even made a system out of the time clock. If you check in by seven minutes after, you get credit for the full fifteen minutes. Eight minutes after, and you don't. He always clocks in late, and at the end of the day, clocks out seven minutes before the half-hour—saving himself fourteen minutes of work each day. Everyone knows it, they joke about it— everybody but the supervisors, that is."

Del took another bite. The grease running down Del's beard was the final blow to my appetite.

"Everyone is headed over to check out the forklift, even some of the guys manning the exit, and Carl just shrugs and says, 'Time to clock out,' turns and heads for the door."

"Except he didn't go empty-handed."

Del shook his head. "He picked up a case like it belonged to him and marched out—right there in plain sight."

"Wheelbarrows," I said.

"Worse," Del said. "But he would've made it, that's the thing. At least until that manager, the one who had been sick, suddenly rallied and decided he needed to come in for part of the evening shift. Didn't want to be derelict about his duty, that's what he was telling everyone later—*after* he'd run into Carl leaving and taken the wine back and fired him."

"Wow," I said. "And the police?"

Del nodded. "The manager was riled up. He didn't like Carl in the first place. After the police came, we all had to be interrogated about what we'd seen. The forklift was still up in the air, but no one was paying any attention to it anymore."

Del gestured to the burger he'd gotten for me. I waved for him to take what he wanted.

"The worst thing," he said, still chewing, "is that I had started to follow his lead. I saw what he was doing, I looked at everyone watching that forklift, and...Louise, it's worse than that. I had a case in my own hands when the manager walked back in, dragging Carl behind him. And even though I put it down like I'd just been moving it, the manager *saw* me with it."

"Oh, Del. He didn't turn you over to the police, did he?"

"I think everyone suspected me," he said. "But it's like shoplifting. It doesn't count 'til you walk out the door, and I never got the box out of the warehouse. I told them I was just moving it. But I don't think anyone believed me. Either way, the manager said he'd be watching me. All these plans we've been working on, obviously everything is off now. And the job itself is short-lived, I'd imagine."

He took another big chomp of the burger. Bad timing no matter when I brought it up, but I couldn't put off my own news any longer.

"File this under one door closes and another one opens," I said. "Seems like I've got a job opportunity of my own."

Taking a deep breath to steady myself, I told him all about my offer. My concern was that Del would remember that first day and the flirting and what he'd said about Trevor being my boyfriend. I could see him getting if not jealous, then at least suspicious about the invitation and about the time I'd be spending with Trevor. I was prepped for opposition, but I couldn't tell from Del's reaction—or lack of it, I mean—what was going through his mind. He just sat and ate and stared across at the table toward the hotel window.

His look was so intense in that direction that it crossed my mind he might just be wondering about throwing me out of it. Or maybe he was just thinking about the fast food restaurants out there, and a run for another burger.

"How many people will be there?" he asked finally.

"I don't know," I said. "I think they'd need a good-sized staff." It wouldn't be just Trevor and me alone, I wanted to tell him, but I didn't want to call too much attention to that aspect of it if it wasn't already running through his head. "I think it would be pretty busy overall."

"Would you be spending the whole day in the booth?"

"No one's talked to me about my shift yet, but I imagine it rotates some throughout the day."

"But you might be there for most of it? Helping them set up in the morning, take stuff down at night? Pretty much the whole day possibly?"

"It's really just for the fun of it, Del. I could probably leave early, if you had something in mind. And I'm sure you could come by while I'm there. I think that would be nice, in fact."

"I might stop by," he said, with just an edge to it like he was saying something he wasn't saying—like stressing he'd be checking up on me. "How much wine do they bring to a festival like that?"

"How am I supposed to know? I've never done this."

"I would think a fair amount," he said. "They would need to stock enough for the tastings, of course—and I would imagine they'd be selling it, right?"

"It is their business, Del."

"Would you need to have a liquor license on hand for that, do you think?"

"Del, really, you seem awfully concerned about it, and if you'd rather I didn't do it..."

"Oh, no, Louise, not at all," he said. "What you're telling me might be exactly what we need."

*   *   *

Once I'd realized that jealousy wasn't the first thing on Del's mind—that he was, in fact, encouraging me pretty heavily to do this and the reasons why—I found myself shifting strategies. When I'd said one door closes and another one opens, I hadn't meant it the way he took it.

"Del," I told him, "if you're abandoning your big 'mastermind' plan because Carl got caught and *arrested*, then why do you think this off-the-cuff idea would work?"

"Sometimes you labor a lot in the wrong direction before the right path presents itself." Del was hunched over the kitchenette table now, making notes. "I'd said all along that I thought a big haul might be easier if the wine was being transported somewhere, if it was off-property. I have a feeling this is right."

"But this is just back to the smash and grab stuff that you used to do at those convenience stores."

"There was no smashing, Louise," he said, only half paying attention, more focused on his scribbling. "There was no grabbing. It was more like a quick stop and shop."

"Stop and steal maybe. What shopping did you ever do?"

He did look up at that. "I always made a point later to patronize the businesses I robbed, did you know that? After you quit that 7-Eleven, I still went in there pretty regular for chips."

"Fine. Steal and shop," I said. "Morality. But Del, those jobs, it was usually only one person on shift. Do you know how many people are going to be there? And I don't just mean people behind the counter, which I don't know, but people at the festival itself? Witnesses? Bystanders?"

"A big crowd might work in our favor." He stood up now, started pacing the room while he talked.

"And Del, you always made it clear that the first rule was that no one gets hurt."

"I'm not going to shoot anyone, Louise."

"I didn't mean hurt physically, Del. I meant hurt in other ways.

It's just a small business—"

"That charges fifty dollars a couple for three swigs of wine. In their salon, remember."

"Of course I remember, Del. I was there this afternoon, like I said."

Del leveled his eyes at mine. "What's this about, Louise? You didn't seem concerned about this when I robbed the 7-Eleven you worked at. You kept telling me you were fine with me being a criminal, no worries, you just wanted to be included in it."

"But Trevor, who asked me—"

"Is that what this is about? All that attention he was giving you?"

"I'm just saying that it's Trevor's family who owns the place, Del."

"And I'm saying that stealing from family didn't seem to be an inconvenience when you and I stole from my own sister."

Stolen goods in the first place, I started to point out, and a situation she'd put her own self and all of us in, but the phone rang first. Carl. He'd gotten out on bail and needed Del to go pick him up.

"I'll be back soon," Del told me.

"I won't wait up," I said.

I didn't want to talk about it anymore. My guts were already twisting up over it all.

After he left, I crawled into bed, put a pillow over my head, and tried to make everything go away.

What I said before about true love being two people looking in the same direction? Despite my best efforts, I could barely sleep that night thinking about that. I lay in bed turning it over and over in my mind, and gripping that old sock monkey in my hand like it might bring me some luck with all this, some guidance.

Because to get that true love, I realized, sometimes, you've gotta turn your own head to match up with where that other person's eyes are focused. And it made me dizzy trying to figure out which of us might swivel our gaze first.

When Del came back and crawled into bed beside me, I didn't look his way, just pretended to be asleep. Soon he was snoring next to me, like he hadn't given any of it a second thought.

I woke up the next day exhausted and ill-tempered. Del didn't say much to me while he was getting ready, and more silence as I drove him to work. Our conversation from the night before hung like a weight between us—at least a weight on my own mind and on my body too. I felt like I'd been sucker-punched.

"Carl okay?" I finally asked, just to break the tension.

"He thinks the charges will eventually be dropped."

"And what did he think of your next big plan?"

"We're on the same team, you know."

"You and Carl?" I asked. "Or me and you?"

Del didn't bother to answer.

After dropping him off, I didn't want to go back to the hotel room, cooped up with these sudden bad memories, and I wasn't in the mood for any more wineries—troubled thoughts there as well, guilt, fear, what have you. Instead, I drove down to the town of Napa and walked along the waterfront, sat for a while by this big tile mosaic near one of the hotels, then splurged on a red velvet yodel from a bakery around the corner—something for me, which usually boosted my spirits but this time just left me feeling sugared up, sickly sweet. I went to Yountville later, browsed some stores, and up to Calistoga too, where I got gypped into stopping by the Old Faithful geyser—laying down the admission fee before realizing that it wasn't the real Old Faithful but just a sad tourist trap.

After that I just went back and slept the rest of the afternoon—getting away from things I didn't want to think about, maybe trying to get away from myself.

*   *   *

I'd always said I was fine with Del being a criminal. Why was I torn up about this now? What had changed? Did I really have feelings for Trevor?

I kept trying to gauge that last question each time I saw Trevor over the rest of that week leading up to Saturday's festival. He'd asked me to stop by the winery for some prep work—no tastings, as it turned out, but mostly just the two of us talking in the salon between customers. He gave me a quick behind-the-scenes tour, shared more stories about the winery and its history, talked about the layout and schedule for the festival, how it was all going to work. When he ran out of official things to tell me, he moved on to stories about his parents and growing up at the winery, what he'd learned along the way about wine-making and wine tasting. He told me again how impressed he was that it all came easy to me.

Whenever a customer came up, he asked me to hold on while he handled the tasting. I settled into the salon, stared out at the vineyards, reflected on all of it. I liked him, I did. He was a good-looking guy, sure, and a good guy too, and I was flattered by the attention. But wasn't it more sisterly than romantic that I felt? Or motherly maybe, even though he wasn't much younger than me? I was sad to see him caught in the middle of this, hesitant about seeing him get hurt.

Still, each night—dutifully, reluctantly—I passed along to Del everything I'd learned. The schedule, the layout, how many cases of wine on hand, where the truck would be parked—all of it.

"You still feel bad about betraying your boyfriend here?" Del asked.

"There's nothing going on, Del. I've explained that."

"He's not flirting with you these days?"

"Isn't that what the plan needs, a femme fatale?" I cocked my hips, tried to look tough. I didn't want to lie to him.

Del chewed at his bottom lip—not just thinking this time, but biting something back.

"You're not cold enough for a femme fatale," he said finally. "But something's going on, isn't there?"

"I'm not reciprocating," I said, enunciating the word.

No matter how many times we talked about it, he didn't seem convinced. The conversation never resolved, just ended.

Carl came over most nights, and he and Del made their notes and charts and diagrams and puzzled over them. Later, after Carl went home, Del and I did some more reacquainting, trying to connect, to prove something to one another, but somehow it didn't feel all that acquainted in the end. After he went to sleep, I sometimes ended up down in the business center, doing those same Google searches on whatever might be happening down in Victorville or just surfing around aimlessly.

One night the searching paid off.

"She fessed up," I told Del coming back to the room, rousing him up.

"Who?" he said, still groggy. He shielded his eyes when I turned on the lights.

"Brenda."

He sat up in bed, just wearing his boxers, leaning against the headboard.

"Where'd you hear that?"

"Online," I said. "The *Victorville Daily Press* had a big story on it. It looks like finally she just admitted to it all, best I could understand."

I handed him the article I'd printed out downstairs. It took a second for his eyes to adjust, his face all squinty—or maybe that look was just surprise playing itself out. Brenda's picture was front and center, and she looked as done-up as usual, but remorseful now instead of that plastered-on smile.

"A terrible error," the article quoted her as saying. She blamed the economy, promised she would do whatever she could to make amends. "I've had a lot of people who've reminded me the right way to do things, and I'm sorry I let them down. I wish I could say thank you."

Her lawyer said that Brenda took full responsibility, planned to throw herself on the mercy of the court, ask for community service. "Someone who has given so much for Victorville can do the same again," he said. Many of the missing items had been recovered. It sounded like a deal had already been made.

"No mention of us in there," Del said.

"Unless you're the one she's thanking. Family looking out for family. Taking responsibility. You taught her that, and it's like she's a changed woman."

"She was always like that," he said, though I'd sure never seen it, except in a lot of empty claims about how she was going to take care of things. "She just forgot it for a while."

"Does this mean we're free again?" I asked.

Del scratched his beard. "Guess we can quit being Bonnie and Clyde and go back to being us."

I touched his hand.

But which us? I thought.

Saturday loomed.

By the morning of the festival, I finally realized I was a changed woman myself—or at least a changing woman, in ways I hadn't expected and in ways I still needed to tell Del about. Trouble was, he was already gone. Carl had picked him up to go borrow a van from a friend, part of the day's big plan.

I thought about calling him on his cell, then didn't. What I needed to tell him needed to be told in person.

I got the impression that folks in Napa aren't used to really hot weather—especially in the fall. Just about anywhere we went, they talked about the shape of the valley and the climate and why it's such a perfect place—not just for wine but for everything, it seemed. The way the valley opens into the bay and the winds from the Pacific or from the river. The way that morning fog rolls in and out. How quickly the ground can cool down, how slowly it warms up. A lot of comparisons to the Mediterranean until after a while it seemed to me that some folks thought they actually were living in Italy or the South of France or wherever. Idealizing it and romanticizing it—selling it too, that's what Del reminded me.

So when the weekend of the festival turned out to be hot as blazes, with temps up in the nineties, no one was ready for it.

I'm not sure if it killed any grapes, which a lot of the vintners seemed to be talking about, but it near about killed some of the folks drinking the wine. These middle-aged fellows wandering up, sweat on their brows and their underarms sopping wet, I felt sure they were gonna keel over with a heart attack, and I just hoped it wouldn't be at my station.

The layout of the festival was pretty extensive. Food trucks, craft booths, a small concert stage with local bands scheduled to play throughout the afternoon—a real mix of stuff, light rock, country, even a little bit of hip-hop. They had a bigger concert planned for the evening, this soul singer who had her last big song back in the eighties but was still minor celebrity enough to draw a crowd.

"You kinda look like her," slurred one man, sidling up to my end of the counter and pointing at one of the posters.

Except she could be my mom, I wanted to say, but I just thanked him and handed him a copy of the page with the day's wines printed on it. The stack was already damp with humidity, and a drop of wine had stained the page I handed him. He didn't seem to notice.

I smiled, I poured, I chatted him up—him and everyone, trying to bring a dose of Southern hospitality to the whole thing. The tables at our booth were set up like an L, with four of us working at a time. Except for Trevor, all of the workers on the first shift were pretty and young, which I took as a compliment of sorts. Brittany and Heather I'd never met before, but Angelique had been working at the winery over the last week and had seemed overly interested in the attention that Trevor was giving me. I felt bad for her, wondered if she was jealous. When Trevor stuck close to me for most of the morning, telling me what a good job I was doing, "just like I knew you would," I pointed out that Angelique had really been doing most of the work. Trevor's hand brushed mine more than once as we reached for the same bottle, and when I saw that Angelique had noticed it too, I tried to watch my own movements even more carefully.

"I'm gonna take a quick break," Trevor told all of us about eleven. "Back in a half-hour."

I felt my breath catch when he told me—not because I was gonna miss him, but because he was taking that break right on schedule. I knew what was coming next—or thought I did.

Several couples showed up right after Trevor left—more of the Mercedes and Acura type we'd seen at the winery that first day, dressed to the nines. These folks didn't seem to mind the heat. Not an ounce of perspiration on them, though they made up for it in attitude. "Tastes flowery," one of the women said, squiggling up her nose about the tiniest taste of one wine.

"Honeysuckle," I said with a smile. I scanned the passing crowd for a sign of Del. He was out there. He was coming.

Just about that time, a large man stepped up to the table at Angelique's end of the L—Del's size, I saw as I glanced over, but then I saw the dark suit and his slicked-back hair and prickly face, all scratchy red around the cheeks. Like he'd cut himself about a hundred times shaving.

When I looked again, I saw that it wasn't just "like." This fellow had indeed cut himself about a hundred times shaving, and my heart went out to him for it.

Without his beard, Del was an entirely different person—but I can't say it was an improvement. Where he usually seemed rugged and confident, now he looked fleshy and vulnerable. Where other times he seemed mostly relaxed and comfortable, now he looked restless and shifty. If he was trying for authoritative, he might've chosen the wrong disguise. Over Del's shoulder, I caught sight of Carl, standing a few yards further back, stepping from one foot to the other like he had to pee.

None of this was promising.

Del didn't turn my way at all, but kept his focus on whatever he was saying to Angelique. Carl jiggled his eyebrows at me. For a second, I thought he was going to wave.

"Excuse me," I told the couples in front of me. "I need just a minute."

"But I'm ready for the next wine here," one of the men said. "The pinot noir."

I pushed the bottle toward him. "Make yourself at home." I headed to the other table.

"Yes, ma'am," Del was telling Angelique when I got there. "ATF. Alcohol, Tobacco, and Firearms." He chuckled. "Though luckily, I'm not representing the T & F part of my position today."

"Anything wrong?" I asked.

"He wants to see our license," Angelique said. She had a bob haircut and a low-cut top.

"A routine check," Del said. "Are you in charge?" The face was transformed but the eyes were the same, of course. Just the slightest glint in the green as he finally looked my way.

"Trevor's on break," said Angelique. "Do you know where the license is, Bonnie?"

I did, of course. I'd specifically found out. That was part of my role here—and it was a simple one really. No mastermind plot. No complex plan. I just needed to spill wine on it and mess it up enough that it was unreadable. Then Del would "impound" the wine while the paperwork got sorted out. He'd drive it off, supposedly to the festival headquarters, then he'd keep on driving, he and Carl would swap the cases into the van, and Carl would deliver it to his connection for relocation.

No way the plan was going to work.

"I'm sure we have it on file somewhere," I said, but I didn't move. "Like Angelique explained, our manager has stepped away. Why don't you go check out some other booths until he gets back?"

"Got a checklist." He held up a clipboard. "I need to stick to my rounds."

"How about a break yourself then? Mighty hot in the suit, aren't you, sir? Wouldn't you like a quick nip of chardonnay to help you cool off?"

"Couldn't drink on the job," Del said, getting impatient but trying not to show it. "Official business and all."

Other people had been listening. At the word *official*, two drunk guys who'd wandered up exchanged glances and headed in the other direction.

Del gave me a sterner look. "Could we expedite things here? I'm on a strict timeline."

Like I've said before, true love is two people looking the same way, and sometimes one of them has to turn their head for it to work.

I sighed. I went and got the license from one of those expanding file binders that Trevor had tucked into the back of the truck. I laid it down on the counter in front of Del, then poured a swallow of wine into a glass and dumped it right in the middle of the license.

"Bonnie!" Angelique shouted. "What did you do that for?" I think I'd splattered her.

"Accident," I said. It was about as subtle as what Del was doing, that's the way I looked at it. "There's the license, sir."

Del had turned about eighteen shades of red—embarrassment or anger, I couldn't tell which. Probably both. Those cut spots along his cheeks flared, like they might start oozing their own red.

From back there in the distance, Carl was straining to see what I'd done. He looked like he *really* needed to pee now.

Some of the wine drinkers gathered along the L were leaning in to check on what was happening. Some of the folks I'd been helping had indeed made themselves at home and poured some hefty glasses of wine, settling in like this was a show or something.

"I can't read this," Del said. "How am I supposed to know it's legitimate?"

Angelique bent down and looked at it. "Sure you can," she said. "It's just wet, but none of the words got smeared."

"The license needs to be in its original form," Del explained—

back on task and determined to stick to the plan, no matter what.

But I wasn't.

"It's not the paper, Angelique," I said. "Whether it's wet or—" I shook my head. I crumpled the wet license, dropped the wad of it on the counter, which got a gasp from Angelique. "It's the principle of the whole thing."

"The principle?" she asked, still stunned, but I ignored her. I wasn't even sure what principle I meant.

"What's your name again, sir?"

Del cleared his throat. "Clyde," he said, uncomfortably.

Angelique laughed. "How about that! Bonnie and Clyde. What are the odds?"

Del widened his eyes with an I-told-you-so look, but I ignored both of them on that.

"Well, Mr. Clyde," I said. "Did you know that this winery is really a family business? Our manager, the one who's stepped away, it's his parents who founded the place, still run it."

"I didn't know that," Del said, though again, I'd already told him. He gritted his teeth. "I've got a sister who runs her own business and—"

"I'm sure she's as sweet as you are," I said. "But we're talking about *this* business right now, and I want you to just imagine it— the folks who started this winery, bought their first batch of grapes and put them in that first tank they owned or those first barrels and then watched over that tank and those barrels until the wine inside was right ready to be drunk. Imagine how they felt putting it into a bottle and passing that bottle along to the first person who drank a glass from it and tasted that it was good."

"Sounds downright biblical," Del said. "As I said, I'm on a schedule."

Back behind Del, Carl started rubbing at his neck something fierce—or wait, not rubbing, he was pulling his finger across it, signaling somehow, though Del, facing me, couldn't see. I needed to accelerate my plans.

"Imagine they have a child," I went on, speeding up my pitch.

"Little boy maybe, playing on some barrels, running around the winery. Or maybe they were still building that winery when he was a boy—the building itself, but the business too, the future. A *fresh start* for all of them."

Del glared at me on that, not liking how I enunciated that turn of phrase. He seemed to be uncomfortable about the people pressing closer against the table, though one of them was nodding at me and my story, so I felt like I had support somewhere.

"The one evening, the boy's up on the father's lap, the two of them looking at that building going up or maybe the grapes on the vine, and the dad says something like, 'Son, one day all this will be yours.' And one day that boy might well be put in charge himself, you know?"

"Bonnie, are you talking about Trevor?" Angelique asked. "Because speak of the devil and all." She pointed behind me. Del was fuming.

Go, I mouthed at him. He shook his head, shaking me off. He may have mouthed something back at me, but I won't repeat it here.

"Is there a problem?" Trevor asked, coming up beside me.

He touched my back as he came up. Reflex? Protective? Either way, Del didn't seem to like that either.

"No problem," Del said. He held up the clipboard. "ATF. A routine check."

Trevor's forehead creased up.

"I've never heard of that kind of routine at festivals like this," he said. "Are you new? You look familiar, but..."

"No, sir," Del said. "You don't know me. New to the area, and this is a new procedure this year, but your license here simply isn't in respectable form." He nudged with his pen at the wet clump of paper in the middle of the table.

"What the—?" Trevor asked, and Angelique and I both tried to explain, though my explanation leaned more heavily on that word "accident" than Angelique's did.

"Whatever happened," Trevor said, "we can work this out pretty easily." He pulled out his phone. "Dad told me to keep the festival organizer's number on speed dial, just in case."

"No need to do that, sir," said Del.

"Don't do it," I said.

"Why not?" Trevor asked, his finger on the call button, but I hadn't been talking to him.

I'd been talking to Del, who had started to reach into the inside of his coat. Did he have his gun in there? Was he just putting his pen away? He wasn't reckless. He wasn't. No violence, he'd said. He wasn't going to shoot anyone, right?

"Because decisions have consequences," I said. "That's the story I'm trying to tell." I caught myself tearing up, despite myself. I had tucked that sock monkey in my pocket, and I reached for it now, patted it to make sure it was there. "Those vines I was talking about, the ones that dad and the son are looking at, they're the past and the future all tangled up together. My point is that the things you do today, the choices you make today, they do make a difference tomorrow. And the things you do, they touch others, all of it connected."

"Is this some kind of metaphor?" Trevor asked.

"Yeah, I'm confused myself," said Del, squinting.

He'd pulled his hand out of his coat pocket. It was empty. Some decision reached maybe, or at least hesitation.

I wiped my eyes. "What I'm talking about is a little boy—or maybe it's a girl," I said. "Either way, a child who's someday gonna want his parents to be proud of him—or her, whichever. And those parents, they're going to want their child to be proud of them, that's what it's all about, isn't it? But then what happens in the meantime?" I gestured toward Del.

"The ATF comes in and gives him a problem?" Angelique said.

"I really do think I should call someone with the festival," Trevor said. He pressed the button on his phone, putting it to his ear.

"Listen to me, Clyde," I said. "What I'm trying to say is this: A boy like that would want someone to look out for him, to want what was best for him, and he'd want someone to *be* the best for him.

Isn't that what it means to be a role model? To do what's good and right and...and...?"

Trevor had gotten someone on the phone, and I heard him asking about the ATF and license checks, then asking whoever it was to come by our booth. If Del had heard all that himself, he probably would've left then, just dodged the whole thing, but he clearly hadn't been listening. He was just looking at me, hard, puzzled.

I searched Del's face—this new face of his that I was seeing as if for the first time—searching for some hint of that anger that might have been there before or even disappointment, but I couldn't tell what was going on in there, even more than usual. I still couldn't tell for sure what was going on inside of me either—felt myself twisting back and forth about what it really meant to do the right thing: for yourself, for the one you love, for everybody.

"Don't worry, Bonnie," Trevor said, putting his hand on my shoulder. "The festival director is—"

He was probably going to say "on the way" but Del cut him off.

"I don't mean to be personal, ma'am," Del said. "But are you by any chance telling me that you're in the family way?"

I nodded. "Yes," I said. "Yes, yes, that's exactly what I'm saying."

But even after I'd said it, Del's expression stayed unclear. *Inscrutable*, that's the word he himself would've used. Then pretty quickly all too scrutable as everyone else's reactions started rolling out.

"Trevor, you're blushing," said Angelique, and I turned and saw it myself—Trevor's embarrassment and confusion, the way whatever hopes he had for me, for us, all that flirting of his, suddenly got ripped away.

Angelique saw something different, of course. She blushed herself, raised her hand to her mouth. "Oh, my God," she said. "I knew something was going on between you two, but I had no idea it had gone this far."

"Oh, Angelique," I started to say, reaching out my hand to her, but then I saw Del's own face reddening—about twenty-one shades of it, and not a one of them embarrassment. I realized too late that Trevor still had his own hand on my back, remembered too late Del's own questions about something going on between us, understood how Angelique's reaction was sparking Del's own.

Before I could stop him, Del threw his clipboard down, pulled back his fist, and slugged the side of Trevor's head.

Trevor toppled back, his arms flailing, and fell across a case of wine just behind him—then knocked over several other cases in the process.

"Del!" I shouted. "No!"

"Who's Del?" shouted Angelique.

"What the—?" Trevor shouted.

And more shouts from most of the people gathered around each side of the L.

Del himself pressed against his end of the table, pushing it back as he tried to climb across it.

"All that flirting," he said—to Trevor, to me, I wasn't sure. "Right in front of me, like I wasn't even there. And now you're *pregnant?*"

"I didn't know!" Trevor cried out—sounding nasally now. Del must have tagged his nose.

"Stop!" I said. "Del!"

"Who's DEL?" Angelique shouted again.

Del meanwhile had made it over to Trevor, who was scuttling backwards, toppling a couple more cases. Del reached forward and grabbed Trevor's shirt, pulling him up. Everyone had stepped back, giving them room—everyone but me, that is.

"Del," I said, pulling on the back of his own shirt. "The baby's not Trevor's. It's yours."

At which point the tension level dropped some—or at least Del dropped Trevor back to the ground, which was some sort of improvement.

As he turned my way, Del's expression was still struggling to figure out his emotions.

"Mine?" he said. "Us? Why didn't you tell me? I'm—"

"I didn't know," I said. "Not until this morning. I didn't know, but you were already gone, and—"

And I didn't see any more how Del's expressions were playing out, because of all the kissing and hugging and squeezing—and didn't get any more words out either, since the squeezing was pretty tight.

But I could hear Trevor's voice right behind Del, still nasally. "What the hell just happened?"

And Angelique's right behind me: "I'm not sure, but I don't think this is the first time Bonnie and the ATF man have met."

I can't say that we explained things adequately to Trevor or to that festival organizer he'd called—a middle-aged woman with dramatically oversized cat eyeglasses that she looked through even more suspiciously with each word out of our mouths.

"You're telling us this was like a flash mob?" she said. "Performance art? Publicity stunt?"

"Improv," Del said—which was true enough in one way. He was improvising even then. "I'm sorry it got out of hand."

Trevor was holding an ice pack against his cheek. "You should've warned me," he said—not the first time.

"You should've told me," said Del—also not the first time.

We were standing about ten feet behind the booth, the four of us. Angelique was stacking the wine cases back up as best she could, while Brittany and Heather struggled to handle the crowds, which had indeed grown quickly—like people slowing to look at a car crash, but in this case they could also stay and have a drink.

No matter that we hadn't really meant it as publicity. Traffic was booming. Sales too. And only a handful of bottles had broken. Good packaging.

"And you're not planning to press charges?" Cat Eye asked Trevor.

He eyed Del from behind the ice pack.

He didn't look sure about it.

"Given the happy news," he said, finally, "I guess not."

Before it was all over, Trevor offered us some confused congratulations, then gave me an awkward and disappointed hug—cut short when he seemed to catch himself that this was part of what got him punched in the first place. Maybe to cover himself on that, he tried to hand me a bottle of the top wine from the Higher Elevation tasting as a celebration present.

I thanked him, but handed it back. "No drinking for me," I said. "Not for a while." That was reason enough, but there was also the guilt that the original plan had been to take all of it from him. And the fact that Del had already stolen a bottle that first day at the winery.

Turned out we got a second bottle of it anyway. In the midst of the hubbub, Carl had ducked in and picked up a case of it on his way back to the van, and this time he got away with it. No one paid him any attention—proof right there that where you're looking is as big a part of what you *don't* see as it is about what you do.

"Guess we'll be letting this one age more," Del said, after Carl had left with the van.

"It's September now," I told him, counting on my fingers, "so at least 'til June or thereabouts."

"Worth the wait," Del said. He was still beaming, kept touching me, giddy with the news.

The two of us were back in the front seat of the Nova. We didn't go anywhere, just sat there where I'd parked, and watched the folks wandering in and out of the festival. In the distance, I could hear one of the bands starting up. Something country, something earnest it sounded like.

"Carl's connection is going to be pretty disappointed about not getting any wine," I said, hanging the sock monkey back on the rearview mirror. "Carl too. He'd expected a bigger haul than just a single case."

"He's fine," Del said. "And he still thinks a festival like this is the way to go—or else holding up a delivery somehow. Not much other choice, now that he's lost the warehouse job. He asked if I wanted to refocus these plans today down the road."

"And do you?"

Del tapped at the top of the steering wheel, gathering his thoughts. "This isn't where I see myself anymore," he said. "Where I see us. We've got bigger plans ahead, don't you think?"

With that freshly shaved face, Del struck me now like an overgrown boy instead of a big man—a younger man, slowly losing the baby fat in his cheeks, smoothing out into someone new but still himself. Everything was changing. Where we were going and what it meant.

"It's like that word *provenance*," he said, echoing my own thoughts. "You try to trace back the full history of something, everything that contributed to it, how all of it affected what came out, but that's just backward looking. It works the other way as well. Like what you were explaining about the vines back there. The choices you make, the actions you take, the accidents too—you have to recognize that each of those steps along the way, and the missteps, they impact the final complexity of it all."

I reached out, put my hand on his leg—that same gesture that seemed to have become the start of each new stage of our journey. "Can you wait nine months to find out?"

"Nine months," he repeated. He put the car into gear. Both of us were looking toward the road ahead. "Nine years. Ninety years. As long as you'll give me. Both of you. I just hope I'll be there to see it all."

THE QUEEN'S PARTY

Our visit to the Little Chapel by the Sea didn't turn out quite like
we'd expected—and not just because Las Vegas is a desert town.

"Del?" I whispered.

"Louise," he said, sort of a half-whisper with a growl on the
weez part, his voice too deep to stay soft.

"Do you love me?"

He was all pity-eyed, but he didn't reach my way. Maybe he
could see who was watching, but I couldn't, not from where I was
laying. "Are you scared, hon?" he asked.

"Itchy," I said. The carpet scraped against my cheek and, up
close and personal like this, I saw it was not just cheap but probably
in need of a good cleaning.

It seems funny now for that to be the thing I was thinking
about, given what was happening, given where it all went.

"I just kind of want to hear it," I told him.

"I do love you, and I promise, I'm gonna get us out of this."

"Will you take me to be your wife?"

"Soon as we get through this."

"I know, but I mean *right now*. Will you take me now?"

"Could you please just be quiet?" came another voice from behind Del somewhere, hissing at me. "He's going to hear."

"Shhh," I told the voice. It wasn't the minister. I didn't think so at least. The tone was off, but he might've sounded different away from the microphone.

"Del," I went on, "do you promise to have me and hold me from this day forward, for better or worse?"

"I think *right now* might be proving that very point," Del said. He wasn't entirely looking at me—glancing up over my head and doing something with his belt, unbuckling it. Trying to use it as a weapon? Or maybe just loosening it up, given the angle his stomach had tilted when he laid down on the floor? We had indeed had a big dinner.

"For richer and poorer?" I said.

"We've already proven that one, but—"

"In sickness and in health?"

"Louise, like the minister suggested there, this might not be the best time."

It was the minister, after all—which disappointed me right then. Seems like if he was really serious about the job, he might've stepped in to officiate himself at some point.

Del was scooting around, trying to pull the belt through his loops. It didn't budge.

And I wasn't going to budge. We might only have the rings for a short time, and I intended to use them while we could. Optimism in the face of adversity, that's what it was.

"As long as we both may live?" I asked, trying to wrap it up quick.

"Oh, hon, I really wish you wouldn't have said that one at this precise moment." He stared past me again, then began to redo his belt, rushing to buckle it back.

I heard the footsteps, a heavy tread coming back down the aisle. I wouldn't have called it ominous, not then.

"Lady, can you just shut up for a second?" said the man looming above us. "I'm trying to work some things out here, and my patience is running thin."

With the black ski mask covering his whole head and the gun in one hand, he reminded me of how Del had looked when he robbed the 7-Eleven that first night we met. About Del's size too. But you could tell from this guy's eyes that he was scared and desperate, and I thought not just how that was different from Del but also that it might be in our favor.

Thought wrong, of course. Scared can be stupid, and desperate can be dangerous, and all of the combination can be—

"She's just talking," Del said. "Leave her alone."

Black Mask turned to him. "Big man," he said. "Knight in shining armor gonna save her?" In addition to the gun, he had a knife in his other hand, and he held it down toward Del's face—trying to look tough same as he was trying to sound tough.

Then a phone rang out in the lobby, and another voice came booming through a loudspeaker. "Attention inside the chapel, please pick up the phone."

Clearly I wasn't the one contributing the most to the noise level—that was my immediate thought, still being the smartass, and I started to say it out loud. But Del let out a howl and jolted back. He banged his head against the pew behind him, let out another yell.

As Black Mask stood up, I saw that Del had yanked his hand up against his cheek. When he pulled it away, blood smears ran across his fingers. A piece of his cheek that had been there before wasn't there anymore.

Some of the other people in the room let out their own cries and shrieks, and Black Mask swung out his gun hand and swayed it back and forth, yelling for everyone to "stay down" and "stay quiet" and threatening "I'll do the same to you and worse." Everyone tried to obey, but somebody laying down on the other side of the chapel kept up a low whine. Black Mask's breath came in and out in deep heaves. The phone kept ringing, then stopped, then started again.

I know mood swings are pretty common for folks in my condition—bun in the oven, as Mama would say. The hormones sometimes have their own way of doing things. But what I felt then was different. A flash of anger had pulsed up inside, and just as suddenly I felt that anger run cold and hard. The confidence didn't seep out of me but just surged stronger.

I hadn't been joking about Del and me exchanging our vows there on the floor, no matter what it must have sounded like to anyone else laying beside us under the gunman's threats. I'd been serious, and in that second Black Mask cut Del, I felt more committed than ever—both to him and to the baby inside me.

I can't say that Del's proposal was the most romantic in history. "We should get married," he said the morning after he'd found out I was pregnant. "Don't you think?" He was talking between complimentary mini muffins at that extended-stay hotel back in Napa Valley. At least with his fresh shave then, no crumbs were clinging to his beard.

Just for the record, I was never one of those women who spent their free time daydreaming about her wedding or setting the bar high about some elaborate marriage proposal that no man could live up to. I've known my fair share of them, sure—picking up copies of *Brides* magazine before they even have a fiancé (some of them before they even have a boyfriend)—but that's never been me, so no disappointment from me that he didn't get down on one knee. I just told him "yes." And I didn't have any big plans myself about what kind of wedding when Del asked me what next.

"Back when we were kids, my best friend Charlene got this Dream Glow Barbie and Ken one Christmas," I told Del, "and we used to hitch them up on a pretty regular basis. We decorated her Legos with some icing from tubes in the kitchen and made a long aisle, and we'd hold Barbie and Ken under the light and shake them to get the glow to absorb quicker. When they strutted down the aisle, their outfits just sparkled."

"It'll be a real challenge to top glow-in-the-dark formal wear, hon," Del said.

"But the reception would be cheap," I said. "While they danced, Charlene and I used to lick the icing off the Legos until we were all sugared up."

"Charlene ever get married for real?" Del asked.

"Not last I heard," I said. We'd swapped some emails and I'd sent her a postcard or two when I was back in New Mexico, but the way Del and I were moving, it was easy to lose touch. "She always had her plans down pat for it. The bridesmaids' dresses would be burgundy, she told us. Not maroon, not auburn, not wine, but burgundy. And she wanted George Michael's 'Faith' as her wedding song—that churchy opening before it kicked in on something you could dance to, you know. But the one thing she didn't have was a boyfriend."

We'd had a falling out about that once, when I pointed out that very thing to her. *Insert groom here*, I'd told her, *and God help him*. She hadn't talked to me for weeks.

"It's the person, not the pomp," I told Del. "That's the way I look at it."

"Do you want to go down to the justice of the peace then?"

"Maybe something more special than *that*," I said.

I'm not *anti*-romantic, I mean.

Del thought. I thought. He had another mini muffin.

"How about Vegas?" he said. "It's quintessential."

Which I took to mean a good thing, and that's how he got my second "yes" of the day.

Vegas turned out to be everything I'd expected it to be—by which I mean both tacky and with that sense that anything could happen. So much spectacle! So much neon! So much dinging and whirring! Gladiators strutting and posing in Caesar's and the women in those white tunics ferrying drinks to people hunched over blackjack tables or the slot machines. With the restaurants and shops and all of it, that place probably stretched on bigger than my hometown back in North Carolina—both the space and the population—and with scads more money. I kept looking at the piles of chips, the jewelry some of the women were wearing, the extravagance.

And then lots of folks with no money who wanted some piece of it all—con men and grifters and pickpockets. I'd kept pointing out to Del all the women who looked like hookers. Too many people looked like their luck had played them wrong. People just jittery with worry and desperation, rushing past us to get to the tables, rushing back out when their last luck had run out for good.

"If you were gonna pull the great Vegas robbery," I said, leaning in close to Del, "do you think you'd try to work my being pregnant into the plan? Folks can treat you different when they find out you're pregnant. They get all gooey-eyed or they feel like they've got to be more careful. It could be an asset."

"It's already been done," Del reminded me. "Julia Roberts in that second *Ocean's Eleven* movie."

"I must have fallen asleep in that one," I said. "Did it work?"

"Not so much."

"Maybe we'd handle it better," I said. "Mastermind."

About that time, a woman passed by with rings on every finger—big honking jewels—and I wondered how somebody slick might ease one away. Like she didn't have enough, like she would really miss it.

We were on our way to get our own rings then—the next thing on our wedding checklist. We'd gotten into town late the night before, had gotten our marriage license first thing in the morning, and were headed to the Forum shops now, basically a shopping mall hooked onto Caesar's. Big columns and statues loomed over the passageway, and the way the lights shifted on a mural of clouds overhead, it was just like the real sky up there.

I let Del pick out the rings. Small silver bands, simple but elegant—at least that's what I told myself—and then I found a dress I loved, one this blonde woman had been looking at herself before she returned it to the rack.

It was wine-colored, not white (and not maroon, auburn or burgundy either, which had me wondering whether we should wait for family and friends), but it struck me as elegant. It had a sash just above the waist—cradling the baby, I felt like—and trying it on made me feel sexy, which I needed, what with all the nausea I'd already been feeling and the bloat.

But it was pricey, and I realized why the blonde woman had put it back.

"Splurge," Del said—not hardly like him at all.

"Aren't you lucky?" said the blonde, circling back like she'd been watching.

"Excuse me?" I asked.

"My man would kill me if I spent that much," she said, then turned and stalked off, like we'd done something wrong.

Before we headed out to the chapel, we grabbed some pizza at an Italian place right by this big statue of Neptune with his trident and some sea monsters spread out all around him. It seemed like everyone in the desert wanted a bit of water nearby.

"What was your daddy like?" I asked Del as we ate—just making conversation. I never expected his face to tighten like it did, his jaw to set.

Del and I had never talked much about the past. I knew he'd grown up in South Dakota somewhere—his "formative years," as he said, but he didn't elaborate much beyond that. Even when we were staying with his sister, I never once heard any reminiscing about their parents or when they were kids. *Estranged*, Del had said about the two of them, and the tone had told me not to ask much more.

But now that I was "with child," the future seemed to be coming at us from a lot further ahead, and the past was calling to me in a fresh way. Little Orange Seed, we'd started calling him or her, after the doctor we first visited tried to explain the baby's size, and the name had stuck. No matter how small, the baby had already become a big part of us—bigger than either of us. When you're bent over a toilet heaving up your guts or stopping to pee about twice an hour, you realize that it's not all about you anymore.

"He was a dad," Del said. "Read the paper each morning, went to his job, came home and had dinner, watched TV, didn't talk much."

"Taciturn," I said. "Like father, like son, huh?" I nudged him, meaning it friendly-like, but he bristled.

"Sometimes I see myself in him," Del said, after a long pause. "Quiet, like you said. Maybe more than that. They say you end up like your parents somehow. Genetics partly. Nurture too. Or lack of it. He likely thought he was a good dad."

Del's beard had already begun to grow back in, but having seen him without it, I still pictured that little boy look. I could see it again now, something vulnerable and faraway.

"How about your mama?"

Del took a deep breath, then another bite of pizza. He was chewing on something else in his mind while he ate. Around us people were laughing and drinking—some of them maybe too much. While we'd been talking, a man had climbed into the fountain by Neptune, and when security tried to get him out, he'd shouted that he could buy them three times over, ten times over.

"When I was a kid, I used to be afraid of the dark," Del said finally. "My mother would come into bed and lay down with me to help me get to sleep, run her fingers through my hair, talk to me."

"Sounds sweet," I said, picturing myself doing the same thing to our child someday.

"Dad didn't like it," he said. "I used to hear them arguing about it, me with the covers pulled up against my chin. My mom saying things like *rough time* and *little boy* and *lonely*. My dad saying, 'If *you* won't teach him, then *I* will.' Sometimes he'd come in and yell at me, and me crying and yelling, and my mom crying. One night my dad lifted me out of bed and held me up high in the air and shook me, shook me hard, and..."

"What happened?" I asked.

"My sister," he said. "Brenda came running in from her own bedroom, not much bigger than me, and just started hitting at our dad, pummeling him with these tiny balled-up fists."

"And that got him to stop?"

"He put me down, yeah. Then he turned toward her." He shook his head, like he was trying to shake away an image. "She was always like that, did what it took."

I thought of Brenda saying those same words—"do what it

takes"—back our first night in Victorville, thought about how where all that had taken us. I pictured her herding those porcelain animals like one might break, remembered her promises that she'd never let Del get hurt, all her talk about taking care of family—and his talk, his decisions too. Del's sadness and his anger seemed deeper to me now—what Brenda's betrayal had meant—and it made more sense his decision to sacrifice himself, how that made him and Brenda even. Taking the high road like she might've done once.

This new story put everything in Victorville in a fresh light—and just family in general. Del's and mine both. The push and pull, the risks and sacrifices, the debts and disappointments.

I thought of Mama. I felt my own belly.

Del wanted to play blackjack after that—a change-the-subject kind of suggestion. He made a joke about a windfall for the baby, but hand after hand, he kept getting dealt fifteens and sixteens, tough cards to play, and the chips kept heading in the other direction.

Same thing everywhere around us. A row of old folks playing their luck against the slots. A couple hunched over a craps table, looking an awful lot like us, with the woman perched just behind him, both sets of fingers crossed. Some people seemed to be having fun—free drinks—but others still struck me as hungry and hopeless, the economy like it was, people praying for a win or a way out. Across the way, two men in suits muscled through the crowd, a thin man held up between them, his feet barely grazing along the floor.

I thought of Del as a boy, held high in the air, his legs jangling.

I was about to nudge Del that we should move on, but he beat me to it.

"It's a losing game, Louise," he said. "No use just throwing good money after bad. Are you ready for some matrimonial bliss?"

As I said, the Little Chapel by the Sea wasn't quite as advertised. No sea in Vegas, I knew that already, but the neighborhood didn't even look remotely resort-like. A bunch of office buildings squatted along the street, and just a few blocks away we'd passed pawnshops, a bail bondsman, and a cement block building advertising peepshows and private DVD booths. Several houses stood on the block where the chapel was, but one of those had a sign out front for psychic readings. The chapel itself was a sandstone bungalow, and on the way to the door, I caught our one solitary glimpse of real water: a small pond out front with a broken fountain in the middle of it. It gave off a dank, swampy smell—the algae, I thought, until I saw the orange fish floating on its side.

"Sure you don't want to get married in the car?" Del nudged my elbow and pointed to the side of the building. A drive-thru window jutted out over a covered carport. Beside it, a big white sign was headed "Matrimonial Menu," with "Happy Meal for Two" as one of the services listed beneath. There was no wait.

"If we had a convertible, maybe," I said.

"You're hard on my Nova, Louise. It's a valuable piece of machinery."

"I'm not saying my vows with a cushion spring pinching my butt."

The big front doors had stained glass windows, but instead of Jesus and the apostles and the good book or whatever, one of them had a bride and groom flanked by palm trees. In the other, the couple stood in front of beach chairs, with Elvis performing the ceremony. Mandatory for Vegas, maybe, but this was the older Elvis and he wore a speedo. It wasn't a good look.

More coastal stuff inside: his and hers Hawaiian shirts tacked up on the walls, a pair of fish sculptures in neon colors—one in a top hat, the other a veil. Beach chairs lined the waiting area, but only two other people sat waiting there—dressed all in black, spiky hair each of them. At the far end of the room, a set of doors stood slightly open, a ceremony already underway inside.

"Welcome," said a woman behind another window, not much different from the drive-thru outside but facing into the entryway. "Happy couple or wedding guests?"

Her voice was thick and raspy, and she held an electronic cigarette. Streaks of purple ran through her beehive hairdo, and a powdery sweet smell drifted through the window. Shalimar, I thought, though my nose had been overactive and unreliable lately—compliments of the little one, I'd learned.

"Happy couple," I said.

Del stepped up behind me and put his hand on the small of my back. "We're ready to be wed."

"Some folks aren't so sure," Beehive said. She pulled out a legal-sized form. Her pen matched the color of those streaks in her hair. "You have your application?"

"We picked it up this morning," Del said, handing it across.

"Will you be needing a wedding dress or tuxedo rental?"

"I think we're looking pretty sharp as we are." Del chuckled. That same blue blazer with the elbows wearing thin, but I hadn't pointed it out.

When Beehive cocked her head my way, her hair swooped out at a precarious angle. "You're okay?" Looking at the dress.

"I got it just for the occasion," I said.

Beehive settled back in her seat.

"Ring purchase or rental?"

Rental? I thought.

"Handled," Del said. As he patted his chest pocket, he craned his neck to see how long the checklist might be.

"Bouquets for you or your bridesmaids?"

"I'm good," I said. "And no bridesmaids."

"Ma'am," Del said. "I thought we'd just be coming in and getting in line to say our vows. I don't think all these accouterments..." He shook his head. "It's about the people, not the pomp."

Beehive leveled her eyes at him, then at me, giving me this look like *grooms*. "This is the most special day of your life. You want to do it right," she told Del. "Plus, I need to figure out how long we'll need to pull your package together, so I can schedule your ceremony."

We let her carry on with the checklist, mostly just saying no and no and no to each thing—no reception time, no limo, no heli-copter, no hotel reservations—except that we did take her up on the discount for paying with cash instead of credit. "Substantial savings for you," she said. "Popular with the high rollers in particular."

We also opted for the standard photo package, but no, not the videography. "The package would save you," Beehive stressed. "If you get video, you also get a simulcast on the web, letting your rela-tives afar view the ceremony as it unfolds, *plus* a private YouTube clip. You or your loved ones can enjoy repeated viewings."

All of it seemed like she was just reading from a pamphlet, but I'll admit, it did give me pause—thinking of Mama again. We hadn't told her anything yet about the wedding or the baby. Her fault, easy enough to claim—avoiding whatever she might say. Or was it our unfairness?

About that time, one of the wedding parties ahead of us came out of the chapel into the hallway, raucous and rowdy and clearly enjoying themselves. The couple was older, the groom rail thin while the bride overflowed her dress in about four different direc-tions. *Jack Sprat*, I thought.

"Come back soon," Beehive called out, which seemed odd. Did they get much return business? Then I remembered what the clerk at the marriage bureau had told us: More than 120,000 applica-tions for marriage licenses each year—and the ones to get a divorce weren't far behind. *The economy these days*, she'd said, and when she'd told us *good luck*, her tone said we sure might need it.

The couple in black stepped inside next. As the bride stepped up, I thought I saw a dog collar around her neck.

"For survey purposes, what attracted you to our establish-ment?"

"The sea," I said.

"Speaking of," said Del, "looks like the sea out front might need some attention."

"Sea's not out there, it's in there," Beehive said, waving her hand more broadly. "Sea of humanity." She took a puff of her elec-tronic cigarette. The tip glowed.

"Let's do get the video," I said to Del. "Simulcast won't be necessary, but..."

"For posterity," Beehive said.

"For Mama," I told Del. "And for..." I touched my belly. No name for him yet—or her, as the case might be.

Beehive leaned out through the window and smiled.

"You're preggers?" she said. She checked something off on her clipboard, then reached behind herself and handed a small package through the window. "You get a special gift for that, compliments of the establishment."

The pocket-sized notebook had "And Baby Makes Three" emblazoned on the cover and a ballpoint pen hooked through the coil.

Del and I settled into those beach chairs to wait for our slot on the schedule. At least it gave us a front row seat to that sea of humanity Beehive had been talking about, which seemed pretty choppy as those wedding parties rolled and tumbled down the hall into the inner chapel for their ceremonies and back again.

One group came through in full formal wear (whether rented from Beehive or not, I wasn't sure), another couple looked like they'd just come from the casino—the woman dressed in this slinky sequined number. I kept picking out other women that looked like hookers, which might explain the ring rental policy.

"Did you see the jewelry on that one?" I whispered to Del.

"How could I miss them?" he said. "Rings on every finger, it seemed like."

"Slip one off, and she'd hardly even notice," I told him, thinking about the woman back at the casino again.

"You shopping for a different ring?"

Even though some of them had indeed looked good, I shook my head. "Just thinking again about how much a big Vegas haul would net. The whole place is thick with riches."

Next up was this big group that had clearly just come from a bar, or a whole bar crawl—groomsmen and bridesmaids and about four layers of family. "Bobby puked," one of the groomsman said, trying to whisper but not, and then Bobby, the groom it seemed like, pulled a flask from his tuxedo jacket and said, "Round Two!" The alcohol smelled particularly strong, which made *me* feel like puking, but I tried to hold it in. The bride was stumbling, and when one woman tried to help steady her, she yanked her arm away: "Mother! Stop fussing and nagging. It's MY party!"

Which also made me think of Mama, this time without the guilt, and about all those wedding plans of Charlene's, how quickly it could all turn sour.

I timed the ceremonies, about twenty minutes a pop. I'd tucked a book of baby names in my bag, and while we waited, Del and I passed it back and forth, then added the names we liked on the front page of that new "Baby Makes Three" notebook. On the girl's side, Del came up with some good ones: Lucinda and Harper, and he circled Harper twice. "We could call her Poppy," he said, which seemed sweet. But when it came to boys, bless his heart, Del kept going after these elaborate names. With a name like Delwood himself, maybe he was thinking of tradition somehow.

Here's the list I was coming up with, if it was a boy:

Jack
Ray

Here was Del's list:

Augustus
Dashiell
Thelonious
Wilberforce

Wilberforce? I wrote in the next note I passed his way.

It means "ditch," he wrote back, as if that explained anything.

Clearly there would be discussions ahead.

Like usual, my mind was already racing even further into the future anyway, testing out each of those names in little scenes. I pictured Lucinda—Cindy maybe—falling asleep on Del's big shoulder. We taught Augustus his ABCs. Poppy became a Brownie, which my own mother would never let me do. Dashiell got his first haircut, rode his first bike, put his first tooth under a pillow. I baked up a big tin of cinnamon buns for Thelonious (just Theo, please!), and when he and Del and I got all sticky-lipped, we just laughed and laughed.

"What was your own dad like?" Del said. "Really, I mean."

"Not the sock monkey version?" I asked. I shook my head. "Even if that story wasn't true, he did leave Mama and me, and she never got over it. I was too young for it to make as much impact."

"What do you remember before that?"

"Magic tricks," I said. "Daddy was a magician."

"Really?" Del said. "Top hat and rabbit and everything?"

"Not professionally, that's not what I mean. He just liked to do party tricks and stuff for fun. Detachable thumb and got your nose. Coin behind the ear. Typical dad stuff."

"Seems like I'm gonna need to learn some of those," he said. "For Wilberforce."

I let that slide.

"Daddy liked card tricks best," I said. "You know, pick a card, and he could tell you what it was or just pluck it out of the deck. Sometimes, he'd even make it rise out of the deck like it was on an invisible string, and I'd squeal like the whole world was magic."

Even as I remembered it, I pictured Mama glancing over at us from the stove or her armchair, tight-lipped already. "A miracle," she'd say, and I could hear the sarcasm in her voice, even if I didn't know that was the word for it.

Thinking of that tone and that look reminded me of another trick he did called Gin and Tonic, with a dime and a penny where the dime just disappeared—and a comment from Mama about him not being able to hang on to his money. "You know what would be a good trick?" she said—more than once. "Getting a paycheck to appear instead of a pink slip."

"Want me to show you my favorite trick?" I asked Del.

"Seems like we've got time," he said.

I stepped up to ask Beehive if she had a deck of cards.

"It's Vegas," she said, and handed one through the window.

"This one's called the Queen's Party," I told him, as I separated all the face cards and the aces out from the rest of the deck, thinking of how Daddy used to correct himself and tell me *Your party* and ask which of the queens I wanted to be that time. Hearts, I always chose, and he'd say *Of course* and *Queen of my own heart*, and Mama would call him a charmer—never a compliment.

Once I had the face cards gathered, I laid out each of the queens one by one on the arm of Del's beach chair. They just barely fit.

"The queens had a party," I said, "and each of them invited a king to join her."

Then I laid out each of the kings on top of the queens.

"Then each of the kings brought a friend," I said. "The troublemakers"—same as my Daddy had said each time all those years ago.

"Does it matter if the suits match or not?" asked Del.

"You're missing the point," I said.

Even Beehive was watching now, peering at us through the window. Another wedding party popped past, a small one. The groom looked nervous.

"Anyway," I said, "now there are three of them at the party, and turns out they got into a little hanky panky"—again, same as Daddy always said.

Hanky panky? I'd asked him one time.

Shenanigans, he'd said.

She's five, Mama had said.

"When the party got out of hand," I went on, "the authorities had to step in."

The cops were the aces, of course—and as I plopped them down, I tapped each of them with my knuckle, which had always been part of the trick. "Tamping down the rowdiness."

After that, I stacked each pile of cards one on top of the other.

"Heading to the hoosegow," I said. "It means *jail*."

"From the Spanish, right?" Del said, perking up at any new bit of vocabulary.

"Loosely," I said. I never knew where Daddy got the word. "But wait up! Along the way, there's a car crash and everybody gets all tousled together."

I held the stack toward Del.

"What am I supposed to do?" he asked.

"Cut them," I said.

Del made a simple cut—an inattentive cut, I could've said. Way back when, I'd always tried to think carefully about it—trying to get dead-even sometimes, or other times just taking the top card or else just the bottom card to try to mess up Daddy's plans.

Cut 'em again, if you want to, honey, he'd tell me. *It was a big ol' crash.*

What was the secret? Was it in the extra cuts? Or was he tricking me there too? I'd second-guess myself, sometimes trying one way, sometimes another. It never seemed to matter.

"Bad as that crash was, you remember that Louise can always set things right," I told Del, substituting my own name for what Daddy used to say. Then I dealt the cards into four piles, the aces all together now, and the jacks, kings, and queens too.

"Sure," said Del. "Because the order hasn't changed."

Beehive didn't seem impressed either. Another couple stepped up to the window—taking her attention completely.

"At the time, it was pretty impressive," I said, folding all the cards together. "I was in awe."

"It was good," Del said, then he went back to the baby name book.

I tried not to be disappointed, tried to keep things in perspective.

What people see, Daddy had said at the time, when I asked how it was done, *that's not the real thing, but it takes on a realness. Do you understand, sugar?*

I didn't then. Maybe I did now.

* * *

Just after an older couple and four or five of their guests stepped in for their ceremony, Beehive called through the window that we were next.

"Want to duck inside for a sneak peek?" I asked.

"I don't think they'd mind," Del said, and we slipped through the door and into the back pew.

The stained glass windows continued in here—one wall of them obviously lit up artificially from the back, and the other facing outdoors. The sun had gone down now and left them lit only by the streetlights, muted and shadowy. The minister was dressed pretty conservatively—no Hawaiian shirt or anything, like I'd wondered briefly about—but tropical flowers surrounded him up there. Birds of Paradise, we'd learn later, the arrangements sitting on top of white columns, all of it bright and colorful.

A photographer moved around the ceremony, taking shots from each side and up the aisle. The videographer perched in one corner, fiddling with her camera. Someone had splurged for the upgrade.

The final couple ahead of us stepped to the altar, the man tall and so ramrod straight that it crossed my mind he looked more like a butler than a groom. When his bride reached to take his hand, her own glinted blue in the light—a big old rock on her finger, and I thought again of heists and hauls, just letting my mind play out. Their friends took their seats, front row, not noticing us. The minister greeted everyone and started talking about how nice it was to preside over a renewal of vows—"a quarter century of married life already," he said, "and a commitment to many more ahead." That got my imagination going in an different direction—thinking that Del and me might someday come back here just like that, with Poppy or Dashiell or—

Someone shouted out in the lobby. Then another shout and sounds of a scuffle. Everyone up front turned to look back—look back at us, caught there in the back row. Then the doors right beside us burst open and Beehive rushed in, followed closely by the man in the mask.

"On the floor," he said, waving a gun. "Everybody, now. And turn those cameras off or I'll shoot them out."

Up on the altar, the tall man pointed a finger at the gunman. "Now see here," he said in a vaguely British accent, which only increased that butler feeling I had. He started to step forward, but Black Mask swung his arm wide. The gun went off, and the bullet shattered one of those vases just next to his wife. The water sprayed all over her, birds of paradise flying high, and her shriek hit such a shrill pitch I half-expected the other vase to burst.

"Back it up, Jeeves," Black Mask said—a deep voice, similar to Del's. Clearly it wasn't just me who saw the whole butler thing going on.

Del's hand squeezed mine, and I'm not sure what else he might've done, but whatever it was the man with the gun caught it.

"You too, big guy," he said. I saw the knife in his other hand then. "Don't want to make her a widow before she's a bride, do you?"

Clearly that's not possible. There's an order to these things. But we got his point. Everyone did.

You might wonder if I was afraid for the baby. Man with a gun bursts into the room—man with a gun *and* a knife—and shouldn't a mom's, even a mom-to-be's, first instinct be to protect the baby first? Find shelter, find safety, roar up with some superhuman strength, something like that?

I'm not sure how to explain this, but I wasn't scared, not at first. Startled, but not scared—and it wasn't just because Little Orange Seed was, well, only the size of an orange seed at that point.

It was because of the story I'd been telling Del, what Daddy had said about what people see not always being the reality of a thing. None of what was happening seemed real to me, at least up until the point that Del got sliced.

Sure, Black Mask seemed forceful and demanding, the way he swung that gun and knife around, the way he shouted at everyone, telling them to get down on the ground, telling them he was going to be taking their money and their jewels, warning them that he wouldn't hesitate to shoot. But I'd seen his eyes, and I thought he'd stunned himself as much as everyone else when he shot that flower vase. And his whole conversation with Beehive seemed like a comedy routine.

"You've already taken all the money we have," Beehive said. "Can't you just leave?"

"Not enough," said the bandit. "And nobody to blame but yourself."

"I already told you—"

"And I already told *you* what I read on the website. Cash only, it said."

"Cash *discount*," Beehive said.

"If you say that again." Black Mask waved the gun again, trying to be forceful, but mostly sounding frustrated. "Either way, I'm not leaving here empty-handed."

As he hopscotched through all of us on the floor, I saw that he wore white boots. Really swanky-looking things, smooth and polished, which added another level of unreality to everything.

And unreal too the way some of these people grumbled about giving up their stuff—like Jeeves saying "See here" again, and his wife crying about "Not my sapphire, it's an heirloom, please" and Black Mask going even more tough guy, "Hand it over"—all of it like something out of a script, when you knew they probably had insurance on it.

I did feel bad when he took the photographer's camera. "I need it for work," the photographer said, but Black Mask didn't care, and I figured those pawn shops right down the street would take it in a heartbeat. The videographer's camera was too big to carry, but I heard her asking Black Mask for some baby pictures from her wallet before he took her purse. Seemed like he gave those to her.

"Who's got the goods here?" he said, when he came to us. "You got the rings, big guy?"

Del reluctantly pulled our new wedding bands out of his pocket, but before he could hand them over, a light suddenly strobed and circled through the room, pulsing through those stained glass windows. A moment later, we all heard a knock at the front door. "Police," said a voice. "Is everything okay?"

Black Mask let out about a half-dozen curses and called Beehive some unsavory names, but he shouldn't have blamed her. More likely it was because some neighbor heard the shot that hit the flowers. As he rushed back down the aisle, he almost stepped on me.

"We're closed," he called through the door. "Everything's okay."

"Could you unlock the door, sir? We received an alert and need to check the premises."

"I don't have the key."

"You don't have the what? Who is this, sir?"

"I'm—Oh, whatever. Back away from the door or I'm gonna start shooting folks here one by one."

"Del?" I whispered then. "Do you love me?" and that's when I began to go through our vows myself. Meanwhile, as I said, Del was taking the opportunity to figure out a way to fight back, but Black Mask came back down the aisle and told us to cut it out and then cut Del himself.

Blood makes everything real.

Cordless phone in hand, Black Mask paced back and forth in the entryway, coming into the chapel to watch us, then stepping away briefly, then back again—nervous, it seemed like. Even though we could hear only his half of his phone conversation, hostage negotiations were clearly already shaping up.

"No, I don't think I want to tell you my name," Black Mask said.

A long pause. Someone on the other end speaking to him, and then his reply: "I hope everybody comes out of this without getting hurt, and me included."

One of the guests from the other party gave out a low whimper. I watched Del. That line had already been crossed. Without anybody getting hurt *worse*, that was the goal now.

"Eight or nine, not counting me," Black Mask went on. "I'd have to count to get it *exact*." Another long pause. "What happened? What happened was I can't feed my family these days. All this money in this town and not a bit of it for me and my wife and my..."

Black Mask's voice kept getting louder as he stepped into the chapel, then softer as he stepped into the entryway. At one point, he came closer to us and tossed a paper towel down between us, some way for Del to staunch the bleeding.

"Are you okay?" I asked Del as Black Mask turned away.

"No time to worry about that," he said, dabbing at his cheek. His eyes watched the doorway. "Primary agenda is getting us out of here. I just wish I'd brought my gun."

"Del," I hissed. "You don't bring a gun to a wedding."

"Either way," he cut me off, hissing louder, "next time he comes in and goes out, next time his back is turned, I'll—"

"Don't you do something else stupid," said another voice not far from us. Hard not to eavesdrop.

Black Mask came in again, quicker than expected. "Seems like I should be the one making the rules here." Then out again.

"You can't try to jump him," I whispered to Del. "It'll just startle him. He'll do something stupid."

Del wasn't listening. He was reaching toward the "Baby Makes Three" notebook that had dropped on the ground near me.

"Give me the pen," he whispered.

"The pen?" I asked.

"Shiv," he said, and when I grabbed it myself and slid it into the sash on my dress, he seemed surprised—which only made sense later when I found out what *shiv* meant. Despite what he thought, I wasn't intending to stab Black Mask myself—much as I wanted to after how he'd cut Del.

"I think we're done talking now," said Black Mask, coming back into the room. The phone clattered across the floor as he tossed it down. Those boots marched back our way. Black Mask loomed over me again. "All right, what else you got?"

It'll probably seem like I wasn't thinking about my baby right then, wasn't thinking straight, but I told myself I was—on both counts. In that moment, I was fast-forwarding again toward the future like I'd been doing earlier. Years later, maybe Del would tell Wilber or Harper the story of how smart I'd been and how brave, and I'd say that I wasn't feeling brave, just looking it, but I wouldn't dispute the smart part, not if everything turned out okay.

I took a deep breath.

"I'm pregnant," I told Black Mask.

"So?" he said.

"So I've got to go to the bathroom. Can you help me up?" Before he could respond, I started to stand up. Not like he could've helped me anyway, his hands full with a gun and a knife and all.

"What?" he sputtered, raising that gun again, and I willed myself not to look at it. I could hear others in the room sort of shuffling and cowering. Del himself started to jump up, but Black Mask screamed, "Stay down! Now!" and swung the knife in his direction. Then back to me: "What are you doing, lady? You can't just—"

I stood up straight—as ramrod straight as Jeeves had before. I looked right in Black Mask's eyes, trying to focus past gun and knife both now, trying to push down the anger I felt at him.

"Morning sickness isn't just in the mornings," I told him. "It would really, really be better for everybody here, including you and those boots of yours, if you let me go to the bathroom."

Every bit of my insides were shaking by that point, but I concentrated all my energy on making my confidence look real.

The hand with the knife twitched and twitched. The gun held steady on Del. I held my own breath, not steady myself, not at all.

* * *

Family, Black Mask had told the police on the phone. He had a family. Wouldn't that count for something?

Dangerous is just desperate, I told myself. *Stupid is just scared.*

I thought about the man that security had dragged through the casino, his feet scuttling against the floor—about those faces hunched over the blackjack tables and the slot machines.

I thought about Del, holding up convenience stores for tuition money—about Brenda and everything she was afraid of losing.

I thought of my own parents arguing about bills and laziness and magic tricks—and the night he came into my room and told me "Daddy's going away for a while" while Mama stood in the doorway with her arms crossed and anger just steaming off of her.

There hadn't been a sock monkey that night, no, but when he brushed my hair back behind my ear, I did expect something—a dime maybe or even a quarter or one of those rubber balls from his magic tricks. But he just pulled his hand away empty.

The only magic there, Daddy's final trick, was to make himself disappear.

Everyone breathed easier when Black Mask gestured for me to go, a tight jerk of the knife toward the lobby and the bathrooms there. He stayed close to me, warned me not to try anything dumb, took his post at the chapel door to keep an eye on everything.

It had indeed crossed my mind to cut and run. Black Mask might turn his back to watch the others. I could slip away. And maybe no one would've blamed me, being pregnant and all, putting the baby first.

But my plan was to get Del out too, all of us—even that minister who shushed me, even Jeeves and his wife with the fancy rings.

From the bathroom, I could hear that things were escalating, both outside the building and in. The phone rang again and that voice on the bullhorn called out about reestablishing contact, veri-fying that everyone was safe, talking things out. A helicopter passed overhead. Through the door, I heard those boots pacing. Black Mask finally banged on the door once. "You done yet?" Antsy, clear-ly. Not without good reasons.

"Almost," I called back.

The note I was writing took longer than I'd expected. By the time I'd finished, that ballpoint was running low on ink and I'd used up four pages of that pocket-sized "Baby Makes Three" note-book.

When I finally stepped out, Black Mask was—to use one of Del's words—apoplectic.

"Despite myself," I whispered, "I'm going to help get you out of here." I passed him what I'd written, the pages torn out of the note-book and folded twice, then handed him my earrings and watch. He put the knife in his pocket to take them. "I'll expect those back later. And let me tell you"—leaning in—"you be careful with that knife and that gun, or *you're* the one who won't be getting out of here alive, do you understand me?"

He jerked his head back—startled, surprised, but anger ready to flare again. "Lady, I..."

I turned back toward the chapel, left him to read what I'd writ-ten while I laid down where I'd been before. Several of the people on the floor looked my way. The minister glared with irritation. The bride who'd lost her sapphire seemed shocked and more than a lit-tle uncomfortable. Maybe she needed to pee herself, but didn't feel as daring.

"You okay?" Del asked.

"Much relieved, trust me," I said. "And we'll get you taken care of soon, I promise."

The puzzled expression must have hurt Del's face, because he winced immediately. That wincing must have hurt too, but before it could go much further, Black Mask came back.

"You there," he said. "Pregnant lady. I'm gonna need some help from you. And you, big man, I'll get to you in a minute." Then he stepped over to Beehive. "Lady, you want to get up? I need a tuxedo, size forty-six long, and you better hope you have it."

Gun in one hand, knife in the other, and that ski mask adding friction, Black Mask struggled to shimmy out of his clothes and put on his tuxedo. Even under the best of circumstances, formal wear can be tough to manage, and it would've been impossible for him to fasten his cufflinks and line up the studs properly and get those collar stays in place without letting go of the grip. He stood in the entranceway of the inside chapel, bending, bobbing, trying to keep an eye on the door, an eye on us, everything covered. He'd piled his loot beside him.

"Help me fold these sleeves up," he said, jerking his hand at me, the fabric flapping. The tip of the knife touched my forearm as I fastened the cuffs. I don't think he did it on purpose.

"Please be careful," I told him.

I had to ease the jacket on slowly, one arm at a time, while he moved the gun from one hand to the other. He put the knife on the floor for that part of it, then picked it up quickly as soon as it was done. I wondered if Del had been watching, if he'd thought about trying anything.

I could've pushed him over at some point. Maybe I should've, but I didn't want to risk him slipping the wrong way, the gun going off, or maybe panicking, reacting. Too much potential for bullets flying.

As I put on the cummerbund, I broke the news to Black Mask. "You're not going to be able to take everything with you." I pointed to the pile of wallets and jewelry, the camera. "They'll be watching."

"Just my luck," he said. "All this, and coming home with next to nothing to show for it. Again."

"Not your first time robbing a chapel?"

"No," he said. "It is. My first. Maybe my last. Bills, bill collectors. Just needed something to make ends meet."

"Desperate times," I said. I thought of Del again, of all of it.

But Del had never hurt anyone. He'd been careful.

As I tied Black Mask's bowtie, I thought about yanking it tight, wanted to, but then wondered what reflex would do. Him jerking his hand up maybe, the one with the knife.

"My wife's pregnant too," he said. "And we've got a three-year-old."

I snorted. "Setting a good example, aren't you?"

He stiffened. I felt his muscles tighten, felt the blade against my side—no accident this time. "Don't judge, lady," he said, quick and gruff. "And don't think you're out of the woods yourself, not yet." Out of the corner of my eye, I saw Del shift on the floor, readying himself in case anything happened. He had indeed been watching.

"You didn't need to cut him," I whispered. "Why did you do that?"

Black Mask breathed heavy through the wool. He smelled like garlic up close like that.

"Forget that," Black Mask said. "Just get me fixed right."

He would've looked sharp when it was done—except for the ski mask, of course, which kind of spoiled the look. He kept his gun on me as he had me empty the money from all the wallets and stack it for him. He left the wallets themselves in a pile along with the photographer's camera—all too bulky to hide in the tuxedo.

He kept the other jewelry, though, stuffing the rings in his pocket. When he came to mine and Del's, I started to ask for them back. But I couldn't yet. It couldn't look like we were in cahoots.

"I've got a phone call to make," Black Mask said when he was done. He swung the knife in Beehive's direction—just pointing, reckless. "You, step up and get that videographer of yours ready. I need you to explain to the police how your webcast works, and hey, big guy"—gesturing toward Del—"you want your fiancée here to be okay, here's what you're going to do..."

*   *   *

It's not the cards you're dealt. It's not how you arrange them or how you cut them. Sometimes they're stacked against you, and that's one thing I learned from Daddy: Those times, maybe it makes no difference how you play them.

But maybe other times it does.

Because that's something else I learned from Daddy: the difference between reality and realness. You can try to fix that last one most anyway you want.

The videographer stood back at her post, panning the camera across the chapel—the pedestal with the flower arrangement still standing on it and the one without, the stained glass windows, and finally the hostages, all of them on the ground but sitting up now, since, as I'd written in my note to Black Mask, they might look dead otherwise.

"Everyone is okay for now," said the man with the gun as the videographer reached him and focused her camera on his face. Except it wasn't Black Mask holding the gun now, but Del. "Nearly okay," he said. "And I aim to keep it that way."

The gash on his face probably added a good touch, much as I hated to think that. It made him look tougher and meaner, suggested things hadn't been going smoothly. Everyone watching would wonder what had happened, what might happen next. If the gunman had been cut like that, what had happened to everyone else?

"We're going to work through this, all of us," he went on. "In a show of good faith, I'm going to let two of the hostages go. The woman is pregnant, and she's pretty shaken up, and I don't want that kind of responsibility on me. Her husband will accompany her out."

It would've been a good touch to have the camera swerve out to show Black Mask and me, but that wouldn't have worked. He had a knife jabbed against my side. One false move from Del, he'd said, and he'd kill me. One false move from anyone. Whether any-one on the other end of the webcast could've seen the knife or not, I don't know, given the angle and all, but Black Mask still had his mask on—not wanting anyone in the room to see his face—and that wouldn't have looked right for a hostage, of course.

I had to keep telling myself that Black Mask wanted to get out of there as much as anyone, because right then, that knife was pressed close enough that any slip, any panic, could be really dan-gerous.

"For your information," Black Mask whispered to me, "I can't worry about being a role model." There was anger beneath his words, spit to his tone, maybe something else. "With my wife and my son and that baby on the way, I need to get the bills paid and food on the table."

"I'm not arguing," I whispered back. "Let's just get this done, and you can get back to them."

"Like she even wants me back," he mumbled. "You know what it's like coming home every day feeling like a failure? Being told you're a failure?" I felt the knife point press gently against my back, not purposeful maybe, but it was there, all the anger, all the frustra-tion. "Not just get a job, but get *another* job. What have you done for me lately, right? And what *am* I supposed to do, huh? Can you imagine how that feels?

I could. I'd lived it, of course—but I'd just been six at the time.

"Maybe your wife doesn't know what to do herself," I said.

He didn't answer—just let out a sigh like the weight of the world had pressed it out of him.

"I'm sorry I cut your husband," he whispered. "It was an acci-dent."

"He's not my husband," I said. "Not yet. But thanks for the apology."

Del was still talking into the camera. "As soon as the two of them are safe, then I want the police to make a show of good faith in return, or the next person coming out won't be walking on their own two feet. I want..."

After that it was pretty much boilerplate. He wanted some cash and a car and a helicopter. "Safe passage," Del said, "and immunity"—ad-libbing that part himself, but it sounded convincing, and his expression had a degree of menace. The cut, and that beard still coming in, maybe even more menacing than if it had been full—rough and dangerous instead of just teddy-bearish. He held up the gun a couple of times. The police had to see it, had to see it in Del's hands, that was key, and it still had five bullets in it. None of it would've worked otherwise.

The bride with the sapphire started whimpering again. "My ring," she said. "Don't let him get away with my ring."

A dumb move. She was going to give it all away.

"Go," Del said, shouting over her. "Go now."

Black Mask tightened his grip on my arm and yanked me around—frightened himself maybe by the suddenness of Del's shouting or worried that the other bride was going to let the truth out.

Nothing stupid, I thought. *Please, nobody do anything* else *stupid.*

Outside, the light hit us first. Two police cars had barricaded the driveway, and their headlamps shined toward the door. A news truck was parked to the side, its own heavy-duty spots lighting up the scene like daytime. The silhouette of a woman stood near the truck, her back to us, and I realized there was probably a cameraman behind her, recording our every step same as that videographer inside had her own camera trained on Del.

Black Mask was no longer masked now, of course, having pulled it off just before we opened the door, but at that distance, they probably couldn't see him clearly.

"Tuck your head down," I told him. "Pretend you're comforting me." He pulled me tighter as we passed the fountain. The scales on that orange fish floating there looked electric in all the light. I finally caught a glimpse of Black Mask unmasked: the swooping sideburns, what was left of a pompadour after the ski mask had done its work.

Those white boots suddenly made more sense. Elvis was indeed mandatory. And with as many Elvises as there were in Vegas, probably not great job security or benefits after all.

Don't forget what he did to Del, a voice told me. I thought of my parents again, of Black Mask and his wife, his own kids. I thought of the baby I was carrying myself.

"Step forward," said a voice from a bullhorn. "You'll be safe now."

"Remember your biggest concern is me," I whispered to him. "Me and the baby. That's what husbands do."

"Lady," Black Mask muttered, "my biggest concern is my real family. That's what got me into this."

"I hope you work that out," I said, and I did. "But in the meantime, you get through this by taking care of me, remember that."

"She's pregnant," he shouted—not to me now but to the policeman stepping toward us. "She might be in shock. I need someone to look at her and check on the baby. I just want you to get that madman in there who did this to us." That crack in his voice wasn't pretend, I knew, but it would've been hard for anyone to know the fear and nervousness that were really behind it.

"Calm down, sir," said the officer, taking my arm. "You may be in shock yourself."

"Don't worry about me, officer," he said. "It's my wife, my wife—she's the one I'm worried about."

My wife, he said, *my wife*. It was the first time anybody had ever called me that. The truth is, things don't always work out like you expect.

Black Mask kept his grip on me as the policeman hustled us toward an ambulance across the street, paramedics waiting at the ready. Several other officers stood behind the police cars we passed, doors open. They had guns at the ready or even aimed at the front door, all of them focused in that direction. I saw a laptop with Del's face on it, the scar gleaming, and I heard him shouting,

"The time is ticking away here. I don't know how much longer this can go on."

Black Mask and I walked right past. Everything was dim and shadowed behind the glare of those headlamps and the TV crew's lights. Even I could barely see his face, except to make out those sideburns.

"We need to talk to you about how things are unfolding in there," said the policeman. "An insider's look." We'd just reached the paramedics then, a man and a woman, and one of them hustled me toward the back of the ambulance. Black Mask held back, away from the light inside the ambulance.

"Just give me a minute to make sure she's okay. That's all I'm asking."

"I understand, sir," the policeman said. "Priorities. But just a minute. We've got a situation on our hands."

One of the paramedics had strapped a blood pressure cuff on my arm. The other pointed a light into my eyes. Black Mask became even more of a blur in the shadows.

"No dilation," said the paramedic. "Breathing seems normal."

"Blood pressure elevated, but only moderately," said his partner. "How far along are you?"

"About eight weeks."

"Should be fine, but let's get you up here and check—"

"Honey," I said to Black Mask. "You didn't let him get my ring, did you?"

He hesitated, but only for a moment.

"Of course not, honey," he said—his own *honey* almost dripping. "You know I'll always look out for you."

He dug into his tuxedo pocket.

"Silly to think about now," I went on, while the paramedics continued to fuss and bother, "but that big blue sapphire means the world to me."

He hesitated longer at that one, hand still deep in his pocket. Even in the dimness where he stood, I could see the crookedness of his smile—a lip curl on one side. Was he the young Elvis? The older one? He was still blurry, but from what he said, I imagined he'd seen better days.

"I don't care what happens to the man who did all this," I said, pressing the message home. "That's up to him. I just want each of us to be safe—and to make sure my ring is safe too."

"Just trying to take care of the woman I love," he said. He pulled out the sapphire, then finally stepped into the light. His eyes looked tired now, bags under them, old Elvis after all.

It felt loose as he slipped it on my finger. I'd need to get it resized.

Just then shot rang out then from inside the chapel, then another that cracked one of the stained glass windows, then three more. "Oh, my God," said one of the paramedics. "What's happened?" He stepped away from the ambulance to look. Even his partner turned away from me. Everyone's attention shifted toward the building. The shenanigans there, as my dad would've said.

Everyone's attention except mine, that is. I knew where to watch this time. Just as the final shot sounded his cue, Black Mask slipped away from the ambulance and disappeared off into the night.

He still had plenty of loot to take home for his wife and kids. No one was headed for the hoosegow after all.

Del and I never did get married in Vegas. As you can imagine, the Little Chapel by the Sea wasn't in the best condition to stay open that night, and no one was keen on finishing up the ceremonies outside. It wasn't that Beehive was mad at either of us for the role we'd played in letting the man get away—I mean, except for those bullets that Del put into the wall and through the window. In fact, she was the first one to explain to the police that Black Mask had forced Del and me into these roles, that Del had no choice but to ensure my safety.

Even when Jeeves tried to argue that Del and I were accomplices, in on it from the beginning, Beehive stepped to our defense again, insisting that we'd helped to get that evil man out of her chapel and get everybody else out safely.

Plus, she had her hands full with that news crew—eating up the attention from the reporter. As they interviewed her about her ordeal, she kept sneaking in snippets of advertising. "I'm not sure why that bandit thought that we would have so much cash, since the Little Chapel by the Sea also accepts all major credit cards, including Discover," she said. "And I'm not sure why he chose to rob us at the time he did, but since the Little Chapel by the Sea is open twenty-four hours, seven days a week, there would have been no *off* hours for him to strike. Still, he should be easy to find, since he's wearing top quality formal wear of the kind you can rent right here on the premises at..." Who knows if they let her say the address on TV or edited it out, but I couldn't begrudge her trying to make the best of a bad thing. Times were tough. Free promotion never hurt.

The officer who'd walked Black Mask and me to the ambulance was less forgiving.

"You could've signaled me," he said. "He was right there, two feet from me."

"He had a knife," I told him, not the first time.

"I never saw a knife," he said.

"I felt it," I said. "And seems like I had the better perspective."

The police set out a manhunt anyway, scouring the blocks around the chapel, street by street, and all the businesses beyond, that pawnshop, that peep show. The bail bondsman even got in on the act, and the psychic across the street, who said from the start, "You'll never find him."

Turns out she was right. The only thing any of us could pinpoint about him were those sideburns, that snarl of the lips, those white boots. The flipside of that glut of Elvises in Vegas: it was easy to hide in plain sight.

I'd thought Del would be impressed by my slick move with the sapphire, but he just gave me a muted smile when I showed it to him.

Was he disappointed that I hadn't just gotten back our original rings? I didn't find out the truth until we watched the evening unfold again on YouTube—not just the clips that had ended up on the news, but the full film, which was automatically saved for posterity, just like Beehive had promised. She'd listed the chapel's website prominently, more free advertising, and it was already racking up views.

Go, the Del on the screen said, looking at Black Mask and me off-screen. *Go now.*

The camera stayed firm on him while a door opened and shut off in the distance—Black Mask and me leaving. Del's expression softened, worry creeping across it.

"I couldn't stand having you out of my sight," he said, the first time we watched it together, "not knowing what might happen out there. I wanted to run after you. I didn't know what to do."

Thank God, Jeeves said after the door closed. *He's gone—* which might've tipped off everyone watching out there, the police, I mean, except that Del's face toughened up again and the gun jumped back into view.

You get back down! Del shouted, loud enough that it startled me every time I watched the film. *No one move.* His eyes gleamed, brimming up with anger. It was scary to watch it, even knowing Del, and I can only imagine what Jeeves must have thought, and everyone there. *You just better hope your luck is as good as theirs,* Del said, *because if I hear anything else from anyone, that luck's going to run out pretty quickly.*

"What were you thinking right then?" I asked Del. The cut on his face was glossy. I'd smeared it with Neosporin, but really no way it wouldn't scar.

"I was thinking that if a man gets backed into an unfortunate situation, there's no telling what might happen."

"You thought that Black Mask might spook and hurt me somehow? You were scared of that?" I asked. "I was just worried you wouldn't trust my plan."

Del looked over at me, reached and touched my belly. "I trust you," he said. "Always. But I didn't trust that bandit, and I didn't...Louise, I realized right then that I didn't entirely trust myself."

I looked into his eyes, not the ones on the screen but the ones right in front of me, and I saw something new in them, and I could hear it in his voice too, the steeliness of it—another glimpse of what I'd just seen on the video that had frightened me.

"If those people in the chapel had done anything to jeopardize you getting out of there," he said, "if they'd made any move to jeopardize you and Poppy, I'd have shot down every one of them."

That's why the sapphire hadn't impressed him.

Once I'd gotten my plan rolling, I'd ended up distracted by baubles.

From first cut to final standoff, the stakes had been higher for Del.

The night before we headed out of town, we drove down the Strip—slow because of all the traffic, the windows down. All the lights reminded me of those winter wonderland things that they set up in the fields back in North Carolina during Christmas time and charge ten bucks a car for families to drive through. Except these lights were brighter and wilder, and it was in the middle of the dessert, and even in early October, the night air was nice and warm, and whatever the ads kept trying to say, this show was clearly not family-friendly.

Up near the entrance to Bally's, just past the Eiffel Tower, I heard someone shout, "You in the Nova!" and my first thought was that it was the police again, that we hadn't gotten away. Old reflexes, like I've said before.

But it was just this drunk guy coming out of the casino, his buddies right behind him. He leaned in the passenger door. "I'll give you twenty-five for the car," he said.

I started to laugh, figuring it was a joke. Twenty-five dollars? Even with the jangly mirror and that spring digging into my butt cheek, the car was worth more than that. It ran okay, it had gotten us where we needed to go and then some. More.

But Del didn't laugh, and when I turned to look at him, he was chewing on that bottom lip.

"*Thirty*-five," he said.

The drunk man leaned back and looked up and down the car.

"C'mon, Harris, let's go," said one of the man's buddies. "You're not seriously planning to buy this, are you?"

But Harris looked like he'd fallen in love. "Yeah," he said, over-loud. "My dad had one like this when I was a kid—same color and everything."

Del revved the engine just slightly, just letting it hum.

"Thirty. Cash," Harris said and he patted his pocket. "I'm on a winning streak."

Thirty *thousand*, he meant, as it turns out. Who knew that Del's old Nova was actually a collector's item?

Turns out Del had known all along.

What you see, as Daddy would've said, isn't always the whole story.

We headed out the next day in a black Mustang convertible. Del bought it at a used car lot for half the price he'd gotten for the Nova—the kind of thing I'd been hankering for, been nagging him for, myself.

"This more your style?" Del said as we buckled up.

It was. Easing the seatbelt across my belly, hugging it around the baby within, having Del beside me—all of it seemed more comfortable, more secure, more promising.

Riding out of town, I waved goodbye to Vegas, to the people we passed. The sapphire was loose on my finger, and heavy in a different way. No matter. I felt like a homecoming queen, maybe even a real one.

THE CHILL

"Hey, Baby Boy," I cooed, rubbing his cheek, cradling him close to me—soaking in the warmth of him, same as he was probably soaking in mine. "Hello, beautiful."

He'd slept the whole ride home—half-slept, drowsy-like, rousing up, drifting off again as I navigated the Mustang extra-careful along Williston's icy roads. February in North Dakota was like nothing I'd ever experienced, none of this was.

By the time we walked through the door, he'd needed changing, and he'd woken up fully as I put on a fresh diaper. Only four left in the bag. I'd send Del out for a package when he got home. Plenty more stuff to pick up.

Baby Boy turned those big blue eyes my way, looked over at the walls, then at his hand, then at my face again. Maybe still waking up. Maybe that's what it's like all the time, every day. All of it new somehow, right? All of it unreal?

I smiled. I could still hardly believe it myself.

Six months old, so he could sit up by himself, even if a little unsteady. I set him down on the floor, steadied him, then sat down myself cross-legged—same as I used to make Mama do for tea parties when I was a girl. No tea set, of course, not that he'd have been interested at that age anyway—maybe at any age.

I'd grabbed the keychains from the spare bedroom—the nursery—both the sock monkey keychain that Del had bought for me in

New Mexico, and the one with the purple teddy bear that I'd stolen myself.

"Now, which do you like better?" I asked him. His eyes darted from one to another, weighing, judging. Not one to rush into things, I was seeing that already. He was cautious. A planner. Which made me think of Del, of course. Made me wonder already what people might ever see of either of us in this little man.

Finally, he reached toward the teddy bear—which gave me a brief surge of disappointment. The sock monkey meant luck, good fortune, something. My talisman, Del had called it. But when I gave Baby Boy the purple teddy bear, his face just lit up so much that it made things feel right again. A new life, a fresh start—that's what we kept telling ourselves. And maybe there had been a good reason I'd stolen the teddy bear keychain, some design to it all.

Then Baby Boy put the metal part of the chain in his mouth, and I had to take it away again.

"You must be hungry," I said. "What was I thinking?"

I picked him up and took him to the table, propped him up on my knee while I peeled a banana and mashed it in a bowl. Yogurt was another favorite, but none in the refrigerator. Another thing to add to the list.

He ate the tiny spoonfuls quickly, hungrily—messily too, of course, as much dribbling out as going in with some bites. He'd just spit out a fresh bit of it when Del came in from his long day at the oil fields, freshly scrubbed but still carrying some remnant of his workday smells: crude oil, ammonia sometimes, sometimes rotting eggs. The cold air rushing in softened it some (more snow that day—again).

Del closed the door, then stopped and stared at us, his brow furrowing. He eyes never left us as he hung up his coat, took off his shoes. He didn't come to the table yet, just stood by the door.

Finally, he pointed to Baby Boy. "Who?" he said, his voice cracking, then "Who's...?" or "Whose?"—stumbling to get it out.

Baby Boy threw his hands in the air and smiled. *Welcome home, Daddy*, I thought, rushing ahead of myself as always.

"Ours," I said. I tucked my nose closer to the baby's head, those wispy curls, that fresh, downy scent. "Ours now."

When Del first talked about heading up to the Dakotas, I thought it was a turn homeward—his home at least—and maybe the chance to meet more of his family. It was something I'd been talking about at least, after our Vegas wedding went sour: the desire to have Del meet Mama before we tied the knot. Given Mama, I was still wishy-washy about how quickly we needed to rush back to North Carolina ("Cora can needle me plenty from afar," Del said), but I thought it was real sweet that Del might be thinking the same thing about his folks. Given what he'd finally told me about his parents, though, I wasn't expecting a warm homecoming.

"Wrong Dakota," Del said when I asked. "I grew up in the South."

By which, of course, he didn't mean the actual South, but just South Dakota. Everything is relative.

Beyond that, he didn't elaborate, and the tone warned me off pushing too much. I just settled back into the passenger seat of that new Mustang convertible (new to us, I mean), clasped my hands over my belly (still not much of a belly at that point), and enjoyed the ride.

Our real destination was up in the northwestern corner of North Dakota—our newest fresh start. "Oil boom on the rise up there," he told me. "This thing called the Bakken Shale. From what I've read in the papers, it's going to be big."

Everything else in the country going down the tubes economically, companies failing and the government trying to bail out everybody, savings lost and people strapped for cash—our own savings continuing to dwindle.

"If there's a boom, more people will come, and they're going to need places to live," Del said. "I know our real estate plans back in Victorville didn't work out, but this is a different place, a different future. Everything that's happening is going to put North Dakota on the map. And we'll put ourselves square in the middle of it, on our terms this time."

Sometimes Del gets it really right. Long after we left Williston, I kept seeing it on the news—the population doubling, incomes skyrocketing. This one story talked about rents there being the highest per square foot of anywhere in the U.S., higher even than New York City or Los Angeles. One article I read used the phrase High Plains Millionaires.

If we'd stayed, maybe Del and I could've been a part of that.

All of it a pretty big "if," as it turned out—looking both forward and back.

For all of our fresh starts, this may have been the freshest—almost everything new, including that new Mustang we drove into town and that new life brewing inside of me.

Del earned a job working the Bakken Shale soon after our arrival in Williston—a temp job, as he looked at it, until he could get his foot in the door with the real estate market. We went together to the uniform supply just off Main Street and picked him up a couple of sets of brown bib overalls with reflective stripes up his chest and around the arms and legs and some gloves and these steel-toed boots that he clinked against one another sometimes when he was just sitting there, contented with himself. The shifts were long, and he'd come home exhausted, smelling like diesel, dabbed with bits of grease, but the money was as good as he'd promised.

North Dakota didn't have reciprocity with California on Del's real estate certification, but he was able to schedule his examination and get his license pretty quickly, and on his free days, he met with realtors and even some appraisal services about coming onboard. No immediate takers, but Del felt confident. "They'll all need significant assistance soon enough," he predicted. "In the meantime, we're more than bankrolling our immediate future."

We moved into one half of a duplex, renting from the landlady who lived in the other half—a rare find, as it turned out. Housing was already hard to come by, the motels filled past capacity, people sleeping in their campers they'd driven into town, in pup tents, in cars.

Our place came furnished too, which was nice, even though a lot of it was outdated. The sofa had this brown on beige pattern, with little scenes of the west: stagecoaches and wagons, cowboys and cacti. First things first, Del put up that painting from Taos, the couple on that misty beach. As fall turned to winter and settled into a deep freeze, I'd watch them and think ocean and sun and warmth. It never worked.

Margaret was the landlady's name—somewhere in her seventies, I'd guess, gray hair in a tight perm, bright red glasses, and a gold cross around her neck. Norwegian stock, she told us. She'd lived in the area all her life and didn't like the oil business one bit, especially the man camps, as they were called, sprawling trailer parks sprouting up for all the single workers rushing into town. "Ghettos for the oil field trash," Margaret sneered, but she smiled quickly to show she wasn't including us. "Not family men, not like Del." That was why we got the place, her holding out for better. The new scar on Del's cheek probably would've been a mark against us, but my belly trumped it. She liked to touch it whenever she got the opportunity—"for luck," she said. "God has plans for this one, I can feel it."

Margaret also knew an obstetrician—Dr. Williams. "Call me Doc Williams," he said, an older man, probably near to retirement himself, but generous and good-natured. "Baby's the size of a plum now," he told us on one of our first visits. Seemed like everyone uses fruits and vegetables to talk about the baby's size and growth, obstetricians, nurses, even that pregnancy book that I'd started carrying around like a Bible. As the weeks passed, I updated Del where we were: lemon, nectarine, apple, pear, girl.

"Girl?" Del said. He'd come home late, bleary-eyed, shaking his head like maybe he hadn't heard me right.

"That's what the ultrasound said. I didn't know today's visit was the one for that or—"

I felt bad that Del had missed it, but he didn't feel left out. He just started jumping up and down, lots of hugging and kissing, like when he'd first found out I was pregnant (without all of the hitting, of course; I still felt bad about poor Trevor on that count).

"We should stop calling her Little Orange Seed now," he said.

"Yeah," I said. "Pretty soon, she'll just be Orange."

I planned to get a job myself, but Del told me not to bother. His salary promised plenty for us, plus enough to fast-track a savings account. I could just stay home—"prep up for the baby," as Del said.

"Kind of old-fashioned, don't you think?" I told him. "Want me to kick off my shoes and go barefoot?"

"Not with a North Dakota winter coming."

Even without a job, I did end up finding work of a sort. When I'd gone to the local hospital for a visit and to sign up for Lamaze classes, I'd seen a sign about volunteers and checked in on it.

The volunteer coordinator had long blond hair—really long, flowing in curls down the full length of her back. When she'd first interviewed me, her posture was so straight I wondered if she'd caught part of it under her rump, curving her spine tight like a bow and arrow. Rapunzel, I probably would've called her at one point, or just Frizzy, but her name was Sabrina. She was excited to have me aboard, said that the pregnancy had given me a welcoming glow.

"I feel goodness coming off of you," she told me. "We have some openings at the front desk, and this is the kind of energy I want greeting our visitors."

Two of us at a time carried each shift there, checking people in, occasionally escorting patients or families where they needed to go—mornings, afternoons, even some evenings as Del's hours grew, his shifts bumping up toward twelve hours some days, him having to catch rides now to and from the oil fields while I kept the car.

I tried to live up to what Sabrina wanted—turning a smile on everyone who came our way, folks who were really struggling. Up to a dozen patients a day stopped by for dialysis, driving from all through the region to get there. People recovering from heart attacks or bypass surgery came in for therapy, to help quit smoking, to change their ways. Accidents aplenty every day, fender benders in the snow, neck injuries, spinouts on those crazy roads. People who weren't recovering too, of course, and who wouldn't. Del and I were lucky, I realized, if luck was the right word for it. I know it probably sounds sentimental, but...carrying our baby, I felt like I was storing up love, had lots of love and good fortune to share, and I tried to share it where I could, how I could.

Whenever a woman and her husband sidled up to the desk, her already going into labor, the two of them getting checked in, heading up to delivery—I saw Del and me there soon and imagined what that day would be like. Imagined it again when those new families went out that front door, the father pushing his wife in a wheelchair, everybody cooing over the newborn in her lap.

Even with my volunteer shifts, I still had time to "prep up for the baby," and truth to tell, I found myself enjoying the idea of domestic life—and more than enjoying, embracing. Albertson's was the grocery store I'd first went to, and I liked it, liked roaming the aisles and stopping in the produce section each trip to track down whatever fruit or vegetable had cropped up on that week's chart, heft it in my hand, hold it against my belly, picture the baby inside. I liked the cashiers asking me about my pregnancy. Boy or girl? When was the due date? Did we have a name?

I made a resolution to learn to cook more—not the pre-packaged, microwavable stuff we usually had, not just take-out or delivery. I kneaded and rolled out the dough for the kind of chicken pastry I used to love as a child myself, tried out three different lasagnas which kept us in leftovers for weeks, branched out into some new recipes like chicken marsala and turkey roulade. Margaret loaned me some of her cookbooks, and walked me through some Scandinavian meals: these thin pancakes made with leftover potatoes, and another time meatballs in a thick sauce that she called *kjøttboller*—which had this funny o in the middle of it and which she pronounced a lot like "shot ball," so it was easy to remember. I pictured the future—me tending to the stove while Del cooed and giggled with the baby after work. I had this big idea about meals that could work different ways once the baby got old enough: a fancy pasta dinner for us and something simple, buttered noodles, for our child.

"Complementary cooking," Del said when I told him—excited not just by the phrase but also by the idea.

I dug into the pregnancy books, peeked ahead at the books for baby's first year—the joys and challenges ahead. Our side of the duplex was two bedrooms, and I'd stand in the empty one, imagining the nursery it would become. Del had seen a rocking chair at a yard sale after we got into town, and he'd bought it as a surprise—the one piece of furniture in the house that was ours, and sometimes I'd sit in it, watch the sunset over the backyard, sometimes feeling the baby wiggle as I waited for Del to come home. The two of us, I corrected myself, waiting for Daddy.

We weren't just making room for the new addition to our lives. We were remaking those lives themselves.

Not everything went smoothly, of course. As my belly plumped out, it felt nice to clasp my fingers across my middle, to see the comforter rising up when I pulled it over me at night. But other times I just felt uncomfortable—in chairs or in bed, in my clothes, in my body. I was also gassy a lot, short ripples of it that seemed to always be working through my system, and constipated. I near bout burned down the duplex when I tried frying chicken myself (we didn't tell Margaret, just cleaned the grease), and I realized pretty quickly that cooking was only part of it all.

"Del!" I said, when we handed out candy for the trick-or-treaters, everybody talking about how lucky we were for a warm night (thirties!) after the snows we'd already seen. "I don't know how to sew a Halloween costume."

"We can buy one at the store."

"Those are always flimsy," I said. "And I've never made a Thanksgiving turkey myself either. Or that full spread of side dishes either. How in the world are we gonna do all that *and* take care of the baby?"

"That's a long way off to worry about," he said.

"We'll need to make a practice run this Thanksgiving. I'll start looking for recipes."

The doorbell rang again. Del stepped up with the candy bowl. "I think you're putting the cart before the—well, the stroller before the baby."

Which, of course, reminded me that we hadn't even started looking at strollers or cribs or bibs or any of it yet—and sent me browsing over at the JCPenney, making frantic lists, firming up everything we'd need.

Some days were a panic, the future overwhelming.

But when Thanksgiving came, Margaret walked me through stuffing the turkey and making the gravy, then joined us for dinner, her own children spread too far and wide to visit themselves. It all turned out okay.

At Christmas, she loaned us ornaments for an artificial tree we picked up, and together the two of us made this Christmas bread with candied fruit that she said was tradition.

It felt like family. It felt good.

And felt bad too, of course, remembering Mama. Those shot balls weren't all that different from the meatballs and pan gravy she used to make. The Christmas bread was fluffier than those dense-as-bricks Claxton fruitcakes we used to pick up each year, but hard not to be reminded of them. I felt like a bad daughter not going home for the holidays, felt guilty generally not having told her about the baby yet—keeping that feeling safe, protecting us from whatever Mama might say about it.

"How's J.R. doing?" she asked when I called her on Christmas Day. Del and Margaret were in the next room, Margaret pressing once more about the baby's name, Del telling her I'd made my mind up on one but hadn't told anybody, not even him. In the midst of that, Mama's question left me disoriented.

"Who's J.R.?" I said.

"J.R. Ewing."

"Oh," I said. "Del."

Mama snickered. "I couldn't decide whether to go with J.R. or Jed Clampett."

"I wish you wouldn't make fun of him, Mama."

"First he's gonna be a real estate mogul"—she pronounced it MOE-GYUL—"and now he wants to be an oil tycoon."

"He still—" I started to say that he still planned to work in real estate, but it wasn't worth it. "He's still the man I love."

"Love," she repeated. She snorted again like always. "What's the temperature like there?"

"It's about ten degrees."

"I mean the high."

"That is the high," I said. "The low was around negative twelve yesterday. We've got about a half a foot of snow on the ground.'"

"Bet that new Mustang convertible is just perfect."

I didn't say anything.

Mama and I sat in silence. Del kept telling me *Don't let Cora get to you, don't let her spoil things*, but I needed to check in, didn't I? The baby seemed restless, twisting, turning, kicking—maybe picking up on my own discomfort. I looked at the Christmas tree we'd put up, the present for Mama I still needed to mail. I traced the pattern of a wagon wheel on one of the scenes on the couch. *Go West*, I thought, and remembered why I had. All of it adding reasons why I shouldn't say anything more.

"I just miss you," Mama said then, almost a whisper, and I let my own breath out, not even realizing I'd been holding it.

Her tone was tender and helpless, so unlike the way she usually was, that I almost broke down and started telling her everything anyway, but suddenly it seemed like too much. It would make her more upset to find out how long I'd hidden things. It overwhelmed me to realize that every new moment I didn't tell her compounded the trouble further. The only thing I could get out was "I miss you too." That and: "I'll try to call more often, okay?" Then I told her Del needed me.

I heard the click on the other end of the line. She hadn't said anything else.

I sat there in silence for a while after that, tracing the edges of horses and cowboys and sunsets. The baby settled down again. I wrapped my arms around myself, hugged my belly, hoped that she and I would always be closer, better.

Two days later, I woke up and knew that something was wrong. The stillness was too still. My body felt tense, cold—not a pain or a discomfort, but an awkwardness, like it didn't know itself anymore.

Del took the day off, drove me over to the doctor, steering that Mustang along those treacherous roads. I clutched the armrest the whole drive, like holding on for dear life—not because of the ice but because I believed if I could just keep my grip steady and firm, everything would turn out fine.

When Doc Williams held the ultrasound against me, I finally relaxed. The heartbeat was there—faint but there—and I could see our baby, curled up and sleeping.

Then Doc's expression told the truth—the way his forehead furrowed, the way his eyes suddenly turned away. A chill shivered up the length of me.

The baby wasn't sleeping, and that wasn't her heartbeat. It was just the echo of my own off in the distance, slowly breaking.

"I'm sorry," Doc Williams said, pulling away the wand and leaving me laying there with that cold gel smeared across my belly, too stunned to cry yet.

"What?" Del said. "You're making a mistake. Try it again. Look again."

But I knew. I'd already known.

"Leave it for just a minute more," I told the doctor.

"There's no movement," he said. "There's no—" *Hope*, I felt like he was going to say, but he cut himself short.

"Maybe so." I reached for Del's hand, clasped it firm. "But that doesn't mean there's nothing to see."

Winter days in Williston are short. Most days the sun doesn't rise until after 8:30, and it goes down again just after five. Even then, snow is more frequent than sun, and the cold is bitter. The door of the Mustang regularly froze shut, and that soft top I'd wanted so badly creaked and crinkled at every turn, like the ice had twisted itself into the fabric. My skin chapped, cracked, tore.

But none of it was as cold and dark as I felt inside.

There's parts of this story that won't be easy to tell and a lot here that I'm not proud of. In fact, anticipating what's ahead, I'm already feeling ashamed—of myself, of Del, of all of it. The worst crime that we committed—that *I* committed—even if it wasn't entirely my choice.

The reasons you do things don't always make up for the doing of them.

I know that some folks who've been reading these stories are gonna be surprised by what happens here. All I can say is that I wish there was a different story to tell—of me and Del having a baby and him becoming all sappy and me giggling and both of us dog-tired and stressed out beyond belief because we're not getting any sleep, just can't seem to change the diapers fast enough, can't figure out why the baby is crying or how to get him to stop. And in the middle of all that, who knows whether one of us might break the baby somehow, especially Del with his big, clumsy hands? But at the same time none of that tiredness and worry and fear would matter because here would be this human being the two of us brought into the world, and a better world for it, right?

That's about as good a happiness as any of us should expect.

And really, if you want a happy ending, just skip ahead. I promise there's better times down the road.

But for me, this story is the truth and it's real and sometimes you need to see yourself, own up to what you've done—not just accept it, but embrace it.

This one I need to tell for me.

"Necessary procedures," Doc Williams had said about the sponges they inserted to dilate me, the medicine they used to induce labor, the realization dawning on me that I'd still have to deliver the baby. Hours of Del clinging to my arm, trying to hold me steady, of the two of us crying and crying and crying and I don't know how many times I can write that word to begin to tell you what that scene looked like.

"Sometimes the body has a mind of its own," Doc Williams said days later when my milk came in. He told me to try cabbage compresses—"four times a day to relieve the pressure," even though both of us knew that was only half-true. The real pressure was somewhere else, and no relief for it.

New start, Del and I had said, a new life—and it felt like someone else's life as I washed the cabbage leaves and flattened them out with an old bowling pin that Del had carried around with us, making the veins crinkle and crack just right. It was someone else who took off her shirt and her bra and laid the leaves across her breasts to wait for them to wilt. I'm not sure the magic ever worked.

I had felt like a different person buying the cabbage in the first place—at a different grocery store too, since I couldn't bear to go back to my regular one, where everyone had been interested in my pregnancy, my progress, where there would've been questions I didn't want to answer. The aisles were laid out differently. It felt like a maze. Just a glimpse of the Pampers and the formula on the baby goods aisle sent my emotions spiraling through most of the five stages of grief Doc Williams had told me about.

"Runzas?" the checkout girl asked as she was ringing up the

third head of cabbage—just like that, with a question mark at the end of it. It could've been a foreign language, and in a way, it was. Even ordinary words seemed to be coming through unclear to me those days, muffled and echoing like across a long distance.

I shook my head. "I don't know what that means."

"You know, the sandwiches." She held her hands up in a rectangle, then pointed at the cabbage. "That's what we called them in Nebraska. There's a whole chain of fast food restaurants that make them, but I think they call them the same thing here."

She was young. Wide-eyed and innocent, the lipstick chewed off her lips everywhere but the center. That and her thick curly hair, bright red, made her look like a Raggedy Ann doll. A few weeks before, another life ago, I would probably have called her that.

I tried to pull myself out of the fog. I squinted at the tag on her lapel. Holly. A nice name. She was someone's child. My own could've grown up like this.

"Coleslaw," I lied—though thinking of Mama's recipe, I would've needed a lot of other ingredients: carrots and onions, some mayo, some buttermilk, some vinegar.

I wondered if Margaret had ever made runzas, if she would've taught me. No reason to bother now.

Holly said some things after that, I don't remember what or what I might've said back.

Those days, whatever anyone said to me, I just nodded or shook my head—not always sure that the motions matched whatever yes or no I happened to be thinking.

Given everything that happened later, Holly probably must have thought I was just being rude.

True love isn't looking into one another's eyes, as I've said. It's looking together in the same direction.

After the miscarriage, Del and I were still looking in the same direction, but mostly it was just at the TV. I left it on most of the time, a distraction, a way to fill the silence while Del was at work, a way to keep us from having to talk when he was at home. Each night, we'd settle down to have dinner and watch the court shows on TV—his choice more than mine, since he thought they'd be a comfort. Truth was, I didn't care.

Back in Victorville when Brenda had asked me why anyone would want to watch people broadcast their dirty laundry and stupidity to millions, I'd defended the shows. I'd told her it was like seeing the full parade of life up there: love and hate, betrayal and greed, kindness too sometimes, a lot of lies, sure, but a dose of hard truth alongside, and lessons to be learned. Now it just felt trivial, a mockery of real life.

"Do you think it's something we did?" I asked Del one night. It was during a *Judge Judy* rerun. "Losing the baby, I mean."

My breasts ached as I said it, maybe because I'd said it. The cabbage again, after dinner.

"Doc said it wasn't anything we did," Del said. "And it's not like we hadn't been scrupulous about a check-up from the start, when we first found out about it. We kept it checked out along the way."

It, he said.

The pregnancy or the baby, I wasn't sure which he meant.

"That's not what I mean." I pushed my fork into the center of my plate. I'd hardly eaten anything. Del meanwhile had shoveled some chicken into his mouth, maybe to avoid talking at all.

We were back to quick meals now. I couldn't even pretend to be up for home cooking. When Margaret brought over food, it felt like casseroles for a wake. "God has a plan," she'd reminded me, patting the cross around her neck, but this time it left me feeling sour.

"Do you believe in karma?" I asked.

Del swallowed.

"That's a pretty wide-ranging philosophical question, hon."

"I mean, what we've done in the past, stealing things and all. Do you think that's why this happened?"

Del chewed on it all. On the TV, the judge was arguing with

someone. *I love the truth*, she cried out from the bench. *If you don't tell me the truth, you're going to be eating your shoes.* I reached for the remote and turned down the volume.

"Louise," Del said. "You didn't steal anything. I did."

"She was your baby too, not just mine." My throat caught on the words. I didn't mean to sound like I was accusing him. "And I did steal something—that sapphire ring. And I've been an accessory all along, and..."

It had been an "us" question.

Del stiffened. "We're not bad people, Louise. And I don't think karma is that simple: quick reward here, quick punishment. Quid pro quo." He thought for a minute. "And even if it was, this would seem out of proportion, wouldn't it?"

"I just feel like I did something wrong. I feel like I've let someone down—everyone, you, me, our baby."

That pang in my breasts again, in my gut.

I couldn't stand being by myself, couldn't stand being *with* myself.

"There's a quilter's bee at Fort Buford," Margaret told me one day. "Not very exciting maybe for a young woman like you, but..." She gave me this pitying look through those red glasses. "It's a warm group. It will be comforting."

But watching those women and their projects, all I could think of was baby blankets. And even when I excused myself for fresh air—drawing the cold in and out of my lungs, walking around on my own, trying to get ahold of myself—I walked right into the cemetery in the back, white boards behind a picket fence.

I tried to keep up my volunteer shifts at the hospital—get back into a routine, surround myself with people who had been good to me during and after the miscarriage. But now I had a different perspective on those dialysis patients and cancer survivors, all those illnesses and injuries. How did my pain compare to theirs? Wasn't mine easier to bear? Shouldn't I feel better?

Envy ate me alive whenever some woman arrived to deliver

her baby. When those couples rolled out with their newborns, my brain clouded up, fizzled, shut down.

"It hurts, I know," Sabrina, the volunteer coordinator, told me. "But it'll get better. Time heals all wounds."

I heard the same thing at the support group I went to, went through the same weighing of my grief against others—comparing and contrasting and cataloguing as each of the women shared her story, trying to find myself in the middle of it.

Loss was the word that was used most. The lost child, the sense of loss and of being lost. Not one of them used the words *dead* or *died*. Their children were *stillborn*. The babies *expired*. One woman talked about her *blighted ovum* and *empty gestational sac*. The pregnancies *weren't viable*, or they had to be *interrupted*. That last one took me a while to catch on to. Genetic disorders, hard choices, choices I was glad I'd never had to make and didn't know how I would've made them.

When it came my turn to speak, I didn't know where to begin.

They'd let me hold her after she was born. She was "complete," as they said. All of her toes, all of her fingers, her fingernails too, just the thinnest slivers beginning to form. She was small enough to fit in one hand.

The size of an avocado that week—such a stupid, stupid, stupid comparison.

"Sometimes it's hard to know how to talk about it," Abby the moderator said—small and thin with sharp features but soft eyes. "Know that listening can also help."

She reached her hand across that big table toward me, but she was too far away, so her arm just stretched out into the nothingness between all of us.

One afternoon at my new grocery store, the produce manager nearly ran into my cart. When I looked into the crate he was carrying, I felt myself gasp.

Avocados.

"Are you okay?" he asked. "Sorry I wasn't watching where I was going."

"They look perfect," I said.

"Used to be tough to get them this time of year, but year-round these days." He put the crate down. "These just came in. Help yourself."

I picked one and put it in the cart, then moved ahead. I had a list with me, but couldn't keep track of what I'd gotten and hadn't. I backtracked the aisles even more than usual, not just forgetting what was where in the new store but forgetting myself.

The avocado sat and watched. Occasionally, I touched it. Finally, I picked it up and cupped it in my palms. It had been cold at first, but it warmed in my hands. Holding it calmed me, gave me my bearings again.

Light bulbs were the next thing on my list, and I hesitated when I found they were on the baby aisle. I thought about getting them another time, but then took a deep breath and pushed the cart ahead, looking at the jars of mashed bananas and beans, the tubs of formula, the bottles of baby wash.

For the first time, I felt in control. It seemed, finally, like healing—like magic. Then, as I waited in the checkout line, I lost control again—or maybe took control too much. While I was unloading my cart onto the conveyor belt, I snatched that avocado up and dropped it into my coat pocket instead of adding it to the pile.

Sometimes the body has a mind of its own.

The man ahead of me had just run his credit card through the machine. Holly was the cashier again, and she was busy telling him which button to press. I glanced behind me, and the woman there met my eye. I still have no idea if she saw what I did. She didn't say anything, just put the divider bar down on the belt and unloaded her own groceries behind mine.

As Holly rang me up, I stared at the exit, gauging how many steps I'd need to push the grocery cart once I was done. Were there cameras? Security? Would someone stop me as I was passing through the door? Would they wait until just after I left?

"You paying for that?" Holly said.

"What?" My hand went to my coat pocket, felt the bulge. Still there.

"Are those yours?" She pointed to the conveyor belt. The separator bar between my groceries and the woman's behind me had turned at an angle. A can of beets had wedged itself near the scanner.

Holly glared at me. Her tone had been abrupt. No time for conversation like that day asking about the runzas—no time or no interest now.

"Those are mine," said the other woman, and she reached across to straighten up her stuff.

Holly told me my total. My hand trembled as I handed her the bills from my wallet.

"That coleslaw make you sick?" she asked. "All that cabbage?" No empathy behind the question.

"It was fine," I said. "Just...I just felt weak there for a minute."

No one stopped me at the manager's counter near the front of the store. No one stopped me at the door. No one followed me out to the car.

I loaded the bags in the back, kept the avocado in the front seat all the way home.

I couldn't eat the avocado, of course. I just let it sit on the counter, touching it as I passed by, cupping it in my hand sometimes.

For several days, I just stayed in. I left the TV off. I made a pot roast for Del and me, and the two of us sat at the table and ate it. He reached out and held my hand and said thanks.

Slowly the avocado turned from green to brown to black. Even after I moved it into the refrigerator, it shriveled, then dented.

"Hon," Del said one night. "Looks like this has soured."

It took every bit of will I had to throw it in the trash.

* * *

The avocado taught me a lesson—two actually. The next things I stole weren't perishable, and I spread out my shopping and my shoplifting even further.

Getting gas at one of the Racers convenience stores, I tucked a Hot Wheels car into my pocket. At the Cash Wise, I walked out with a travel-sized baby powder in my purse. Back at the grocery store, I grabbed a trial size of Johnson's baby wash.

Here a jar of baby food. There a plastic bag of tiny fabric balls that expanded into full-sized washcloths when wet. The keychain with the purple teddy bear had seemed a special treasure even from the moment I dropped him in my pocket.

Nothing I took was ever much more than a dollar, I only took one thing at a time, and I always bought something. At the Cash Wise, I picked up about two weeks' worth of groceries, and the baby powder was barely a buck. That's part of the way I rationalized it. Either way, I hid it all from Del, tucking it into the closet in the room that would've been the baby's. Sometimes I'd pull out all of it, whatever I had, and line it up, then just sit in the rocker and look at it. I added the sock monkey to it—all of them talismans maybe.

It wasn't kleptomania, that's not the word for it. It wasn't irrational or impulsive, not after the first time, and it wasn't unconscious. I could've stopped at any point, I could've.

But it felt good to take instead of having something taken from you.

Baby tweezers, a thin carton of Q-tips, a plastic teething ring.

"Do you think that karma works in reverse?" I asked Del another night, the pile of stolen good growing bit by bit in the closet of that empty room. He'd gotten home later than usual, his shifts getting longer. I'd already eaten. He warmed his plate up. He looked exhausted and frustrated.

"How do you mean reverse?"

"I mean is the stuff we're gonna do in the future already known somehow, and it's connected to what happens in the past."

"Some kind of predestination, you mean?"

"Maybe," I said. Then, "No, not really. What I mean is: do you think the things we do in the future can affect the things that happened in the past?"

Del scratched his head. "That's a whole 'nother level of philosophical, hon."

It didn't stop me from stealing, just slowed it down some, spread my crimes even further—to Watford City, to Tioga, not instead of, but in addition to. Spacing it out, same as Del tried to do back in New Mexico.

"Just keep focused on the future," Sabrina told me back at the hospital, swishing that long hair behind her as she took the seat beside me. The other woman on my shift had escorted a patient to Respiratory Care—Sabrina's cue to check in on me. "You can try again. A lot of women have miscarriages the first time. By the second, the pregnancy goes fine."

I couldn't help thinking of the cat Mama and I had lost when I was about eight. Trixie was her name, and she got hit by a car, and one of our neighbors asked immediately how soon we were gonna get another one—"for Louise," she'd said, "or maybe a new toy?" like you could just sub in something new or shiny for whatever was lost.

"We hadn't even been trying before," I admitted. "It just happened, and now when we do want it...Doc Williams said that I might have the same risks with another pregnancy. Del and I might just not be able to have kids." The first time I'd said it aloud. It made it sound real.

An older couple came up to the desk to check in, and Sabrina stood up to help them. In my pocket was a pacifier I'd swiped the day before. I reached into my pocket to give it a quick rub—comfort, luck, I didn't know.

"You could adopt," Sabrina went on, after they'd left. "Later on, I mean, nothing too fresh. You'd be a good mother, I know. I can feel it."

"I don't know," I said. "Maybe."

"It's a shame that some people want a child and...struggle. Or just can't. Meanwhile somebody else out there who can't take care of a child, they..." She toyed with the cord on the phone at our desk, unraveling it, twisting it back. She seemed to be tearing up. "Parenting's not something you do lightly."

"What's wrong?" I asked.

She waved her hand at me. "Just thinking about the Baby Moses case."

"In the Bible?"

She laughed, wiped away a tear. "No, dear," she said. "Over near Manatee, back ten years ago now. A rancher found a boy's body, a newborn, barely a couple of weeks old, in a suitcase, wrapped in plastic, starved, dehydrated..." For a moment she couldn't speak, just sat there. "Murdered in slow motion, that's what they said. The mother, as it turned out."

"That's awful." I could feel my insides churning, my emotions going into overdrive. I thought about what I'd gone through, giving birth, holding our daughter, letting her go.

I reached again for the pacifier in my pocket, squeezed it tight.

"The FBI finally solved it, about a year and a half ago. DNA testing. The mother was still living right there, charged her with murder. She got sentenced to ten years, last summer it was, all over the news. Not enough, some people said, but...it was a sad story all around, her already with three children, and her husband on drugs and alcohol."

She shook her head again, that long hair twisting back and forth. Shaking off the memories.

"That's why we've got that sign out there," she said. "I think about it every time I pass it."

"What sign?"

"Sure you've seen it," she said. "The hand cradling the baby's head. We're a Safe Haven site, for mothers to give up their children if they need to. Avoid another tragic story." She patted my hand again. "And, who knows, maybe pass that child along to a woman like you. You've got a lot of love to give, anyone can see that."

My shift mate returned then. Sabrina got up to make the rounds of other volunteers.

When I reached for the pacifier this time, pressing it hard, it felt like the plastic nipple had started to rip.

"We have cameras, you know."

"What?"

"Your pocket."

Holly again, another trip to the grocery store. Valentine's Day, I remember, because I'd added a bottle of wine to the cart, something special for Del and me that night, a surprise after he got home from work, after my shift at the hospital—something warm and good, especially with the temperature outside dropping to something like fourteen below, especially with how I'd been feeling about us.

None of it was as cold as Holly's tone right then, and the way she was chewing at her lip this time made it look like a sneer. She nodded her head down toward the pocket of my coat. One of the corners of a wipes package was sticking out.

"I had these in my pocket when I came in."

I patted them like they belonged.

She shook her head, two quick shakes.

"I can see the baby aisle from here. I watched you put them in there."

The store wasn't busy that day, which didn't happen much. Usually there was a line at every register, but today no one was behind me.

I turned and looked. Straight perspective, a clear view. When I turned back, I saw the manager watching us from his counter at the front.

"Oh," I said, "these." I pulled them out, handed them over. "I usually do keep them in my pocket at home. It must have been reflex."

"Baby wipes," she said. She didn't scan them, just held them in her hand. "In your coat pocket at home."

"It was a mistake," I told her. "I'm sorry."

"Is everything okay here?" The manager stepped behind Holly. He was balding on top, paunchy around the middle.

Holly stood there with the wipes in her hand, like she was weighing them. Clearly she was weighing something.

"I made a mistake," I started to say, to him this time, but Holly cut me off.

"She thought it was discounted more," she said. "Almost like we were giving it away."

"Need me to do a price check?" the manager asked. Stan was his name.

"It's fine," I said. "Whatever the cost, I'm fine to pay it. I was just confused."

"I don't mind checking," he said.

"It's fine," I said again. He shrugged. Holly scanned the wipes and tossed them in one of the bags with my other groceries.

I was beginning to feel grateful to her, started to say "thank you." But she spoke first.

"I've never even seen you with a baby," she said, as she finished ringing me up. There was no warmth in her voice. Just spitefulness, a sense that she was one up on me somehow. "But you should know, if you're breastfeeding, you shouldn't be drinking that wine in there. And those Twinkies are bad for you."

On my way out of the store, heading back into the blistering cold, I pulled the wipes out of the bag and hurled them in the trash.

I had another shift at the hospital that night, filling in time until Del got off. The information desk had been decorated with a red garland, and the folks in cardiac rehab had printed a "Matters of the

Heart" flier, urging everyone to be heart-healthy not just on February fourteenth, but all year-around.

The afternoon was busy, the evening had been slow. I'd fumed about how Holly had treated me, how embarrassed I'd felt. I wished I could tell Del about it later, but he didn't know about all I'd taken before, and it would've meant explaining all that. I focused on what was ahead—the Valentine's Day surprise, a change of pace, another kind of distraction.

When the woman came in with a baby cradled in her arms, I felt those twinges of envy creeping in again, same as usual. The other volunteer at the desk had stepped away, just to the bathroom, or I'd have let her handle it.

"Can you take him?" the woman asked—a girl really, I saw up close, hardly out of her teens probably. Her eyes were puffed and red. Her hair was stringy beneath a Denver Broncos hat. Her baby was wrapped tight in blankets, two of them, each a different shade of blue. A plastic grocery bag was looped around her wrist.

"Is he sick?" I said. "Or hurt? The emergency room is—"

"He's not sick," she said. "I just can't—I can't take care of him, and my mother, she..." She propped the baby up on the desk between us. He seemed to be sleeping, but roused briefly, moved his head, before settling back in. Blue pajamas peeked out from his blanket—everything blue. They had elephants on them. She put the plastic bag up beside him, a loose jumble of diapers, a carton of wipes. "They said any hospital would take him. He's only six months. He's within the limit."

"Within the limit?" I said, then, "Safe Child," remembering what Sabrina had said. "You're just giving him up?" I didn't mean to make it sound like an accusation, but it must've.

"Please don't make me feel bad about this." Her eyes were pleading, miserable. "I called the 800 number. They said no questions. They said no one would make me feel bad, that I was doing the right thing."

"Yes," I said, "yes." This hadn't been part of our training. No one had told me what to do, or how to handle it. The emergency room, I thought, that's still where she should go. I'll send her that way. "I need you to—"

"Please," she said, pushing the baby closer toward me, beginning to pull her arms away. I reached for the boy to steady him. She was openly crying now. She wiped the sleeve of her parka against her nose, smearing tears and snot. "If I don't do this now, I'm not going to be able to do it. Just...just take him. Just take care of him."

She ran then, across the room and toward the door. At the door, she stopped, turned back to look at me. I thought she'd changed her mind, but she only called to me, "He likes yogurt, and mashed bananas." Then she was gone, back into the chill of the night.

It took me a few moments to realize I'd already picked up the child and was cradling him in my arms.

There are rules about leaving the desk unattended.

There are bigger rules, written and unwritten both. I know.

I walked off anyway, not toward the emergency room but out and away, hugging the baby tight against my chest.

All babies are beautiful, each of them in their own way. But this baby—Baby Boy Blue, in his blue pajamas and his blue blankets—he had something magical about him, that's the only way I know how to explain it. Was it the unexpectedness of it all? Was it those wispy blond curls all over his head? The puffiness of his cheeks and the way his mouth hung open just slightly like he was getting ready to speak? Those long eyelashes, unbelievably long, it seemed like, and those eyes—the blue so deep and dark they seemed unreal somehow.

All of it unreal maybe. I stared down at him with a sense of disbelief as I played with him that first night.

Disbelief too when Del first walked through the door, but of a different kind.

When I'd handed Baby Boy to Del, he'd taken him in his arms, awkwardly—all the questions he'd been asking still playing through his puzzled expression. How and why, whose and who—not just who was the baby and who did he belong to, but who was I now, this person who had brought him home. Valentine's Day surprises all around, just not the ones I'd planned.

"She was just a girl, Del," I told him again. I'd already explained about Safe Child, about how it had all played out. "Young and scared. Torn up about it, the decision she was making. She needed help."

"What did you tell her again?"

"We didn't talk much. I didn't have time. I just...reacted."

"And how did you get him back here?"

"Oh, Del, it was wrong," I said, truly ashamed. "I know it wasn't safe, but I put him on the front seat. I held him there with my hands, held him in place. He was asleep. I drove slowly, the whole way. What choice did I have?"

He shook his head. I knew what he was thinking. A lot of other choices I could've made. The same thought that had been running through my own mind on the drive home, kicking myself for the risks I was taking with the baby, watching the road, watching ahead for the police, watching the rearview mirror—a life we kept trying to put behind us, but a different life this time, different stakes.

"We'll need to get a car seat," I said. "A proper one. And a crib of some kind."

"You're intending that we keep him."

I didn't answer. He hadn't meant it as a question.

Too late to get a car seat that night, too late to buy a crib. Penney's was already closed by the time Del got there. But he swung by the store and picked up diapers and baby wipes, some milk, more bananas, a half-dozen pouches of yogurt. I mashed another banana and fed it to the baby bite by bite with the tip of the spoon.

"Hungry," Del said, watching him gulp it down.

"Is he supposed to eat that fast?" I asked.

"Maybe that's how they eat."

Baby Boy stared at me with eagerness, wonder—maybe a little fear? Or desperation? Or maybe it was my own feelings reflected there.

"Making a mess," Del said.

"Del," I said, turning the tables on him for once.

I gave Baby Boy another spoonful, then more. He finished nearly all of it. When we were done, I marked the time and the amount in the "Baby Makes Three" notebook we'd gotten in Vegas, feeling like we should keep track, figure out a schedule.

"We'll need to find him a doctor," I said, knowing that if I'd passed the baby along to the hospital like I should've, he would've had an immediate check-up. I was cradling him in my lap again, running my fingers through his thin hair. He seemed peaceful, full.

"How are we going to explain that?" Del asked.

"We haven't had a pediatrician before. We'll just say we moved into the area just recently. What would we need to explain?"

"What if the doctor we choose is the one he's already had? What if someone recognizes him?"

"The baby comes *first*," I said—knowing it, but then knowing I wasn't being honest with either of us, already ashamed by that.

We would have to explain him somehow—if not to a doctor then to others. To Margaret next door, to Mama somewhere down the line. Or would we even get that far? I couldn't remember if there were security cameras at the hospital, had never been concerned about it. Would someone have seen? Was the video already with the authorities? What would we do if the mother changed her mind, came back to the hospital? What would she do if she found out that no one knew anything about him?

After being restful in my arms, Baby Boy cried and whimpered whenever I tried to put him down in the makeshift crib that Del fashioned out of sofa cushions and spare pillows. Del and I took turns rocking him, but when we passed him from one of us to the other, he fidgeted, and we were clumsy and uncoordinated, me trying to put my arms between Del's for the hand-off and Del trying to put his between mine, and it only made things worse. When Baby Boy stayed fussy, we fed him again—yogurt this time—after which Del carried him around, a circuit from bedroom to living room to kitchen and back, singing "Twinkle, Twinkle Little Star" and some old *Schoolhouse Rock* songs: "Conjunction Junction" and "Lolly, Lolly, Lolly, Get Your Adverbs Here." It was the last that seemed to settle him finally.

We didn't drink that bottle of wine I'd picked up for Valentine's Day. Instead, I took down the stolen bottle from Napa—the one Carl had given us. "Seems like the special occasion we've been waiting for," I said, but when we toasted the night, the future, it was more uncomfortable and uncertain than celebratory.

"Are you sure about this?" Del asked. "Are you happy?"

The wine felt warm inside—a warmer feeling still having a baby just down the hall. But questions raced and ricocheted through my mind. A thin chill crept over me.

"I don't know the word for it," I told him.

I'm not sure whether he took that as a good thing or not. The baby cried before Del could say anything else, and I rushed down the hall to comfort him.

One night back in New Mexico, Del and I had stayed up late watching *Raising Arizona*, and we'd laughed our butts off at it. It was fun and madcap and crazy, over-the-top unbelievable. "Caricatures, not characters," Del had said later, his mini-review, and that was the thing: Caricature meant that we never really took any of it seriously.

But the crazy here was sure of a different magnitude, and the seriousness too. None of it seemed funny. Even as part of the world seemed to be righting itself—this was what we'd wanted, a family, a baby, all of it almost literally delivered into my arms—not a minute passed that I didn't also think *wrong wrong wrong*.

We were up several more times with Baby Boy Blue, up fretting about it all even when the baby did sleep, and a restless night turned into a bleary-eyed morning. Del fed him another banana while I made a list of things to get at the store. I turned on the morning news, keeping an eye out for a picture of myself or of Baby Boy. Nothing like that in the headlines.

After breakfast, Del called in sick and headed out to run his errands.

"You going to be okay?" Del asked at the door.

"We'll be fine," I said.

And we were. Not that we did much. Stayed inside because of the cold and snow, and for other reasons, of course. Long stretches of me staring at Baby Boy, and Baby Boy staring back, some eating, some pooping—and whether it was the bananas or not, a baby can be messy, let me tell you. I kept a record of each of those, recording it dutifully for when we figured out how to get to the doctor.

I played with his fingers and toes, trying to get him to giggle. I tried to sing the *Schoolhouse Rock* songs like Del had, but ended up making up lyrics because I didn't know the words. I gave him tummy time, because I'd read about it back when I was glancing ahead at my own baby's future, and he surprised me by trying to crawl—thrashing his arms and legs out as best he could—but he was only able to push himself backwards, which frustrated him. After a while he just started crying. I set him up right again.

"You're a very serious child," I told him, as I set him up. "And very determined."

I wondered what he thought of this new face looking down at him, if he missed his mother. I thought about her, sitting in some living room of her own right now, somewhere else in town, lonely now like I'd been lonely before, listening to the silence. Everybody's feelings seemed complicated about that, I would imagine. Something about Baby Boy's expression left me wondering if he knew it himself. I gave him a bath with the trial-sized Johnson's I'd stuffed in my pocket at the grocery store, soaked myself thoroughly in the process, then freshened him up with the baby powder I'd taken from Cash Wise.

I began to rethink that whole karma thing. Somehow the world might really be falling again into order—even with me being drenched from the bath. Maybe, rather than all my shoplifting reflecting back on what had happened, that reverse karma I'd asked Del about, it was looking forward—making the space for the little boy here in front of me, conjuring him up.

When Baby Boy drifted off to sleep after his bath, I called Mama.

"I know it's a weird question," I said. "But do you think I'll be a good mother?"

"Don't tell me you're having a baby?" she said.

"I meant someday."

"Nine months someday?" she said.

"I'm not pregnant." A twist in the gut as I said it.

"I hope not," she said.

"You hope not?" I said. "You don't think I would be?"

"Don't put words in my mouth," she said, snappy. "I just mean...you and Del. You're not settled enough for that. You're moving all the time. He can't keep a job. You're not married."

No use trying to set her straight on any of that.

"Did you ever worry about it with me?" I said. "Worry about being a good mom yourself?"

She didn't say anything at first. I could picture her there on the phone, sitting on the recliner in the living room. There was a photo of the two of us on the end table beside it. I imagined her picking it up and looking at it, looking at me. Weighing things. Or maybe she already knew the answer in her head and didn't want to say it.

"I still fret over it," she said finally. "You never know if what you're doing is the right thing or the wrong one, Louise. Not 'til after. Sometimes not even then." Another long pause—so long this time I wondered if she might have hung up again. "Seriously, Louise, I think you'll be a fine mama. But don't rush on it. Whenever there's a grandbaby on the way, I want you closer by." A catch in her voice. "I wouldn't want to miss a minute of it."

*   *   *

The list I'd given Del had been a long one: a proper car seat and some kind of a crib, a diaper pail, a stroller too, even though we probably wouldn't be needing it for a while with the snow and all. Some clothes, enough to get through until I could pick out some myself, bibs and baby wash and washcloths. More bananas and yogurt from the store, and other soft foods, whatever he saw.

Baby Boy was up when Del got home, and he seemed fascinated as Del unloaded everything—a giant bearing gifts, looming above him with each pass.

As Del assembled the crib, someone knocked at the door. Baby Boy and I were playing on a blanket in the living room. Both of us looked up. Del stepped into the room, screwdriver in hand.

I peeked out the window, worried that it was the police or someone from the hospital, maybe even the mother herself, irrational as that was.

Margaret stood at the door. Before I could duck back, she saw me and waved.

"I heard crying," she said when I answered. "Last night and again this morning. I didn't know if you had someone visiting with a baby."

"It's fine, Margaret, it's just—"

"Oh, how precious," she said, peering past me through the crack in the door. Her face lit, her voice too. "You two do have a baby here. May I come in?"

Before I could stop her, she'd pushed past me and knelt to the floor, cooing at Baby Boy, who seemed to be eating up the new attention.

In the doorway just beyond her, Del held his hands up in a "what now?" gesture. Like I knew.

"It's just temporary," I told her.

"Someone visiting?" She looked from me to Del.

"No," I said. "He's...from the hospital."

"From the hospital?"

"We're taking care of him," Del said, still leaning in the door-way.

"For who?"

My brain was scrambled, and I was doing a little scrambling myself. Margaret stared up at me from the floor. Baby Boy was looking too. I had that feeling again that he understood.

"A foster program," I said. "It's something new. I mean, not the foster program, of course." I sat down beside them, putting my own hand on Baby Boy. "It's a program for women who've miscar-ried."

Margaret's eyes scrunched up behind her glasses. "Oh, my. I would think that would be harder on you."

"They said it might be therapeutic," Del said. He stepped clos-er to us, crouched down beside us around the baby.

"Doubtless *they* know best," she said, not looking convinced—about the therapeutic part of it? About whether there was a *they* at all? "And you said temporary, but so much is required to take care of a child, even for a short time."

"The program provides for it all," I said. "They have supplies on hand."

"But I saw everything Del was unpacking," she said. "It looked brand new."

That scrunched look again, maybe something else behind it. What was the line between kindness and curiosity? Between curios-ity and challenge? The screwdriver jostled in Del's hand, and I re-membered what he'd said back in Vegas, how he'd have killed eve-ryone in the chapel if he thought the baby or I were in jeopardy. Would he do the same for this baby? Were we in jeopardy now? Was Margaret?

"They provide the funds," I said, watching Del, watching the screwdriver. "An investment. The idea is that it wouldn't be a one-time occurrence."

"With that kind of investment, I'd certainly hope so," Margaret said. "He'll be with you through the weekend then?"

"Yes," I said, my guts twisting. "I don't see why not."

"It's settled then," she said. "I'll bring over dinner tomorrow night—something special."

"That's not necessary," Del said, tapping the screwdriver. "We'll be fine."

"Nonsense." She cupped her hand under Baby Boy's chin. "It's the least I could do while you and Del have your hands full."

"That's so nice, Margaret," I said. "That'll be fine. Won't it be fine, Del?"

She stayed a while longer, each minute exhausting, even though Baby Boy seemed tickled. After she left, I watched through the window as she stepped back around to her side of the duplex, looking for a backward glance, a change in her walk. Del came up behind me.

"You wouldn't have hurt Margaret, would you?" I asked him.

"Like you told her," he said. "Everything is going to be fine."

In my arms, Baby Boy cooed and gurgled and vomited up about a half a banana.

Del finished putting together the crib while I cleaned up the baby. All afternoon, I caught myself stealing glances out of the window after that, keeping one ear turned for the sound of steps on the sidewalk, some knock on the door, that other shoe dropping. I left the TV on, the volume down, still waiting for news to break.

Del went back to work the next day. My day at home with Baby Boy was mostly the same—same play, same food, same worries. I had a volunteer shift scheduled at the hospital that morning, so my turn to call in sick. No hint from Sabrina of anything wrong, of any trouble at the hospital.

In the evening, Margaret called Del to help her ferry over the feast she'd made—a big pot of lamb and cabbage stew, a dish of boiled potatoes, and a basket of fresh bread. "Hearty fare," she said, "strength for these cold days—and busy days, with this one now."

She'd made a cream porridge for Baby Boy, made thin like she'd fed it to her own children at that age, she said. She'd brought him a wooden car too, and he seemed delighted as she pushed it back and forth on the table in front of him.

The cabbage brought back sharp memories, then just as quick I felt my pride swell when I fed Baby Boy some porridge and Margaret commented on his good appetite, praised me as a natural. Emotions veered from one extreme to the other, and in the middle of it, I kept waiting for Margaret's suspicions to show themselves again, for more double-edged questions.

When she asked about how Baby Boy ended up at the hospital, I just told her the truth—or at least some version of it. The mother who brought him in and how torn up she'd been, how the Safe Child program worked, what I'd heard of it, even the story of Baby Moses that Sabrina had told me.

"Oh, I remember that story," Margaret said. "Awful." She looked at Baby Boy. "Hope, that's what people need. Hope instead of fear."

Something we all wanted.

"But all this time and you haven't even told me his name," she said.

"The mother didn't give it," I said, pretending to concentrate on cutting a piece of lamb, putting it in my mouth.

"Louise has been calling him Baby Boy," Del said.

"Of course," Margaret said. "The parents who ultimately adopt would likely want to name him themselves, I would think."

The meat lost its flavor. It stuck in my throat as I swallowed it.

"Are you okay?" Margaret asked. "I hope the lamb isn't tough."

"It's fine, Margaret," Del said. If he meant to sound reassuring, he didn't succeed.

"The whole idea behind this therapy," she said, watching me as I drank water to clear my throat. Whatever thought she had, she never finished it. She just kept watching—concerned, curious, I wasn't sure which—until Baby Boy swatted his hand down, slapping the table.

"Do you know what I need to do?" she said. "I need to call that foster service myself."

"What?" I said.

"Don't try to stop me," she said. "I'll phone tomorrow and tell them what I've seen tonight. And I'm going to suggest that you two should be *permanent* parents for this child."

"Oh, Margaret," I said. "Please don't." Baby Boy had spit up, and I was wiping his chin.

"Why not? You're clearly good parents, and you'd wanted a child of your own, and they're already invested in all those supplies for you, and..."

"She already asked you not to do that, Margaret," Del said, softly but with its own edge behind the words. "You don't know what the consequences might be if you try to interfere like that." He'd stopped cutting his own meat but kept the knife poised in his hand.

Margaret looked back and forth between Del and me, caught me shaking my head.

"You seem...upset," Margaret said, reaching for the cross around her neck. "Both of you. I'm only trying to help."

"You've helped enough, I think," Del said. "Don't you, Louise?"

The scar on his face was flaring bright red. Margaret, meanwhile, had begun to turn pale. Even Baby Boy seemed to be holding his breath.

I laughed, hoped it didn't sound nervous. "Oh, Del, it's sweet of you to be worried about things, about me. I—" I turned to Margaret. "He's just being protective. Like you said, the whole idea of the therapy here, it's...it's new territory. For all of us." I put my hand on Del's arm, pressed firmly with my fingers, felt the muscle ripple. "We don't want to rush things. We just need to take it slowly, prove things—to ourselves, to others—one day at a time, isn't that right, honey?"

Del nodded, didn't speak.

Baby Boy began to cry. I let go of Del's arm, picked the baby up and nestled him against me. "It's okay," I whispered in his ear.

"Everything's going to be fine." I hoped I wasn't lying.

"Programs like this move at their own pace, I understand that," Margaret said finally. She sounded sincere. "A waiting list to adopt—a long one, I can only imagine. People as eager as you for a child of their own, who've been waiting even longer."

Del cleared his throat. "Feelings run strong," he said. "You don't want to get in the way of something like that."

I leaned forward. "What Del means—"

"Of course," Margaret said, waving off my words.

I thanked her, stroked Baby Boy's back. He was tired. We all were.

Later, at the door, Margaret apologized again.

"I only meant well," she said. "God has plans here, I believe that. It's just that sometimes they need a push." She touched at the cross again. "I'll wait for now, but I won't be giving up on you two."

"What were you going to do, Del?" I asked after she'd left, whispering because we were trying to get Baby Boy to sleep. "Kill her right there? Bury her in the backyard?"

"You do what needs to be done," Del said, then after a long pause, "It wouldn't have come to that."

I sat in the rocking chair, Baby Boy cradled in my arms. Del sat on the floor, leaned back against the crib. The lights were out, and the darkness stretched between us.

"We're going to have to move," I said.

"Move where?" he said. "Across town? We were lucky to find this."

"Out of town," I said. "Far away."

I heard a sound, something tapping on wood. Del tapping his head against the crib rails. "There are opportunities here," he said. "Even if I don't get a real estate job, the oil fields pay a superior wage, and there's an opportunity for advancement. The fresh start we've wanted, the stability."

"And what do we do if Margaret *does* try to call about him?" I said, lifting Baby Boy up just a little. "Or what if the mother goes back to the hospital? What if she sees us one day at the grocery store? Are you going to keep threatening people until—"

Baby Boy shifted and fussed, struggling against me.

"He knows we're arguing," I told Del.

"We're not arguing," he said. "And threatening doesn't accomplish anything. I just..." The exasperation in his voice said it all, even without whatever words would've come next.

"We can't live like this," I said. "We need a fresh start for *him*."

Del caught a ride in to work the next day, back to his routine. Nothing resolved. I called in sick again, left apologies on Sabrina's voicemail. I'd be in again soon, I said. At some point I'd just need to tell her that I'd quit.

I gave Baby Boy another bath, we pushed around the car Margaret had brought him, I gave him tummy time again and watched him flail in place, frustrated at going nowhere fast. I understood the feeling.

I'd just barely gotten him down for a nap when the doorbell rang. Margaret again, I knew. More questions? Real suspicions this time?

But it was Sabrina standing there—her long hair bushing up around the fur-lined color of her parka.

I'd opened the door too widely at first, I closed it back too quickly. Just as quickly I realized how rude that was. The cold was bitter as always.

"I'm sorry," I said, through the crack in the door. "I'm afraid I might be contagious."

She laughed. "If I worried about that, I wouldn't be in the job I'm in, would I?"

Still, I didn't open the door any further.

"The house is a mess," I said. One of Baby Boy's blankets was on the floor behind me. The toy truck was on it. Del had propped the stroller in the corner. The house smelled like baby now—some mix of baby wash and diaper rash cream and dirty diapers. "I'll be back in soon, I promise."

"I'm not worried about the shifts," Sabrina said. "I'm worried about you."

The wind picked up. Bits of snow fluttered through the crack in the door.

"I'm fine," I said. "Just not feeling well. It's not a good time."

"Something's wrong," she said. "I could hear it in your message. You seem like something's wrong."

"Everything's fine," I said, trying to be firm like Del would've been. "Please, I'll call you later."

I closed the door on her. All of it rudeness she hadn't expected, I knew, not from Louise with her welcoming smile, right? She'd been worried about me, and I'd probably made it worse. She'd be suspicious now, same as Margaret, maybe worse.

Through the crack in the curtains, I watched Sabrina wait at the door, like she might knock again. Finally, she turned to leave. But she'd barely taken a few steps when Baby Boy started crying back in his bedroom. Did Sabrina hear? Or was it just another round of second thoughts about knocking again? She paused, I knew that. Only for a second, but she did stop.

I rushed back to Baby Boy's bedroom, scooped him up in my arms, tried to shush him, felt my frustration rising when he just got louder. I reached up to hold my hand over his mouth, stop him however I could—then caught myself before I did it.

What was it Sabrina had said? Some people want a child so badly. Other people out there who just can't take care of the one they have.

Parenting was nothing to be taken lightly.

By the time I peeked out the window again, Sabrina was gone.

Just a moment of relief in that. Then I realized that she'd had to pass the Mustang—that she might have seen the car seat Del had installed in the backseat.

*   *   *

I couldn't reach Del on the phone—either his cell phone or through the main work number. But I couldn't wait until I'd reached him. I had to go ahead and get my plans in motion.

I packed our suitcases with our clothes, gathered Baby Boy's things in some grocery bags, piled some groceries in another sack. Too much of what we had was perishable, not enough for a good getaway. I stacked it all together near the front door. We could hit the road as soon as Del came back—head out with him or without him, if it came to that. I didn't believe it would. I hoped not.

I tried his phone again, but didn't get an answer—left a message for him through the main number. "It's urgent," I told the man who answered.

I stared out the window while Baby Boy sat on the floor. He wasn't happy, kept whining, wanted more of my attention. Both of us felt restless, trapped. Waiting for Del on the one hand, waiting for the inevitable on the other.

I told myself that we needed more provisions for the road, but it was probably that trapped feeling that really drove us out—that need to dodge whatever was coming, to feel like we were moving even if we were still waiting.

It was our first trip in the car together since that first night, and I was already uneasy about that, putting him in the car seat, navigating those roads. He seemed fine with it, making happy sputtering noises all along the way, but I felt myself getting more and more nervous. Each time we passed a woman in a car, I wondered if it was *her*, if she'd look my way, if she'd see her child in the backseat. For all Williston's boom, it was still a pretty small town. It was hard to go unnoticed.

Several minutes from the grocery store, a police cruiser turned in behind me. In the rearview mirror, I saw that it was a woman behind the wheel. She seemed to be watching me. Had Sabrina called someone? Or maybe the police had already been told about the baby, and they'd just kept it out of the news. Maybe that was why Sabrina had come over in the first place. She'd known.

"It's okay, Baby Boy," I said. "Everything's okay."

Several blocks later, the cruiser turned off, went in another direction.

At the store, I struggled to get the car seat balanced in the shopping cart, tried to shield Baby Boy from the frigid wind, tried to make it look like I knew what I was doing.

"Do you like shopping?" I asked him as we went through the front doors—whispering it so that no one would suspect how little I knew about him, this child supposedly my own.

He was looking around like he'd never been in a store before. I touched his hand. He curled his fingers around my index finger. His touch felt comforting, calming. I remembered what Del had always said about keeping your cool in times of crisis, pretending nothing was wrong.

Inside, I loaded up the cart with food that could travel easily—no refrigeration, a long shelf life. Bananas would turn, yogurt would spoil, but jars of baby food could be kept in the back of the car, or maybe those food pouches I'd seen. They could last as long as we needed.

I grabbed canned goods for Del and me—a lot of them, as if planning for Del to join us would help to make it true. I tried to think healthy, restarting my resolution for us, for our new family. I steered clear of cans of ravioli and beefaroni, stocked up on vegetables instead: beans and peas and beets. All of it ridiculous when I look back on it now.

"Let's see," I said when we reached the baby food aisle, sorting through the pouches, looking for anything with banana in it. "Would you like...peach, apricot, and banana? Pumpkin banana? Berry, banana and beet?" I was talking to myself as much as him, of course, trying to act normal, keep calm. Whichever ones he seemed to reach for the most, I just added to the cart. I did get the one with beets. It seemed like a sign, since I'd already added beets to Del's and my groceries, and I also got zucchini, banana, and amaranth, even though I still don't know what that last one is.

Baby Boy didn't want to let go of a pumpkin banana that he'd grabbed. He whined for it, pushed my hand away when I tried to take it from him, calling attention to us. Someone was going to see him, someone would see that he wasn't mine. "Okay, okay," I said, opening it for him. He finally quieted down.

Once I had everything, I headed for the checkout line—Holly standing at the head of the shortest one. I felt my irritation flare from the last time, the wipes in my pocket, as I steered into her lane. But this time I'd show her—my last chance to do that.

"Usually he doesn't come shopping with me," I told her as she began ringing up the groceries, forcing myself to sound nonchalant, chipper even. "It streamlines things for me to come on my own"— throwing in a Del word. "But you'd shown such concern for him and what I was buying last time I was here, I thought I'd bring him in."

"Seems okay now. Eating and all."

She rang up some packaged cheese and crackers, a can of Vienna sausages. Baby Boy sucked on his pouch, contented.

"He's a good eater. Seems happiest then."

Which was true. I was beginning to know him.

Holly kept glancing back and forth between me and Baby Boy as she rang up the groceries and packed them away.

"Must look like his daddy," she finally said.

I didn't answer. I just reached down and touched his check. It kept me from slapping her.

"Anything else?" she asked.

The fogginess was coming in again, the fear. I needed to get out of the store before anyone else saw that he didn't look like me. "Not a thing. Just time to get him back home."

She gave me the total, a smirk playing across her face. I gave her my cash. I pushed the cart out of the door.

But no sooner was I through it than the manager stepped behind me.

"Just a minute, ma'am," he said.

The manager's voice was stern, commanding—but that wasn't what sent Baby Boy crying again.

It was just that the pouch he'd been eating was empty. The pouch I hadn't paid for.

Baby Boy and I both sat in the back of the police car. In front was the woman I'd passed on my way to the store, the officer who'd followed us those short tense blocks.

"I forgot that he had it," I had told them when the officer first arrived, kept telling them. "An honest mistake."

The manager had glared at me, leaned in toward the officer, whispered something. I heard "not the first time" and Holly's name.

They knew I was lying, that's all I could think. Not about the pouch—that really had been an accident—but about Baby Boy. He was perched on my hip now, hugging close to me. But I felt sure I must have looked awkward, not used to carrying him, holding him wrong.

I could feel my face going white—transparent. They could see right through me, I knew it.

"I'll write it up," the officer had said, shaking her head as she turned to escort me back to the car. Officer Landis, her badge read. When I'd seen her earlier, just a glimpse, I'd thought she looked stocky behind the wheel. But standing up, walking, she seemed thinner, busty up top and wide in the hips but with a figure, not barrel-shaped like I'd expected. In the car, she started filling out the paperwork—name and address, everything.

What were the odds? All those times Del had gone out, and I'd wondered if he'd be coming back. Everything that had happened with his sister that could've landed him in trouble with the law. Time after time when I worried about the risks we were taking, and now—

"The cashier says you've done this kind of thing before."

"I'm sure."

"You're sure she said that, or you're agreeing that you've done this before?"

Outside the car, shoppers were glancing our way as they

passed. Curious stares, accusing one, lots of judgment. When a girl riding in the front of a cart waved at me, her mother swatted at her hand and turned them both away. Another woman slowed and stared openly. Again, I wondered how close Baby Boy's mother might be.

"It was an accident today."

"And it wasn't an accident on other days?"

"I just needed to get home."

"What's the rush?"

Baby Boy gurgled and smiled. He was a good boy, I could see that already. We were lucky, I thought, and just as quickly realized how absurd that sounded. Karma and fate again, what we did and the consequences of it—rethinking it all a third time, or a fourth. I'd lost count.

I looked at the door handle. I could try it. I could run across the parking lot with Baby Boy, take both of us away as fast as I could. But the door would be locked, of course. Even if it wasn't, we wouldn't make it far.

Then I thought of what life would be like for him even if we did get away, this life on the run.

"Have you ever done things," I said, "that you don't know exactly why you were doing them?"

"How's that?"

"Reflex," I said. "Or instinct or...no, that's not what I mean. I just mean without thinking about it, without thinking it through. Not just not knowing why you were doing it but even not knowing what you were doing."

This time it was Officer Landis who didn't answer. Her radio squawked. A mumble of words there, cut off as she turned down the volume. Her eyes met mine in the rearview mirror. I was ready to let it all out, confess what I'd done, finish it. Baby Boy was more important than me. Making sure he was okay, that was the main thing.

"How old's your son?" she asked.

"Six months," I said. "Just over."

"I'd have guessed younger."

I looked at Baby Boy. That's what his mother had said. Maybe she was rounding up. Who knew? We didn't know his actual birthday. Maybe they could find his mom, find out.

"He's just small for his age."

"It's not him made me think that," she said. "It's you. I can see it in your eyes."

I held Baby Boy tighter. I looked again in that rearview mirror, adjusting my head to see myself this time. My eyes seemed tired, beaten. I looked guilty.

"I've got two myself," Officer Landis said. "A boy and a girl. Seven and three. First pregnancy seemed easy, but the second...wow. For a solid four months after she was born, I hardly recognized myself. The postpartum hit me out of nowhere." She laid the clipboard on top of the dash. Put the pen on top of it. "Maybe it was having two of them and trying to keep track of it all, maybe something chemical with having a girl instead of a boy. Who knows?"

Baby Boy had grown quiet. I thought he was asleep, but when I looked down, he was staring up wide-eyed, like he was listening. Attentive again, and again I wondered how much he understood.

"It comes with a stigma, you know. Inevitable probably, but you see it different from the inside than from out. People trying to help, asking you about it, or asking *around* you about it, asking my husband, like I was under a glass and everybody was looking at me and watching and waiting." Her eyes met mine again. "Even the support came across as judgy somehow. Either way, attention we didn't need. My husband was tiptoeing around me a lot, like he didn't know what to do or how to begin to help. One day he finally said just that to me—said 'I don't know what to do here, but I know you. You're a fighter. Strongest woman I know, that's why I fell I love with you, and you're a great mother and...'"

She stopped talking. I didn't say anything at all—same as with that support group I'd been in, except this time, I felt like someone really was talking to me.

"Seems to me like this was just a mistake today," she said. "New moms are always juggling. You had your mind on your baby first, right?"

I nodded, pulled Baby Boy closer.

She pulled the clipboard off the dash, tugged the top sheet off of it, crumpled it up.

"I'll explain things to the manager there. He's a feisty one, uptight, and he'll probably give me hell about it. Not doing my job, miscarriage of justice, whatever."

I felt my insides twist at the word *miscarriage*. She didn't notice, hunched over writing something else on the clipboard. She got out of the car, opened my door, handed me a piece of paper.

"This is my doctor. She was a big help to me—me, my baby, my husband. You'll call her?"

I took the paper, stared at it. It didn't seem real. None of it did.

I started to get out of the car, but when I looked down, I saw that Baby Boy had fallen asleep. I tried to scoot out gently, but the seat creaked and the angle was bad. When he shifted and fussed, I settled back down.

So close to getting away, and so far.

"Their needs come first, don't they?" said Officer Landis, whispering. "Just hand him my way."

I hesitated. It was the very thing I feared, handing him back to somebody in a uniform. But she was right—and not just about that being the easiest way to get him out of the car.

I eased him toward her. She took him gently into her own arms.

"What's his name?" she asked.

I stumbled as I was getting out, stumbled over the response.

"My boyfriend's name is Delwood," I said.

"Delwood Jr., huh? Men are funny that way, aren't they?" She laughed, handed him back. "He's a beautiful boy. Got your eyes, I think."

*   *   *

Sometimes the body has a mind of its own. Sometimes the heart knows best. Del had never gotten any of the messages I'd left. He just came home at his normal time, and I had a big dinner waiting for him, a vegetarian lasagna from another of the recipes I'd found back before I lost the baby. A healthy recipe, using a bunch of those perishables that I hadn't been able to pack. I'd heated that can of beets on the stove too, because I'd earned them, but neither of us liked them. They just sat there on the plate, adding color and at least the look of goodness. Baby Boy had another banana and his pick of all the pouches we'd bought. He chose kale, sweet corn, and quinoa—seemed to like it, though neither of us knew what quinoa was any more than amaranth.

Baby Boy sat on Del's lap, all of us around the table, just like a family. I felt a tugging and a pressure in my breasts—this time something the cabbage wouldn't have helped.

No one came to the door. No one called. I left the TV off.

After dinner, we all played on the floor. Spread out the same blanket, wiggled our fingers and made faces and tried to get Baby Boy to giggle. We played with the teddy bear keychain again, but he got frustrated when we wouldn't hand it over. That gave Del an idea, and he laid Baby Boy down on his belly, then dangled the keychain in front of him. Baby Boy's arms and legs started scrabbling just like before, but this time he moved forward—which tickled him so much he started to laugh, and Del and I cheered, and pretty soon all three of us were laughing and cheering and crying until we didn't know which was which.

It was a milestone, but I didn't write it down.

Instead, I told Del my plan—my new plan.

"Are you sure about this?" Del asked, same as he asked the night I'd brought Baby Boy home.

"No," I told him. Then "yes."

Sometimes I wasn't sure whether my answers matched what I was feeling inside. This time, they did—both of them.

At the hospital, I tousled Baby Boy's wispy curls, fell into those deep blue eyes one last time, then gave him a kiss before Del took him in. Del wasn't the one everyone knew, after all, and Safe Child promised no questions. Even so, I was sure I'd hear all about it when I returned to the volunteer desk the next day.

I sat in the car, watched the two of them walk through the falling snow, felt the cold seeping around the edges of that convertible top and even deeper inside. I thought of the support group I'd been to, the child I lost, everyone's sense of loss, sense of feeling lost. I thought of Baby Boy's real mother, and how she'd probably watched that same hospital entrance from her own car before she brought him in.

I wondered what she'd told him before she got out and started her walk.

My heart went to her.

I'm ashamed even now of what we did, but grateful too for the time we got to spend with Baby Boy, short as it was. I hope he's found a real family. A good one. Not a day of my life passes that I don't remember him.

I never thought of him as anything but Baby Boy Blue, of course—maybe knowing all along, deep down, that we couldn't keep him. It's a mistake to name something you're going to lose.

My daughter, our daughter, the one who died: Her name was Cordelia—partly after Mama, but with Del closest to her heart.

WEDDING BELLE BLUES

"So you're the man who stole my daughter's heart," Mama said that first afternoon, all of us finally sitting down together after those first hellos and hugs, after Mama had said how good I looked with a little extra weight, after Del and I had unloaded our bags into my old bedroom. Mama had made coffee while we unpacked, set out mugs and snacks.

"And you're the woman who made her who she is," Del said.

"Smooth talker, huh?" Mama said, missing the double meaning I thought I'd heard in Del's words same as hers—or maybe I was already being oversensitive myself. "I've known every shape of smooth talker there is. Hope you'll amount to more than any of them did, especially if you intend on marrying this one."

Home meant Mama's wingback chair and the naugahyde La-Z-Boy Daddy left behind and the green gingham couch, one arm frayed silly by the cat we'd had from the time Daddy left until it got hit by the neighbor's car. Home meant those Little Debbie cakes I used to crave when I was a kid that Mama still stocked by the drawerful. Home meant Mama herself, her hair pulled back in a tighter-than-ever bun, her tongue just as sharp.

"Some sugar for your coffee, Mama," I said. "Because it sounds like you need some sweetening up already."

She snorted at that.

"You know I take mine straight."

"In that case, Cora, I'll give it to you straight," Del said, leaning forward. "I'll do my best by Louise, always, and that's a promise."

"Sounds like a plan," Mama said, "depending on what your best turns out to be." Her smile didn't look like a smile.

When I took her aside later about that, she'd said she was just taking the measure of the man—good-natured banter, she called it.

Later that night, we found she'd short-sheeted the bed. She dismissed that as old-fashioned fun.

"Skirmishes and standoffs"—that's how Del explained our visit with Mama. "Stalemate" got thrown in there alongside, like it was a game and everyone strategizing somehow.

To me it was just sullenness and sarcasm, too much nitpicking, too many no-win situations.

Every morning at 7:07, we'd hear the alarm go off in Mama's bedroom and the creak of her mattress. Some mornings we stayed in bed, and Mama would sniff and grumble later about us sleeping in. If we got up and joined her in the kitchen, she acted like we were in her way at every turn. Each of us shuffled around the other as we reached for the bread on the counter, a mug in the cabinet, the butter in the refrigerator.

"Do you mind if I get some of that coffee for myself there, Del? Since I made it and all."

Del scooted down the counter as quick as he could, leaned by the sink instead—the sink Mama inevitably needed next.

"Mind if I put my spoon in there?" she asked, done stirring her coffee.

Del didn't say a word. He just shuffled back to where he'd been standing before.

It was all bumping heads both figuratively and—at least once—literally, when Mama and Del cracked skulls as they both knelt to pick up a fork that had slipped off Mama's plate.

"I was trying to be gallant," Del told me after Mama headed off to work—her part-time job, taking classifieds at the twice-a-week paper—but Mama had glared at him at the time.

"You're like that Visa commercial," she'd told him.

"Visa?" Del asked.

"Everywhere I want to be."

She didn't like the way he chewed his food—"like a cow with its cud."

She gave him a hard time about the Mustang—flashy and indulgent and it didn't matter that I was the one who'd wanted it.

She didn't like how he loaded the dishwasher—"you can't put a plate in there with that kind of crud stuck to it," and forks went prongs *up* not *down*, at least when Del did it the other way.

But if he didn't offer to load it, he was *shiftless*. And even when we tried to make sure we pulled our part by picking up groceries before she got home from work, she found fault. The wrong brands, too big or too small a carton, and where was the money coming from anyway?

"If you've got dollars going out and no dollars coming in, then eventually the money is going to run out for good," she told me. "Doesn't that boy understand basic economics?"

"We're just here for a visit," I told her. "Are you wanting us to find short-time jobs?"

"Hasn't seemed to be a problem in any of the other places you've been traipsing off to all this time. Selling houses, stocking shelves, working in a mine."

"It wasn't a mine, Mama. It was an oil field."

"Ask me, it's indecision and a lack of commitment to anything." She snorted. "My thought is, you make your bed and you lie in it, though I hate for you to be stuck yourself." Only later did I catch on that it was jab at our wedding plans, plans she hardly seemed to want to be a part of.

Del and I finally agreed on two rules. Number one, if Del couldn't say something nice, he wouldn't say anything. Number two, if it got bad enough, he'd just walk away. And Del insisted on a "corollary:" We'd move on right after the wedding.

He bided his time with a new laptop (a Dell, of course, which he thought was funny) and a Nikon camera that he'd picked up with the extra money he'd made back in North Dakota. Lots to learn about the camera, lots of new terms right up his alley: *aperture, focal length, shutter priority.*

Another thing for Mama to pick at: "Wish I could spend my whole day learning some hobby. It's like your daddy was with those magic tricks."

As for me, coming home was like a return to my high school years. When things got tough at the house, I went out with the girls.

The night we went for drinks at the new Mexican place in town, Charlene and Daphne kept insisting it was a bridesmaids' bash. Actually, every time we'd gotten together in the two weeks since Del and I arrived in North Carolina, they'd called it a bridesmaids' something. Bridesmaids' breakfast, bridesmaids' lunch, bridesmaids' coffee, bridesmaids' trip to the convenience store for a case of beer.

"But I'm not having any bridesmaids," I kept telling them, and I told them again that night.

"Maybe no *de jure* bridesmaids," said Daphne, slurring as she leaned toward me. "But *de facto*..." She'd been working at a law firm for a couple of years, a paralegal taking night classes for her law degree. She wagged a finger at me when she spoke, which wouldn't have been so bad except she had her fourth margarita in the same hand.

"Daphne!" Charlene shouted—not the first time she'd called her down. "Do you know how much it costs to dry clean a dress like this?"

The guys at the next table turned to look our way—also not the first time. Daphne's left boob had been almost hanging out earlier. I think they were hoping for more show.

"That's dry clean?" Daphne said. She waved her hand at the dress, this slim paisley pattern that seemed to be coming back into style. More tequila spattered. "Check if it says Dry Clean Only or if it just says Dry Clean."

"What's the difference?"

"About twelve bucks a cleaning, I'd imagine." Daphne adjusted her shirt. The men at the next table turned back to the ball game on the big screen, cheated of a fresh peek. "If I've learned anything at the firm, every word counts."

"Thanks for the tip," Charlene said, not meaning it. She brushed at her dress again, twisted back my way. "If we're not bridesmaids, we're at least bachelorettes, right?"

"Cheers to that," Daphne said, and we all clinked glasses—even though I'd said no to a bachelorette party as well, at least not a *de jure* one.

The Mexican place, La Poca Cocina, wasn't new to town but it was new to me—built right after I'd moved out west and clearly pretty popular now. Daphne and Charlene both knew the bartender by name, and Charlene had waved at some clients from her insurance office—"PR with the policy holders," she said. Wherever we went, I caught looks from people who seemed to recognize me. *Is that Louise back in town? And where had I gotten off to in the first place?* Leaving home had been sudden. Cutting off ties had been pretty absolute. So coming home to get married meant more than just coming back to Mama. With most of those folks who thought they recognized me, I just didn't return the look.

Meanwhile, the attention Daphne got was definitely not business-related. Several men had already come up to chat. The classy ones offered to buy drinks for all of us.

Another one was heading our way now—tall and thin and walking like a foal taking its first steps. He wore a straw fedora and a polo shirt tucked into jeans that had been ironed into sharp creases. His shoes clacked as he walked—boots as it turned out, the silver tips of them glinting in the light.

"Buddy," Charlene whispered to me. "He keeps sending Daphne these elaborate love notes, calligraphy and everything."

"She interested?"

On the other side of Charlene, Daphne had already pursed her lips.

"Says not. Says because he gets the cards at a discount where he works, it's all show. He's a little odd, but a good guy at heart."

"Evening, ladies," Buddy said.

"Private party," Daphne said. With her foot, she scooted the extra chair under the table.

"Daphne!" Charlene said—the trend continuing. "Manners."

It was dark, so I couldn't say for sure, but Buddy may have blushed.

"I was going to ask if I could buy y'all a drink," he said, "but don't mean to interrupt."

"We'd appreciate that, Buddy," Charlene said. "Just having a celebration." I think she kicked Daphne under the table.

Daphne rolled her eyes, pushed the chair out again, and patted the seat, like Buddy was a dog.

Buddy sat obediently. Charlene introduced us more formally.

"Another round," he said to a passing waiter. "What's the celebration?"

"Louise is getting married," Charlene said.

"To a hunk," Daphne said. "Hunka hunka burning love, that's what he is."

"Daphne," Charlene said.

"I'm serious," Daphne said. "He wants to sow some wild oats before settling down, you can call me a field, right?"

"Daphne!"

Buddy definitely reddened that time. I heard him clacking the tips of his boots together, a nervous tic maybe.

Daphne had been doing that same routine for a week or more. I'd tried to ignore it, figuring any reaction would just encourage her further, but I'd begun to think I needed to deal with it more direct- ly. First time they'd met, Del had reached out to shake her hand, and she'd leaned in for a hug, and then kept leaning in, chest for- ward, every time they were in a room together.

"You hit a home run, Louise," she'd told me. "It's not just the physicality of him, but he's got such a way with *words*"—which was funny since Del usually went out of his way *not* to talk to her. In fact, it had gotten to the point that as soon as she entered a room, Del slipped out the other side. Now I felt like slipping out myself.

Daphne had always been the good girl back in school. Straight-A student, never an ounce of trouble in her teen years, graduated cum laude from a women's college in Raleigh—"got my MRS degree," as she said, "set myself up as a design consultant, and settled down to be Martha Stewart...until I realized I didn't like to cook, didn't like to clean, and didn't want to be a mom." No way out, she'd figured, until it turned out her banker husband didn't really want a Martha Stewart himself. In fact, he wanted a Mark Stewart—whose name Daphne found on some torrid emails in her husband's computer.

"Salacious stuff. Not just inculpatory but incendiary," Daphne said (no wonder she liked Del), "which gave me plenty of leverage for our parting of the ways."

After the divorce, she got a job and set a plan. She seemed happier for it. Unattached, unbridled, out of control, and about eighty times more attractive for it.

Trouble was, she knew it.

As for Charlene, she'd never found a man to insert into that dream wedding of hers. No one quite good enough? No one quite interested enough? The very thing we'd had a falling out over back in high school—me pointing out that none of her plans would be any good until she had someone to share them with. Charlene had gotten a job at an insurance agency, risen the ranks, was set to take over the firm when the boss retired. Along the way, she'd also gone through a handful of long-term relationships that eventually petered out. The latest boyfriend, Ned, was a stockbroker, and everything seemed more promising.

"No ring on the finger yet, though," she'd told me, wistfully.

"It'll happen," I said. "He's a great guy, what I've seen of him."

"Nothing's ever guaranteed. But I'm not nagging, not this time."

Across the table, Buddy stirred his drink and stole glances at Daphne—puppy dog again—while she seemed to be scoping the bar for someone else, maybe anyone else. Poor Buddy. I felt like he didn't know what he was getting himself into.

Around us, a lot more of the same—couples drinking, men stepping up to women, women stepping up to men, a lot of flirting, a little arguing. Everything the same somehow, and yet different. The Mexican place used to be a barbecue spot back when we were in high school. Sweet tea and a combo plate of pork and chicken had been replaced by tequila and tacos. "The New South," Mama said, and she didn't mean it in a good way.

And I'd changed—and not changed. Earlier in the evening, I'd caught sight of families in the dining part of the restaurant—young parents with their kids in tow—and felt my heart splintering. Not a day that I didn't think about the baby girl I'd lost, and the baby boy we'd had and given back.

I hadn't told Charlene or Daphne about any of that—wouldn't. We hadn't become strangers in the time I'd been away, but despite all the bridesmaid bonding we were supposed to be doing, I didn't really feel as close to them as I probably should.

"How's Del doing with your Mama?" Charlene asked.

"Turns out the road to hell is really paved with *bad* intentions," I said. "I don't want to talk about it."

"Weddings bring out the worst in people," Charlene said. "But speaking of disasters you can control...don't mean to be all businessy about things, but have you thought about wedding insurance?"

"Wedding insurance?" I asked.

"Really cheap, and covers it all," Charlene said. "Limo doesn't show up, you get another one free. Dress rips and you need a last-minute alteration, it's covered. Can't do anything to stop the weather really, April showers and all that, but it could cover a back-up location."

"How about if someone makes off with the groom?" Daphne said. "Because I'm telling you..." She raised her latest drink. Buddy looked away—polite, perturbed, I couldn't tell. I tried again to ignore her.

"I don't hardly think I need all that, Charlene. We're getting married in the backyard at Mama's place with just a handful of people. Not much room for anything to go wrong."

"The way this world is, sugar, you never know what might happen."

"Truer words," Daphne said, and she pointed with her drink hand toward the doorway, where my own ex had come in—tall and lean and his eyes landing on mine about the same moment that mine caught his, like he'd been looking for me.

Maybe he had been.

When I climbed into bed with Del that night, I was wearing my wedding dress. Well, Mama's dress, that I'd asked to wear down the aisle myself—another way I'd tried to make her feel more invested in the wedding.

"You're crinkling," Del said.

"It's the petticoat," I said.

"You're not superstitious about this sort of thing?"

I tried to get under the covers, but the skirt was flaring up under the comforter. When I looked down—a mound of fabric rising up around my middle—it reminded me of when I was pregnant, of laying my hands across my belly, of feeling contented and hopeful. After the miscarriage and everything after, I'd kept asking Del about karma and reverse karma and how every choice meant something. It had torn me up.

"Whatever bad luck we're gonna have," I said, trying to shake it off, "we oughta earn it."

I tucked myself in closer to him.

"Late night," Del said.

"Later than we'd expected. Drank too much."

"Tequila, right?" Del sniffed the air. "Smells like you brought the bottle home with you."

I punched him under the covers.

"You didn't drive home, did you?" he asked.

"Charlene's boyfriend played taxi."

"Ned seems like a good guy."

"He's nice, but dragging his feet. Charlene is more than ready for the next step." I tried to turn, but got stuck midway and gave up. "I think our wedding has got her thinking about things more."

"Maybe it will nudge Ned along."

"Maybe," I said, but I doubted it. "How was your time with Mama?"

"Spent the evening in front of the TV," he said. "There was a *Forensic Files* marathon."

"Better than court TV shows?"

Del gave a sideways shrug against the pillow. "Like mother, like daughter."

"You think?" I wasn't sure whether that was a casual remark or if it had some bite to it.

Another sideways shrug from Del. I elbowed him, best I could, given the angle.

Odd to be beside him in my wedding dress, but odder still to have him in the room where I'd grown up, in the same bed. Same as everywhere we'd moved, Del had hung that picture he'd stolen in Taos, that couple sitting by the ocean, the sea spray making it all misty, but the rest of the room was like a museum of my teen years: a Bryan Adams poster on one wall, my old high school yearbooks, a lava lamp that had once seemed the coolest thing ever. Mama's house smelled like her now, face powder and Pine-Sol, and having Del's smell in the middle of it, musky and earthy, still startled me. Not in a bad way.

"You had a good night overall?" he asked.

"It was good seeing everyone." I told him about the evening and how everything wound up: Buddy trying to make a last pitch for some attention from Daphne and her brushing him off, Charlene and me guiding Daphne to Ned's car, how Daphne had reminded me twice to pass along her regards Del's way.

I didn't tell him about my ex, about how Winslow had joined us at the table, about my conversation with him. How he'd heard I was back, how he'd been thinking about me ever since, how he'd meant things different than I'd taken them all those years ago—the promise ring that he'd given me right after our high school graduation and that I'd just as promptly given back, telling him we weren't in junior high anymore. I'd truly expected that we'd go from graduation to the altar and straight into building a family—more commitment than he was ready for at that age.

And now? Lines around Win's eyes, both of us growing up. And his hair was combed—combed straight I mean, instead of loose and ragged, which he might have worked at just as hard way back when.

Too late for a second chance, Louise?

We've both moved on, Win.

I never did. I'm still here, here right now. And now you're back.

"Pretty insistent, huh?"

"What?" I said.

"Daphne," Del said. "Telling me hello."

"I must have been drifting off." Which was true. The margaritas were working on me, the lateness. "I'm glad you and Mama are getting along better."

"Détente at least."

"What's that?"

"I didn't ask her to change the channel."

"That's a successful evening."

Charlene had talked to me on the drive back. *Don't let it get to you, hon. That's the way men are. They realize they're losing something and they want it all the more, even if it's something they lost a long time ago.*

And then Daphne: *But if you do decide to hook up with Win, just remember I've got dibs on Del.*

Daphne!

Lying beside Del felt reassuring. I did feel myself drifting off, but something was waking me up too. Having him in my old room and my old bed brought out the naughtiness in me, like it was high school again and Del and I were going to fool around right under Mama's nose. The wedding dress added an adult level of raciness. I started rubbing his chest, I pictured twisting myself and that wedding dress up on top of him somehow, but that was the last thing I remembered. Before it could go any further, I must have fallen asleep.

I slept all night in the dress, wrinkled it up even worse than how it had looked coming out of the garment bag in Mama's closet. It didn't matter. Mama had already said it would need to go to the cleaners.

That détente didn't last even twenty-four hours. No surprise really.

That next day Del followed Mama downtown to get an oil change on her Buick and help her run some errands while her car was being serviced: dropping off the wedding dress at the cleaners, stopping by the tailor's for alterations on the dress Mama was gonna wear for the wedding, popping into the stationery store for some thank you cards Mama thought I'd like. (They had dandelions on them, I found out later—which had been my favorite flower when I was, like, eight. I wasn't crazy about them, but welcomed any positive move Mama made toward the wedding.)

Del had seen it as a good deed. I'd thought it was a chance for them to get to know one another better. And in the meantime, I'd tried to reminisce about better times, going through some old boxes I'd brought down from the attic and wanted to share with Del. School stuff like old report cards, a trophy for perfect attendance, year after year of school photos, including one of me all snaggly-toothed and with what looked like a mullet. Photos of Mama and me together over the years, and pictures of us with Daddy, and it was like I could trace the decline of their whole relationship in the way Mama looked in those photos—the twist of her mouth, those tightening expressions. Daddy looked different than I'd remembered. In one he wore this red suede jacket with what looked like a shag carpet lining around the collar, and he was looking away somewhere off-camera. The way his profile turned made him look all movie star or maybe just TV star: chiseled chin and crisp cheekbones and his hair just wisping up at the front like the breeze had caught it. He looked young—younger in the picture than I was looking at him, I realized, which put things in perspective.

I found one of his old magic tricks in the box—a penny and a dime, or what looked like a dime, since the backside was painted like a penny and the penny itself was hollowed out for the dime to disappear inside of it. That's how he did it. A mystery finally solved.

I was holding it in my hand when I heard Mama bursting through the back door.

"...like I had all afternoon to revisit every place we stopped," Mama said, slamming the door behind her. "And me with a hundred and one things to do these days."

Then Del's voice. "I just wanted to try to get to the bottom of it, Cora. That's all."

"You could've dropped me at my car first, couldn't you?"

When I walked into the kitchen, Mama was opening up a mesh bag of lemons. She pulled two out and put them on the counter. Del stood to the side. Neither of them looked happy.

"What's wrong?" I asked.

"Flat tire," Mama said.

"Punctured," Del corrected.

"Flattened it, didn't it?" Mama rapped her knuckles on the counter. "Honestly."

Del didn't answer. Rule #1: If you can't say something nice...

"Did you run over a bottle or something?" I asked.

"Probably a whole bunch of bottles the way he drives," Mama said.

"Del is a fine driver, Mama, you know that." Hands at ten and two, always.

"It wasn't a bottle," Del said. "It was a slit in the sidewall."

"A blowout waiting to happen," said Mama. "Which just goes

to show you what you get for choosing flash over substance."

"It wasn't that the tire had poor integrity," Del said. Mama gave me a sidelong glance at that word. "It was cut."

"It was about $170 is what it was. For *one* tire, which I would hardly call e-co-no-mi-cal"—mimicking Del, it felt like.

"Cora, it wasn't an expenditure I'd planned on." Mama looked my way again. She mouthed the word *expenditure*. Del saw it, but kept his cool. Rule #2: If you need to, just step away. "I'll be outside."

"Running off," Mama said, after he was gone. "Same as always."

"Maybe if you were nicer to him," I said, turning to follow Del out.

"If you can't take the heat," she was saying, but I let the door close behind me.

By the time I reached him, he already had the trunk open. It wasn't the new tire he was looking at, but the old one sitting in the trunk. He had that new camera out and was taking pictures of it from several angles.

"Purposeful, all this," he said, digging his finger inside of the tire. The slit was only about an inch long. "The man at the tire shop said it had to be vandalism. Not the first he's seen either, it turns out."

"Who would do something like that?" I asked. "Kids?"

"I don't know," Del said, but he was looking at the house as he said it. I followed his look, saw Mama watching us back. The same pinched look of hers that I'd seen in some of the photos with Dad I'd been looking at.

"You think *Mama* did it?"

Del clicked his eyeteeth together. "She keeps talking about the car, criticizing it," he said. "She short-sheeted the bed, she gave me salt instead of sugar for my coffee. Maybe this is just upping the ante."

"But you were with her the whole time, weren't you?"

"Your Mama wanted some lemons for a pie," he said. "I figured

I'd make myself useful, what with that grocery store right there downtown. While she went on her errands, I picked up a bag of them. By the time I got back, she was already standing by the car."

"Doing what?"

"Just standing there. On the passenger side," he emphasized, pointing to the tire that had been cut. "Waiting for me to unlock the door."

"And that was it?"

"She called me Moneybags when I handed her the lemons, said she only needed two of them not a full tree's worth. We were barely out of town when I felt a shimmy on her side of the car. I pulled over and..." He pointed again to the tire.

"You think Mama did that?"

Del shrugged. "Maybe, maybe not." He poked at the tire again. The rubber was about a quarter-inch thick at that point. "To tell the truth, I'm not even sure she could if she tried. This would need considerable force. And it's possible that it might've happened anywhere along the way, a slow leak like that. Who knows? Might've happened right here."

He bent down to look around the car, which he'd been parking in the same place every time.

"What are you looking for?" I asked.

"I don't know," he said. "Piece of metal maybe? Something like that? I looked around at the dealership, after we'd gotten the tire fixed and I went back to drop Cora off."

"And did you come up with anything?"

"Just a lot of grief." He kicked at the dirt around the tire. "Done now."

But we weren't done, none of us. Not at all.

Mama's house was out in the country, a good nine miles out from the city limits—and *city* would be an exaggeration. *Town* was more like it, and Mama's house wouldn't be suburbs, just rural. Fields stretched behind the house a good ways—not Mama's, someone else's, the family that Mama and Daddy had bought the house from years and years before. Collards were growing there now, and spring peas—rows of each. That family had let Mama have a corner of it for herself, and she always put in a plot of tomatoes, peppers, and cucumbers, none of which would show until later in the season. West of the house stood another small field, which belonged to the neighbors just beyond. All woods on the east side, a dense patch of them, and woods across the street too with a creek running through it.

Living in New Mexico, I'd gotten a better sense of perspective, how big a distance there could be between things, but when I was younger, our house felt remote and isolated. Those wouldn't have been the words I would've used. *Bored*, I might've said. *Lonely*, I might've thought. I remember standing in the yard and staring at the empty road, no one passing by, nothing happening, and feeling like I was a world away from what my friends in town might be doing. All of which is to say that it's unlikely that someone just passed by the house and decided to slit the tires on the Mustang. And given the distance from town, it was unlikely that Del could've driven around on all Mama's errands with a tire that had been cut in the backyard.

But next morning, Del was out there again poking around for more clues or fresh signs of damage—which didn't surprise me, really. But what did was the sheriff standing beside him.

I joined Mama at the window. "What's going on?" I asked her.

"Maybe that fiancé of yours is testing out lawman for his next big career move." She sipped her coffee. "One of these days you'll see him for what he is."

"I hope *you'll* sometime see him for what he is," I said. "A good man."

I stormed out before Mama could answer.

Del was kneeling by the back fender of the car. He had his camera slung over one shoulder and a yardstick in his hand, measuring something on the ground. The damaged tire was propped up against a shed.

The sheriff tipped his hat. "Morning, ma'am," he said. "Welcome back." He rested his hand back on the butt of his gun, like it felt most comfortable there.

"Long time, no see," I said, not that I'd particularly missed him. Earl Griffin was his name—short and stocky, liked to get in everyone's business. Years back, he'd been one of the cops who'd made a habit of sneaking up on teens rendezvousing in the backseats of cars. He'd interrupted Win and me more than once, cold-hearted that way, and I hadn't forgotten it.

"Find anything new?" I asked Del.

"Mr. Delwood here found a footprint," the sheriff said, pointing. "Took a picture of it."

Del tapped his camera.

I looked at the footprint, then looked at the sole of my own shoe. I put my foot down just alongside the print. The length and the tread matched.

"Sorry, hon," I said.

The sheriff sighed. "I'll take down the report anyway," he said. "Like to keep detailed files on anything happens in my jurisdiction. Could be part of a spree."

He pulled out a notebook, asked Del and me for information, finally looked hard at Del.

"That scar of yours," he said, pointing his pen at where Del got cut in Vegas. "That's not from this skirmish, right?"

Del's eyes narrowed. "There wasn't any skirmish," he said. "And the scar's old."

The sheriff nodded, wrote something else down.

Mama came out then.

"Don't let me disturb the crime scene," she said. "Just heading to work."

Del chewed at his lip as she walked past, his eyes still narrowed. The sheriff watched too, but his look was more generous—admiring even.

"I didn't do it, Earl," she told him. "In case you were wondering."

"Would never have crossed my mind, Ms. Cora," he said, smiling. "Hope you have a good day at the paper."

"Another day, another ad sale," she said. "Sometimes two."

"May need to bring you some business myself one of these days," he said. "Y'all still run personals in the back of the paper?"

"The lovelorn were getting overly frisky," she said. "Had to shut it down." She shut the Buick's door as she said it, shut down the conversation.

The sheriff blushed—seemed human for a change.

"I'm surprised you called the law," I told Del after the sheriff had left. "Especially if you still think Mama might be behind it."

"Could have been anyone," he said, not looking at me. He'd settled down in the living room, was looking at the laptop he'd picked up.

"And if it was her?"

"Then maybe she'll come to understand these pranks of hers are serious."

"Please, Del," I said. "Let's try to keep the peace."

"Rule 1, don't say anything to rile her," he said. "Rule 2, turn and walk away if she gets riled. Nothing in there about not protecting our property."

I shook my head.

"OK to disturb the crime scene now?" I asked, purposefully echoing Mama. "I need to take the Mustang into town."

"Where you headed?" he asked, looking up.

"Errands and lunch," I said.

"Want me to join you? I'm starved."

"My lunch is with Daphne."

He bit the corner of his lip.

"Your Mama probably has leftovers in the refrigerator," he said. I thought about what Mama would've said: Not too upset with her to not eat her food. "And anyway, I've got some research to do."

"Tire forensics?" I asked.

"Our future," he said, which made me feel doubly guilty for the white lie about lunch with Daphne.

I headed for the door. "Back later."

"Hey," he said. "Do you think it was odd that the sheriff asked for my social security number for the report he took?"

"Probably just part of the paperwork," I said. "Who knows?"

Del's research about *our* future was really for *me*—looking for some alternative to what he really wanted to do, which was head back to Williston, North Dakota, the good money in the oil field, the prospects in that business or in real estate there. The boom money.

But the memories of everything that happened in North Dakota still overwhelmed me sometimes. I needed a break, I'd told him.

"A break like a getaway for a while?" he'd asked. "Or a break like making a break, calling it quits with North Dakota?"

I hadn't known how to answer that question then, didn't now, which meant Del tried to balance all of it: searching job listings in North Carolina as well as back in North Dakota and a little bit of everywhere, real estate trends, shifts in the economy. He read the paper online now, since all Mama took was the community news where she worked—and she didn't subscribe but just brought it back on the days she worked.

Del had made enough in our six months there to carry us through the rest of the year, maybe more—"a buffer," he said, "but no reason to squander it." He'd calculated things pretty elaborately, even if Mama called it blatant irresponsibility, but what seemed like a budget at first pretty quickly became a countdown—not toward the money running out but toward a decision about what next.

That decision hung heavy. Every decision seemed to.

"Do you remember that time we made prank calls to all those 800 numbers?" Win asked. "What kind of stupid stuff were we asking them?"

"We called Crest, I think," Daphne said. "Asked them whether it was true that Tartar Control stripped the enamel off your teeth. And another time you called about the bottle of Raid that was left on top of a radiator and—"

Win was already laughing. He pressed his nose tight and said in this whiny tone, "It's really hot to the touch, ma'am, and it's starting to vibrate. Is it okay to pick it up or should we call the fire department?"

"You kept that woman on the phone for ten minutes," I said. "If you'd kept it up a minute longer, I think she would've called the fire department herself."

"You and your voices," Daphne said. "Whoever was on the other end must have heard us all laughing in the background."

"You called up Mr. Wickham, the biology teacher," I said, "and—"

"Frog in the road," Win jumped in before I could finish.

I don't even remember what "frog in the road" meant anymore, but over the years it had turned up as a punchline to most anything that came up.

Daphne, Win, and I were at Ester's downtown, a sandwich shop that had been there as long as I could remember. Those same Formica tables, those same red leatherette chairs that would stick to your bare legs in the summertime. It wasn't too far from the law office where Daphne was working, one of the reasons she'd picked it. Ester's for lunch, the Mexican place for drinks and dinner, all of it right there together. Most of the traffic at Ester's was quick, though—lots of takeout orders, the tables turning over quickly. Meanwhile, we'd lingered.

Daphne had been the go-between—and was serving as chaperone now. Win told her that seeing me had brought back a lot of memories, a lot of regrets. He wanted to talk some. "He needs closure," she said, but I got the feeling it was still second chances he was after.

"Different kinds of party games back in junior high than in high school, huh?" Win looked at me as he spoke.

A sly grin turned up the corner of those lips.

"I wouldn't know," said Daphne, taking the last bite of her sandwich. "Y'all had more fun back then than I did."

"You were always the goody-two-shoes," Win said. "Not like Louise."

My turn to look Win's way. "We all make mistakes," I said.

"Ouch." He leaned back in his chair, grabbed at his heart.

A lot of guys our age had started developing a paunch—those beer guts from high school and college turning into full bellies and already easing over into a sag. As Win leaned back, his shirt lifted to reveal ripples of muscle. Not an ounce of fat on him.

"No girlfriend these days? No wife?" I asked.

Win grinned, leaned forward again. "Are you checking out the competition?"

"Just small talk."

"No one special right now," he said, like it didn't matter.

"Win's working so much," Daphne said, "I'd be surprised if there was time for anyone."

"Aren't you still at Henderson's?" The sporting goods store had hired him on back during his high school football days. Small town celebrity had suited him.

"Catch up, honey," Daphne said. "Win is an entrepreneur."

"I've got a graphics business," he said. He'd taken a straw from the dispenser and was twisting it into a triangle. "A lot of logo work. Cups, t-shirts, keychains, bumper stickers. Henderson's was actually my first client. Still a good relationship."

"A good relationship with lots of businesses," Daphne said. "He's even had some clients up in Raleigh."

Win picked up a French fry. "It's just talking to people," he said. "Just turning on the charm."

Had he given a quick nod to Daphne as he said it? Just my imagination? Either way, Daphne excused herself pretty quickly and went to the bathroom. Win eyed her backside with the kind of attention that seemed to be glaring, but which turned out be just patience. The second she rounded the corner, he leaned my way.

"It's not making you nervous, is it?" he asked. "Being here, with me."

"Not a bit," I said. "Old friends, right?" I picked up my Orangeade, pulled the last sweet bits from the bottom with my straw.

"You tell your boyfriend you and me were getting together?"

"I wasn't getting together with you," I said. "I was meeting Daphne too."

"He the jealous type?"

"Nothing to be jealous about," I said. It felt honest.

Somebody across the restaurant called his name—somebody behind me. Win eased back, waved, said he'd see them later. I didn't look over.

Win leaned forward again. "I'm just asking. Are you sure this Del is the right one for you?" He'd lowered his voice, maybe so the folks at the next table couldn't hear us.

"Del and I have been through a lot together," I said.

"We went through a lot together ourselves," he said. He dropped the twisted straw on the table between us, held out his hands like he was negotiating.

"I've done a lot of growing up since high school, Win."

"Both of us have." He reached out and took my hand, and the touch sent shivers through me, despite myself. Those hazel eyes of his didn't waver, didn't blink.

Around us, people kept eating and talking. Through the plate glass window behind Win, I watched people passing on the street, going on about their lives. I was trying to go on about mine.

"Daphne told me you wanted closure," I said. "This sounds like wanting to keep your foot in the door."

"I'm just saying, who knows what might happen? With the wedding, with us."

It sounded like what Charlene had said. *You never know.* Preparing for the worst in her case. Hoping for it in Win's?

"Look, Win," I started to say, not sure what my next words would've been, but then I noticed with relief Daphne was looming over us.

"Am I interrupting?" she asked.

The look in her eye made me wonder again if her trip to the bathroom had been coordinated somehow. Win gave a little shake of his head—answering her question or signaling that things hadn't gone as planned? Maybe I was just being hypersensitive to all of it, reading too much into it.

Just chitchat after that while the bill seemed to take an eternity to come. Talk about Win's work and Daphne's and about the wedding just days away—which seemed to add insult to whatever injury Win was feeling. He stood up suddenly and said he had to head back to work—then leaned down for a hug.

"See you again soon?" he whispered in my ear. His lips brushed against my hair—not a kiss, but not *not* one.

I took it as a rhetorical question. I told him bye.

Daphne stood up for her own hug, said something herself that I couldn't hear.

"Everything okay?" she asked after Win was gone.

"Just a lot on my mind."

"Win?"

"More like everything I still have to do." I picked up the straw Win had dropped, unfolded it straight again. "The dress wasn't ready at the cleaners. I swung by before lunch, but they said try back after four. I'll probably go home, come back. Hurry up and wait."

"Don't worry about it," Daphne said. "Let me pick it up for you. Charlene and I want to come out tonight."

"Out to Mama's house?"

"I'm putting on my design consultant hat again," she said. "We've come up with a craft project. Did you have plans?"

"Not hardly," I said. "Trying to keep Mama and Del from bickering." Which was probably plans enough.

The craft project was homemade paper lanterns for the backyard.

When Daphne and Charlene arrived about seven, Daphne had

several rolls of old wallpaper tucked under one arm. Her other hand carried a bag overflowing with bits of fabric at the top and weighted down with several glue guns at the bottom. On the same arm she'd hung a bunch of old embroidery hoops. Charlene meanwhile was toting Mama's wedding dress, fresh from the cleaners in a sheer white garment bag.

My wedding dress, I thought, as Charlene draped it across Mama's wingback.

Before I could look at it, pressed and ready, Daphne unloaded some of her own gear into my hands and steered me toward the dining room. "How about a round of drinks for the crafting seminar?" she said, dumping the rest of it onto the table.

"Daphne," said Charlene. "We could've picked up something ourselves. You can't just come in demanding drinks."

"I already picked up a bottle of wine," said Mama, who'd done even more as soon as I told her who was coming over. A pork loin was roasting in the kitchen, and scalloped potatoes with pimento cheese. Seemed like having company might indeed soften her up, at least for the night.

"Bless you," said Daphne. From how loud she was and how red her cheeks were, it seemed pretty clear these weren't her first drinks of the evening.

"I stopped by for a margarita after work, that's all," she told me when I asked about it. "What's the use of becoming a lawyer if you can't get liquored up pretty regularly, right?"

"As long as you're steady enough to operate the hot glue," I said.

"If I get a GWI, I've got friends in high places in this town," she said.

"GWI?" Mama asked, coming into the room with a bottle of red.

"Gluing While Impaired."

The gun wobbled in her hands.

The wine Mama opened was from that winery out on the by-pass. *Cloying*, that was the word they would've used in Napa, but I appreciated it. It reminded me of being young and silly, and it meant something, Mama making efforts like this.

Daphne led us through each of the steps. Cutting the wallpaper into strips, looping the strips into teardrops, gluing them together bit by bit. "It'll accordion out when you're done," she said.

I pulled the materials to make a lantern myself, but really I was just savoring the moment, surprised by it. Back in high school, whenever friends volunteered their houses for group projects, I'd never jumped up to offer that we could meet at our place. I'd said it was because of the drive—easier to meet in town, easier to just walk to someone else's house right after school—but I was embarrassed about how messy Mama kept things, embarrassed about that rotating door of boyfriends, worried about how word might get back to everyone at school about...something.

Looking around now, though, I realized this was the kind of scene I'd wanted all along. Mama's house was cleaner than I'd ever remembered it. No boyfriend around, and no complaining from her about it. Just her and my friends and me all around the table, talking about everything and nothing, everybody working together, focused on something productive and beautiful. And the way Mama chewed at her bottom lip as she tried to line the edges up properly reminded me how Del did the same thing and gave me hope that they might still get along fine if she'd give him a chance.

The whole place seemed homier than it ever had when this had actually been my home.

Then Mama spoke.

"This was a real fine idea, Daphne," Mama said. "At least the wedding will *look* nice."

"What's that supposed to mean?" I asked. "That *look*?" I looped another swatch of paper around on itself.

"I didn't mean that it wouldn't *be* nice," she said. "It's just different, the way you're approaching things. No church wedding. No sit-down dinner afterwards, just a 'selection of hors d'oeuvres.'" That had been Del's phrase, which made Mama hate it doubly. "No family at the wedding."

"We'll have family at the wedding," I said. "You'll be there"—though honestly I was thinking twice about that.

"What about extended family?" she said. "What about Great Aunt Grace?"

"I thought Grace was dead," I said.

"And what about Del's family?" she said. "It says something, a man who won't invite his own kin like that."

"Now, Cora," said Charlene. "Not every wedding is the same."

"Del's sister can't make it," I said—not elaborating on why. "He's not close to the rest of his family."

"Which says something itself," Mama said. She focused on her fabric, gave it an angry twist. "Is it wrong for a mother to be concerned?"

"You're not being concerned," I said. "You're being critical."

Mama yanked up her lantern. "And what's this supposed to look like again? An accordion?" She thrust it out on the table. It looked more like a bagpipe.

Whatever homey feeling I'd felt was long gone. Charlene leaned in to help salvage Mama's work—save something about the whole evening.

"Speaking of popping up...is Del around?" Daphne asked, not hardly as innocently as she was trying to make it sound. "Doesn't he want to join in here?"

"That'll make things better," Mama grumbled.

"He's in the bedroom." I turned back to my lantern. "Catching up on some work." We'd planned to let him stay back there, out of sight, out of mind. Rule #3 maybe—preemptive this time.

"Work?" said Mama with a snort. "About the only effort I've seen him make since he got here was about that dang tire."

"What tire?" Charlene asked.

I filled them in on it all. "Del thinks it was probably vandalism."

"And Del thinks the vandal was me," Mama said. "Called the sheriff on me, don't think I don't know it, Louise. But I've said before and I'm saying again that I didn't have anything to do with it."

"It's done," I said.

"You can say it's done," Mama said, "but—"

"No, I meant *this*."

As I held up the top string of the lantern, the rest of it fell out in this cascade of ruffles. Each of the loops was shaped like a teardrop, a whole series of them latched from the wooden hoop at the top to the bottom layer, gathered together with a loop of twine.

"Exactly," said Daphne, clapping her hands.

"How'd you finish so quickly?" asked Charlene.

Mama reached out and touched the edge of it. "It's just beautiful, honey."

Was it? The loops of wallpaper seemed uneven, lopsided even. But Mama's saying it was beautiful—sounding sincere about it—that made it all worthwhile.

"I'm gonna show Del," I said—breaking our plan, I know, but I did want him to see it. And Mama's comment seemed to have softened things.

"Ask him if he can tear himself away from his 'work' for dinner," Mama said, as I stood up. On her way to the kitchen, she muttered, "You can bet your last dollar that man won't miss a meal."

So much for softening.

"Oh, just call him out here," Daphne said. "Del! Louise has got a surprise for you."

The house wasn't big. Our bedroom wasn't far away. Del had probably even heard Daphne ask about him the first time, and he definitely heard her calling out to him. I pictured him cringing, looking for a way out, the window maybe. I heard the door open, heard him walking down the hallway, but he didn't make it into the dining room.

"Is this your wedding dress?" he asked.

"In the bag on the chair?" I said. "Yeah."

"Don't look, Del," Charlene called over me. "It's bad luck."

I started to tell her he'd already seen it, but Del spoke again before I could.

"What happened to it?" he asked. "Is this paint?"

In a second, all of us jumped up and headed his way.

Del was holding the dress up and away from him. The bag wasn't entirely see-through, but what he was talking about was clear enough: a big black splotch that looked like it was bleeding through the fabric and the plastic both. The way the bag wrinkled, it looked like the splotch was sticky too, the whole mess of it clumped together.

"Oh my God," Daphne said. "It wasn't like that when I picked it up at the cleaners, I know it wasn't."

"Oh, no," Mama said coming behind me, heartbreak in her voice—the same heartbreak I was feeling—but something else laced inside of it. "Del, what have you done now?"

"Cora, I just walked in and—"

"Just walked in and did *what*?" Mama said.

"Mama, could you let up for even one minute?" I snapped. "Here, Del, let me." He was unzipping the bag. I snatched it away from him, opened it the rest of the way. The stain was still wet and sticky, bluish-black.

"Careful, Louise," Charlene said. "You're getting it on your fingers."

Daphne checked the back of the chair. "Did something from here get on it?"

"It's inside the bag, Daphne, not outside," I said, feeling my eyes tighten, the tears coming, as I handed it back to Del.

"Looks pretty viscous," Del said, which I mistook as *vicious* at first. He tucked his hand in an odd way inside the bag, gave me a look I didn't understand.

"Maybe something went wrong at the cleaners?" Charlene offered.

"First the tire and now this," Mama said, then half under her breath. "Trouble seems to hover close to you, Del."

"Could you just stop? For one second?" I was full-fledged crying now, couldn't help it. Everything felt like it was raining down on me all at once. All the tensions and bickering and nagging. Everyone doing what seemed the exact opposite of what we needed and wanted. And suddenly I didn't even know what that was anymore, what we wanted, what I needed. "Could everyone just stop, for once?" I didn't care I was making a scene. They were all staring at me, surprised possibly at my sudden hysterics.

I ran out, back to the bedroom.

A minute later, Del was next to me on the bed.

"I'm sorry," I said. "I just—"

"Nothing to apologize for."

"We have the worst luck," I said.

"Not luck." Del opened his hand to show me a small crumple of soft plastic, about two inches long, wrapped loosely in a Kleenex.

"What is it?" I asked.

"Some kind of ink packet," he said. "It was tucked inside the dress. And look." He pointed to one side of it. The ink whorled slightly. Some corner of a fingerprint it looked like.

"Proof that someone did this on purpose—and now we need to discover who."

The ink packet had given me a sudden idea about that "who," of course—and I don't know which feeling was stronger in me, relief that Mama might not be behind it all or anger at the person who probably was.

What Win had said about his feelings, about not giving up on me, about who knew what might happen next—all that gave him motive. What he had said about running a graphics business. Wouldn't they use paint and ink there?

See you again soon, he'd told me. That whisper of a kiss. A promise? A threat?

Lots of headshaking and hugging from Charlene and Daphne when I went back into the living room. Apologies on all sides, including mine. Then some head scratching alongside the headshaking, when I saw who was standing there with everyone in the living room.

"Evening, Ms. Louise," said Sheriff Earl, standing just to the side of Mama's wingback. Mama hadn't gotten up.

The sheriff was out of uniform now, except for the hat. He gave a quick tip of it my way before he stepped forward to shake Del's hand—then stopped when he saw the stain there.

"This part of the evidence?" he asked. Del shrugged. I started to mention what he'd found, then didn't when Del gave me a quick shake of the head and cut his eyes toward either Daphne or Charlene, I couldn't tell which.

"We hadn't even thought of this as a crime," Daphne said. "Not until the sheriff showed up." She and Charlene looked confused—or unsettled. Maybe both. I felt the same myself.

"Vandalism," the sheriff said. "Not the first we've had here this week."

"You think this is connected with the tire," Del said.

The sheriff shrugged, propped his arm on the top of the wing-back. "Trouble seems to follow you pretty close these days, Mr. Delwood."

"Same thing I was thinking," Mama said.

"Not sure the trouble is mine," Del said. "But none of this seems happenstance."

"Happenstance," repeated the sheriff.

"I mean coincidence," Del said. "None of it seems an accident."

"I went to school," said the sheriff. "I know what the word means. Anyway, back to what you were telling us, ma'am." He gestured toward Daphne. He'd apparently been walking everyone through the events of the evening.

"There wasn't anything wrong at the cleaners," she told us, "at least not that I saw."

She'd gotten there just before they'd closed, but they hadn't been rushed bringing it out from the back, and she'd been equally careful taking it out to the car—"like it was my own," she said—and she'd even cleared out all the junk in her backseat so she could lay it flat and not wrinkle it.

"Maybe there was a tear in the bag," she said. "Maybe there was grease on the door or something."

"No tear that I saw," said Del. "And this doesn't appear to be grease." He held up his hands, which prompted the sheriff to turn a long gaze at those purplish stains again.

"We'll examine the car in due time," he said. "Go on, Ms. Daphne."

"While I was putting the dress away, some folks from the office came up," she said. They'd asked her to join them for a drink at La Poca Cocina, so she'd walked over there.

Charlene picked up the story then.

"Daphne had planned to run by my house on her way out here, but she called and told me to meet her there instead."

"How long were you in the restaurant?" the sheriff asked.

Daphne shrugged. "Two drinks." Which didn't answer the question entirely.

My own question would've been whether Win was there, but I needed to hold off on that. Too much to explain about Win and how we'd seen one another and what had been said. Too much to explain with Del there.

"The cleaners closes at five, and I met her at 6:30," Charlene said.

"A lot of time unaccounted for," Del said.

The sheriff rubbed at his chin, kept his attention on Daphne. "You left the car where it was?" he asked.

"It's a short walk," Daphne said.

"Locked?" he asked.

Daphne pulled out the keys from her purse.

"Keyless entry," she said. "It's habit to press the button."

The sheriff took the keys, kept on with his questions. What time did they get to our place? How long were we working on those lanterns? Had anyone come back in the room where the dress was? I sat and pinched at my leg as they went through it all, trying to distract myself from everything else I was feeling, trying to keep from breaking down again.

"Let's go take a look at Daphne's car," Sheriff Earl said finally, then motioned toward Del. "Want to join me, Mr. Delwood?"

"Absolutely," Del said—and he did seem eager.

Mama's eyes followed the two men as they walked out. When they were gone, she leaned forward, like she was waking up.

"Anybody ask Del what all he was doing while we were making those lanterns? A lot of time 'unaccounted for' there, seems to me like."

"Mama," I said, and even I could hear the layers of exasperation in the word. "And why on Earth would Del do this?"

"Always defending him," she said. "Can't he ever speak for himself?"

"Not when you're talking behind his back, he can't."

"He wants to be talked to face to face, Earl can take care of that."

It dawned on me then why Earl was there. Charlene must have seen something when I turned toward Mama, because she stepped between us. "Let's all try to take a deep breath and—"

"You called the sheriff?" I said. "Another escalation between you two? Did you even hear me before, what I said about all this?"

"You want to know why he might do something like this?" Mama said. "No backbone. Fear of commitment. Something like this dress fiasco would fit him just fine—the coward's way out."

My head felt like it was about to fly off. All of this was too much to believe. "You don't know when to stop, do you, Mama? How about if I left too? And I don't mean just back to the bedroom. I mean for *good.*"

"Whoa," Daphne said. "I think Charlene's right. We should all take a step back and—"

"That's all you two do, isn't it?" Mama said. "Same as you running West the first time, and then the two of you gallivanting across the country, him quitting jobs as fast as he gets them. Quit you sooner or later too, you mark my words." She plucked at the arm of the chair. Then almost to herself, "Maybe a good thing that mess happened. One more reason to cancel the wedding. Give you time to come to your senses."

A smugness about the way Mama sat there after she said it, like she'd not only made a point but gained one. All the bickering with Del, all the nit-picking about our wedding plans, all of it came to this.

"Cora," Charlene said.

"You know you don't mean that," Daphne said.

But I knew she did, and suddenly I wasn't convinced that it was Win behind it all.

"That really is what you want, isn't it, Mama?" I said, softly. "You're not even upset about the dress itself, are you?"

"It never brought me anything but trouble." She wouldn't look at me as she spoke. "I just don't want you to end up unhappy."

"Then why are you trying so damned hard to make me that way?"

Finally, Mama looked up, like she'd honestly been startled by the idea. "Oh, Louise," she said. "I'd never want that."

Del and the sheriff came back through the door. I could only imagine what the scene looked like to them: me looming over Mama, my face revealing who knew what about how miserable I still felt—felt afresh—and everyone else sitting around with an even bigger wedge of uncomfortable between us.

Then I saw that Del's own demeanor had shifted. His jaw was set firm, anger simmering in his eyes. The sheriff's brow had furrowed.

"Any chance you could see the car from the restaurant?" the sheriff asked.

"We were in the back," Daphne said. "Why?"

He held up the keychain, pressed the buttons on it. "No grease on the doorjamb, but your keyless entry doesn't work. The lights blink and the horn sounds when you hit the button, but the locks themselves don't budge at all. Need to get that fixed."

"Always something with that car," Daphne said, then the realization seemed to hit her. "Oh, wait. You mean while we were in the restaurant, *anybody* could've gotten to the dress."

"I wouldn't think *any*body," the sheriff said. "And wouldn't think it necessarily happened then. Just something to get fixed."

Del's expression deepened, like he'd been kicked in the gut.

*   *   *

I should've left again. Del and I both should've.

But Mama's words about taking the coward's way had me hesitating—how she'd crow about having been right. And in the hesitation, Mama stood up and touched me on the arm.

"C'mon, let's eat," she said. "Everybody's just hungry. Dinner's getting cold."

Truth was it had already gotten cold, and the pork had dried out some, and combined with the tension lingering in the room, none of it went down smoothly.

"We'll find you another one," Mama said at one point, breaking the silence. It was like she was speaking to the bowl of potatoes. "There's lots of dresses."

"Cora's right," said Charlene. "We need to make a fresh start on all this." But she didn't look any more convinced than I felt. I knew from experience how quickly a fresh start could fall back into old ways. I'd believe it when I saw it.

On a side table, Daphne had propped up the lanterns we'd made—the one I'd finished, Daphne's and Charlene's only half done, then Mama's own little failure. She'd tried there too.

Mama had invited Sheriff Earl to join us, and he seemed to be the only one to take any pleasure out of the meal.

"Been some time since I've had a roast this good, Ms. Cora," he said. "Your bad fortune is my good luck."

Somebody else thought that too, I figured. Win. Or Mama. Or...

At his end of the table, Del had settled into a dark brood.

It wasn't until everyone left and Del and I were back in the bedroom that I found out the reason why.

"That sheriff barely looked at the car," Del said. "And he didn't give me an opportunity to examine it myself. He just wasn't interested."

"What was he interested in?"

"Me," Del said. "What I'd been doing back in the bedroom while you were working in the dining room. If I could prove I'd come out at any point. Was I hiding something back there? Hiding something in general? Why was I the only one with stained hands? And where did I get this scar anyway?" Del was pacing from one side of the room to the other.

"What did you tell him?"

"The truth. I was looking at the dress and my hands got smeared. I got cut in a Vegas hold-up. Nothing to be ashamed of there. We weren't the ones holding the place up."

I thought about the sapphire I'd taken. Del didn't mention it, and neither did I.

"But here's the thing," he went on. "The sheriff already knew about it. And about my sister in Victorville. He told me he'd done some poking around about me, that he liked to keep track of the people spending time in his jurisdiction—and that it sure seemed like I'd had a passel of bad luck for just one person."

Del emphasized the word *passel*, but for once, it was vocabulary he didn't seem to savor.

The wedding dress was beside me on the bed—pulled fully out of the garment bag now, and all of it laid out on top of an old blanket to keep the comforter or anything else from getting stained too.

"Why didn't you just show him the ink packet you found?"

"I'd planned to tell him, soon as we were outside," he said. "But when he focused in on whatever crazy case he's building against me, I couldn't. My own fingerprints might be on it where I picked it up. It would just confirm what he's already thinking."

"Why were you gonna wait until you got outside? Why not show everyone?"

Del hesitated on that one, and I had the sudden sinking suspicion that I knew.

"Hasn't it occurred to you," he said finally, "that it might be one of the women in that room behind all this? The dress and the tire both?"

"Please don't, Del," I said. "Please don't go after Mama again. I can't take it."

But it wasn't Mama alone that he was considering. It was all of them.

Del was logical about it, methodical, tallying up all the motives and opportunities—cobbling it together from stuff I'd mentioned about Charlene and Daphne and from what he'd seen himself. Daphne's office was downtown, hadn't she said? Near where he and Mama had been the day the tire was slit? And she'd had the easiest access to the dress, had actually volunteered to pick it up. Plus she had a crush on Del, which he said might be motive.

"Seriously?" I asked him.

"The heart works in mysterious ways," he said. And he didn't trust the "case of the malfunctioning key," as he called it; a convenient way to deflect suspicions, he thought, given that she wasn't very surprised by the news.

As for Charlene, she'd been the one to carry the dress in, and she'd been the one to keep pushing me on wedding insurance—a recommendation I'd failed to take, a premium she didn't get, and maybe she wanted to prove a point on that? Plus, hadn't I been the one to talk about how she'd always wanted to get married, and now her latest boyfriend was dragging his feet? How did envy play into all this? Spite?

"And I'm sorry, but we can't rule out Cora," he said. "It's me she's after, not you, I know, but..." On and on, all the ways these people who were supposedly my closest friends, my family, could've betrayed me, undermined me, attacked me. I hadn't even told him what Mama had said about this being a good reason to cancel the wedding. Imagine the ammunition that would've given him.

The bedroom was the place I'd run to get away from it all. Now even this wasn't safe.

How could you find the line where Del crossed from doing this because he cared about me to just going after some other person who supposedly cared about me? Even if Win was indeed behind it, none of the rest of it felt good.

And why hadn't I just mentioned Win? You make your bed and you lie in it, Mama had said, and I sure had. The troubled part about hiding something is that you usually have to keep hiding it. Win was someone I'd need to handle myself.

At some point in all Del's talk, I just shut him out, shut out my own thoughts. I stared at the painting above the bed instead, the couple with their backs to us, the waves drifting and crashing. The mistiness there wasn't just in the painting now. It was welling up in my own eyes.

"Do you ever wish we could just go away?" I said, pointing to it, wiping at my tears. "Just turn your back on everybody, on all this. Make it just you and me again."

"Elope, you mean?" Del asked.

"That or..."

The same instinct I'd had earlier that night, and those same words of Mama's about a coward's way. It wasn't just that we'd be proving her right. I truly did want things to be better for us. A lot to handle here, and all of it on me.

Del and I both jumped when the phone on the nightstand rang. I was closest to it and grabbed for it.

"Hello?"

"Is Del there?" The voice was familiar but muffled, slurred.

The question startled me as much as the ringing. *Who's this?* I should've asked, but I just handed it toward Del. "It's for you."

"Hello?" Del said, then he held the phone away from his ear and looked at it.

"Hung up?"

"No," Del said. "Whoever it was told me to leave his woman alone."

That was why the voice had sounded familiar. Maybe I'd known who it was even when I answered.

A familiar voice. Disguised but not entirely. Still sounding like itself underneath it all.

Win and those pranks of his. This was just on a whole 'nother level of serious.

He couldn't get away from who he was, I thought—then realized maybe none of us could.

"You want a cup of coffee yourself?" Mama asked Del in the kitchen the next morning.

"I'm good," Del said.

The two of them were sitting at the table while I washed up the pork pan from the night before. A new era of civility, I hoped.

"I'd be happy to pour you one," Mama said, "The way you're eyeing my mug, I get the feeling you might need a jolt of caffeine your own self."

"Just admiring the design," he said.

I turned to look. Mama's mug said "Southern Belle Raising Hell." I caught Del's eye, pulled a soapy finger across my throat, trying to signal for him to cut out whatever he was doing. A new era of civility on Mama's part, maybe, but fresh trouble from his direction.

Finally Mama pushed the mug toward him. "Admire away," she said. "I'm going to work."

After she was gone, he picked it up with a paper towel. Looking for fingerprints.

"I asked you not to do this, Del. I asked everyone to just stop—all of it."

"Maybe this will clear her," he said. "You'd be happy about that, wouldn't you?"

"You think she's the one who called last night?" I asked him. "Disguising her voice?" But he was already sifting together some mixture of cornstarch and candle soot to make the fingerprint powder he'd found the night before, Googling recipes on his laptop.

"Maybe she put Earl up to that too," he said.

"I'm not waiting around for this nonsense," I said. I cleaned my hands and told him I was going out for a while—not that he noticed, him playing junior detective and all.

* * *

All of which worked somewhat in my favor—Del not asking where I was going.

Win's business was a squat warehouse with corrugated aluminum siding and a gravel parking lot out front. The lot was empty when I got there, and I swung the Mustang in sharp enough to raise a cloud of gravel dust.

I must've swung through the front door the same way, since the receptionist there widened her eyes and buzzed Win as quick as I asked for him and pointed me back down the hallway like she was glad to pass me on to someone else.

"Couldn't stay away, huh?" Win said as he showed me into his office.

"Seems like someone can't control himself, that's for sure."

"What's that supposed to mean?" He gestured toward a seat, but I didn't take it. Both of us kept standing.

His office was nicer than the aluminum siding outside might've suggested. The chair rail reminded me of Brenda's office back in Victorville, and the wooden shelves along the walls gleamed like they'd been sprayed with Pledge. A whole line of merchandise filled them—cups and koozies and water bottles, tote bags and Frisbees and umbrellas and a whole lot of other crap, different logos all down the line. Pennants filled another wall—most of them samples, but some of them familiar from our own high school days. Vintage now, maybe. Behind Win's desk stood his own football trophies, polished to a sheen.

Talking about moving ahead, but still living in the past, that's how it struck me, same as that lunch at Ester's.

"What I mean is this," I said. "You tell Daphne you want closure, then you blindside me with this pitch to give you one last chance. You ask if Del's the man for me, then start talking about what might happen if the wedding falls through for some reason. And all of a sudden, we've got—" I pointed to the wall of cups and stuff. "What kinds of ink do you use for all this printing?"

The question seemed to surprise him. "I wouldn't know," he said. "Some of it is heat transfer, some of it is laser printing, but as for the ink...I just buy the equipment. The tech folks handle all the production and the refills and all."

I stared at him. "You're telling me you couldn't get your hands on some ink if you wanted to?"

He shrugged. "I guess I could if I had to—"

"And how about late yesterday afternoon. Where were you then? Maybe somewhere near the Mexican place downtown?"

"Yesterday?" he said, like he really had to think about it. "Yeah, I was at the Mexican place yesterday. I go there pretty regular. Everybody does, it's a good happy hour. But what difference does that make?"

"What *difference* it makes," I sputtered, and then I told him, all of it.

"Sounds like somebody doesn't want y'all to get married," he said when I was done.

"And I think we both know who that someone is."

He held up his hands.

"Whoa whoa, sugar," he said.

"Don't you call me sugar," I snapped.

He kept his hands up, but didn't say anything—just nodded. Trying to calm me down maybe, but it didn't work.

"You're right," he said, finally. "About everything you're saying, you're right. Losing you back in high school, seeing you with those guys you dated after me—all that broke my heart. And seeing you again, back here...it's just brought back a lot of memories, a lot of feelings—good ones. We had something, Louise, something real, and if there's a chance to figure what might still be there for us, then...Look, I don't want to lose more years here."

It was the kind of thing that might've melted my heart if I'd seen it in a movie, might've done the same in person all those years back, if he'd said any of this instead of just yelling at me that I was being stubborn, that he hadn't done anything wrong, all that frustration and anger.

"So you try to sabotage my wedding, same as you tried to make my life hell back when we broke up?"

He didn't seem fazed by the accusation. "That dumb kid isn't around anymore, Louise. Like I said, I've grown up. And whatever chance I want for us now, it wouldn't mean much, would it, if it ended up built on a lot of heartache."

He sounded sincere, he did. More of the kind of thing that might've softened my heart once upon a time.

But at that point, I didn't care.

"Del's not just the man I'm *with now*," I said. "He's the man *for* me—now and forever. Whatever you do, whatever anyone does, we're getting married, and we're going to be happy. If you *are* doing something, then stop it. You got that?"

I didn't wait for an answer. The receptionist still had that scared expression when I passed her on my way out.

Del had finished his fingerprinting by the time I got back.

No match. *Of course.* I could've told him. In fact, I had.

"Satisfied, Sherlock?" I asked—probably sharper than I would've asked other times, but there was still momentum from my conversation with Win.

But Del wasn't satisfied.

"Cora only used her right hand to hold it," he said. "I need to figure out a way to check her left."

"You are incorrigible," I told him. But big words seemed to have lost their weight with him.

"Weddings bring out the worst in people," Charlene said again the next day. "That's a universal truth."

Del and I were out to dinner with Charlene and Ned—a steak-house chain near the Walmart on the bypass. When we'd planned it, we'd wanted it to be a leisurely night out—away from the wedding planning, away from the troubles surrounding the wedding—

but as soon as we'd placed our orders, those were the first things on everyone's mind.

"That may be true," said Del. "But this seems worse than most people's worst."

"Were the cleaners able to fix the dress?" Charlene asked.

"Not enough," I said. "The stain will always be there. Faint, but there."

"How's your mama taking it?" Ned said.

"What do you mean her mama, Ned?" Charlene asked. "How about how is Louise taking it? This was *her* wedding dress now."

"I'm just saying it was her mother's dress first, a lot of memories, I'd think."

"Ned's right," I said. "I'll be fine. I've got another dress I can wear." The one that I'd been wearing in Vegas on what would've been our wedding night there. My only hesitation was that it was wine-colored—not because it wasn't white, but because Charlene had claimed a similar color herself for bridesmaid dresses, and I didn't want to offend somehow. "But I can't tell how Mama's doing. She keeps saying that the dress never brought her any joy, what with how things turned out between her and Daddy. Good riddance to bad rubbish, she said."

"She was looking at me when she said it," Del added, and it was true. She had been. I'd ignored both of them and ignored Del again now—making a practice of it really, since I'd already had to ignore the way he'd been eyeing Charlene's wine glass, like he couldn't wait to powder it up.

"But the fact is," I went on, "she seemed pleased when I first asked her about wearing it. She must have had *some* feeling for it."

"I hope you can find out what happened to it," Ned said.

"Thus far our investigations have been inconclusive," Del said, shooting me a sidelong glance—confirming our agreement not to say much more.

Charlene shot me her own look. Was my own expression giving something away despite myself?

"Everything's a mystery." I folded up my napkin and laid it on the table. "If you'll excuse me, I'm going to step to the restroom before the food gets here."

Dutifully, Charlene followed.

In the bathroom, we leaned against the sink, and I admitted my suspicions about Win.

"And are you going to confront him about it?"

"I already did," I said, propping a hip on the sink. I told her about my visit—nothing answered, nothing resolved. "And don't tell Del I've been in contact with Win—at all. No use stirring up even more trouble."

"You know me, Louise. I'll take a secret to the grave. You can trust me on that."

I looked at Charlene in the mirror. Her smile was sympathetic. Did something else hide beneath it? Del always said that anytime someone asks you to trust them, don't.

Back at the table, Del and Ned had moved on from talking about our wedding—but not too far.

"Charlene and I are in no rush," Ned was saying. "Wouldn't you agree, Charlene?"

"With what?"

"Getting married ourselves," Ned said, but he didn't wait for her to answer. "I mean sure, we've talked about it, but what's the hurry? Each of us is busy with our work, and we're not in a rush to start a family, and it's not a matter of commitment really. We know we want to be with one another."

"We're together most of our free time anyway," Charlene said. "Staying at one another's places and all, so we might as well be married."

Her tone made it sound like she was agreeing with Ned, but the words said just the opposite. Maybe I was the only one who noticed. I thought of Daphne's phrase, *de jure* versus *de facto*.

"And I'll tell you, the whole idea of a wedding gives me the heebie-jeebies anyway," Ned said. "Not the being married part, but the whole rigmarole of the ceremony. And I hope that you won't be throwing your garter, Louise, because that's the worst of it. It's like telling every single guy there to step up, drink the Kool-Aid, join the cult, and the women use that kind of thing to twist their boyfriends' arms. Am I right, Del? I go to whatever lengths it takes to steer clear of that—sometimes feel the same about going to a wedding in the first place."

"Ned," Charlene said softly. "Surely you don't mean that, not with all Louise is—Hey, where's my wine?"

"Oh," said Del. "The waiter must have taken it by mistake."

Which interruption was at least good because it stopped Del's eyebrows from twitching. They'd been downright jittery at everything Ned was saying.

Mama was already in bed by the time we got home, but she'd brought the latest issue of the paper from work—opened to the crime blotter column, which had write-ups about the vandalism to the tire and to the dress.

Sheriff Earl was quoted as saying he was investigating "West Coast interests," which probably seemed absurd to anyone else reading it, but Del took it as a pointed message—from the sheriff and Mama both.

"He's just a small-town sheriff," I told him. "And maybe Mama didn't mean anything by it."

Del shook his head. "On a mission," Del said. "Both of them."

Del's own mission wasn't coming to much. No match on the fingerprints from Charlene's wine glass.

Of course, I wanted to say again, but after what Charlene and Ned had said at dinner, maybe it wouldn't have surprised me.

"But she only held it with three fingers," Del said. "The index, middle, and thumb of her right hand. I was watching."

"Seven more to go," I said. "Plus Mama's left."

"And Ned's maybe," Del said. "And Daphne's." He shuddered at the last one.

All this time, Daphne had wanted to get her hands on Del. Finally, he was returning the favor—even if reluctantly.

Same as Del's and Mama's détente had ended after the tire, the new era of civility came crashing down as soon as I showed Mama the dress from Vegas—and this time it was me she was after, not Del.

"A bride wears *white*," she said, storming out of the bedroom where I'd modeled it for her. "It doesn't have to be *pure* white, I'm not a prude, but off-white at least, is that too much to ask for?"

"I think it looks good on me," I said, following her out.

"It's slinky," she said.

"It's summer weight!"

"It's scandalous."

Del had been sitting with his laptop when we stormed into the living room. Already he'd sort of half-risen out of the chair—leaning forward to launch himself out of the La-Z-Boy. Jumping straight to Rule #2. Up, up, and away.

"I think I'll step out now," he said.

"Just like your daddy," Mama muttered, plopping down into her chair. "Carbon copy." Back to square one.

"Del is *not* like Daddy," I said, standing my ground. "He's a good man." I turned to Del. "Stay here." He went back to the recliner, but he didn't look happy about it.

"Love makes you blind," Mama said. "You can call him a good man all you want, but how has he treated you? He won't keep a job, hasn't given you a home, the two of you are moving all the time. You called me from North Dakota to ask if I thought you'd be a good mother, but how in the world are the two of you supposed to settle down and build a family at all the way you're going?"

Which stung more than Mama knew, needless to say—stung twice because it was my fault she didn't know about the baby.

"When I see Del tinkering with that camera of his, all I see is your Daddy teaching himself useless card tricks. All that time he spends at that computer looking for y'all a *future* is no different from your daddy walking the pavement and finding more distractions than opportunities every time. Mr. Big Shot taking us nowhere, and once he'd got us nowhere, all he did was turn tail and run the other direction himself."

Del was bouncing his foot like he was still thinking of jumping up, and I wouldn't have blamed him. I thought of what he'd asked me about taking a break versus making a break. Sometimes it was hard to tell one from the other—and hard to know which one was the right one. I thought of Daddy, thought of him leaving, and couldn't entirely blame him either.

It made me feel sorry for Mama, it did, and for Daddy too, hearing it like this. For all of us, really.

"That's not how it all happened," I told her, sitting down myself now.

But how was I supposed to explain what *had* happened: Del robbing those convenience stores, the trouble with the law in Victorville, the heist he'd planned in Napa, the Vegas wedding we were going to have without her, everything about the baby...

"I'll tell you what happened, exactly how," Mama said, holding up a hand. "You moved West because of me. Now don't you deny it, because it was a good thing. You kept talking about making a fresh start, and meantime, here I was in the same old place, doing the same old thing, I thought I could maybe get on the right path myself. But it took losing you, thinking I was losing you, to see it."

That's why there were no boyfriends anymore. Why the house was clean and fresh. "I'm glad of that, Mama," I said. I started to reach out and touch her hand, but she pulled away before my fingers met hers.

"How do you think it felt every time I heard about your *newest* fresh start, and the new one after that, Del doing you just like your daddy did me, and you staying with him despite it, and the two of you aimless and wandering and wasting your life on a fast car and frivolous stuff like stupid teenagers? And now you're here the two of you, making a joke out of your wedding, out of all of it." Mama shook her head. "You're just being stupid, Louise. As stupid as I was at your age, but with a fresh coat of it now because *you* should know better."

"I've had enough of this," Del said. He stood up.

"And there he goes," said Mama, smug. "Walking out at the first sign of trouble, just like I said."

"I'm not going anywhere, Cora." But he did. He went across the room toward Mama.

"Del," I said. "Don't. I'll—"

"I'm sorry, Louise. I know you asked me to just stay quiet, and stay out of the way, and I've done that, but not anymore."

Mama just glared up at him as he squatted down to face her eye to eye.

"You listen to me, Cora, and you listen good," he said. "You can talk about me all you want. That's your prerogative. Our car, our wedding plans, what time we get up in the morning, what we buy at the store, whatever you want. And you don't have to like the dress either, but as for the woman wearing that dress, Louise is as fine a woman as I've known and better than I deserve probably. I love her and I'm not leaving her, not now, not ever, and I'll tell you something, I won't tolerate anybody talking bad *to* her or *about* her, and that includes you, do you understand me?"

Mama's jaw was set as firm as Del's did sometimes, and her eyes had narrowed to pinpoints same as his. Something about her just burned hard.

When she raised her hand up toward him, I thought she was going to slap him, and Del must've too, because he flinched back.

Mama just laughed and patted him on the cheek.

"It's about time you showed some gumption," she said. "I appreciate that in a man."

In retrospect, maybe Mama was right about a few things—first on the list, formal wedding invitations.

Our wedding day turned out beautiful. It was like spring broke just on that afternoon, the azaleas lining Mama's front porch coming into full bloom, the tulip tree in the side yard bursting out pink and fragrant, and the sun shining down from a cloudless sky—no April showers, so some turn of good luck there.

Charlene and Daphne came over early to help us decorate the backyard. We'd set up some folding chairs Mama had borrowed from the church and attached white ribbons to the ends of each row. After that, we stretched twine here and there between several of the trees to hang those wallpaper lanterns we'd made. A light breeze sent them swaying sweetly.

"It's lovely," I told Mama, and I meant it.

"But where's Del going with that chair?" she asked. "He's messing up the rows."

It was one that Daphne had handled, I felt sure. I just let him go. I still didn't know who to trust, but it was my wedding day, and I'd decided to let it go as best I could.

"If I told you he was dusting for fingerprints, would you believe me?"

Mama snorted, but—I don't know how to explain this—it was a sympathetic kind of snort.

"He's determined," she said. "I'll give that to him."

No matches on the chair there, Del told me later, but the fingerprints had been smudged.

"She's a slippery one," he told me, and I couldn't have agreed more.

After that we'd all gotten ready for the big event. Mama had come to terms with my dress, and she'd added brown patches to the elbows of Del's blazer, which he insisted on wearing. Charlene and Daphne had decided if they couldn't be bridesmaids, they'd at least look like they were. They wore the same dress: navy blue satin with a black lace mesh, knee-length, one shoulder bared. I had to admit, they looked good.

By the afternoon, we realized that the chairs we'd laid out weren't hardly going to be enough. With no list of invitations mailed or RSVPs received, who was to say what had brought each person to the backyard? Word of mouth had spread further than I'd expected, that's what I thought, but then I found out that Mama had placed an announcement in the paper—not necessarily inviting people but just saying "will be held tomorrow," which some people apparently took as a welcome.

Despite my best efforts to dodge some of the folks I'd gone to school with, several of my old classmates turned out, and I spent a good chunk of the time before the ceremony introducing them all to Del. Meanwhile, Daphne was doing some dodging of her own, since Buddy had shown up too, sporting that same hat of his and those same boots but a crisp linen suit. He glommed onto her almost immediately—one person at least that Del and I didn't have to entertain.

Some folks from Mama's work came, and Great Aunt Grace proved she indeed had not died—and proved in that process that Mama had decided to take care of extended family herself if we weren't going to. Grace also brought a guest of her own, one of her grandkids who drove her the two hundred miles to get there—a second cousin of mine, or third cousin, once or twice removed, I didn't know and didn't remember him. He seemed like a nice guy, clean-cut, handsome and polite, but when Aunt Grace made a comment about my "lovely gown," it came out snarky. I used the same tone to compliment her floral hat—god-awful ugly. It felt like we were even.

Then, just as Del was checking whether we could get more folding chairs, I caught sight of Win on the other side of the yard, talking with Charlene and Ned, all three of them set off from the crowd.

I tried to keep a smile as I made my way toward him, but from his own reaction when he turned my way, I'm betting that my smile didn't look any more sincere than it felt.

"Let me guess," I said. "Next thing, you're going to be the one who stands up and objects as soon as the minister gives you an opening."

"I'm not trying to sabotage your wedding," Win said. He glanced toward Charlene and Ned like he was looking for support.

"I just figured I'd be here to deliver some good wishes in person once it's done."

There had been a time when that sly smirk of his seemed cute.

"If you think I'm going to put up with anything *else* from you," I said.

"Hold on there, honey." Win held up his hands in surrender. "I told you already that—"

"Don't you call me *honey* either," I said, dropping even the pretense of a smile.

I didn't realize I'd moved toward him until Charlene reached out to hold me back.

"Let's take a walk, Win," said Ned. "Cora's got some punch laid out over there, and—"

"And keep him walking," I said. Neither of them answered me, but Win went off without a fight.

Charlene didn't release her hold on my arm 'til they were out of earshot. "Just before you walked up, Ned and I told him it maybe wasn't the wisest move, his being here."

"Some gall," I said.

"You still think it was him?"

"Everyone seems like a suspect these days."

"Except me," Charlene said.

Before I could answer, Del stepped over.

"No more chairs," he said.

"Ned and I are glad to stand," Charlene said. "Or heck, Louise, if you make us bridesmaids, that'll open up even more room in the crowd. There's still time!"

The ceremony itself went pretty much like they all do. He will, I will. He does, I do. And a kiss. Del and I wrote our own vows, which were about as lean as you could make them, even if some of the words on Del's side leaned overmuch on the thesaurus: *endearment, constancy, perpetuity, perspicacity.* (I'm not sure Del used that last word correctly, but I didn't want to spoil it for him.) Either way, the ceremony was quick, we said what we needed to say and we meant it. We'd bought new rings after the ones Black Mask had stolen in Vegas, but as a souvenir of our adventures I wore the sapphire I'd earned from that haul, and I even surprised Del by sneaking the little sock monkey between our hands when the minister wasn't looking. It all went off without a hitch. Well, except for the obvious one. We did get hitched—finally and, hopefully, forever—and for a moment, it was like nothing else in the world existed except the two of us.

But there's two sides to that situation, of course—to feeling like you're the only people in the world, to focusing just on one another, and really to having most everybody else focusing all their attention your way and their goodwill too, at least you'd hope.

One side is philosophical, the idea of being alone or almost alone with your fiancé as the two of you become something else—start of a big journey, maybe the biggest of all, and it really is just the two of you, both literally and metaphorically.

But there's also a practical side—and that was the downside in this case.

If we'd been facing the crowd, or if they'd been facing anybody but us, then maybe Del or I or somebody would've caught sight of who stepped away from the ceremony and stole a big chunk of our presents from Mama's front room.

One thing you don't want at a wedding is for everyone to think you suspect them of having committed a crime. Needless to say, it adds a layer of awkwardness.

The good news was that hardly anyone knew the presents had been stolen.

After the ceremony, Mama had asked for fifteen minutes to set up the table for the reception, and everyone had milled around outside, kissing me and shaking Del's hand and offering congratulations and best wishes, until Mama had stepped back out and invited everyone in to a couple of full tables of food.

Whatever her disinterest and reservations and obstructions had been before, Mama more than redeemed herself with the reception she laid out for us. Daylilies stood in vases at the center of each table, and the spread of food was just outrageous—the hors-d'oeuvres we'd supposedly agreed on and a whole lot more. She'd made a big pork shoulder with rolls and two kinds of mustard. And if that wasn't enough, there was a three-tiered tray right beside it with ham biscuits on one level, chicken salad sandwiches on the next, and a mix of open-faced tomato or cucumber sandwiches on the top. There was potato salad and slaw, and a big tray of cut vegetables and dip, and a crabmeat and cream cheese spread with crackers, and I don't know what all else, everything labeled with little calligraphied cards—another of Daphne's craft projects, I felt sure.

With Mama setting all that up so quickly, wouldn't people assume she'd also moved the presents out of the way?

"Weddings spark an appetite in me," Del said as we came in, loosening the button on his blazer. "Especially when I'm in them."

"First, I need to borrow the happy couple for a second," Mama said, leading us into the kitchen. Del glanced back with envy as the first guests dove into the feast. Once we were behind closed doors, Mama told us what she'd found.

"Someone absconded with our presents?" Del said.

"If that means took off with them, then yes," she said. "I've done called Earl, but he's on the other side of the county. He said he'll get here as soon as he can."

Which is another thing you don't want at your wedding, of course: a police presence. And Del and I wanted it even less than most, since Del was convinced that the sheriff would come up with something incriminating if he kept looking.

"Who in the world is doing all this?" I said.

"Did you see anyone leave the ceremony?" Del asked Mama.

"I was front row," she said. "But even if I hadn't been, that crowd out there was swarmed all over the backyard. Hard to keep track of anyone." She leaned back against the counter. "But as I stepped inside to set up, I did see Ned and Charlene slinking off behind the house." She waved her hand. "But that's silly. She'd be the last person to have anything to do with this, wouldn't she?"

Del stole a glance my way. Ned's comments from dinner and his reluctance to get married. Charlene's eagerness and her jealousy (maybe) about our wedding. That wedding insurance I'd refused to buy. Charlene had seven other fingers that could've handled that ink packet, and Ned had ten.

Then there was Win, not just showing up like he had but standing with them, like they were all together.

Maybe some people could've waited for the police to show up and sort it all out, but that wasn't me. When it comes right down to it, much as I said I didn't care about the wedding, I sure didn't want it to be ruined—and Earl showing up would almost surely do just that. I figured we could solve this ourselves before they arrived, then everything could go back to normal.

Del had the same idea. Before we left the kitchen, he ducked down the back hallway and returned with the camera looped around his neck. We headed out into the crowd—into the crime scene.

Every hand I shook, every smile someone gave me, I wondered what was behind it. Who were the people I didn't know? And what was the truth about the ones I thought I did know, like Charlene and Ned? And where was Win—still my chief suspect?

Del took pictures of everyone he could. "Preserving the memories," he told people as he snapped the photos. "Organizing a gallery of suspects," he whispered to me between shots.

But organization would be tough. The crowd overwhelmed the house. It was tough to stand, much less move. ("Would've been easier on everybody to have it in the church and the reception hall," Mama reminded me later. "At least I had my slinky dress and no train," I told her. "Better maneuverability, right?") Finding Charlene and Ned was going to be tough, and no guarantee that they held the answer.

"I don't know some of these people," I whispered to Del when I had a chance. "Mama may, but some could be complete strangers, walking in off the street for all we know. It could be anybody, couldn't it?"

"It would have to be someone who knew you, who was out to get you," he said. "If it was just a robbery, that would be one thing, but the tire, the dress, that phone call..."

"Either way, we've got to go quick, before Earl gets here."

"Y'all make sure you try my potato salad," I heard Mama call out behind us to the people pushing against one of the food tables. "And we've got cake later, made it myself, so I expect everyone to stick around." Just being a good hostess as far as anyone knew, but she'd promised to make sure no one left the scene.

"What a beautiful bride," said one of my mom's coworkers from the paper. Martin? Marvin? "And what an interesting dress. The big city sure has changed you, hasn't it?"

I just smiled and thanked him. No time to explain that none of the places we'd lived had been in a big city.

Across the room, a flash of blue satin. Charlene and Ned huddled together, making kissy faces at one another.

"There," I told Del.

"It looks conspiratorial," he said. "Come on. I'll be bad cop."

He took off, pulling me behind him, but even getting across the room was a chore. We had to wend through a lot more hand-grabbing and kisses on the cheek and good wishes. When one of Mama's friends stalled us by the other food table, Del took his picture then leaned in to grab a bite. "I'm starving," he said. "What does that say?" He stooped to read the cardboard sign. "Tea Taffy?"

"Tassy," I said. "It's like a tiny pecan pie."

Another handshake, a slap on Del's back. He almost choked on the tea tassy, sprinkling some pastry crumbs across his lapel. Then an opening in the crowd, and Del dove ahead again.

Bad cop meant just what you might think: Del puffing up his chest, getting right in Ned's face, and launching into more of a challenge than a conversation. He yanked up the camera first, like capturing a mug shot.

"I hope our ceremony didn't cause you any kind of pressure," he said. "Hope you weren't incited to do anything rash or sudden."

"Del doesn't seem like himself," Charlene said to me.

"He's just hungry," I said.

But Ned surprised us both. "In fact, I did do something rash, though it might not seem sudden enough for some people." He smiled at Charlene. Del was right about that word *conspiratorial*.

Before either of us could react, Ned took Del's hand and shook it. "I just want to say thanks," he said. "This is the first wedding that's been less about the big dog and pony show and more about the people. What the two of you said up there to one another...I'll admit, Del, I'm not sure I understood everything you said, but it seemed like you felt it—right there." He tapped Del's chest. Del was too stunned to react. "Felt it in there, and I did too." Tapping his own chest that time. He turned to look at Charlene, his eyes big and gooey like he was looking at her in a different way.

Charlene was pretty much bouncing up and down at this point. "Maybe weddings bring out the worst in people, but they can also bring out the best, can't they?" she said. "Oh, honey, I know it's not right to announce our news at your wedding, but as soon as the ceremony was over, Ned pulled me off to the side of the house and popped the question. We made out like teenagers. I just hope no one saw."

"It really was just an inspiration," Ned said. "I hope we can do something simple like that ourselves, though I'm not sure if Charlene has any plans of her own in mind."

I remembered the Dream Glow Barbie and Ken, the song list that Charlene had been making since middle school, the running list of bridesmaids and guests she kept. Charlene's smile told me that there would indeed be discussions ahead. But neither of us wanted to spoil the momentum.

"Felicitations," said Del, disappointed, and he went through the motions of having them pose for an engagement photo of sorts.

"You don't know how happy I am to hear this," I told Charlene—not just the news of their engagement but also what sounded like a pretty good explanation for that slinking Mama had seen—and a pretty firm alibi.

"You don't look happy, Louise," said Charlene. "What's wrong?"

"I'll be back," I told Del. I dragged Charlene into the bedroom and filled her in.

"Oh, Louise, I'm sorry," she said. "But I do have some good news—though I'd hoped I wouldn't have to tell you. After what happened with the dress, I bought you some wedding insurance myself, as a kind of safety net, just in case. I hope it helps."

And there went the rest of my suspicions—at least about Charlene.

"Did you see Win?" I asked her.

"He left," she said.

"I'll just bet he did." I pictured him making off with the loot, one last punch at Del and me, one last punchline to his big joke on us.

"He couldn't have taken the presents," Charlene said, "at least not during the ceremony. He was standing with us the whole time. In fact, right after Del kissed you, he muttered, 'It's done.' He was there through the whole thing."

"How about after the ceremony?" I asked.

"He went looking for Daphne," Charlene said.

"Sounds like I need to find Daphne," I said, my next stop anyway.

As soon as we'd stepped out of the bedroom, I caught sight of that other blue satin dress—on the side of the room now where Del and I had started, of course. She stood by the first food table, chatting up that second or third cousin who'd driven Aunt Grace down. She'd already told me that weddings were a good place to get lucky, and now she'd zeroed in on her mark. He was indeed pretty good-looking, though maybe young for her.

"Let's go, Del," I said. "We probably don't have much time left."

We made a beeline for her—by which I mean a lot of zigging

and zagging, starting and stopping. Del's camera swung from side to side on his neck, hitting one man and spilling a drink.

He had his bad cop persona back in place by the time we reached Daphne, though it was spoiled by the fact that he'd grabbed a pig in a blanket and was chewing it while he talked.

"Where were you during the wedding?" he asked, his mouth half full. He didn't bother taking a picture this time.

"Finally *you* come searching *me* out?" Daphne said. "Sorry, Del. You missed your chance. I draw the line at married men. But Louise, your cousin Justin is simply charming."

"And Daphne is a spitfire," said Justin. "It was just chance that had me sitting beside her at the wedding, but we've hardly left one another's side since."

"Hardly?" said Del.

"Not at all," said Daphne, with a wink. She patted Del's chest. "Can't be jealous now."

Del stepped back, almost by reflex, and someone stepped through between us and Daphne, everyone taking advantage of any break in the crowd.

Del leaned toward me. "She's out?" he asked, popping the rest of the pig in a blanket into his mouth.

"Looks like it," I said. "Just get something to eat, and we'll talk in a minute."

Del grabbed a plate and joined the guests making their way around the table, searching the rest of Mama's spread. I maneuvered back toward Daphne and Justin.

"Charlene said Win went looking for you after the wedding," I asked her.

Daphne turned red—like she'd been caught at something.

"Is he the guy who was sitting with us?" Justin asked.

"No," said Daphne. "He came up afterwards."

"Oh, the other one." Justin wagged his finger at me. "The one whose heart you broke."

"I have to fess up, Louise," Daphne said. "I feel bad about it, but I told Win I'd help him make one last pitch for himself. I didn't really think you should get back together with him, and you know I wouldn't condone chasing after someone who belongs to someone else—"

My jaw dropped. "You wouldn't?"

"Of course not!" she said. "Not really. But Win asked for a favor, and he's a friend too, and I thought there wasn't any real harm in y'all talking."

"Why did he find you after the wedding?"

"To thank me for trying," she said. "I think he really did still love you, Louise, and he said to tell you best wishes."

"He did seem pretty torn up about it," Justin said. "I told him to stay, have some drinks, but he said it was better if he left. We walked him to his car."

Circling the table again, Del nudged me. "Louise," he said. "I can't read your Mama's handwriting. Is this chicken salad or tuna?" He held up the card, pointing it my way.

Like I didn't have more on my mind right then. "That's not Mama's handwriting," I said, taking the card from him. "And it's chicken." Del dove in again.

"Careful with that, hon," said Daphne, taking the card from me by the corners. "Looks like it's still wet."

I looked down at my fingers—a bluish-black smear. *Viscous*, as Del would've said. *Vicious* too, I thought.

"Daphne, you made these cards, right?"

"If I had, I guarantee it wouldn't have smeared," she said. "No, that's Buddy's work. I'd recognize his handwriting anywhere. Same fancy swirls and everything that he uses on all those sappy love letters. He does calligraphy for stuff like this as a sideline."

I remembered what Charlene said about Buddy's elaborate love notes when he'd shown up at the Mexican place. "A sideline?" I asked Daphne.

"Sure, he runs the stationery shop downtown—right there between the cleaners and the restaurant."

Right by the cleaners, in full view of Daphne picking up my wedding dress. And probably the same place where Mama picked up those dandelion thank you cards. But why would Buddy be after Del and me? Then I remembered how embarrassed he'd seemed when Daphne went on about liking Del. Then there was that late-night phone call to Del, warning him away from "his woman"—which I'd assumed to be me, but with Daphne acting gaga about Del...

"Where's Buddy?" I said.

"Who knows?" Daphne waved her hand out at the world. "I think I've finally convinced him to give it up. He was sitting with me during the service, just leeched onto me, that same routine. I don't even remember what I said, but he suddenly got up and left, and good riddance."

Del had completed his next circle of the table. "Let's go," I said, taking his plate from him and handing it to Daphne. He only managed to grab a handful of broccoli before I pulled him out the back door.

I expected that Buddy would be long gone, but when Del and I walked outside looking for him, he was just stepping out of the back of a van on the far side of the yard. The side of it read "Steed Stationers" in big letters. The logo was a horse, galloping to the rescue.

Somebody's gonna need rescuing, I thought—and truth be told, Buddy already looked like he might need it. His linen suit was crumpled and wadded, and his hair looked wild. What had he been doing in the back of that van?

"Buddy!" I called. He saw us, and immediately turned tail and headed for the driver's seat. Whatever suspicions I'd had pretty quickly seemed confirmed.

Del called his name a second time, but Buddy had already cranked up the van. The engine roared. Del started to run after him, but I stayed put. Buddy would be gone before either of us ever reached him.

Then I saw our Mustang. The top was down, and somebody had scrawled "Just Married" in some kind of red gel on the door.

Streamers were attached to the side mirrors and to the rear spoiler. Lines of string hung from the spoiler as well, tin cans attached to the end of them.

"Del!" I called. "This way!" And as Buddy's van pulled back, we were already headed for our own getaway car.

The country road in front of Mama's house had probably seen its share of fast cars and dumb stunts. Moonshiners maybe back in the old, old days. Drunk drivers swerving and weaving and maybe crashing on those sudden tight curves. Kids opening up their engines on the straightaways, flooring it just to see how fast they could go. Heck, I'd done that last one myself, more than once.

But I'll bet no one has ever seen the likes of our car chase that day.

Our tires squalled and smoked as Del swung us out of the yard and onto the road. He drove with one hand, trying to push away the streamers that were flapping into his eyes. I had streamers punching at me too, and my hair flew in about eighteen different directions. Behind us the tin cans sounded like cymbals clanging.

About a half-mile ahead of us, Buddy's van swayed wildly from side to side with each turn, the whole thing top-heavy, like it would flop over any minute. We lost sight of him on the sharper curves, closed the distance on some of the straight stretches. Even there, Buddy struggled to keep it steady. I wondered if he was drunk.

"Who is Buddy again?" Del shouted over the roar of the wind. "And why are we chasing him?"

"He stole the presents!" I shouted back. We were getting closer to the van. "He messed up Mama's dress."

"Why?"

Daphne, I started to say. But I realized that wouldn't be enough to make sense of it yet. Before I could say anything, Del stepped on the gas, and we surged forward into the left lane, like he was gonna pass Buddy. Buddy swerved, Del hit the brakes, I lurched forward, then back.

"Where's he going?" Del said.

"Beats me," I said.

We never found out. Ahead of us, lights flashed at a railroad crossing. The gate was already lowering. Buddy sped up like he was gonna try to beat it, but he was too late.

Just as the train crossed the intersection, Buddy screeched his brakes, coming to a stop at such a hard angle, I'm still surprised the van didn't topple into the tracks.

Del sidled the Mustang up beside the van, those cans skittering around the car. Buddy had already jumped out of the van, and Del wasn't far behind him. Me either.

I expected Buddy to run, but instead he turned and put his fists up. He was too spindly to really seem threatening, especially the way he seemed to be doing this high-step with his feet, like a little dance. He kicked toward Del's middle as he came up, and that's when I saw that the tips of Buddy's boots weren't just metal but had knives jutting out from the toe—sharp enough to have sliced through the Mustang's tire, I'd imagine. Sharp enough to slice through Del next.

"Del!" I shouted, but I don't know if he heard me over the sound of the freight train thundering past. Buddy and Del circled one another, those knives making it tough for Del to bridge the distance. Del jabbed once and again, then ducked away as Buddy threw more kicks, his face twisted into a snarl. About the third time, one of the toe knives caught Del's blazer, ripping a gash in one of Mama's new patches. Del spun, the momentum slinging him to the ground. Buddy almost lost his own balance, but managed to catch himself before falling flat.

The train rushed out of the intersection, leaving silence in its wake. Del lay on the asphalt, dazed. Buddy pushed himself upright again, moved toward Del, pulling his right boot back for a final blow.

But Del wasn't going to get cut—not again, not if I had anything to do with it. I reached over and grabbed one of those tin cans, yanked it free of the spoiler.

"Hey!" I shouted, rushing up behind Buddy. He made a hard turn toward me, just in time for his chin to meet the can I was swinging toward his face. "Not on my wedding day! And not to my husband!"

I hit him again to make sure he hit the ground.

He probably would've gotten up again, except as the gates of the railroad crossing rose up, the sheriff's cruiser pulled through from the other side.

Before any of us knew it, Earl darted out of his car and had his gun on Buddy.

That habit the sheriff had of sneaking up on folks? That time, I welcomed it.

"First, I get a call that your wedding presents have been stolen," Sheriff Earl told us, as he was handcuffing Buddy. "Then dispatch radios over reports of newlyweds in a Mustang drag-racing a delivery van. I stand by what I said before. Trouble follows you pretty closely, Mr. Delwood."

Del pointed to Buddy, silent and sullen and looking like he still wanted to take a swing at someone. "At least you've got proof now that it wasn't me."

"But why?" the sheriff asked. "That's my question."

When Buddy didn't answer, I said it for him. "Daphne." The snarl on Buddy's face deepened. He opened it like he was going to say something, then didn't.

"The pretty girl put him up to this?" the sheriff asked.

"Made him do it," I said. "Even if she didn't know it."

"You've got that right," Buddy said finally. "The way she treats me, the way she went on about *him*." Buddy cut his eyes at Del behind me. "Him already engaged, hasn't been in town a month, and she's falling over herself talking about him—me right there beside her, but it's like she can't even see me. When he parked that flashy convertible of his right in front of my store, like he was flaunting it..."

"But why'd you ruin Louise's dress?" Del asked. "Cora's dress. Neither of them did anything to you."

"You'd have thought it was Daphne's." Buddy spat out the words. "The way she was holding it in front of herself, looking into that front window of the cleaners, admiring how it was going to fit her."

It didn't surprise me. I could see her doing it. "And you wanted to get her back."

Buddy nodded.

"Then today at the wedding, sitting beside her," Buddy said, "I asked her how she pictured her own wedding, but she didn't even hear me—busy flirting with someone new now, this guy she'd just met. When I asked her again, just trying to get her to look at me, to see that I was there, that's all, she told me she pictured it with me in the pews—if I got invited at all."

Even with Charlene getting proposed to, she'd been right the first time: Weddings bring out the worst in people.

"What happened to the presents?" Del asked.

Buddy glanced at the rear door of the van, then pretended that he hadn't. "I just lost it after what Daphne said, how she treated me. Leave it at that."

But the sheriff wouldn't. "Open the door there, Mr. Delwood," he said, and Del stepped toward the van.

I'd been watching Buddy's face, the way the anger suddenly drained out of it. The snarl sagged. Something deeper inside him seemed to be crumbling.

"Just leave it, Del," I started to say—but he'd already opened the door.

What had me trying to stop Del was a sudden memory from middle school: a diorama project that each of us had to complete—great scenes from American history—and we'd displayed them all around the classroom. I'd made Betsy Ross sewing the U.S. Flag, using a Barbie doll and a handheld flag we'd gotten at the dollar store on July 4th. I lost points because it was a contemporary flag—too many stars—and several people had done even worse, just throwing their projects together, but the teacher, Ms. Whittle, had gushed herself silly over this one girl's diorama: the Declaration of Independence handwritten on sheet of poster board, Lego men gathered around a cardboard desk. Each of them had a cotton ball glued to his head, and the pen John Hancock was holding looked like the tail feather from a real bird.

After lunch, when we got back to the classroom, there was a big empty spot where that diorama had been.

Ms. Whittle had the principal open up everyone's lockers, determined to find out who had taken it. I don't remember the name of the girl who did it, only the look on her face and what she said— "I just lost it a little"—right before her locker was opened. Inside those Lego men had been ripped apart, the diorama thrashed and shredded, the poster board marked up with the words "I hate you" and "Teacher's Pet."

The presents inside Buddy's van had the same look that the diorama in the locker had, like they'd been caught up in a whirlwind of envy and rage and hatred. No wonder he looked like he'd been in a fight even before we got to him.

"It seemed like you and Del had it all," Buddy said. "And what do I have? Nothing, not even a hope at anything like what I want? A woman who can't see me, a future that's..." He looked at the handcuffs Sheriff Earl had put him in.

Maybe his future was coming into focus.

While we'd chasing down Buddy and dealing with Earl, Mama had brought out the cake. It stood three layers. On top of the first layer, Mama had written: "Congratulations, Louise." On the next level, "Good luck, Del." And on the very top these bride and groom figurines: the groom sitting with a ball and chain around his leg and the bride standing tall with a key in her hand.

It probably would've been funnier if we hadn't just seen Buddy being led off in handcuffs.

At least Charlene had lightened the mood in a different way:

Dream Glow Ken and Barbie stood near the cake, a little worse for the years, but still with those crazy outfits just waiting to shine. Charlene was shining herself, linking arms with her new fiancé.

We'd decided not to mention the stolen presents or Buddy's arrest, but what with Sheriff Earl showing up and the way my hair looked after the convertible ride, the news could hardly be contained. No one had ever heard such a story—or at least lived it. Most memorable wedding ever, someone told me later. Other folks said they thought about leaving but were glad they stayed to hear what happened. Del and I were like celebrities, and Sheriff Earl too. The fact that all the presents were covered by Charlene's insurance took the edge off, let people just ride the drama.

"I always thought of Buddy as quirky, but never dangerous," Daphne said. "I'd even considered just going out with him, giving it a chance. Why not? Now I feel lucky I didn't."

Part of me felt lucky for Buddy that she didn't—and then not, of course. Poor Justin, I thought now, looking at how Daphne had adhered herself to his side. He didn't know what he was getting into.

"I'm just impressed at Louise for figuring it all out," Del said, coming back from the buffet table. He finally had a full plate in his hands.

Sheriff Earl was behind him with an even fuller plate. "And I'm impressed with Cora's cooking," he said just as Mama came from the kitchen with another tray of biscuits. "You've outdone yourself with this fine spread."

"Slick talker," she said with a snort.

But this snort was sympathetic too, and there was a smile on each of their faces, and I wondered what might be brewing between the two of them.

Del's research about a next job or next place to live never turned up anything "substantive," as he said—but he did find us a nice honeymoon spot.

He'd rented us a cottage at the coast—beachfront even. "A steal in the off-season," meaning that word figuratively, of course. Given Del's background, it was good to clarify.

All we had to do was step down the porch stairs and across the yard and we had sand in our toes, a little dune that rose up just beyond the backyard before dipping down to the beach. That early in the year, it was too cool for swimming or suntanning, but the beach is still where you'd find us most of the time, towels laid out on the sand, me flipping through some magazines. Beside me, Del "rested his eyes," snoring despite himself. Every once in a while he'd reach over and put his hand in mine.

"That was some mighty good investigating, Louise," he'd say.

"Luck," I'd say—that loaded word.

Evenings we sat out and had drinks on the back porch (white zinfandel and I didn't care who knew it). It became an evening ritual, watching the ocean as the sun went down. One evening, Del picked up the idea again.

"Seriously," he said. "We could go professional. Grayson and Grayson, Investigators." He'd been relishing my new married name.

"Make it Grayson and Co.," I said. "And you're the 'and Co.'"

"Or maybe Del and Louise, Licensed Detectives—friendlier, more inviting."

"Louise and Del," I corrected. "Or just L&D, Licensed Detectives. We could make a logo out of our initials."

"I like the alliteration there. L&D, LD."

I only stumbled into the truth about Buddy, of course. No real investigation, nothing to take credit for. Even Del's detective work—all that fingerprinting—had ultimately been for nothing. But when somebody's dreaming ahead like Del was here, it's best not to spoil the fun.

Even that early in the year, folks walked the beach late afternoon and evening. Couples strolling hand in hand, a family or two taking advantage of the off-season rates like Del and me were, an occasional runner sprinting full speed across the sand.

Del pulled out his camera to take some pictures of the ocean, like he had been every evening around sunset—trying out different exposure settings to catch the light just right. I sipped my wine, watched the tide rolling in, felt the sea spray in the wind.

"C'mon," I said to Del, and I picked up my wine and started for the stairs.

"Come where?" he asked.

"I wanna feel the sand in my toes."

We didn't go far, just to that dune at the edge of the yard. I plopped down at the top of the rise, right in the middle of the path that folks had made through the sea oats.

"More comfortable up in those chairs," Del said, squeezing tight to fit beside me. I knew he was sitting on a bramble or two over there. The ones under me had me thinking of Del's old Nova—missing it for once.

Down on the beach, I watched more people passing by. It wasn't idle now. I was looking for the right one.

"Hey!" I called down to a boy, sifting through shells.

He looked up like he wasn't sure I was talking to him.

"Yeah, you," I said. "I got a favor to ask."

He came up, a thin kid, pimply-faced and his blonde hair all tumbled in the wind, sand in the curls. His blue eyes made me think of Baby Boy, how couldn't I?

"What are you looking for?" I asked.

"Coins," he said, still keeping a little distance.

"You a collector?" Del asked.

"You never know what you might find." He shrugged. "Could be treasure out there."

As soon as he said it, the boy looked embarrassed, like he'd been caught being foolish, but Del just said, "I can't argue with that." He put an arm around me, tugged me closer—a sappy move, but you wouldn't catch me complaining.

"Can you take our picture?" I said. "My husband's got a camera."

It still felt funny saying *husband*, but it felt right now.

Del gave me a surprised look, like he wasn't sure about handing over his new camera. The boy hesitated as well.

"Are you worried he's going to run off with it?" I whispered.

"L&D, LD would take care of it, if he did," he said. "Just trying to remember which settings would be best."

Del adjusted the buttons, handed it over to the boy, pointing out which button to press. The boy stepped back toward the beach to take aim.

"No. Not there." I pointed over my shoulder. "Take it back there, from behind us."

The boy looked puzzled. "Your backs?"

"Yeah. And make sure you get a good view of the water."

The boy had to step through the sea oats to get around us. Del chuckled as he passed.

"You know it won't look the same as that painting I got you," he said. "The mistiness and all, the camera won't pick that up, I don't think."

"I know, I know," I said. "But that painting..." As I leaned into Del, a bramble bit into my backside. The sand was all gritty, and the sea oats swatted at us, and I thought that's how life is—not always as easy as it looks. "That painting was just romance, just a dream, and this...this is real, this is you and me."

"And you like it like that?"

I heard the camera behind us click.

"You bet."

ART TAYLOR

Art Taylor's short stories have won many of the mystery world's major honors, including the Agatha, Macavity, and three consecutive Derringer Awards, in addition to making the short-list for the Anthony Award. A native of Richlands, NC, Art lives in Northern Virginia, where he is a professor of English at George Mason University and writes frequently on crime fiction for *The Washington Post*, *Mystery Scene*, and other publications. He's married to the writer Tara Laskowski, and together they spend most evenings chasing a toddler (or being chased, depending). In his free time...wait, what free time? Find him at www.arttaylorwriter.com.

Henery Press Mystery Books

And finally, before you go...
Here are a few other mysteries
you might enjoy:

THE AMBITIOUS CARD
John Gaspard

An Eli Marks Mystery (#1)

The life of a magician isn't all kiddie shows and card tricks. Sometimes it's murder. Especially when magician Eli Marks very publicly debunks a famed psychic, and said psychic ends up dead. The evidence, including a bloody King of Diamonds playing card (one from Eli's own Ambitious Card routine), directs the police right to Eli.

As more psychics are slain, and more King cards rise to the top, Eli can't escape suspicion. Things get really complicated when romance blooms with a beautiful psychic, and Eli discovers she's the next target for murder, and he's scheduled to die with her. Now Eli must use every trick he knows to keep them both alive and reveal the true killer.

Available at booksellers nationwide and online

Visit www.henerypress.com for details

WHEN LIES CRUMBLE
Alan Cupp

A Carter Mays Mystery (#1)

Chicago PI Carter Mays is thrust into a house of lies when local rich girl Cindy Bedford hires him. Turns out her fiancé failed to show up on their wedding day, the same day millions of dollars are stolen from her father's company. While Carter takes the case, Cindy's father tries to find him his own way. With nasty secrets, hidden finances, and a trail of revenge, it's soon apparent no one is who they say they are.

Carter searches for the truth, but the situation grows more volatile as panic collides with vulnerability. Broken relationships and blurred loyalties turn deadly, fueled by past offenses and present vendettas in a quest to reveal the truth behind the lies before no one, including Carter, gets out alive.

Available at booksellers nationwide and online

Visit www.henerypress.com for details

ARTIFACT

Gigi Pandian

A Jaya Jones Treasure Hunt Mystery (#1)

Historian Jaya Jones discovers the secrets of a lost Indian treasure may be hidden in a Scottish legend from the days of the British Raj. But she's not the only one on the trail...

From San Francisco to London to the Highlands of Scotland, Jaya must evade a shadowy stalker as she follows hints from the hastily scrawled note of her dead lover to a remote archaeological dig. Helping her decipher the cryptic clues are her magician best friend, a devastatingly handsome art historian with something to hide, and a charming archaeologist running for his life.

Available at booksellers nationwide and online

Visit www.henerypress.com for details

THE DEEP END

Julie Mulhern

A Country Club Murders Mystery

Swimming into the lifeless body of her husband's mistress tends to ruin a woman's day, but becoming a murder suspect can ruin her whole life.

It's 1974 and Ellison Russell's life revolves around her daughter and her art. She's long since stopped caring about her cheating husband, Henry, and the women with whom he entertains himself. That is, until she becomes a suspect in Madeline Harper's death. The murder forces Ellison to confront her husband's proclivities and his crimes—kinky sex, petty cruelties and blackmail.

As the body count approaches par on the seventh hole, Ellison knows she has to catch a killer. But with an interfering mother, an adoring father, a teenage daughter, and a cadre of well-meaning friends demanding her attention, can Ellison find the killer before he finds her?

Available at booksellers nationwide and online

Visit www.henerypress.com for details